Murder ...
Technically

A Report on the
Neighbor from Hell

By Steven J. Sokkal, PhD

The Phoenix Group

Murder ... Technically
A Report on the Neighbor from Hell
By Steven J. Sokkal, PhD

Copyright © 2004 Michael Sadler
First printing: August 2004

ISBN: 0-9708747-5-8

Published by
THE PHOENIX GROUP
PO Box 20536
San Jose, CA 95160
Phone/Fax: 877-594-9076
Email: info@tpgpub.com
Website: www.tpgpub.com

Cover design: Michael Graham (www.michaelgraham-art.com)
Editing & layout: Tony Stubbs (www.tjpublish.com)

Printed in the United States of America

Dedication

For Mark and Jaci Mohler, friends I'd never met … until they just showed up in the hospital prior to my open heart surgery. It's good to be vertical again, eh, Mark?

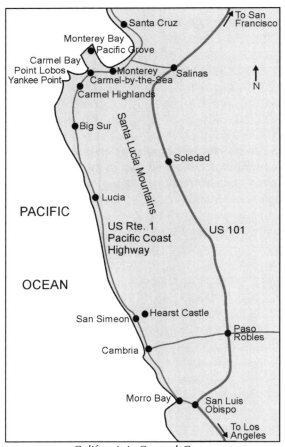

California's Central Coast

1 Report Introduction

The natural gas flowed for thirty minutes at full volume into the various rooms of the newly constructed 2-story seaside home of Gil Nortze. Spewing forth in a continuous *whoosh* from a broken ¾-inch line, the gas/air mix finally reached critical density. And that critical density came into contact with the hot blue flame of the water heater in the garage. There followed an explosion of unimaginable ferocity that lit up the morning sky at Yankee Point. It blew out the windows on both floors and quickly set the house ablaze.

Neighbors in the Carmel Highlands area within a half-mile radius of the explosion reported to 911 on that morning in May, 2002 either the noise, the rising smoke, or in one case from two miles up the coast, the actual flames. Of course, everyone at first suspected a terrorist act, but that was quickly dispelled. Al-Qaeda terrorists have only fundamentalist fervor to get them motivated. Some of the people in Carmel Highlands at the time had something much more powerful—fundamental body chemistry fueled by passion yet ruled by chromosomes.

The nearby Carmel Highlands Fire Department was, however, late in arriving. A huge pine tree had fallen an hour earlier and completely blocked Highway 1. It wouldn't have mattered, really, as the house was quickly gutted. Fortunately, no one was in the house at the time of the explosion, although there was a murder … technically … just before that, plus three other murders even before that. Two counts of vehicular manslaughter that weren't even filed, plus a suicide, should also be mentioned. And what happened after the explosion is important, too.

Had the surprise party Gil Nortze planned for his new girlfriend, Trudy, gone off as originally planned, there would have been seven people in the house later that same day. Some might call it good timing. In its entirely, however, events and prior criminal acts leading up to and after the exploding house incident suggest one of those double-edged sword scenarios, but one has to know the people involved to better understand the true situation.

2 Ken Easton

It was just after eight o'clock on Friday, November 24, 2001, on one of those breezy crisp mornings for which the central California coast between Monterey and Big Sur is famous—taking your breath away. Cold winds were just picking up out of the northwest, already at 23 knots, and expected to hit 40 ahead of the monster storm heading quickly toward the coast—and the steep cliffs— of Yankee Point. It is an area where spectacular scenery along a rugged coastline is the norm, not the exception. Granite rocks out beyond the little headlands stand sentry duty against a relentless sea, eroding away a nanogram at a time with every wave. Northwesterly winds carry away the sea spray towards the cliffs where, beyond the bluffs, steep mountains and deep ravines hold firm. One day, far in the distant future, they, too, will succumb to the sea and the force of gravity.

Whitewater pounded so hard against the forty-foot, west-facing, vertical cliff that the thunderous sound in Ken Easton's ears easily masked the vibration under his swim fins. In a full neoprene wetsuit exposing only his slightly nervous hands, his ankles, and face, a six-foot, 200 pound, 35-year-old tanned and healthy man stood on the outcrop near the southern end of his Yankee Point property. Ken needed a distraction.

For nearly a month, post-9/11 world events had dominated Ken's, and the rest of the country's, attention. Mazar-e-Sharif in northern Afghanistan had fallen to the Northern Alliance, and some areas were under control, but Osama bin-Laden hadn't been captured, and fierce battles raged across the country. Closer to home, Ken had spent too much time worrying about the vacant lot next door.

Ken had to close his eyes and cover his ears to concentrate on the vibration. He felt it again— that quick buzz through the swim fins on the soles of his feet—dissipating up through his calves, finally dying out around his knees. He waited for the vibration in his feet to stop, and counted to himself, timing the wave set: *One-one thousand, two-one thousand*, up to ten. Opening his eyes, Ken felt the slight sting of the salty mist, and then he leaned forward, bent his knees, and sprang off the cliff into a swan dive, calculating after a quick glance seaward that the next wave was a fifteen-footer.

Forty feet doesn't look like much on the ground; it's about the length of two tandem curbside parking places. Even vertically, it is only about seven feet higher than the highest platform from which Olympic divers twist and somersault. But then again, Olympic platform divers don't have to worry about cold churning currents, rapidly changing water depth, no exit ladder, the lack of assistance if trouble arises, and the occasional hungry ten-foot tiger shark.

For ninety-nine percent plus of the human race, Ken's leap of faith would represent the scariest, not to mention longest 1.25 seconds in their lives and, considering the local circumstances, probably fatal.

Ken locked his elbows, overlapped his hands into a horizontal triangle to break the surface tension, and hit the 59-degree water at exactly 34.1 mph.

Yeeow, that's cold! Cold seawater definitely wakes a body up, wetsuit notwithstanding. With submarine canyons a mile deep just offshore, the waters around the Monterey Peninsula are always cold.

On a flat, still surface (high surface tension), and with *im*proper hand placement, hitting the water with one's forehead at that speed is like getting smacked real hard with the flat side of a ping-pong paddle; stings like a bitch, not to mention Excedrin Headache Level Nine (see your neurologist if symptoms persist). In this case, with low water surface tension caused by the churning action and eddy effect, Ken hit his little triangle perfectly and made a soft entry.

Eight feet underwater, the undertow dragged Ken down towards the start of the offshore canyon, then sent him seaward. He swam with the flow, frog kicking and swimming the breaststroke for a good hundred feet out to sea. The exertion also helped him warm up as cold seawater infiltrated his wetsuit. Ken then felt the impact of the wave crashing twenty feet above, and quickly darted at an angle up to the surface, and smoother water, just behind the 15-foot wave, both fins working hard now.

Once on the surface, Ken wasted no time in swimming freestyle, breathing every fourth stroke, in a straight line out to sea. He felt the next sixteen-foot roller lift him and then drop him down the backside, and he stopped to check his position, treading water. The center of the break was directly over the start of the submarine canyon, and he knew where that was in relation to the cliff. The next wave was bearing down, so he swam sidestroke ten feet to the left and stopped again, lining up for the right-break. This third and largest wave of the set was an eighteen-footer.

Given the choice between swan diving off a 40-foot cliff into a churning ocean with all the aforementioned uncertainties, or facing an 18-foot wave looming ahead, most people would be wise to opt for the former. It had been his personal experience that there are so many more things that can go wrong with that much mass moving so fast, bearing down on a swimmer like a hungry liquid mountain and eager to swallow up and keep underwater any challengers. A splat from 40-feet high is far more preferable.

At the age of sixteen and already a strong and proficient swimmer, Ken Easton's wave timing was not very good one day. On a 10-foot day at Zuma Beach above Malibu, and without swim fin assistance, he dove down underwater too early and too shallow ahead of a Zuma monster. A 10-foot wave at Zuma is akin to a 20-foot wave anywhere else due to its mass, form, and speed.

Misjudging the distance and depth of the impact zone, Ken found himself in a washing machine. He desperately needed another breath, but the churning whitewater wouldn't let him up. In fact, he was being dragged seaward by the undertow. He kicked his feet and flailed his arms trying to surface. Before he could get a breath, the next monster crashed on top of him.

Ken's prospects for survival quickly became exponentially problematic. He was alone in the water, out of breath, and his whole body was in a state of one big muscle cramp. When that next wave took him down and under, and whipped him around like a piece of kelp, Ken found himself in Part 3 of the crunch/no-breath/crunch cycle. There are, for most swimmers at Zuma, only five parts before it's over. But Ken got lucky. As the undertow dragged him downward and toward the next monster coming in, he felt his toes scrape a bit of sand. He pushed himself down to the sandy bottom, and with one final desperate effort, pushed off from the bottom and shot to the surface ten feet above his head.

Ken managed to take three gasping breaths to be ready when the next wave crashed in front of him. When it was ten feet away, he pushed himself back to the bottom and counted to five, and then pushed off again, shooting up like a dart. He came up in calmer water just behind the wave, and then he managed to swim to shore. It was a valuable lesson.

Off the cliff of his Yankee Point home, the huge wave climbed higher and higher, and Ken swam head down at full throttle ahead of the wave to catch it. His feet went from horizontally behind him to nearly vertical over his head as the wave picked him up and pushed him forward. It was one big-ass wave.

Don't screw up, man. And no heroics!

The wave launched him down the smooth green face. His head popped up, and before the water drained from his eyes so he could see, he jutted out his right arm, palm down and body rigid, fins pointed, and started to plane down and across the wave face. When he could finally see where he was going, it was pretty much like watching himself go over Niagara Falls ... without the barrel. It was a controlled freefall.

Surfers have The Tube, but they are standing atop a surfing "device." Bodysurfers, with their bodies in full water contact, call it The Zone. There's a world of difference, mainly attitude, and many a fight has broken out between bodysurfers and "device" surfers over the years. Surfers usually win, though, because there are usually twenty-five surfers to every bodysurfer. And they have firepower and not much true remorse. "Oh, sorry, dude, I thought that was a seal my board hit."

The wave crested behind and launched Ken ahead of many tons of curling water, and in an instant, he was in a six-foot diameter curl. The sound of the cascading water over and behind him was almost deafening. Inside the zone, Ken was focused, alert, calm, ecstatic, and bursting with adrenaline, all at the same time. Between drop-in and bailout, this is what a bodysurfer does, and what he lives for. He rode up the steep face and turned back down, all inside the curl, then whip-kicked his fins and shot out from inside the curl to sunshine. Seeing the closeout ahead, Ken dove down and came up behind the wave.

The ride didn't last long, but if 1.2 seconds in a swan dive seems a long time, six seconds on that wave, most of it locked in the curl, is an eternity. Inside The Zone the first time or the hundredth, it's all about time and motion.

Ken surfaced, right fist in the air, and screamed, "Yes!" to no one but the sea. That was his best wave all year. He was also slightly winded, and his time was up. He had but a few precious seconds to breaststroke toward the cliff, his head out of the water, and catch his breath. The next wave crested and crashed twenty feet away, and the 10-foot wall of churning whitewater came at him like a roaring freight train. Three feet before it enveloped him, Ken dropped straight down, kicking and pulling his way ten feet through the already turbulent water and towards the base of the cliff just ahead. He could see nothing, but he knew exactly where he was. It was all by feel.

Ken slid his hands across the submerged cliff face and felt the familiar knobby protuberance, gripping it tightly just as the washing machine action from the wave above reached him. He then swam under the ledge and kicked with his fins. He was in a narrow rock chamber and had to keep his ascent accurate to avoid scraping on the rocks.

At the surface, he popped his head up and took in a welcome breath of some of the twenty cubic feet of air available inside the rock chamber. He hooked his right arm around a rocky pinnacle and waited to regain his breath.

It was low tide, and a slanted vertical crack in the rocky ceiling three feet overhead allowed just enough light to see the calmer water level changing with the rising and falling tide. He lingered a few moments, checking the colony of sea anemones to be exposed for only a few more hours, and spotted a tiny one starting to grow.

"Hello, little one," his voice echoed, only slightly out of breath now, "Welcome to the world. You make it an even dozen." He touched the tip of a tiny tentacle, and it withdrew for protection, the other tentacles on full-out sensory alert for something either above it or below it on the food chain.

This was Ken's secret place. No one on Earth but him knew of its existence at the time, and he planned to keep it that way. He figured there were just some things a man keeps to himself.

The next wave smacked against the rocks, sending a clap echoing throughout the confining chamber, and the water level rose a few inches. At times of high surf and high tide, there was just enough headroom below the rock ceiling to catch some air before the water level rose up for a few seconds into the light crack, and then receded. Ken had experienced that only once, and it was spooky enough to last forever.

Ken lingered until the next rising of the water level, and then it was time to go.

He took in a gulp of air and pushed off against the narrow rock walls to send himself straight down, and when clear of the outer overhang, he found bottom with his feet and shot to the surface. He had about fifteen seconds to swim north, parallel to the cliff and around the Yankee Point headland, where a rocky shelf just below water level allowed him to quickly remove his fins and scramble up and out before the wall of whitewater from the next wave could snatch him. He continued to climb until he reached a ledge ten feet above the water. He leaned back against the rocks, his wetsuit protecting his back against scratches, and rested a moment to catch his breath. He removed his hood, exposing his sandy blond hair.

From the south side of a small cove, Ken had a commanding view of Point Lobos State Park to the north, and the headland of the peninsula to the south. Looking west out across the ocean for as far as he could see, the ocean was in turmoil, whitecaps blowing their tops like millions of little volcanoes. Above the horizon, a thin waning crescent moon hung above rain clouds moving in from far out at sea, so he could look forward to a rainy, moonless night.

A big storm was fast approaching from the northwest, and by five p.m., right around dark, high tides and large waves would be influenced by the steeply inclined submarine canyon starting just 25 feet offshore from where Ken dove in. The funnel configuration was just enough to push up incoming waves to over thirty feet and cause them to break right onto the cliff. Ken grew excited about what was to come: A sound like a huge explosion every time one of those puppies hit home.

Being an engineer and problem solver, Ken Easton had done the math. The amount of energy dissipated by the volume of a thirty-foot high wave, along a thirty-foot breaking section is enormous. Without going into the joules of energy and kilogram-meters per second and square roots of this and that, Ken Easton calculated that it was basically as if a 3,000-pound SUV (or a dozen Yugos) hit the cliff doing about 150 mph. With apologies to Bulwer-Lytton, it was looking to be a dark and stormy night ahead—perfect weather, according to Ken Easton's standards.

Swim fins in hand, Ken climbed the remaining thirty feet of near-vertical rock, well worn hand and foot holds facilitating the ascent to the plateau above. At the top, Lindy was there to greet him. Ken was temporarily out of breath and bent over, hands on knees and an easy target for Lindy, who began licking his face. He grabbed her jowls, kissed her on top of her nose, and then let her lick his face some more. He couldn't help but laugh. "I'll bet you're hungry, aren't you, girl?"

The four-year old Border collie was well-past ready for her breakfast. "Ten minutes, okay?"

Ken headed toward the spa, Lindy trotting along behind. Ken was proud of that spa, having done all the work himself. He had dug the hole, run the lines for water, gas, and electricity, and then had cut and placed the rebar and cemented and plastered the inside. A flatbed truck had delivered the heavy flat Travertine stones, and Ken set them into wet cement, one grunt at a time. It had taken almost a month, but it passed inspection at every phase. He and Valerie had spent most of an entire day in it, fingers and toes pruning away after first firing up the spa heater.

Stripping out of his wetsuit and hood, Ken stepped naked except for his wristwatch into the 104-degree swirling water and sank up to his neck. "Oh, yeah," he said, letting out a deep breath. He spent the first five minutes going over that wave ride in his head, critiquing but mostly commending himself, with thoughts for an even better ride next time. For the second five minutes, Ken thought about his little wave impact experiment he'd set up for that evening, expecting heavy surf.

After a soak in the spa, Ken Easton was ready to go to work … and since he worked at home, his office was a minute's walk away. He grabbed his wetsuit and fins and scooted off toward the house before the cold breeze could get to his gonads.

Ken's 2,000 square-foot home stood on a 30,000 square-foot lot, most of it east and up the hill towards the highway. It was the only house seaward of Spindrift Road on the little headland, cut off from casual view from neighbors by trees and bluffs. Ken's father and mother, both now deceased, had built the rectangular, single-story redwood-siding ranch-style house in the late sixties with a view of the ocean from every room. Ken's older sister, Laura, had had the room with a better view, but it was only a matter of degree. Even after twenty years in the alpine forests of Switzerland, Laura had written to Ken that she still missed that awesome ocean view. The next lot south, and up above on the next bluff, was slightly smaller than his and the only other buildable lot on the headland still zoned R-1—single family residential.

For ten years, Ken Easton had been actively trying to buy that lot because he didn't want to have anyone building so close. Ken's lot ended to the south in a sloped face, at the top of which and beyond was the prime spot for a house on the adjacent lot. But it was the potentially intrusive view down onto his whole backyard that raised Ken's hackles. "I'm not a nudist," Ken had recently told his colleague, Greg McAferty, "but if I feel like walking naked to the birdfeeder, by God, Greg, I want the option of walking naked to the birdfeeder."

What began with concern about a potentially intrusive view would later turn into a nightmare. The lot's owner, however, a certain Robert Sparks living in Las Vegas according to the records, had refused Ken's offer ten years ago on the basis that it was his retirement property. Sparks said he could not even think about selling it for at least a couple more years.

Every two years, Ken had called again. In 1997, Ken called once more. This time Sparks acted very coy, saying it was a possibility but not at that time. Ken tried on half a dozen occasions over the next three years to negotiate. He offered twice, and finally three times what the property was worth— $250,000 at the time, and now even more—figuring there *must* be a number that would satisfy the guy. Even three-quarters of a million dollars for a vacant lot apparently hadn't been enough.

And now, just the week before Thanksgiving 2001, first in a letter and then to an answering machine that cut him off after thirty seconds, Ken made an offer of a cool million, an offer that would mortgage him to hilt. He told Sparks that if he wanted to build a showplace, this was not it, as no one could see it from the highway or from most of the way down the treacherous access road. Heavy cement trucks would also have one helluva time … dial tone. It had all been to no avail.

After a quick shower, Ken slipped into his favorite, albeit tattered, sky blue sweatshirt and sweat pants, a gift from his wife five years back. He fed Lindy and made coffee, and then headed into his office at the far south end of the house, cup in hand, ready to start the day. He booted up his computer, sorting out and prioritizing information in his head.

Ken Easton was a consulting acoustical engineer, at the time just starting work on a six-month project with Donne & Maris, a big engineering firm headquartered in San Jose. D&M was under federal contract to devise a system that would detect three different levels of structural damage in multi-story buildings during an earthquake, and send a warning signal, hopefully before the building's occupants were trapped inside a collapsed structure.

San Jose was in earthquake country, and right on top of the granddaddy of them all—the San Andreas Fault. The complicated San Andreas Fault system runs from the Gulf of California north by northwest to the coastal region north of San Francisco and out to sea. Fault branches can be found all along the coastal range, including Paso Robles, Santa Cruz, and cities like Cambria on the coast.

Where there are earthquakes, there is ground acceleration, or lateral g-force. It's the old tablecloth analogy—a sudden jerk leaves everything with weight (plates, knives, and glasses) in place. But in an earthquake, it's as if the table settings (buildings and homes) are glued to the tablecloth (via foundations) and can't avoid the high acceleration. High g-forces cause structural damage, sometimes structural failure, and on occasion complete building collapse. Ken's job was to come up with a system that would "know" the difference between the three states of damage after a building experienced a seismic event.

If damage was light, occupants could still work in the building during repair. If some non-critical structural elements failed but would not cause complete collapse, occupants could still work inside but with certain restrictions. And if there was sufficient structural damage—cracked or broken steel beams or connecting flanges, damaged foundations and the like to suggest imminent collapse, occupants and officials would know that, too.

The trick was to determine, on a sliding scale, where the "transition points" were. Ken had written the proposal in a single weekend, having come up with an ingenious scheme to embed optical and acoustical sensors into the buildings at the construction stage, all pre-wired to a fail-safe alarm system inside the building and transmitted to the city engineer's office.

Part I was a simple idea. Three 40-foot long steel pipes, one-inch in diameter, would be laid in near the top of a building's concrete foundation footings in parallel, one each on the eastern and western foundations and one down the middle section. On one end of the steel pipe, an optical laser light emitter would shoot a beam down the pipe, where at the other end a receiver, like a shooter's target, picked up the beam.

In an earthquake, the whole structure usually moves as a single unit. However, if the beam shooting down the pipe were somehow deflected, different amounts of deflection would infer differing amounts of damage along the length of the foundation. If the beam were to be deflected by a maximum of an eighth of an inch, it would mean, based on the structural calculations for the hypothetical building, the foundation had deflected, perhaps even settled on one end, but the structure above was in no danger of imminent collapse.

If the beam were deflected by a quarter inch to three-eighths of an inch, trouble was brewing. The occupants were probably safe from collapse, but other critical components would have to be checked by a structural engineer before an all-clear signal could be given.

And finally, if the beam were deflected by more than half an inch over forty feet, on any one of the three foundations, it was time to evacuate, as not only had the foundation fractured, but also there were probably other serious structural problems above. Ken had worked up a program to equate the amount of deflection in the forty-foot tube to the probability of serious structural damage above. But that was the easy one.

The idea that made the feds sit up and take notice was the embedment of acoustic sensors to pick up the deflection, cracking, or actual failure of critical structural components. Each type of failure has its own unique acoustic signature, mostly in the strength of the signal, or waveform, generated. The cracking of a steel I-beam has a unique sound associated with it. And it is very much *un*like, say, a snapping 5/8" stainless steel bolt, which is a completely different sound altogether, and with a different acoustic signature.

The problem could, theoretically, be pinpointed accurately to a specific joint, connection, or structural member. The problem to be solved was to pinpoint the location of the damage and how the acoustic signature changed—speed and wave form— between structural elements, such as beam to flange, flange to vertical post, post to foundation, etc.

As in using many geosynchronous satellites— the Global Positioning System, or GPS—above the Earth to pinpoint one's position on the ground, Ken's proposal for a Building Acoustic Warning System (BAWS) showed engineers a three-dimensional picture of a given failure's general location and how much of a problem was predicted as a result of it. When all of the building's BAWS sensor data were compiled on a computer monitor, it would pretty much isolate the problem(s). And a yet-to-be-worked-out warning system of bells and alarms would deliver one of three messages, the intent of which would be clear to all:

1) No Problem (back to work);

2) Some Problems (an engineer is on the way);

3) Go For Outdoors Now (GFON)

The transition point of the GFON option (euphemistically referred to by the inner circle of D&M engineers as *Get the Fuck Out Now*) would be the trickiest of all to determine with any degree of accuracy. The whole project hinged on the margin of error around that now merely theoretical number. Too low and people might die; too high and it's useless. And yet the final number had to incorporate some degree of allowable risk. Most importantly, it had to be able to withstand altogether withering cross-examination, not to mention bald-face misrepresentation, by a future litigant's attorney(ies).

Both Ken and Greg were well aware that, of the many problems facing structural engineers in a seriously litigious society, most people really don't understand physics, or math, or materials science, or much of anything about hard science. People want to live and work in safety, but they have no clue as to how all this mysterious engineering stuff comes together. Also, both consumers and businessmen always want construction done at the least possible cost.

So, when a building collapses in an earthquake, Ken knew how easy it was to bamboozle a jury into awarding huge sums of money *from* engineers and firms who did the best they could, given the science and the construction budget, and *to* people who may or may not really deserve it. In most cases, there is an out-of-court settlement. Application of the law is not about seeking truth; it is, rather, about getting maximum dollar for your client and one's firm.

Ken was also aware that anyone could write the script on what would sway a jury: "The little dead girl, Becky, cradled in her mother's arms ... I couldn't get the picture out of my mind." The jurors might listen to the scientific explanations, but it is the suing attorney who holds strong emotional sway with, "They could have built it stronger, and they failed to do that based on cost, not the life of Becky Jones." And the lawyer would always get across the point, "That's why you carry insurance, right?"

What Ken knew would fly right over the jurors' heads was the simple proposition that if given, say, $10 billion, one could build a small office building that would be, for all practical purposes, nuke proof, let alone earthquake proof. "The Pentagon has probably done it already," Ken said to his colleague, Greg. Furthermore, he knew that society doesn't permit the worst-case analysis to be used as the basis for every building ever constructed. The country would have gone broke long ago, and it would be small comfort knowing that no building had ever collapsed.

Ken stared at his desktop with thoughts of voracious attorneys exposing, *ex post facto*, purported flaws in his design. After a moment, he knew such negative thinking was unproductive, so he glanced over towards the bookshelf, above it a Henry Miller painting, entitled, *Amour Toujours* ('love always,' or 'eternal love'). Viewable in its original form on the Internet, the Giclee print was still severely damaged from so much time exposed to seawater, but Ken preferred to leave it that way. Under the piece was the framed photograph of him, Valerie and their two-year old son, Tyler. The photo held his stare, and the memories began. Ken still missed them very much. It was going on a full year now. The emotional pain wasn't so much a lesser one now as it was locked

21

in at a certain plateau, like a chronic disorder, rising and sinking as thoughts make their way to the surface, fueled by past conversation. "Analytically emotional," he had said recently to Margie, the lady who owned a bed & breakfast up the highway and who had asked, standing in line at the grocery store, how he was holding up.

"One does not 'get over' such tragedy," the grief counselor had told him. "One merely moves on with a much heavier heart that gets lighter only with time."

The ringing phone brought Ken mostly back to the present. He recognized the caller I.D of his colleague up in San Jose. Greg McAferty was a structural engineer at D&M, and head of the acoustic sensor project. Ken pushed the speakerphone button. "Morning, Greg."

"Good morning, Ken. Thought you might like to know I just confirmed some of those GFON echo location parameters you sent over yesterday." Ken had just returned from San Jose and crunched some numbers two nights before on D&M's Cray supercomputer, having e-mailed the results to Greg just the afternoon before.

Ken responded, "I was going to start with turkey overdose yesterday and the effects of post-9/11 on the airline schedules, but I'll go with acoustic emission signatures, if you insist."

"Oh, yeah," he said with a guilty chuckle, "I heard how your flight got delayed." It was noticeable in his voice that Greg had unintentionally glossed over the small talk— a sleight regretted. Greg correctly surmised that Ken had spent Thanksgiving alone. They did the small talk, got down to business on the numbers, and ended with the Ken's answer to Greg's question about the coming storm. "The sensors are set, and the program is up and running, ready for the real thing tonight."

*****

Note to John: These periodic notes are to answer questions I feel you may be asking yourself as you are reading. I know you suggested not getting into too much detail on the historical material—and the DNA, too, as I recall—but I felt compelled to combine the science with the historical record, plus a little dramatic license, to fill in report details where appropriate. Reports like this can be so stale and impersonal, so I am trying my hand here at a narrative format. As far as Ken Easton and his bodysurfing are concerned, I know what you're going to say: "This could never happen." But it did—the guy's amazing. He was both a diver in high school and a champion swimmer at UC Santa Cruz (he once held the world record for the 400-meter Individual Medley at the NCAA prelims for *almost* an hour). The engineering information was all on computer disk. I spent an entire week going over it before it made sense to me. I think the time was well spent. Steven

3 Nortze

The Nortze family name (the "e" in Nortze is silent) had been associated, at least since the 1880s, through incomplete records and questionable associations, with failure at every possible turn. Only superficially related to business or financial failure per se, although those were undoubtedly part of the mix, the Nortze failure was of a different ilk altogether.

In a continuing quest for personal perfection, the actual always seemed to fall far short of the ideal for the Nortzes. Beginning with George "Papa" Nortze, family members from that point on looked to their patriarchs for savior status, and the imperfections—read failures—detected would be incorporated into their respective psychological wiring. Not in a direct, confrontational *J'accuse!* sort of way, but rather deep down in the psychological mix. There was a general feeling of being let down, even a sense of betrayal, for not being provided with whatever it was that members of the Nortze clan thought they deserved.

In late 1883, George "Papa" Nortze noted in his diary that he had bought into a "sweet deal" as a partner in the first (and last) whaling station in Monterey. Seasonal migration of the gray whale along the California coast has occurred for millions of years, from calving grounds in Baja to the plankton swarms of Alaska's Bering Sea.

Beginning in 1854 in Monterey, the goal of whalers had been to kill every whale possible—grays, humpbacks, even the occasional sperm or right whale—for their blubber, rendering them down for oil. In a few short years, whales had been hunted almost to extinction.

Almost thirty years after the whale slaughter began, George Nortze set out to catch every remaining whale lumbering by in order to reap his fortune in whale oil. He figured that many others before him had done so, so why not him? The problem was simply that there were not many whales left when Nortze tossed his harpoon into the ring, so to speak.

In the abstract world of George Nortze, catching a whale was a simple notion of harpooning the beast and hauling him back to shore for rendering. In the real world of diminishing numbers of whales in early 1886, and plying the windy, cold, and usually treacherous outer waters off Monterey Bay in 28-foot rowboats, whaling was anything but simple.

George Nortze's little fleet caught very few whales the year before. The financial picture had also started out bad in 1886, with no whales caught since early January, so George volunteered to go out and help land a whale. It would, as it turned out, set an example for others not to follow. After a three-day trek by ten boats in monstrous seas with howling, bitterly cold winds, the whalers harpooned a single bull gray whale.

George Nortze had nearly died of exposure on the hunt, but his hopes were buoyed at the sight of the whaling station ahead and thoughts of a warming fire. Crowds of Montereyans, including his then 18-year old son, Duane, waited anxiously on the docks as the boats hauled the carcass toward shore. Due to a favorable change in weather, practically the whole town showed up, people expectant that this one whale would signal better fortunes for the people of Monterey. Everyone, including Duane, cheered as the whalers neared shore. A minor victory seemed at hand.

Disaster quickly snatched defeat from the jaws of victory. George, despite his exhaustion and near freezing, hoisted his hauling rope high in the air for all to see, arms visibly shaking from exposure. By something exceeding coincidence, it and another carelessly maintained rope broke apart from the strain just offshore from the docks. The whale quickly and unceremoniously sank. Even so close to shore, the deflated whale carcass settled a hundred feet down on the bottom, virtually inaccessible.

George Nortze couldn't believe his "bad luck." He cursed the whale, the ropes, and his fellow whalers, leaving no room for self-blame in starting this doomed venture in the first place. George tended to demand perfection from others, but never took blame himself for the consequences of his own actions.

A pall quickly settled in over the docks, people looking as if they had just witnessed the sinking of the entire town into those same ocean depths. As if on cue, the Presbyterian Church bell struck noon, and most people realized this was the death knell for Monterey whaling. The onus of blame quickly fell on George Nortze, symbol for the failed whaling enterprise in Monterey. His diary contained the notation: "By comparison, Ahab had an easy time with Moby Dick."

George Nortze stood in familiar entrepreneurial posture looking out to sea from Point Piños, on the rocky northern shore of the Monterey Peninsula and what is now part of Pacific Grove. It was a cold late-January day in 1886, and a light rain was settling in like a sick and cranky relative staying the entire weekend. George was, despite the elements, all confidence in the presence of his son, Duane, but the Nortze family mentality under all that red hair revealed more ambition than common sense ... at least if family history was any guide.

Standing on the Peninsula at low tide on that cold and rainy January day, George and Duane discussed their common future. "We have to do something, and quickly, son. Our operating capital is quickly running out."

It's a good thing there was no commercial potential in butterfly wings or body parts, as the grove of eucalyptus and pine trees a quarter mile south from where he stood—where millions of Monarch butterflies came every winter to rest in a unique microclimate—would have quickly fallen victim to the Nortze clan's rapacious appetite for financial success.

George assumed that all his problems would be solved by the acquisition of money. Of course, the problems went directly to more personal matters, such as perhaps not getting what he needed as a child. Since there is no mention in the diaries and journals of a Mrs. Nortze—Duane's mother—it's all informed speculation.

It's pretty safe to say that George and/or his wife might very well have walled themselves off to those they cared for the most, including Duane, their only son. But the psychological notion of what should be (the ideal of parental bonding), as opposed to what was (little bonding but actual financial failures) had to have a profound effect on young Duane in the manner in which he bonded—first to his parents, and later to his own children. And from those children who later became parents to their children, the cycle continued. It's a murky business in that realm of the subconscious, different for each person on all but the most fundamental level.

Duane glanced down at his feet and stepped away a few inches so as to get better purchase on the rocks, nearly every inch covered with abalone. He then had an epiphany. "Papa, how about if we built a processing plant for these abalone, right in the center of town? People love abalone, and we could export what we don't sell locally."

George was dumbstruck. "You're right. The gold isn't in the hills, Duane, but right here under our feet!" Abalone were so plentiful along the central coast near Monterey that even the thousands of sea otters plying the regional waters could not keep up with the abalone population.

Abalone were on the exposed rocks for the taking, and taken they were, quickly and in mass quantities by the newly formed Nortze Abalone Cannery. It would later prove to be one of the nation's first environmental catastrophes.

"Nature has provided an endless supply of these tasty arthropods," George wrote in his diary. He didn't quite understand the concept of diminished supply. After all of the easily obtainable abalone shells had been pried off the local rocks, it became apparent to the most casual of observers, and only later to George and Duane Nortze, that if one wanted more abalone, one would just have to search further up and down the coast, and into deeper water as well. Like the slaughter of the whales, and with no lessons learned, the pillage of abalone had the same result.

The waters off Monterey Bay are some of the coldest in the world at that latitude, caused by deep submarine canyons in places over a mile deep just a few miles from shore. With all the local abalone picked clean, George Nortze began dumping more and more money into the cannery operations to offset the higher and higher cost of getting the abalone back to shore for processing.

First it was a matter of sending boats further up and down the dangerous coast. And after that, divers had to be outfitted in semi-protective (and expensive) suits to collect near-shore abalone. The upwelling frigid water is ideally suited for passing whales, or furry sea otters dining on abalone, but human divers, even with protective but primitive suits, were dying off faster than they could be replaced. Hypothermia, suits ripped by jagged rocks, air hoses snagged or ripped from their connectors by rough seas—these things and more were the cause of angst to George Nortze. Not because people were dying, but because the venture was fast becoming an increasingly futile outlay of capital.

The divers also had to dive deeper and deeper to collect what was left of the abalone, which wasn't much. George Nortze did not know, nor did he care, that natural replacement of abalone took many years, sometimes decades to grow to maturity, but certainly not months. Nortze had wiped the central coast clean of abalone, and the sea otters began leaving the area for other feeding grounds.

Papa George was torn between the near-perfection of wiping out the abalone population with the financial crises he faced. "Success is measured by the numbers accumulating in one's bank account," he wrote, "which is inversely proportional to the number of surviving abalone." He decided to leave the day-to-day cannery operations up to his manager while trying to come up with another way to make his fortune.

Sleeping 20 hours a day for nearly a year did wonders for George Nortze, if not his family and fortune. George had plenty of time to think about his future, and he planned his financial strategy accordingly. He wrote much and often in his diary. Early on in Papa George's "sleep and think strategy," as he called it, he came up with the idea that Duane should get a job and help support the family. "The perfect solution," he wrote.

There were undoubtedly other Nortzes in the bloodline back in Europe, but the first mention in the American press was of one Duane P. Nortze, 19 years of age, of Monterey, California, in 1887. As the night desk clerk of the luxury resort Hotel Del Monte, law enforcement authorities questioned Duane about the fire that razed one of the largest and certainly most elegant seaside resorts in the country.

A big spring celebration at the Del Monte began at sunset, signaling the opening of the season, with dignitaries from San Francisco and important townspeople in attendance. On that cool April Fool's evening seven years after the hotel's grand opening, Mr. Drake, one of the hotel owners, was in a tizzy with all the preparations. He dashed by the check-in counter in search of more table linens, shouting behind him, "Red, look sharp and *be* sharper." Duane's shock of red hair had made the nickname stick. He was a stocky boy, and not all that handsome or extraordinary in any way, seemingly just a regular kid starting out in life.

"Yes, Mr. Drake." Duane continued his efforts to sort out newly forged extra room keys. He was stuck on which was Room 6 and which Room 9, turning and comparing the numbers repeatedly, looking for any slight difference. Then he spotted it.

"Good evening, Duane." The familiar voice caused Duane to raise his eyes just enough to see a huge spray of daisies below an ample bosom. He smiled officiously. "Morning, Consuelo." Duane returned to his thinking only about the key comparison.

At eighteen, Consuelo Marasco, of Mexican descent, was the only child of a farmer and his wife up in Carmel Valley. They supplied seasonal vegetables and flowers to the Hotel Del Monte and other local outlets.

Not by any standard the most beautiful young woman Duane had ever laid eyes on, Consuelo was short and stocky, a bit like Duane, but she had a round face that sloped a bit to the left side, and her front teeth were crooked. She did speak impeccable English, an advantage she hoped to use to catch a rich husband someday. There were a lot of rich gold miners at the time, so at least the dream was there. Duane was not a prospect, being just a clerk and all, but she could at least practice her feminine wiles on him, especially on this All Fools day.

Over the past year, Consuelo had used on Duane what little physical charms she possessed, subtly flaunting her body in a manner that Duane found harder and harder to ignore, even as he quashed his impulses for so unattractive a young woman.

Like so many people in the late 19th century, Consuelo kept a diary. "I think I'll stir up a little trouble today," she had written that morning at home, "Duane is such a handy target." It was an innocent notion on her part, meant to merely test the waters of passion in a climate of a little practical joking. That day's would be her last entry.

Consuelo leaned across the counter, lowering her flowers just so, exposing her cleavage only to Duane. She whispered, "Got an extra room for us?" She was clearly enjoying teasing the sexually inexperienced young Duane.

Duane knew at that moment that if he didn't respond to Consuelo like the man he supposed himself to be, even though he had no desire for her, he would never be treated like one. "Nine," he blurted out. "I go on break in fifteen minutes." Duane slid the key to Room 9 now attached to its leather holder across the countertop to a very surprised Consuelo Marasco.

"You *are* an aggressive young man, after all, aren't you?"

Duane ignored the tease. "It's Room 9, not Room 6," Duane added, almost to the point of insult. It was a poor defense against hope. There sat an air bubble in Duane's chest the size of a grapefruit. He had never done such a bold thing with a girl, and he thought about what might happen if he proved to be a less than an accomplished lover. Duane contemplated full retrenchment, but the need to lose his virginity outweighed his lack of desire for Consuelo, as well as outweighing any fears of intimacy, or sexual failure, should that opportunity arise. It was, in his mind, an opportunity to act on what he believed was the "perfect" opportunity.

Consuelo rose to the challenge. She scooped up the key and slipped it into a pocket. "Fifteen minutes, then." She primped herself and walked off to deliver her flowers to the dining room. Meanwhile, the minutes passed by like hours for Duane, who kept busy whipping his libido into shape, one fantasy at a time.

First, there should be flirtatious small talk, something about the quality of the room, the bed linens, antique furniture, whatever. And then it will be on to touching, holding perhaps, all leading up to that first kiss. I will have to pretend she is far more beautiful to get past that phase. Mrs. Drake, now there's a perfect woman. The blonde hair, the curvaceous body—yes, she will do nicely. Consuelo will feel my passion, and she will respond in kind.

And so his fantasy progressed, all the way up to, but not including the final act itself, which Duane wanted to leave as a mystery to be solved in the moment. It was a pretty good plan for someone so inexperienced. It just wasn't perfect.

After what seemed to Duane an eternity, the assistant manager finally relieved him, and Duane made his way circuitously to the south corridor. All but a few of the guests had already made their way to the banquet hall for the festivities. Duane nodded to the last two as they passed, pretending he was just checking up on things. His heart raced as he pulled out the key to Room 9, checking to see that no one was watching. He opened the door.

Inside the room, sitting in profile on the end of the bed, Consuelo had her hand under her dress and was masturbating herself. *Perfect!* To Duane, it was a sight nothing short of an open invitation, so he stepped in.

Consuelo turned her head and saw Duane, and her eyes flashed in anger. "Get out, you idiot!" she shouted. "Did you think I was really serious … with you, a desk clerk?" It was a bit over the top, but she wanted to test some limits here. Besides, she figured, he could come over to the bed, wrestle her down and take her at his will. There were all sorts of interesting possibilities running through Consuelo's head.

It all had quite the opposite effect on Duane Nortze. In a state of shock at the disconnect between his perfect opportunity and abject failure, he gathered up what was left of his senses and backed out of the room, closing the door behind him.

Rejection. Abject embarrassment. Total sexual frustration. Failure. *Serious … with you, a desk clerk?* The phrase jabbed him sharply. Consuelo would rather pleasure herself than have Duane enjoy at least part of the fun. And all this, he concluded in a blinding fury, with a homely, wholly *im*perfect girl like Consuelo.

Who the hell does she think she is?

When Duane's giddy expectation met with unfathomable sexual shock, there had to have been some sort of internal physical reaction. At that very moment of psychotic break, it may have been that a bolt of negative mental energy coursed through Duane Nortze's physical body and settled somewhere in his brain, the exact place a mystery. A synapse deep in his gray matter, perhaps. "The pain was akin to electrocution," Duane wrote of *something* that happened that day.

That synaptic junction must have overloaded and exploded, sending hormonal shrapnel into a particular cellular array, perhaps damaging a chromosome. That implies gene-level corruption at least, but more probably an effect at the lowest possible level—particular DNA sequences on the helical strand.

There are four amino acids, called nucleotides, linking the two strands together: Adenine always pairs with Thymine, and Guanine with Cytosine. Putting one or more of the amino acids out of commission on one or more strands will not only affect the matching amino acid forming the direct link, but will also and forever after alter one's DNA during replication.

Few mutations are beneficial, and most are fatal. And there are mental illnesses, like depression, that can be currently directly traced to genetics (production/blocking of brain chemicals, for example). But for that to happen, there are always corrupted DNA sequences involved.

In Duane's case, one can think of it in terms of the phrase coined by the late renowned zoologist and author, Steven J. Gould: *punctuated equilibrium.* In short, it means that an organism plods along like normal for a lot of generations, even eons. It may undergo minor morphological changes along the way as a result of random and non-fatal changes to its DNA that prove beneficial. And then, WHAM! Something big happens, such as a freak meteor impact leading to global extinction and the rise of mammals adapting to new conditions.

On the human level, a psychological meteor impact during a psychotic episode might prove just as destructive, especially for succeeding generations. It could be termed Punctuated Psychogenetic Equilibrium. The human mind is a formidable force.

Whatever the exact cause of the Nortze family line's punctuated equilibrium in the brain of Duane Nortze, the effect would prove permanent, manifesting itself in many ways over the years, particularly with women. At least that's what one could reasonably conclude by a careful reading of certain cryptic entries in his diary and others.

And when one puts together the behaviors of his and later generations of Nortzes associated with issues of personal attachment, a psychological profile emerges—the makings of antisocial citizens. But the problems were intergenerational and went so much deeper than the "environment" of dysfunctional personal attachments. That at least infers a genetic aberration.

Most importantly, the genetic aberration that passed itself on to future generations was bound to express itself somewhere down the line. At one time perhaps deeply embedded in a recessive gene, the evil in Duane Nortze was somehow brought to life by the words and deeds of Consuelo Marasco. Sent up a few hundred floors to the executive suite of Duane's subconscious, it was time for evil to take a peek at the hostile world outside and get it back under control.

On this first occasion, the little voice in Duane Nortze's head, the same as in all of us saying its first hello in the morning and the last goodnight, dredged up the rationale for a particularly heinous act.

Duane walked down the empty corridor and out the back door, and a few paces ahead opened up the storage shed. He retrieved a full gallon gasoline can used for the generators and, covering it with an old blanket, walked back to the door of Room 9. With festivities now underway in the banquet room, the corridor was empty.

Duane quietly slipped his key into the lock and turned it, leaving it in place so the door could not be opened from the inside. Duane then folded the blanket and placed it just in front of the crack under the door. Covering the end of the spout with his palm, he tipped up and lowered the gallon can, and then removed his palm, allowing the gas to pour freely under the door. Some of the gas reached the edge of the blanket. Three-quarters of the can was empty before he heard the foot-steps, first away from, and then towards the door.

When the can was empty, Duane took out a match, struck it against the wall, and dropped it near the bottom edge of the door. The volatile fumes now circulating in Room 9 exploded in a fireball that Duane could see reflected under the door.

Muffled screams never made it past his ears. He picked up the blanket, partly in flame, and beat it against the hallway rug until the flames turned to smoke. Duane then turned and calmly walked to the exit door, rolling the blanket as he walked, and returned the gas can to the shed. When he returned and unlocked the door to Room 9, the room was fully engulfed in flames, and he tossed the rolled up blanket inside. But that was then.

A few minutes before, after Duane had made his awkward and humiliating retreat, Consuelo had sat down at the foot of the bed, giggling at her devious ways with poor Duane. When she first smelled the fumes, she walked to the window to find the source, but it was closed and all she could see was the next building just beyond. She then retraced her steps around the foot of the bed and was almost to the door when the fumes ignited. Standing in a pool of gasoline, her clothes quickly burned off, and soon thereafter the flame and smoke in her lungs seared shut her esophagus, shutting off her air supply.

Duane now stared from the open door at the charred, still burning body lying on the floor, barely recognizable as a once-human being. His uncontrollable anger had been dissipated by actions matching an idealized solution. So, without a hint of remorse, Duane thought to himself: *At least it was a dry heat.*

Duane Nortze suddenly saw himself not only as his own emotional savior, but that there were others to save, too. It was hero time. The room was filled with dense black smoke that began to pour out into the hallway and into Duane's face. He took in a healthy gulp of smoke, exhaled with a fitful cough, and turned towards the office. His face now sported a thin layer of smoke, and he purposefully streaked it with the back of his hand. "Fire!" he yelled, then coughed again and again as he ran down the hallway to warn the guests. "Fire ... fire ... everyone get out ... fire."

The hotel burned to the ground, but with no loss of life reported, as Duane never mentioned Consuelo. It was arson, to be sure, but since no one had seen anything, and arson investigation per se hadn't been invented yet, Duane played dumb with the police—by no means a stretch of character.

It would be a week before her father, Pablo Marasco, away in San Francisco obtaining seed stock, returned to find his daughter missing. Try as he did to equate the fire with Consuelo's sudden disappearance, Pablo couldn't get to first base with the hotel owners and managers who wanted the incident quickly forgotten. Mr. Drake threatened to cut off his flower business if he so much as talked to the police, and further suggested to the grief-stricken Pablo that he look for his daughter elsewhere.

It would be forever lodged in the newspapers and history books that the fire had, miraculously, not taken a single life. Duane Nortze wrote in his own journal that night a psychologically coded message beginning with: "The gasping, almost a scream—maybe an apology?" and ending with: "Consuelo missing in fire. At least it was a dry heat."

The hotel was quickly rebuilt, and Mr. Drake even gave Duane his old job back as night desk clerk, he being the hero who called the warning, thereby saving many lives. A certificate from the Monterey Fire Department was on display over the rows of mailboxes, and it said so. Duane also kept the newspaper clipping.

Here, finally, was external recognition for a solution to a particular problem, and executed with perfect results. The perfect crime.

Having learned a valuable lesson, the management made sure there were ten full water buckets stashed for future emergencies in the closet behind the mailboxes.

Duane never anguished about the death of Consuelo by his hand, and in point of fact, never thought about it at all, except that everything had gone "perfectly." Consciously, anyway. Unconsciously, however, his actions that night back on the first day of April gnawed away at his psyche minute-by-minute, hour-by-hour, and day-by-day. When the ecstasy of perceived perfection meets head on with the reality of critical and unfulfilled emotional needs, there is no lasting satisfaction. Internal conflicts arising from that can be devastating. No one can say for sure, but the notion of negative gene reinforcement could apply here.

One might fairly ask where in the Nortze family history such disregard for human life originated. Unfortunately, the available records other than diaries do not provide details, but this could have been merely the first outward manifestation of evil, embedded way, way down in the deep recesses of the Nortze genetic code.

Nine months later, in the pre-dawn hours after a bitterly cold December night in 1887, and with few customers in the hotel, Duane Nortze decided on his own volition, yet with no experience in such matters, to clean out the huge fireplace in the hotel's main dining area. He wished only to start a new one to be fresh for the few breakfast patrons braving the wintry coast. Properly using the metal hopper to gather up the ashes (and hot embers), he went back to the office and promptly dumped the hopper into a trash container half-full of paper.

By the time he had gone to the back of the hotel for firewood and returned, the office was ablaze. With the aid of the water buckets, Duane helped put the fire out this time, but like the possibility of Consuelo's death in the previous hotel fire, any mention of this latest incident was kept secret. Mr. Drake quickly realized that if the press got hold of news of a second fire, it would be very bad for business, perhaps enough to shut them down altogether.

It was Drake himself who confronted Duane about his exact activities. When Duane began dissembling and acting evasive, Drake recognized the signs and cornered Duane into a confession. It wasn't arson, just a stupid mistake, and Drake insisted that no charges be filed—bad press and all—but he had to let Duane go.

Duane took his certificate of heroism and returned to the family home overlooking the rocks of the peninsula. He wrote in his diary that night, "Heroes abandoned, managers promoted. They will pay, someday." He began immediately looking for a new job. George "Papa" Nortze, renewed after all his "sleep and think" time, supplied it.

George Nortze had found another venture in which to sink his quickly diminishing capital. Together with three others, Papa George helped form the San Carlos Gold Mining Co in 1888, each of the partners dumping $12,500 apiece into the project in hopes of cashing in on the gold fever that had swept the state since 1849. He desperately wanted to be one of the "millionaire vulgarians" talked about in the newspapers.

As was the case with his whaling venture, George was a bit late—by thirty years—in joining the gold hunt. What San Carlos Gold Mining Co. found was not gold but rather coal, discovered inland from Point Lobos, just south of the Monterey Peninsula. Not the good anthracite coal, but the lousiest bituminous coal with high sulfur content running in a single seam down a hundred feet underground before leveling out. It was a lot of hard work and expenditure of capital for not much product.

George's business acumen was, in all likelihood, unrelated to some mysterious genetic predisposition to failure. But it sure seemed that an almost innate lack of common sense ran in the family.

The mining company employed Chinese laborers, and it fell upon Duane Nortze ("Mista Led" as he was called by the workers due to his shock of red hair) to whip them into shape. Duane made a rather curious entry into his diary: "The laborers seem entirely self-motivated, as their wages are based on tonnage of coal hauled up to the surface." Despite this reality, Duane took particular pleasure in shouting at the top of his lungs, showing them (and his father) just who was in charge. "More coal!" he would shout, "Bring up more coal."

"Yes, Mista Led," was the standard reply, and they went about their business as usual.

Duane became convinced that the workers were loafing down in the mineshaft, and one day decided to get down and dirty and see for himself what was what. Once in the mine, he began by assigning himself the task of placing the heavy coal buckets onto the engine-driven winch. "My hands became raw and bleeding after less than half an hour," he later wrote. Sitting down to rest, he fumbled with sore fingers to pull out a cigarette. He was about to strike a match, and one man shouted, "No, Mista Led!" Three Chinese laborers tackled Duane before he could turn the dust-filled shaft into a deadly fireball. Again with the fire thing, but who's counting?

It was quite a humiliation for Duane. More than that, however, six laborers down in the shaft—amounting to half the crew—quit without explanation, getting their wages only after the whole crew threatened revolt. Fingers were properly pointed at Duane, but Papa George would hear none of that. Duane seemed settled by what he deemed a plausible explanation, shrugging the whole thing off in his diary: "They're a lazy lot and want to shift blame to someone else. Good riddance to them."

After two years of marginal existence, George Nortze was quickly going broke, and this hemorrhage of mineworkers came at a particularly inopportune time. There were bank failures in the East, and capital was drying up all over the country. The fact that the coal was dirty and not of the highest BTU content didn't help. For three more months, George tried to make a go of it, but the company eventually went under.

Papa George immediately regained control over his still-failing cannery business, promptly throwing good money after bad into new machinery and other technical means of production. In the final analysis, however, it wasn't the technical aspects of cannery processing causing the Nortze cannery to go under, but rather aesthetics. By 1910, after twenty years of continuous but only marginally profitable operations, the cute little sea otters loved by the tourists were all but gone, along with their primary food supply—abalone.

Worst of all, however, was the stench. The whole town of Monterey stunk to high heaven. Thousands upon thousands of abalone shells drying in the summer sun were enough to put one off any meal, but particularly lunch at one of the quaint seaside restaurants. George and Duane Nortze hadn't even noticed the smell.

The merchants and residents all began to complain that tourism was in steep decline. The stated cause of dismay from many who flocked to (but mostly away from) Monterey was the awful odors wafting in the breeze from the direction of the Nortze cannery, dead center in town.

While other more remote canneries would last until 1928, the Nortze Cannery was forced to shut down in 1910, and Nortze went belly-up. Again. So crestfallen was George Nortze that he took to his bed. He died a month later, leaving Duane, now 41 years old, in charge of the rapidly diminishing family fortune. George's last diary entry read, "I am finished with an imperfect life. I trust the afterlife will be as perfect as advertised."

Taking the many clues given thus far, the following should come as stale news: The Nortze family was trouble posing in human form. It's a tough thing to impugn about an entire family, but what else can one say, given the facts? Every Nortze venture seemed to sour, a decidedly anti-Midas touch, if you will. And they were also just not very nice people. Chicken-and-egg there, but the probabilities skewed data to the preliminary conclusion that the subject of *monetary losses* was the causative factor. Perhaps, perhaps not.

By 1915, the now 46-year old Duane Nortze had married twice. Since the fiery death of Consuelo, Duane had developed a certain secretive persona regarding women. He was simply afraid of them. Yet they viewed Duane as a mystery man—and hero, according to the certificate—eligible for marrying, and he did have money, or at least what was left of the family fortune. Duane just never did anything with it. No investments, no joint ventures, nothing. He even wrote in his diary of his reluctance for further risky investments: "Why bother? Investing in fire insurance policies? Sounds promising—will reflect." It was "sleep and think" time for Duane Nortze.

During his two marriages, Duane had been a real miser. His two wives discovered only too late what a miserable skinflint he was, and they fled to parts unknown. The last wife did not even bother to file for divorce. And neither former wife had dreamed him capable of an actual murder in what was thus far the perfect crime—no one knew there had even been a murder.

Selfish desires at the expense of everyone else around him had been the cause of much misery for Duane. In addition, where fortunes made other men brave and willing to take risks of all sorts, Duane Nortze's family misfortune, and the death of his father (for which he rightly blamed his own hare-brained abalone idea), had the singular effect of turning Duane Nortze into a sniveling recluse. He was afraid of making even the smallest decision, preferring instead to have others take the blame for things gone wrong. His housekeeper, Maria, soon became "the decision-maker in my life," Duane wrote, "Who else can I blame if things go wrong?"

By late 1915, at age 57, Duane knew the potential for a good alliance when he saw it and raised Maria's salary to $50 per month, an un-heard of amount in those days. She was a native and quite beautiful 25-year old Carmelite Indian, and Nortze showed her off like a prized cow, much to the horror of all right-thinking and morally blessed Montereyans. It was even a scandal in the 13-year old city of Carmel-by-the-Sea, just over the hill from Monterey. Yet it was Maria who would, ironically, later bring some genetic strength into an otherwise doomed lineage.

Maria was devoted to Duane, as he treated her well, but for reasons other than altruism. He needed her far more than she needed him, so he had trodden carefully while developing an alliance. She ended up in his bed willingly, as she wanted a child, but love? No. Maria also didn't attach too much import to their age separation, and Duane wasn't at all sexually demanding.

As time went by, Duane grew standoffish, which was fine with Maria as she had a private life apart from him. She also knew instinctively that the community around her was wholly uninspired by her presence, so she willingly stayed in the shadows.

Maria spoke no English at first, for the simple reason that Duane rarely spoke to her. He slept with her when the urge struck, which wasn't often. Maria was, however, a quick study, and she learned the rudiments of conversation through attentive listening. She was also an avid reader, having basically taught herself the new language. Even Duane was impressed. "Ever try that?" he wrote in his diary, "Not a lot of people make it past the threshold of minimal literacy."

By choice (not to mention community preference), Maria didn't get out much, enjoying instead her readings of local history to bide her time and hone her English skills. Like nearly everyone else, Maria also kept a diary—a cowhide leather bound folio she used for notes, sketches, new words learned, anything coming to mind. She especially enjoyed reading about the role her native people had played in developing the central coast region since the 17th century, and she made notes in her own diary on that as well.

Duane and Maria had a child in 1916, a red-headed boy named Cecil. Maria called him Cecilito in gentle whispers and old Indian songs, but only out of Duane's earshot. It is difficult to assign genetic predetermination too quickly in matters familial, but Cecil Nortze seemed, at least outwardly, about as dissimilar to his father as an offspring could be.

Individual character is noticeable at times even in infancy, after which personality becomes merely refined as the years go by. Some personalities reveal gentle generational swings, others nothing short of wild, perhaps senseless ones. For Cecil Nortze, it was as if his genetic magnet had suddenly reversed polarity.

Where Duane was reclusive, cerebral, and had a nasty temperament, Cecil proved himself early on to be assertive, even combative (but on a friendly level) and definitely competitive. He was a Nortze, no doubt about it, even with red hair tinted with auburn, compliments of his mother's contributing chromosomes in that area. As Maria wrote, "There is a soft side to Cecilito. He is warm-hearted and strong of spirit. Must be from my side of the family."

Yet with all the promise of a new generation, Cecil Nortze spent the first years of his life with two heavy burdens to bear, both related to his parents. His father's name had become synonymous with business failure, and his mother a failure in polite society. No one at the time knew too much about specific genetic influences, so it was never a subject of discussion.

Since Maria and Duane never married, as he was never properly divorced, the sins of the parents were foisted upon their only son, Cecil. Try as she did to make a better life for her son, Maria knew early on that Cecil had been collared with a rather large albatross.

That gene within the Y-chromosome, corrupted earlier in his father and passed down to Cecil, finally began to unshackle itself from the ones around it, starting its path of domination in Cecil at the ripe age of five. Duane and his mother were walking hand and hand in downtown Monterey. It was a cold late-autumn morning, and the wind-swept Monterey pines bristled in a steadily increasing wind. Through the window of a local bakery, Maria could see men and women sipping coffee, children drinking cocoa and munching on pastries, all the while talking and gesturing and smiling. Maria led Cecil by the hand into the shop, both eager for some hot cocoa.

Upon their entry, the room temperature seemed to drop 50 degrees. *Silent hostility* is the only term that fits little Cecil's first impression of Monterey society. It's a good thing he couldn't hear their thoughts: *Fucking Indian whore. Little bastard. Who let these scum into our exalted midst?*

Maria also felt the chill, but she stepped up to the counter and forced a smile. The owner, an otherwise gregarious Italian man named Franco, stared her down, saying nothing.

"Two hot cocoas, please," Maria said in perfect English.

Franco shook his head. "All out," he said flatly. He then began drumming his fingers on the counter and cocking his head toward the doorway in a manner unmistakably suggestive of a quick exit by Maria and her son.

Maria glanced over to the cocoa maker and saw the steam rising. There was plenty of cocoa. She then turned her eyes to each of the patrons, and some looked at her with disgust. Others merely averted their eyes, engulfed in an awkward silence.

Taking in everything, Cecil discovered at that moment the feeling of blind hatred, hatred directed at he and his mother for what he ascribed to no reason whatsoever. Cecil's nerve synapses promptly exploded, registering the painful rejection in the same place within his brain as his father, Duane, when Consuelo had rejected him 34 years prior. With no other outlet for his emotion, Cecil began to sob. Quietly at first, his sobs soon turned into a plaintive wail.

Maria led Cecil out the door without any cocoa. She could handle such treatment, but Cecil could not. At home, Cecil ran to his father, Duane, and related how mean everyone had been to him and his mother. Maria reluctantly filled in the details, and even summarized it in her diary. Duane wrote cryptically, "Time waits for no man but me."

That one incident, more so than all the others that followed, stayed with Cecil for three more years, buried down deep somewhere in his gray matter. Apparently, his father, Duane, never forgot it, either, nor his promise made after being fired from his job at the Del Monte.

By 1924, Franco the baker had moved his whole operation to the Hotel Del Monte. On a chilly, late-September night, and for the second time in its forty-year history, the Del Monte burned to the ground, this time truly without the loss of a single life. The fire was of suspicious origin somewhere near the front desk. And no one could seem to get the door open to the closet behind the wall of mailboxes where the water buckets were stored.

Sitting on a nearby hillside nestled amongst the Monterey pines, Papa Duane held Cecil between his knees, and they watched together as the flames seemed to lick the stars in the cold night air.

According to his diary, Duane let Cecil hold the matchbox, and he said, "Don't play with matches, son—unless you're going to use them."

At that moment, Cecil's intense brain activity probably turned what was previously the damaged but recessive Nortze gene segment into a dominant one. With prior facts and circumstances coming into play here, it undoubtedly had something to do with temperature, if not fire itself, although it is admittedly unclear from current scientific literature precisely how that physical process might have taken place.

In any event, the Nortze family went flat broke after that, and it would be 72 years before the Nortze family curse—the financial part, anyway— finally ended with a Straight Flush.

*****

Note to John: Maria's journal is as straightfor-ward as she was. George and Duane Nortze, on the other hand, wrote about all of their activi-ties very cryptically, almost in code. And George did not feel it necessary to make any mention of his antecedents, so they are lost to history. Much of what I wrote (and will write) in the form of specific dialogue and motivation is ad-mittedly my own speculation, but it is, I believe, soundly based.

For the Nortze male descendents, it was as if the noble human spirit had somewhere, some-how, and under mysterious circumstances abandoned the entire family line—or was snuffed out. Perhaps a creeping incivility grew into outright contempt for the rights, privileges, feelings and hopes of those around them some-where back in time, and became codified in the family gene pool. One thing is clear: This Nortze family trait, just as in eye color, stat-ure, and skin tone, revealed itself in a specific way. "Attachment problems" is too general a

term. A more fitting description might be intergenerational evil brought on by Punctuated Psychogenetic Equilibrium—my own term. Once active, the gene stays active until the hereditary line dies out. The gene never "repairs itself."

While the specific genetic coding probably does not include the more general order to "correct emotional attachment problems," that same coding very well might include the instruction to, for instance, "use prior successful strategy to get desired results." The gene does not consider itself "evil," merely successful—it is an amoral entity.

It took a long time to get all this information together, John, but I think it works. Rather than use terms familiar to me, such as "intrapsychic structures," or go on about "psychobiologic vulnerabilities" and "temperamental predispositions," I tried to put matters in a layman's context.

BTW, John, once I started in on this narrative format, I just got carried away, so I'll try not to take your comment, "Don't write a novel!" too literally. But I found it absolutely critical that you understand the Nortze family background in more than just dry technical jargon. I know we both agreed, "Less is more," but in this case, less is just less. Steven

4 Gil Nortze

"You ain't gonna believe what happened last night, Sparky—a perfect night at the tables!" Gil Nortze had one of those slightly hyped southern drawls, although he was, at least for five years prior to moving to Las Vegas, from *southern* Arizona. On this same day that found Ken Easton bodysurfing off Yankee Point, Nortze sat at home shuffling poker chips with one hand. His new sapphire ring—purchased as a reward for his latest gambling accomplishment—glistened dark blue in the morning sunlight coming through the window.

"With you, Gil, I'd believe anything." Sparky knew he was in for some gloating before Gil got down to brass tacks about the due-date on his promissory note.

"I'm putting you on speakerphone." Nortze pressed the button with a stubby forefinger and continued, very excited, sipping on his morning coffee with one hand and with deft fingers on the other shuffling a stack of chips. He stopped shuffling the chips long enough to pick up the remote and get the fire started in the fireplace, the flames quickly spreading in and among the concrete logs. Glancing to his bookshelf, he felt comfort in seeing the four family diaries—from George, Duane, and Cecil Nortze, and the other Maria's. Gil Nortze had never started a diary, nor did he intend to. "What if someone else reads it?" he had said to his younger brother, Harry. What Nortze had was his gambling log, just as informative if one takes the time to understand it. He picked up the log-book and opened it to the last entries—notes he'd made on the game the previous night.

Nortze then ran his fingers unconsciously through his shock of red hair. "Okay, it's 2 a.m. and I can't sleep, so I go over to Caesar's and find a soft seat with three amateurs at table three, and I'm on the button."

A *soft seat* was Nortze's chance to play with people who knew little or nothing about the game of poker, and the *button* is the dealer's position, with the house supplying the actual dealer.

"What are beginner's doing at table three?"

"Have no idea. There were eight of them origi-nally—all from the same company. The others bailed early 'cause they lost their asses to some outsider. I knew they were raw when I heard one of 'em say, 'Texas Hold-*on'* instead of 'Hold-*em.'* Anyway, it's a thousand/two-thousand limit, and like I say, I'm on the button. For the pre-flop, Little Blind and Big Blind come in for their five hun-dred and two-thou each. Then I'm dealt a pair of sixes in the pocket."

(The first two cards—the pocket—were dealt face down.)

"Oh, you gotta know first off, Sparky, they didn't muck their losing hands after—I asked and they actually showed them to me. Got it all burned in my memory now." He was actually referring to his notes, but it made him feel better to let Sparky think he had it all in his head. "Little Blind has ten-eight suited in clubs, Big Blind has king-ten unsuited, and Calling Station has jack-three unsuited." Nortze was getting excited all over again.

(The Calling Station is a player that, no matter what, calls the bet, even with a bad hand, never raising on his own. He often goes to the last card hoping for some kind of miracle. On the rare occasion when such a miracle occurs, it seems to somehow justify the lack of winning strategy. Calling Stations rarely win; their stakes just dwindle to nothing.)

"Now, Calling Station calls two grand, so I raise a grand. At this point, both Little Blind and Big Blind should have re-raised, but they call instead. The pot is sixteen grand now."

Nortze saw the log notation: *CS—pw?*

"At this point," Nortze said with a little chuckle, "Calling Station is fidgeting like he has to pee and says he wants to get back to his room. But it's not the cards, it's his wife is pissed that he's spending so much time at the tables. The guy's so pussy-whipped he's not even thinking about the cards." Nortze shuffled one-handed his little pile of chips, this time from the bottom up.

Sparky knew that with a quarter-million dollar note coming due to Nortze before midnight, this conversation wasn't about winning or losing the previous night. It was about rubbing salt in the wound.

"So, the Flop comes out," Nortze started in again, "and it's a two-club, nine-heart, and the ace of spades. I've got my pocket sixes, but I'm worried now, 'cause if anyone has an ace, I'm toast at this point."

"Did king-ten raise?" Sparky asked, referring to Big Blind.

"Hell no!" Nortze said dismissively, "Not until it was pointless. Little Blind bet a grand and the next two called, so I raised a grand. Everyone called, so I knew no one had an ace yet. The pot's now at twenty grand.

"Now comes 4th Street," Nortze said with grandeur, referring to the fourth card, also known as the Turn card. The raising now moved up to the max, two grand per for a maximum of three raises per player. "It's a two of diamonds. I'm looking at two pair now, and I can see glory ahead. Unless by some impossible stupidity someone actually has an ace and aren't betting it, but I'm pretty sure they don't."

Sparky was silent, just waiting for the story to end.

"Little Blind's got two clubs in the pocket and one on the table, and with only one card to go. No flush or straight possible, but he bets anyway. Now Big Blind with his king-ten and no hope in hell comes along and raises. I'm thinking maybe he's holding an ace, but my instincts tell me there's something wrong with the way these guys are betting. And lo and behold, Calling Station sees the light and folds.

"Now I'm really stumped, but I raise a grand. Little Blind raises me, and Big Blind raises him! I am in a state of total shock here. I raise again, but this time everyone calls. The pot's now up to forty-seven thousand."

Sparky chimed in just to sound interested, "So, they're all going for some kind of gut-shot?"

"I guess so, but I can't for the life of me figure what the hell they're doing. So out comes the River. It's a fucking six."

"No way!" Sparky said, laughing. He *was* impressed.

"Way! So I'm looking at a boat—three sixes and two's. What do they do? Little Blind bets two grand—don't ask why—and now Big Blind calls. I raise two grand, and both of them call. The pot is fifty-nine grand now, mind you, and they don't have shit."

"But you don't know that," Sparky said.

"Right, but call it a hunch. When they saw my boat, you'd have thought they all had seen a fucking ghost. Combined, their best hand was a pair of two's, king high. But here's the kicker. They were so excited to be playing with a pro, they didn't care how much they lost. I cashed out and went back home up forty-four g's, thinking it doesn't get any easier than that. Like I said, it was a perfect night."

Nortze paused a moment, dredging up something his grandfather, Cecil, the first professional gambler in the family, had once written in his own gambling log. "I was glad to play the toilet on that peel and flush."

The Nortzes seemed always to have a crude way of expressing themselves, but being crude men, it was at least fitting. The crudeness was not a result of being gamblers. A cross-section of gamblers reveals human behavior— attitude, political persuasion, sexual proclivities, and all the rest— throughout the spectrum. It's just that most people consciously temper their inner thoughts, while others like to be crude right out in the open.

"That's amazing, Gil," Sparky said, flatly.

"Tonight," Gil said, with a lilt in his voice, "I think I'll play the nickel slots at the Luxor."

Sparky couldn't stifle a laugh. "Yeah, and I'm getting breast implants this afternoon."

Nortze let out a hearty laugh. "*If* you had great tits, Sparky, I *might* cop a feel and take a bit off your note."

Sparky knew that Gil was waiting for the question: *How much?* It was as if there could be some bargaining. Too late. "Gil, you wouldn't take off a nickel from the IOU of *woman* if she was the best piece of ass on earth."

"Well, maybe a nickel," Nortze said, snickering. "Obligations *is* obligations."

"I'm aware of my obligations, Gil." It was time to get down to it. "So, I guess you're going to call it in?" Robert "Sparky" Sparks had come to the end of the line.

"I think I've been pretty patient, considering, Sparky." Gil stood and walked to the shelf and fingered the diaries. "Could have sold it for cash, you know. But your five years are up tonight, Sparky. If I don't see two hundred and fifty big ones, not a penny less, by midnight tonight, it's all mine." Nortze paused for effect and poured a shot of scotch. "Haven't been back almost a year, so I may have to go out soon and take a look at the property again. Yankee Point is nice this time of year."

Nortze hadn't been back to the central coast since Christmas of 2000, when he had taken a weekend trip to see a woman and also take a first look at his poker winnings—the Yankee Point property that he suspected would shortly be his.

There was silence at Sparky's end, then, weakly and with great remorse, "Yes, it is. I wish I could have paid off a little at a time, Gil, but I've got less than half the money. So, unless I pull off a rush this afternoon, it's yours."

Robert Sparks the man (as opposed to Sparky the gambler) tried to act like the worst was all behind him now—the heartache, the memories— but it wasn't. It was only the middle rounds of self-recrimination that usually last a lifetime.

"Are you coming to the tables tonight?" Nortze asked.

"I doubt it. My son's arriving this afternoon from New York. He's already pissed that his college fund was gambled away, so for me to go to the tables would be like rubbing salt in the wound." With nearly everything else lost, the one thing Robert Sparks valued most of all now was maintaining a relationship, tenuous as it was, with his son.

"Whatever you say. Hey, gotta run." Gil was really thinking: *Take that, prick.*

"See ya, Gil." Sparks had long ago signed over the quitclaim deed, so when he woke up tomorrow he would be short one piece of fabulous oceanfront property.

In high stakes poker, there are only winners, losers, and those who never sit down at the table. Sparky was a loser. Not at first, but it only took one bad night to lose everything of monetary value, and the rest quickly followed. It's what a man does after he's lost big that is the true measure of the man.

Five years before, to the day, Sparky was playing Texas Hold'em with Gil Nortze and a set of 40-year old, heavyset twins—Dan and Dave Snowden—at Sparky's apartment in Vegas over Thanksgiving weekend, 1996. They all hailed from California's central coast, and they had played poker together for years, both at the casino tables and in private.

Dave was a bottom-rung high roller, called a Loose Aggressive. He was inclined to raise, reraise and cap hands that he shouldn't. He always played like he had great cards. Dan, on the other hand, was almost a pro, a Tight.

The joke was that if the twins were wearing the same clothes and everyone had a few drinks, you couldn't remember which was which, a potentially costly mistake. In Texas Hold'em, there is one critical commandment: Know Thy Opponent.

Gil Nortze was pretty much of a Tight Aggressive, a pro. Guys like him are the ones who win tournaments. They adapt, back their confidence with chips, and can even play weak cards for winning hands. And they know when to fold. Sparky was a Rock, a passive player with Tight leanings. Each man had his own particular way of playing the game, and they were all also more or less successful in their particular strategy. Nortze had lost about $50 grand in 2001 to the twins, but mostly to Dan, although Nortze was up overall.

The table limit that fateful night went from a thousand dollars to ten thousand, then pot-limit, then finally to no-limit. Sparky was drinking heavily, a no-no when serious money was on the table. The twins drank beer, while Gil Nortze was as sober as a church mouse, and he took every advantage possible of his clear head.

On what turned out to be the last hand of the night, there was a $400,000 pot staring up at Sparky, and he saw, or thought he saw, victory at hand. He had gone all in on the Turn card, with just the River to go, praying everyone else would fold. They didn't.

To make a long, sad story short, Sparky had four jacks—two in the pocket and two on the table—a very solid hand, beatable only by a straight flush (or five of a kind if playing with wild cards). But he had no more cash to bet with.

So, Sparky had staggered off to his bedroom safe and returned with a sole-ownership, clear-title deed to his undeveloped oceanfront property south of Carmel, then worth $200,000.

Both twins had tactfully tried to warn him off the bet, an unusual move for gamblers. "Fuck you both!" Sparky had retorted, throwing the deed into the pot. "I call." He nearly died when Nortze turned up a straight flush in clubs on the River card, using one the Flop jacks and two other clubs on the table—a nine and a seven— plus his two pocket clubs—a ten and an eight.

There was no *do over,* no *take back,* as everyone played for keeps. It not only ruined Robert Sparks financially, but also was the moment that turned everything around for Gil Nortze. That night marked the end of the Nortze family financial curse.

After five years at the agreed-upon 5% simple interest, and having not paid back a dime of interest, let alone paying off any of the principal, Robert Sparks had a quarter-mil nut to crack in 15 hours if he ever wanted to see that deed, and his property again.

Although Sparks had had clear title as sole-owner, a hand-me-down from his parents, it was supposed to be the retirement property for him and his wife, Sharon. Sharon finally divorced him over his foolish loss that night, a night like hundred others just like it, and she got half of what he had left, which wasn't much. His son, Peter, got the shaft, too. Instead of having all his Harvard tuition paid, plus walking around money, Peter had to work both at McDonalds and shipping and receiving in Wal-Mart to help fray expenses at a second-rate business college.

Sparks' spirit was broken after that. He still played poker for a living, but he lived at the margin. He made enough to squeak by most of the time, playing more out of habit and to pass the time, and trying unsuccessfully to forget that it had cost him not only his money, but his family as well. And Ken Easton hadn't helped by pestering Sparks about selling what wasn't really Bob's anymore, or not likely to be, anyway.

Gil Nortze, on the other hand, was now a winner. Not hugely so, just nicely comfortable. He had a knack for poker, not the least of which was a steely demeanor that gave nothing away to other players. He played strong hands well, bluffed like a champ, and folded when he should. The only game he played now was Texas Hold'em poker.

Texas Hold'em is about as close to the game of chess as a game of chance gets. Chess is *all* strategy, and games of chance are mostly just luck. But Texas Hold'em poker is an interesting combination of the two. It ends up the same as regular poker—the best five cards win—but it's how one gets there, if at all, in Hold'em that is the challenge.

For those beginners who don't understand statistics—the odds—and play against those who do, those neophytes might as well stand at the toilet and do a peel-and-flush until all their money is gone. Nortze had played a game of peel-and-flush the previous night, only with thousand-dollar chips instead of hundred-dollar bills. It was, however, the neophytes who had done all the peeling and flushing.

Statistics are not the only factor in the game, however, as strategy plays large. And reading one's opponents—how *they* play the game—is almost as important as the cards dealt. As Nortze once said to his younger brother, "Harry, everyone gets the same chance to get good cards. The difference is in knowing how to read the ones who do, and clean house on the ones who don't." It's the player who combines a working knowledge of Hold'em statistics and strategy that comes up a winner.

Over the past five years, Nortze had bet a total of $18.6 million. He had won $20.7 million, leaving him $2.1 million to the good, averaging about $400K per year. His worst had been $300K, his best $800K, including Robert Sparks' property that same year. But 1996 had been the start of his winning streak.

Gil Nortze had gone up against some of the best Texas Hold'em players in the world, and he had come out about even, which was a compliment to his talents. He once bluffed six grand out of Phil Ivey, the young "Tiger Woods" of poker. On another occasion, Nortze beat back the stare of

Howard Lederer holding two pair and won a hand with trip sevens.

All in all, it was a damned good living for a 37-year-old man, even after taxes, which he cheated on with both relish and regularity despite lucrative investment returns from the Hi-Tech boom. He sold two-thirds of his stock portfolio the month before the start of the tech decline, and then began shorting the market. It was a gamble that paid off.

But while Nortze was a pretty good gambler, he was also a pretty lousy human being. No real friends, only gambling buddies. Again with the problems with attachment rooted in family history. Nortze had grown up in Cambria, 100 miles south of Monterey on Pacific Coast Highway—Highway 1. His folks had moved for good from Phoenix when Nortze was a year old. A family tragedy one year later made him an orphan.

Gil Nortze was five-six, short with a waxy complexion. He had short red hair and light red eyebrows that made a thin, straight line on his lower forehead, so he looked fairly comical. Women liked Nortze for his money, and he hadn't had a serious relationship since his first and only marriage when he was 24, resulting in two kids. He'd had many one-nighters, thought, mostly with high-priced hookers.

With the quick rewards from gambling—adrenaline as well as money—Nortze had quickly grown tired of home life and all its obligations and restrictions. He just wasn't a family man. So, after seven years and two kids, one day he filed for divorce from Sandy. He hooked up with a Vegas showgirl and flew in secret to the East Coast, settling in Atlantic City, New Jersey, his lawyer-brother Harry handling everything until the divorce was final. Nortze convinced Sandy not to get a lawyer, that he would take care of her, and she got custody of the kids but not a dime in court-awarded child support.

Nortze quickly reneged on his promise of money for Sandy and the kids. Realizing too late her mistake in not hiring a lawyer, Sandy promptly drank herself into oblivion. One July afternoon, she got drunk and walked out into the desert on a 110-degree day and passed out, dying of exposure and dehydration. Gil Nortze's only response to Harry when he had heard the sad news, coming as it did from a place way, way down in his psyche was, "Well, at least it was a dry heat."

Gil Nortze never came back for the kids, justifying to himself they were old enough—seven and six, respectively—to be cared for by Sandy's sister, Eve, out on the coast. They would just have to fend for themselves. Nortze never gave a thought to the possibility that Eve might not be able to deal with the kids.

Nortze sat one-hand shuffling his pile of poker chips and stared out the window of his tenth floor condo, the new day breaking in Las Vegas. The fireplace, now at full throttle, gave off a warm glow. Tomorrow being Saturday and in the middle of Thanksgiving weekend, Nortze figured he'd better go on-line and book a private flight to Carmel and a night's accommodations nearby. A weekend visit to his new property was just what he needed. He saw on weather.com the Doppler radar, the expected weather coming in, and also that it was going to blow out by early Saturday.

For the coming holiday weekend, Nortze also wanted to invite a few people along to make it a full-blown celebration, maybe even have a barbeque, like old times. That would mean he needed a couple of rental vans for the trip down to Carmel Highlands. Robert "Sparky" Sparks, born and raised in Carmel Highlands, would not be on the list of invitees.

*****

Note to John: I had to learn poker to first understand, and then write this, so again it took considerably longer than first anticipated. But I think it gives the best take on what happened, and I'm happy with it. Steven

5 Sam Wynette and Margie Swanson

Sam Wynette, 42, sat in his California Highway Patrol car on the southern end of the Point Lobos State Preserve south of Carmel, finishing up data entries for the previous survey stop. A good-looking man with close-cropped mustache and regulation haircut, Sam was a by-the-book guy on most things related to law enforcement. But he had a knack for reading people, as did his brother, Chuck. When you know what the other guy is thinking, it's a huge advantage—in law enforcement and in life. A family trait, perhaps.

It seemed the State of California had suddenly become interested in the possible nexus between cell phone use and highway accidents. It was part of a 2-year study to write a law mandating hands-free cell phone use throughout the state. Sam had heard on good authority that vote counters in Sacramento were in a state of orgasmic epiphany after reading two professional journal articles. All Sam was told at that morning's briefing was that stats showed a distracted driver on his cell phone to be much more likely to be involved in an accident than someone not distracted.

Duh.

And they had said other stats showed that fatalities for drivers using cell phones, over those who don't, are nine times greater.

Double Duh.

Sam wasn't a statistician, but he had a bit more common sense than God granted geese or statisticians. Even without a government study, Sam knew that drivers who are distracted—by anything—are more likely to be involved in accidents, fatal and non-fatal alike, than those who pay attention. A no-brainer. Sam's brother, Chuck, a retired ChiP, worked for the Department of Homeland Security in Washington, D.C. They had just that morning spoken by phone and exchanged memories over a few well-intentioned, although still mostly inane, studies of human behavior that were supposed to make us all better drivers.

"Remember the one about rain after a dry spell?" Chuck had asked.

"Oh, yeah," Sam said, "The guy actually proved, beyond all statistical probability, that more accidents occur within six hours of the official onset of rain than in any comparable six-hour period at any time of the year, and I believe I'm quoting that."

"You are," Chuck said with incredulity. "Cost the taxpayers about a hundred and fifty thousand dollars for the study, then came the ad campaign, and then the next rain. There were more accidents then than at any other post-rain time, and I'm convinced it was because the people who heard about the study went out and tested it out for themselves, and promptly got in accidents."

Regardless, in support of the assembly bill, on state highways running through state parks on three consecutive Fridays, starting on this, the Friday after Thanksgiving, 2001, Sam and other officers would be making survey stops to acquire the requisite data.

Sam looked up and immediately recognized the battered blue pickup belonging to Margie Swanson, owner of a Margie's Bed and Breakfast in Carmel Highlands, just south of Carmel-by-the-Sea. Margie was also a prime candidate for the poster girl of distraction-related accident statistics. Sam spotted her on her cell phone, but his instincts told him it was worse than that.

Sam caught up with her, ten miles an hour over the posted 55, and turned on the lights. He could see her reaching to put down her coffee and try to stub out her cigarette before making her way to the roadside, swerving a bit in the process. Sam saw her put on her seat belt, too, but only after she had stopped.

Sam took his pad and pen with him and approached. "Morning, Margie," he said with a hint of a smile.

Cigarette smoke billowed out the window, and Sam could see steam rising from the cup holder. The years had not been kind to the face of Margie Swanson, a 35-year-old woman who looked ten years older. Underneath, however, was a sweet woman with one hell of a body. Even Sam couldn't help noticing that. Margie's husband of ten years had, six years before, found a younger, more attractive woman who had more family inheritance (financial and facial beauty) than Margie. She quickly realized why he had never wanted children—with her. It had been devastating to her self-image and esteem. Her family had a history of twins, and Margie had wanted them.

In her gravelly voice made possible by six years of never giving in to a consciousness of health,

Margie said, "Hi, Sam. Was I speeding?" It would have been her fourth speeding ticket in two years, two issued by Sam.

"Yes, but that's not why I stopped you, Margie. We're doing a little survey, and I need to ask you a couple of questions. Do you mind?" All the ChiPs were told that if anyone refused to answer any questions, for any reason, let them go. Everyone knew the legal implications of a perp getting off for unreasonable suspicion. Even a stinking drunk was to be let go on his way, so that a hundred feet further he could be legitimately stopped, tested and arrested.

"So, I'm not getting a ticket?"

"No, but talking on the phone, drinking coffee, and smoking a cigarette—all at the same time and without your seatbelt—puts you in a pretty risky driving category, Margie. But you know that."

Dents and dings all around her truck were silent testimony to the numerous times she banged into things—parked cars, trees, steel posts—all the while encountering one of a number of life's little distractions. She ran her Bed & Breakfast with great care and compassion, but once on the road, she was pretty much a threat to paint jobs everywhere.

Margie feigned guilt. "Yes, I know. It won't happen again."

Sam knew different, but he nodded politely. "Try harder, Margie."

"So, what are the questions?"

Sam began writing. "Well, I can see it's a Ford F-150, and you live in Carmel Highlands. Your age?"

"Don't you remember from the last ticket?"

Sam wasn't about to ask for her driver's license, and there was no need for overt hostility. Sam smiled, offering, "Twenty-nine?"

"Oh, you are a dear. Close enough."

"Last question. Would you support a hands-free law on cell phones given affordable technology?" They expected most drivers to say *yes,* but they weren't sure.

"A law? Hell, no! That's why I have this pickup truck, Sam. In case I get in an accident, it's probably them who gets nailed, not me. I'm thinking of a big ol' SUV for next year, if the B&B does well." She quickly raised and lowered her eyebrows. "It's already booked up for the weekend by a group coming in from Las Vegas, so let's cross our fingers." She held up the crossed fingers of her left hand.

Sam nodded politely, holding his tongue about the SUV-as-battering ram scenario and wrote *no* to the last question. "Thanks, Margie. Please drive safe."

Back in his car, Sam began to add Margie's data into the dashboard computer. After Margie, six more stops and Sam would fill his quota of ten for the day. Glancing up as Margie drove away, he saw her put the phone to her ear with her left hand and take a puff while turning, swerving actually, out onto the pavement, and finally the coffee cup came up to her lips.

Sam thought about chasing her down and actually issuing her a written warning, but his own cell phone rang. The caller ID said it was from home, and since the kids were in school, it had to be his wife, Darcy. "Hi, honey, what's up?"

"Hi, Sam. Can you stop by the school at lunch?" She sounded harried. At 39 and with a history of heart problems, she was supposed to avoid undue stress. Two teenage kids did not help.

Sam bit his lip and shook his head. "What's he done now?"

"They didn't say, specifically. Something about bullying. Cheryl stayed home, um, sick, so could you go this time?"

Sam knew the code. Cheryl, thirteen, had just started getting her period, and it was more of a head thing than physical, but Darcy was trying to be sympathetic and helpful.

"Yeah, I'll go." He usually took lunch at noon, 90 minutes away. "I've got a couple more stops to make before lunch—a cell phone survey—but call 'em back and say I'll be there at noon."

"Thanks, hon," Darcy said with relief.

Bobby had been having discipline problems in school for over a year now, and there was little that Sam or Darcy said or did on important issues to alter their son's fourteen-year old brainwaves. Or at least this one's. Darcy had offered that it was merely the trials of puberty, nothing to fret about, but Sam had his suspicions that Bobby's problems ran deeper.

Sam made his nut on the survey stops by 11:30, so he drove slowly enough down the highway to appreciate the sights. Highway 1 snaked its way down the coast past steep mountains to the left and pounding seas to the right. A big storm was coming, that much he could tell. Sam checked the barriers on all of the outside curves for signs of a car going through or over them—*none today, maybe one tonight.*

6 Bobby Wynette

At five minutes to twelve, Sam walked into the school administration office, and the receptionist smiled and cocked her head toward the vice-principal's office. "He's in there, Sam."

Head lowered in supplication, Sam offered a muted, "Thanks, Yvonne."

Inside the waiting room to Vice Principal Daley's office sat Bobby Wynette, curly reddish-brown hair a bit longer than regulation. He was a good-looking youngster and only slightly smaller and heftier than most boys his age. Bobby fiddled with his backpack and held fast his stoic facial expression even as Sam looked him in the eye, saying only, "Hi, Dad." He motioned with his eyes toward Daley's door. "Mr. Daley wants to see you."

"What about, Bobby?"

Bobby shrugged. "I think I'd better let him tell you."

"I want to hear it from you first," Sam said, and he sat down on the bench next to Bobby, "*Then* I'll see Mr. Daley."

Bobby, cornered, let out a sigh and leaned back against the wall, and he chuckled under his breath. "I don't see what the problem is. I borrowed Mark Toleson's Game Boy, and I accidentally dropped it. It didn't work after that so I offered to pay him for it. But I only had five bucks, so I offered him that. Since it was broken anyway, he took the money. And last night, it started working again, so I took it to school today. When Mark saw me playing on it, he accused me of cheating him on the deal, and I guess I got mad and slugged him."

"Is he okay?"

"Yeah, sure," Bobby said, "It was just a glancing blow."

"And you say you *guess* you got mad?" That had been the first clue.

Bobby did a little retrenchment. "I got mad."

"How much is the Game Boy worth?"

"Maybe twenty bucks."

"When you say it *started working again,* what does that mean?"

Again Bobby shrugged and turned his eyes away. "It just started working, that's all." For Sam Wynette, it usually took about three or four questions to know if someone was lying to his face. In this case, Sam knew after two.

Sam could read people as well as Gil Nortze could read poker players. As in a case where Sam asked a motorist to show him his license and registration, and the guy fumbled around like he was actually looking for it when Sam knew damned well he didn't have either in the car. For Sam, there was a mechanical feel to it when a motorist was stalling, lying, and generally being evasive, almost as if big red letters showed up on his or her forehead, stamped: *Guilty!* There are few people who could get past the tell with Sam Wynette, and Bobby was not one of them.

Sam nodded. "Okay, why then didn't you give it to Mark and get your money back?"

"Because ... um ..." Bobby's brain was on overload trying to conjure up a justification. Looking down at his lap, he offered weakly, "Because I'd already paid him for it, and I really didn't think about it."

"You just did think about it."

"No, I mean I didn't think about giving it back because I'd already paid for it."

"Well, there's a distinction without a difference if I ever heard one."

Caught in his own dissembling, Bobby turned to Sam, wetness forming in his eyes. "I swear, Dad."

"Okay, son, I'll take your word on that—for now. But if your story doesn't hold water, you're grounded for a month." Sam knew the crocodile tears were starting to flow only out of fear of discovery, not false imprisonment, and that Bobby was now trying to manipulate him with emotion.

"Who are you going to believe? Them or me?" Bobby asked plaintively.

"Depends on who's telling the truth." Sam knew that whole truth was not issuing forth from Bobby's lips, so it was time for a word with Mr. Daley. "I'll be back in a few minutes." Sam arose and walked to the door with that feeling every human being experiences at being purposefully lied to. It's like a blow to the gut. Sam knocked, heard a "Come in," and left Bobby to his thoughts and quickly drying eyes.

"Thanks for coming, Mr. Wynette, said Daley, a bookish man in his mid-30s. You spoke with Bobby?"

"Yes, I did. What's the other side of the story?"

"Well, it seems Bobby made it appear that Mark's Game Boy was broken so he could acquire it cheap. It magically fixed itself overnight, and when Mark confronted him on it, Bobby hauled off and hit him in the face."

"Is he okay?" Sam asked.

"Oh, yeah, but that's not the problem, Mr. Wynette … "

"Sam is better."

Daley relaxed a little. "Okay, Sam. I've seen this type of behavior many times before, and it seems that bullying is becoming a way of life for Bobby, plus—"

Sam had to stop him. "Actually, Mr. Daley—"

"Paul, please."

"Okay—Paul. Actually, Paul, it's more about manipulation than bullying, or lying for that matter. He's got it in his pubescent head that he can get what he wants by skirting the rules. Rules of behavior I'm talking about. He's a smart kid, and that's why he gets away with it ... most of the time, anyway. The lying comes only as an after-thought, but the bullying is reflex, I'm afraid."

"You seem quite up on human behavior, Sam."

Sam fidgeted nervously for a brief moment. "Comes with my job, Paul." He looked Daley squarely in the eye and asked rather matter-of-factly, "How many unpaid parking tickets do you have in your glove compartment?"

"None," Daley shot back, "And you can look that up on your computer later. Why did you ask that?"

"I know you're telling the truth because of how quickly you answered, and with such conviction, all *before* you thought I could have find out on my own."

"Oh," Daley said, eyebrows arched and much relieved, because he didn't realize it was so easy to tell in so short a time, "I guess you're right." He was buoyed by all this new information. "So, what can you or I do about Bobby's manipulation thing?"

"Well, based on my experience and in this par-ticular case, punishment of the offender only shows to other people that the rules are being applied without favoritism, but it doesn't do much to alter the basic behavior. Oh, Bobby's going to be grounded, mind you, but he's also going to have to learn that getting what he wants by any means is not the best course of action. I have some work to do in that area. My wife, Darcy, too, but she's on heart medication, so I have to take up some slack here."

Daley nodded, his relief palpable. "I must say, Sam, that I was all prepared for a major confrontation here, but I am grateful for the way you're handling this." He shook his head in minor disgust. "I wish other parents were so accommodating when their kids screw up."

"I know, Paul. It's about taking responsibility. It's never their kid, or even themselves who are at fault. It's always someone else. And you guys do yeoman's work as mediators *and* educators, much of it unappreciated from what I can see."

"Tell me about it." Daley was glad to have an ally. "Any time you need to talk to someone about Bobby, please feel free to give me a call. Together maybe we can make some progress."

"One step at a time, as they say." Sam stood and they shook hands. "Oh, and by the way," Sam said, sheepishly, "I saw your name on the wall in front of your parking spot, and I *did* look up your license on the computer. It must be your wife who has the unpaid parking ticket from Ocean Avenue in Carmel last month." He winked. "Better see that she pays it before it goes past sixty days." He left John wide-eyed but smiling.

In the waiting room, Sam walked towards the exit and said to Bobby in passing, "Let's go." Bobby said nothing while they walked to the parking lot. Sam opened his patrol car door and leaned on the top of the window frame, thinking about how Bobby might have rigged the Game Boy. He stared silently at Bobby, who now had his pack on and was fiddling mindlessly with the straps, anxious to get back inside the building, and to relative safety. "Your mother is not going to take this very well."

Finally, and with much resignation, Bobby said, "So, what's the verdict?" He knew in his heart the hammer was about to fall.

"Son, you being so good with electronics and all, today I'm buying you a kit to build a two-way radio—a walkie-talkie—from scratch. You'll have plenty of time over the next four weekends to work on it. It's either that or *stargazing* for a month."

Bobby wisely opted for the former. At least he wouldn't have to spend hours standing in one spot, head back and looking up at the sky until his neck vertebrae froze in place. That punishment was an insidious torment called *stargazing,* invented by Sam Wynette specifically for kids behaving badly.

After so many hammers falling on him, stemming principally from disciplinary actions at four different foster homes in the greater Cambria region, and only partially offset of late by the love of exasperated adoptive parents, this punishment showed up like a cakewalk for Bobby Wynette, the chunky fourteen-year-old redheaded boy formerly known as Bobby Nortze.

7 Cheryl and Darcy Wynette

"Mom, do you ever wish you didn't adopt us? I mean, like, with all the problems."

Darcy Wynette was gentle in her response. Just having turned 39, Darcy was, as they say, pleasingly plump—just the way Sam liked her. Her brown hair was always nicely coiffed, and she radiated a mother's warmth in her bright smile. She'd been home all day catering to the needs of her daughter, and they were sitting on Cheryl's bed putting together an Emergency Girlie Kit, as Darcy called it: A couple of tampons, some Advil tablets, and a lavender-scented mini-douche.

"Of course not, honey. Problems are just part of life." Darcy smiled and tousled Cheryl's auburn hair, thinking about how her own physical limitations were not the end of the world. "But the rewards are worth it. You're worth it, Cheryl."

Cheryl Wynette's lightly freckled face permitted a smile, but she wasn't so sure about her own self-worth. The realities of personal history—and genetic coding—dominated hopes and dreams.

The abandonment by Cheryl's father and subsequent death of her mother had battered Cheryl's self-esteem. On the environmental front, by not getting the critical emotional support she needed at an early age, Cheryl now had, on the surface, difficulty with personal attachments. And while she had remained close to Bobby throughout the ordeal, the people in their foster care world had been like aliens. Some were harmless gawkers, others actually mean to Cheryl and Bobby. And more. With no parents—perfect or imperfect—no one but Bobby was in Cheryl's sphere of influence to act as her emotional savior. Her exclusive reliance on Bobby's leadership and oversight would later prove to be a large part of her undoing.

On their first "placement," a temporary arrangement with her mother's sister, Eve, Bobby and Cheryl had come to the small Cambria home of the middle-aged couple, Eve and Steward Orson. They had two kids of their own, Jason and Troy, two boys aged five and six, respectively. It didn't take long—three months—for the attentions paid to Bobby and Cheryl to have a decidedly negative effect on the younger boys. They felt as though Bobby and Cheryl got all the attention from Mom and Dad, although the perception was, of course, highly exaggerated. They conspired and acted out with passive aggression nonetheless.

Cheryl, then six, was in her private room, converted from Jim Orson's study, doing a picture puzzle on a Sunday night when Jason and Troy entered without knocking. Troy stated boldly they wanted to talk, as if he was the spokesman.

"When are you going to find a real mom and dad?" asked Troy.

"Yeah," little Jason chimed in, pouting, "How long are you going to be here?"

It was obvious to Cheryl that the two boys wanted her and Bobby out of the picture. She could have said something like she didn't know, or that the people at the agency were looking, but instead she hardened defensively. "Actually, it's you two who have the problem, not me. I hear Mom and Dad might give you two up so they can be our parents." She purposely used *Mom and Dad* to put them on the defensive. Looking up and around in a grand gesture, she added, "There just doesn't seem to be enough room in this house." That's a tough thing for any kid to hear when already struggling with basic insecurity.

Troy and Jason both ran screaming and crying from the room, begging their mother not to send them away. When Cheryl and Bobby talked about it later that evening, Bobby shrugged it off. "Maybe next time they won't be so mean."

Eve Orson had some wicked nightmares following that incident, and she couldn't shake the bad vibes about the whole arrangement. Stewart felt the same. So, despite the blood relation, an agency rep came to the house on Tuesday morning while Bobby and Cheryl were in school. That evening, the Orson's told Bobby and Cheryl that, sadly, they were unable to care for them any longer, and the two would be going to a foster care facility the next day. Neither Bobby nor Cheryl asked for specifics, and they packed their bags.

It must have come as quite a blow that the very people depended upon to provide emotional stability were now casting them out like boxes of old clothes. Their individual senses of betrayal must have gone off the emotional Richter scale.

"We need parents who don't have any kids," Bobby had said to Cheryl as they waited for the agency car to pick them up. He was just trying to buoy her spirits.

"Yeah, and maybe they'll have a bigger house."

Bobby laughed out loud. "Don't count on that!"

Bobby was right. For the next three years, Bobby and Cheryl bounced around four different foster care homes, and none of the houses were bigger than the Orson's. The caretakers filled the spectrum between laissez-faire to strict disciplinarians, but as time went on, the only bond strengthened was between Bobby and Cheryl.

It was in the third year of foster care living in Cambria that a special bond between Bobby and Cheryl became defined. Bobby was eleven and Cheryl ten, and they were in a foster care home run by an elderly couple, Mr. and Mrs. Stokely. The Stokely's spent more time trying to game the foster care system out of money, however, than providing proper oversight to their charges.

The other youngster in the Stokely's care was a 13-year-old boy named Trevor. With Mrs. Stokely upstairs watching TV and Bobby and Mr. Stokely off grocery shopping, Trevor entered the downstairs bathroom while Cheryl was taking a shower. In three short minutes, Cheryl Nortze was transformed from pre-pubescent girl into a victim of sexual assault. With fingers probing and fondling all of Cheryl's privates, Trevor warned Cheryl that if she cried out for help or told anyone he would kill not Cheryl, but Bobby. The immediate vision of a life without her older brother permitted the assault on Cheryl to happen without external protest.

Later, Cheryl did tell Bobby. He did not become angry, or upset. Neither did he run to Mr. and Mrs. Stokely with a tale of woe. Instead, Bobby went with his instincts—something deep within him telling him what was the right thing to do.

That night, Bobby lured Trevor into his downstairs room with the promise of showing him an exciting new game, called, "Tie-up." But Bobby said he had to show him, as opposed to just explaining the game. Trevor was very interested, and as instructed he lay down on the bed facing the foot of the bed and allowed Bobby to tie one wrist with rope to one bedpost.

Acting quickly, Bobby then wrapped the rope around Trevor's other wrist and stretched it towards the other bedpost. Bobby pulled up a chair and placed it in front of Trevor.

Before Trevor could protest, Bobby placed a gag in Trevor's mouth and wrapped several turns of duct tape around the boy's mouth and head. And then Bobby called Cheryl into the room and made her sit on the chair facing Trevor. Trevor was horrified, but he couldn't move or scream loud enough for anyone to hear.

"Okay, Cheryl," Bobby said, "tell me again how long he was doing those things to you in the shower."

"Three minutes," she replied, staring unblinking at Trevor's panic-stricken face at eye level, watching his expression.

Bobby pulled a carrot from his pocket. It was about ten inches long and over an inch in diameter at the fat end. It tapered off to a blunt half-inch that Bobby had whittled down with a paring knife. He held it to within a foot of Trevor's face. "Well, then, Trevor, it looks like it's going to be an inch for every minute, then."

With that, Bobby climbed on the bed and sat across the back of Trevor's knees, pinning him to the bed. Bobby pulled down Trevor's trousers and underwear and exposed Trevor's bare butt.

Trevor struggled and tried to scream, but it was no use. He pleaded with his eyes to Cheryl, mumbling through the gag, "I'm sorry ... I'm sorry. Please don't."

Bobby leaned over closer to Trevor's head. "What was that you said, Trevor? Please don't? I think that's what my sister said, too. And what did you do?"

Trevor stopped struggling and started whimpering. He knew what was coming.

Bobby spread Trevor's butt cheeks and inserted the end of the carrot like a corkscrew until it was in Trevor's rectum about an inch.

Trevor fought it the whole time, and he started crying in pain, but it was a futile effort, and his pained expression was revealed to Cheryl from just a few feet away. Again, he muffled a plea to stop.

Cheryl held up her hand to Bobby. "Wait, Bobby. I think I may have been wrong about something."

"What's that, Cheryl?" Bobby asked.

She leaned in close to Trevor's anguished face and looked him straight in the eye, whispering, and, "I think it was more than three minutes, Trevor. More like five minutes—maybe even six."

Trevor was totally catatonic the first of the three days he spent in the hospital, after which he spilled his guts to the attending physician. He was assigned to another foster home. One could rest assured Trevor would never be the same again. Trevor's own moment of PPE, perhaps. Maybe his offspring, too, if he ever has them.

*****

Note to John: As far as the incident at the foster home, if Cheryl's recessive evil gene had not expressed itself before that incident, it was cer-

tainly somehow zapped into dominance as she sat watching with fascinated glee Trevor's pain and torment. When one incorporates a strategy that mollifies, even briefly, the little voice that laments imperfection at all conscious levels, it is a need fulfilled. It may not be *the* critical need, like forming strong emotional attachments, but it shows up as a success. A secondary gain, if you will. And success cries out for repeat performances.

It took some digging and a little logical deduction on my part to piece it together, but I'm pretty sure that's the way it came down. Also, this important psychological background ties in to later events.

Since relationships get more involved now, I need a mnemonic device to keep the sections straight in my head. I've come up with film titles, which I hope you of all people will find helpful in your screenplay if you need to refer back to something. Steven

8 Children of the Corn

It was Darcy who had first broached the subject of adoption with Sam. They had tried for years to have a child, but Darcy was infertile. It was hard on her, already limited by her weak heart valves. She dreamed of being a mother, and knew she was meant for the job. Having that taken away from her made Darcy feel less a woman, and it gnawed away at her day and night. She blamed herself, God, her genetic lineage, everyone. And she knew that Sam wanted children, too. Darcy even told Sam they should separate so he could find someone better suited to motherhood. Sam, of course, would have nothing of that, and he told her in no uncertain terms to never bring up that subject again. Sam loved Darcy very much.

Darcy finally asked Sam about it over a special meatloaf dinner. "Sam, should we think about adoption?"

"Already have," he said with a wink. "There's an Oakland Raiderette I have my eye on." He smiled a toothless grin and blushed.

Darcy laughed. "Oh, you!" She pointed her fork at Sam. "I'm serious, mister."

"I know, hon." Sam came back to reality. "If you're up to it, so am I."

Both Sam and Darcy were well aware of the time and energy involved in such a venture. So, they began to talk, and plan, and Darcy began making phone calls. Sam and Darcy had at first wanted a baby less than a year old, but that didn't work out. But it all finally came together more quickly than either could imagine when Bobby and Cheryl came into the picture. It was still a tough call.

The Wynettes were skeptical at first that it would work at all. Bobby and Cheryl's critical formative years—aged two through six—were behind them, and with it the opportunity to help shape them, at least environmentally—behavior, manners, sense of discipline—according to Sam and Darcy's own particular standards and ways of doing things.

In the end, it was Cheryl who captured Darcy's heart. They all had spent the day together, just to get to know each other before a final decision was made. Strolling on the beach in Carmel-by-the-Sea, Sam called Bobby to look at a fish washed up on shore. This left Darcy and Cheryl together, standing side by side at the high tide line.

Cheryl spotted something. "Oh, look," she said, and took Darcy by the hand. Darcy would say later that it felt so natural, like it was her own daughter wanting to share in the discovery of one of life's bounties. Cheryl picked up the abalone shell and looked it over, and then handed it to Darcy. "This is for you," she said with a bright smile, "for taking us to the beach today."

Darcy was almost moved to tears. And Darcy actually cried when she told the story to her friend and neighbor across the street, Marcie Avery.

And that settled it. Sam and Darcy signed the papers and in late October of 2000, it was official: they were the proud parents of two kids. Bobby and Cheryl thought themselves fortunate, too, and they vowed to do everything in their power "not to be sent back to the pound," as Bobby put it.

Sam and Darcy Wynette were far from rich, but they tried to make up for it with the love and respect kids need. In some ways, they succeeded. Over the past three years, Bobby had learned some discipline. Or at least how to avoid punishment, which was a good start. Meanwhile, Cheryl was coming into young womanhood, with all the physical and emotional changes made a little less hypercritical by the love and understanding ways of a very motherly Darcy Wynette.

One might think that they would forever appreciate the love and concern of Sam and Darcy Wynette towards two adopted children. For most children, that would be true. But they had adopted Bobby and Cheryl Nortze, children with a family history of viewing the world radically different than most. Searching for the perfect parents yet unable for reasons of trust to form primary attachments, Bobby and Cheryl were in simultaneous states of delusional fantasy.

Sitting on the bed with her mother that Friday afternoon, Cheryl tried to submerge painful realities of her personal history. She tucked the Emergency Girlie Kit into her purse and stood up. "Thanks, Mom. I'm feeling a lot better now, so I think I'll go for a little walk."

"Be back in one hour, before it gets dark or starts to rain, okay?"

"Okay, Mom."

There were two more things Cheryl needed doing before going for her walk. She waited until Darcy left the room to retrieve an item from her private bathroom and slip it into her kit. It was a small bottle of bright red nail polish, the perfect tool, or one might say weapon, to use against Tory.

Tory, a classmate who lived down the street, had teased her mercilessly about the onset of menstruation. Tory had made quite a showing right in front of the other girls, and Cheryl, of writing down her musings in her diary, a tome Tory pulled out and read to anyone who would listen.

With the nail polish now safely in her kit, the last thing Cheryl needed to do was bring into sharper focus the betrayal of so many people in her miserable life. She held the single-edged razor against the tender skin of her inner thigh and pressed firmly.

On her walk, Cheryl wondered why would anyone would want to write their thoughts in a diary. *What if someone else discovers all your secrets?* Cheryl figured out how Tory wouldn't be writing any more in *that* diary.

When Cheryl returned home around 5 p.m., Sam and Bobby were both home. Sam had given Bobby a box from the hobby shop containing the complicated makings of a two-way radio. It was in very small pieces, and required the use of a soldering gun. The assembly instructions and diagrams ran thirty pages.

"I'd read the instructions first," said Sam. "You should know them inside and out before you start."

Standing next to Sam, Darcy nodded in motherly confirmation.

Bobby scanned the pages for something really complicated, or that might overtax his abilities. "No problem," he said with assurance.

The rain began shortly after, and the wind began to pick up, too.

9 The Two Jakes

The first big wave, a twenty-footer, crashed into the cliff and sent little shock waves that Ken Easton, a hundred feet away, could feel through the concrete slab under his feet. He slipped a new battery into the camcorder and plugged the end of the 120-volt adapter into the wall receptacle as well. Just in case the power went out, he had backup.

Even in his thermal underwear and heavy clothing, Ken turned up the heat in the cold room. He had cranked open the south window both to run the lead wires and to get an unobstructed view of the sloping cliff near the end of his lot. A 1000-watt quartz/halogen shop light aimed toward the south lit up the entire area, including the birdhouse centered in the garden.

The extension cord for the shop light also ran over the windowsill and was plugged into the wall outlet. Ken set up the tripod facing out the window, and he mounted the camcorder, tightening both together with the plastic wheel under the tripod's platform. The final touch was to start the CD player, Kenny G doing his thing on the alto sax.

The wind was from the northwest, and together with the roof overhang, Ken was protected from the weather. He saw the rain lit up by the light. Opening the hinged viewfinder on the camcorder, Ken was not surprised to see Jake, the little sea tern, dive into the hole of the birdhouse.

"Just in time, Jake," Ken said aloud, "It's going to be a doozey tonight."

Jake the Tern had shown up in early January of 2001, just two weeks after the accident that had taken Valerie and Tyler. With an injured left wing, Jake wasn't much of a talker, but he was good company. At first there was only a little perch and bird feeder. After Ken built him a birdhouse, Jake the Tern became a permanent resident, chirping away in the mornings and fluttering his injured wing in the foggy—some would argue healing—mists coming off the ocean. Jake flew with a slight but noticeable hitch after that.

Ken pushed the camcorder record button, an hour of 8 mm tape inside, and sat down at his computer already booted up with his acoustic program running. The wind howled outside and the rain beat on the roof mercilessly. To his right was an oscilloscope, connected to the computer with nine low-voltage pickup wires that ran out the window, through the garden, and out to the nine sensors. They were capable of detecting extremely small sound vibrations through the rocks.

The first three sensors sat atop the sloping cliff, the second at its base, and the third set was mounted by epoxy on the little rocky outcrop that Ken used as his diving perch. Within each of the sets of three, one sensor was in direct contact with the rock. A second had a thin neoprene wafer between the sensor and the rock, and the third had a wafer of stainless steel between the sensor and the rock. Because sound traveled at different speeds through different materials, it would be a preliminary real world test of both acoustic dampening and proliferation, with three of the sensors attached directly to the rock at the three different locations acting as controls.

On the oscilloscope, a wide and narrow band of static narrowed and sharpened as Ken adjusted the attenuation settings. Instantaneously with the clap against the cliff of the next wave, a spike on the scope jumped off the scale. Ken decreased the sensitivity one click and waited. Fifteen seconds later the next wave hit the cliff, and the waveform spiked again, but this time within the bounds of the scope.

Nine little windows on his computer screen registered the impact, in three sets of three. All were clustered around 27 megajoules of energy. The cliff had absorbed most of it, but with the hoped for distinguishing characteristics within each grouping, it was a good start.

For nearly an hour, the ever-increasing wave impacts registered on Ken's computer, and the camcorder caught the sprays shooting up to twenty feet above the top of the cliff. A stiff breeze forced the spray into his garden and onto the birdhouse, but Jake the Tern was protected from the on-slaught. And then things began to settle down. The quickly moving front had passed, and left over was a violent sea and big waves, but nothing like in that first hour.

Ken reviewed the data, did a little first-order statistical analysis, and decided to call it a night. He had all day Saturday to massage the data, so he wasn't in any rush. He first copied the 8mm tape onto a new six-hour VHS tape. While in duplication mode, Ken removed the lead wires from the oscilloscope and dropped them outside the window. Just as he was about to bend down and unplug the extension cord to the shop light, he caught a glimpse of the birdhouse. Jake the Tern had his head out the little hole, checking on the state of the world. He still hadn't touched the seeds that Ken had left out for him.

Ken smiled. The snug and secure world of Jake the Tern had not ended, but for Ken Easton, it was about to.

10 Love Amongst the Ruins

What was all warm and fuzzy on a warm summer day at the beach less than a year before now began to be questioned, deep down, with or without logical justification, by two orphans discussing life on the eve of a stormy November night. Something in the atmosphere, perhaps, like charged ions. Or maybe it was just Cheryl's conflict with her classmate, Tory, and Bobby's resignation to his fate with building the walkie-talkies over the next month.

"We've been abandoned before," said Cheryl. Intentionally by their father, and stupidly drunk by their mother. "Who's to say these grownups are any different?"

"Yeah," said Bobby. "Maybe we'll do something wrong and they won't like us anymore." Somehow he knew the word *love* didn't quite fit that into that sentence. He and Cheryl both felt the love from Sam and Darcy, and that was just the point: not being liked seemed somehow worse. Bobby grew silent for a moment, then added, "And what if they do something stupid and get divorced, or killed even? It's back to the pound for us," he said with finality.

They also knew, and had even discussed previously that the California age of legal consent—eighteen—and with it freedom, was a long, long way off for the both of them.

"We've got to keep our eyes peeled for danger signs, that's all," said Bobby. "And opportunities, too."

That type of thinking was not exactly conducive to forming a permanent bond of trust any time soon. For her part, Cheryl analyzed the emotional impact—anticipatory anxiety—that came with her thinking. Expecting the worst every time, she was bound to be right once in awhile.

As for Bobby, he had been thrust into the role of problem solver at a younger age than most. What he saw at the end of the day was a way to internalize the uncertainty of this adoption thing, but openly express, at least to Cheryl, his take on possible solutions as they arose. He protected Cheryl, and that had come to be a major role in his life, for a few critically formative years, anyway. It had the result of forcing Bobby Nortze-Wynette to be vigilant 24/7 for people and situations conflicting with basic survival, particularly in regard to the emotional stability of his younger sister.

To those two separate little voices waking them up and putting them to bed that and every night since the abandonment by their father and death of their mother, it was all about the fear of failure, and of being wrong—about anything. Normal everyday degrees of human failings or wrongness were just not part of the conversation, especially in ones so young and so vulnerable to irrational fears of parental dispossession.

*****

Note to John: Interviews and records were hard to come by, and again time consuming, but I did the best I could. I know you said, "Stick to brief summaries of main characters and event sequences," but some recent info (detailed later) compels me to include the material. Again, I think the extra time spent was worth it.

BTW: I had to spend a lot of time making sense of all the engineering info, too, but without it, there's a big technical gap. Stephen

11 Little Big Man

In a shouted whisper, as if he was trying to be polite, Nortze said, "How the fuck do you expect to cram all six of us, plus the lumber and all the other crap, into this one stinking minivan?" Nortze was thinking primarily of the overweight twins, Dan and Dave, as he stared at the little green van in the parking lot. With everyone dressed against the cool temperature and overcast skies, it would be more than a tight squeeze just to get the people inside.

Margie Swanson was clearly intimidated. She had done everything to make Gil Nortze happy, and now this. "I can see now that is impossible. Again, I'm sorry, Mr. Nortze." She had already explained to Nortze that the other van—the only one available—had broken down on its way over from the rental agency and was, at this very moment, being towed back to the shop.

Out of the blue while standing in the parking lot, Margie hit upon a solution and forced a smile. "Instead of waiting around for them to send another van, how about this: We can do it in two vehicles, as Yankee Point is just a mile down the road, and I'll drive my pickup. I'm sure that between the van and my truck we'll get everyone and your stuff to Yankee Point in plenty of time."

Gil Nortze did not like such clear thinking in the midst of his outburst, for the simple reason that it usually threw most people into a mental nosedive. He liked doing that. Also, he had not come up with the solution himself, and was annoyed by his inability to show someone up. Nortze checked his watch showing just past 3 o'clock. He threw his hands up in the air and shouted, "Whatever! Let's get outa here before it gets dark, for Christ's sake."

In addition to the gambling twins, Dan and Dave Snowden, were their wives, Carrie and Patty, and Tristin Barnes, the property management specialist "assigned" to the trip by Stu Adams, the head honcho of Nortze's financial advisory firm.

With a head for details and a memory like a steel trap, Tristin Barnes was quickly making her way up in the world of property management. Adams hadn't wanted to make the trip himself, but as Gil Nortze was an old customer, Adams felt he had to make good somehow. So he had called and begged Tristin, a member of the firm since February, to go for the sake of the firm. With no ready excuses, Tristin had agreed.

Tristin had stood at the bathroom mirror that morning getting ready to go to the airport. She was a 30-year-old natural blonde, her hair cut fashionably short around a beautiful Scandinavian face, with light blue eyes that flashed every time she smiled, which was often. After putting on a light pink lipstick and fluffing her hair, Tristin had looked in the mirror and said to her reflection, "Take one for the team, girl. It's only one weekend."

Tristin was trying to steel herself for the overnight trip to the coast with Gil Nortze, not knowing what to expect from him, except his usual pompous, arrogant, self-absorbed attitude. Gil Nortze gave her the creeps. But still, she had done that one desperate thing the previous Valentine's Day to get that one critical job interview with Stu Adams, and she would have to live with it forever.

When asked to go on the trip, Tristin had told Stu Adams she had a boyfriend, something she expected Stu to pass along to Gil Nortze, just in case the man had any ideas.

And now, they all stood together in a little group in the parking lot of the Carmel Highlands Bed & Breakfast as the alpha male took charge of the situation.

"Okay. Tristin, Dan, and Dave—you come with me in the van." Nortze took in a deep breath and turned to Margie. "You *do* have all the stuff I ordered, right?" Margie turned and started to point to the pile of goods, but before she could answer in the affirmative, Nortze added, dismissively, "Good, I'm paying enough." He'd seen the pile. Nortze pointed to the second group. "Then it'll be Carrie and Patty in the pickup, along with the big stuff in the back."

To the Moon, Alice! That's what Carrie and Patty were both thinking, harkening back to Jackie Gleason's *The Honeymooners*. Each was ready to take off the gloves at Nortze's rudeness to Margie. But as Margie began taking inventory next to the utility shed, Carrie and Patty calmed down.

There was a pile of pine logs for a "beach fire," according to Nortze's instructions, stacked by the gas meter. The head-scratcher for Margie was that she knew of no beaches at Yankee Point—just rocky cliffs. Included in Gil Nortze's pile was a gas barbeque grill with full propane cylinder; a dozen Douglas fir two-by-fours and a roll of twine; two shovels; a thick white canvas tarp; six aluminum beach chairs; a big ice chest filled with beer and soft drinks, raw steaks, potatoes, and coleslaw; and a sack of pots and pans and eating utensils.

"Okay, folks," Nortze called out, "let's pack it up."

Once everything was loaded into the two vehicles, the lumber jutting out two feet over the top of Margie's tailgate, Nortze wasted no time. "Follow me. I know where the hell I'm going."

Gil drove the van and Tristin sat shotgun while Dan and Dave took up the second and third row of seats, respectively. There was a little room in the back left over for some of their gear. Out on the highway, Nortze began by saying, "You're going to love this place, Tris."

Tristin couldn't help but be in awe of the natural beauty, but she had her suspicions that based on one prior conversation, Nortze thought of it in purely financial terms. No matter. What he did with his money was his decision, although Tristin would try to help determine what the property was now worth. She had brought a few comps with her picked off the Internet, so it was a matter of looking at the property, taking pictures, and talking to a few real estate agents on Sunday to come up with a number.

"It's beautiful," she said, passing a tight grouping of Monterey pines, their long branches swept up and back from a lifetime of stiff sea breezes.

"Lots of old money here," said Nortze, oblivious to the real treasures. "And the lot is probably worth close to a million."

"We'll see," Tristin said with a quick smile.

Following in the pickup truck, Margie asked Patty, squeezed in between herself and Carrie, "So, who is this Gil Nortze, anyway."

Patty was diplomatic. "Oh, he's just a lot of hot air, mostly. Harmless, too. He just likes to show people he's in charge."

"The boys," Carrie said, referring to their husbands, "have known Gil since they were kids down in Cambria." She sighed heavily. "We didn't meet him until the wedding." It sounded to Margie like Carrie might have liked to know beforehand.

"You both got married at the same time?"

"Yes," Patty answered, "Double wedding."

"How nice," said Margie. "They seem like nice fellas."

"Yes, *they* are," said Carrie. Both she and Patty had felt awful about the news that Robert Sparks had lost his property to Nortze in a poker game. And they were more than queasy about coming on the trip, but the boys had insisted. Nortze had put a lot of bread on their tables in the past two years, to the tune of almost a hundred thousand dollars to the good in private gambling winnings. Carrie's husband, Dan, was a very good player.

Nortze spotted the road sign and turned right onto the narrow Spindrift Road, winding his way through the tall pines. Only a few of the houses were actually visible from the road, a sure sign there were some great houses set on the numerous little jutting headlands with an eye to privacy.

A small sign read, "Private Driveway," and Nortze turned down. It was a steep, narrow driveway, made slightly awkward by the tight turns. After a hundred yards, the road opened to a fork, and the view of the ocean, the sun low on the southwestern horizon. A single mailbox sat on the far side of the road. The right fork was paved, but the left fork was still dirt. Nortze veered left and down the hill, coming to a stop as the driveway leveled out.

"Wow!" said Tristin. "This is gorgeous." The seas were calm now, with two-foot waves breaking against the rocky outcrops just off the headland. Tristin spotted a sea otter lying on its back atop the kelp bed, eating something. "Oh, look at that," she said, pointing. "Is that a seal?" Dan and Dave craned their necks for a look out the windshield, too.

"Sea otter," said Nortze. "Eats on his back. Probably an abalone." And he couldn't help himself adding, "*My* abalone, now."

Tristin's stare was transfixed on the little sea mammal. "How cute is that?"

"Make a nice fur," said Nortze without emotion. "When my great grandfather had his abalone cannery, the little bastards were always making off with the profits."

Tristin turned in shock. "How can you say that, Gil?"

Nortze laughed, having successfully gotten a rise out of Tristin. He opened the door and stepped out as Margie's pickup pulled up alongside. When everyone had spilled out of the vehicles, Nortze shouted, "Well, folks, not bad for a straight flush, huh?"

Margie had been impressed by the take-charge attitude of Gil Nortze. To her, Gil Nortze wasn't handsome or refined, but he was a winner—powerful in a certain way, too. She figured maybe a little flirting was in order—maybe get laid if she was lucky. She asked herself, "Hey, how bad could it be?"

*****

Ken Easton was finishing up making a fire in the fireplace. He turned the key and heard the hissing gas, and then flicked the long lighter close to the logs. Instant fire. Ken went to his easy chair and picked up the folder off the side table, sorting through it until he found the GFON printout from Greg. He sat down, eyebrows furrowed, trying to make some sense out of it in light of his own measurements the night before. He'd been at it since mid-morning and wasn't making much real headway.

There was one easily recognizable problem in need of resolution, but he wasn't so sure he had the answer, or at least one that wouldn't add huge costs to a construction project. The one redeeming factor was that at least this would be a demonstration-of-concept project, and costs would not be all that critical. If the system worked, that's what counted at this juncture. Later, in the real world, costs would become very important.

This main sticking point was the acoustic change between structural connections, places where things usually started going south after a major seismic event: Steel I-beam to welded flange, welded flange to steel or wood post, post to anchor—what is called a hold-down—and hold-down to foundation. There were many paths along which the sound waves traveled, some of them overlapping from different directions, but only one path led directly from the source, through the given connection to the next structural member, and a sensor. In between the sensors was a lot of what is called *noise*.

The true signal—associated with a cracked I-beam flange, for example—would surely be buried beneath other signals, most likely echoes, coming from other I-beams, some perhaps only shifting or flexing, while others perhaps failed. Ken suspected that separating the true signal out from the noise would require that, at minimum, a sensor be placed at the center of every single steel I-beam and post. Better yet, two per beam and post, each close to the connection on that end. That way, if a flange cracked and/or separated, sensors close by on each side of the damage would pick up the strongest signal, other sensors further away picking up merely the echoes. Ken wrote up a paragraph on that concept.

Of course, it was also critical that any low voltage wires leading to the sensors would not become crimped, or stretched out too far, or even broken. Ken thought of how oil and gas pipelines snaked their way across the landscape, with even a loop put in every so often to give the pipeline room to flex and shift without harm to its integrity.

Ken sketched out on the back of his printout a looping zigzag pattern to run the wires, with a little extra loop at the connections in case there was movement. It was all he had at the moment, and he doodled in his notebook for an hour, showing himself and others how it might look and work.

Lindy barked three times, and Ken stopped his doodling and went to the south window, cranking it open. She was at the far end of the garden looking up the sloping rocks. Ken couldn't see anyone, but he did see the black smoke rising from beyond the top of the bluff, and he heard clearly a female laugh.

"What the ...?" Ken grabbed a jacket to put over his sweats and walked into the garden. He stopped by to check on Jake the Tern, but he wasn't home in the birdhouse. Seeing the column of smoke rise, Ken figured maybe it was some kids with a late afternoon campfire, so he climbed the rocks with Lindy tagging along behind.

At the top of the bluff, he stopped. A single green minivan was parked at the base of the driveway. Four people sat in a semi-circle of chairs around a makeshift fire pit, and a redheaded man tended to meat on a barbeque grill. A pretty blonde woman was bent over searching a bag for something, and as she straightened up with a basting brush in her hand, she spotted Ken. She immediately smiled and waved, then said something to the man at the grille while still looking at Ken. Ken forced a smile and a little wave back while he approached.

Nortze turned his head to Ken, long meat fork in hand. "Howdy, neighbor!"

Neighbor? Oh, man, it's him—Robert Sparks.

It was all quite a shock to Ken's system. "Afternoon," he said, approaching with a forced smile frozen on his face. "Saw smoke and thought it was some kids up here."

"Nope. Just us chickens," replied Nortze. "I think your dog smelled the meat." Lindy sniffed the ground and stopped next to Tristin.

Nodding respectfully to the twins and their wives, Ken then turned his attention back to Nortze. "Are you Robert Sparks by any chance?"

Nortze snickered, "You missed him ... by sixteen hours, I'm afraid, since midnight last night."

Ken was confused. "I'm sorry?"

Nortze put down the fork and walked over, his hand outstretched. "Gil Nortze. I'm the new owner of this here property."

The bottom fell out of Ken's stomach, but he shook hands anyway. Only Tristin Barnes noticed the change that came over who she viewed as one good-looking hunk standing nearby. "Ken Easton. I live over there," he said, cocking his head. "Did Sparks sell it to you?"

"Sort of," Nortze said with a shrug. Ken then caught the expressions on the twins and their wives, all momentarily uncomfortable. "The point is," Nortze continued, gesturing widely with an outstretched arm, "it's all mine now."

For Ken, there was no use in fighting it, as the battle was now over. "Then welcome to Yankee Point." Ken assumed that the pretty blonde was Nortze's girlfriend, as she wasn't wearing a ring.

"Thanks, Ken." Nortze turned and introduced everyone, with Ken insisting they stay seated. Dan and Dave appeared to Ken more like a twin wrestling tag team on WWF Smackdown than gamblers. Carrie Snowden was a little on the overweight side, but she deflected attention to it behind a huge smile. Patty Snowden, Dave's petite wife, was almost invisible to Ken in the late-afternoon shadow of her 275-pound husband. When Nortze got around to Tristin, their eyes met for the first time. "This is Tristin Barnes, my property consultant." Lindy was already on her haunches next to Tristin.

Ken smiled warmly, feeling the friendliness, and something more, in her blue eyes. "Nice to meet you," he said, adding, "and that's Lindy." For reasons unknown to him at the time, Ken was glad she wasn't attached to Nortze. "How long are you staying?"

"Just overnight," she answered, reaching down and petting the top of Lindy's head. Lindy was in doggie heaven after that.

Ken was taken aback. "Here?"

Tristin laughed. "No, silly, not here. At the little bed-and-breakfast up in the Highlands."

Ken recoiled in embarrassment, shaking his head. "Oh, of course, Margie's," said, finally letting loose a chuckle and playfully slapping the side of his head. "Like you guys were going to camp out here in this weather."

"Maybe in the summer," she said. It was the wistful way she said that, as if she would like to come back, that caught Ken's attention. Tristin felt

Lindy's head nudging her leg, and she reached down and stroked her head again.

"Hey, Tristin" Nortze yelled, seeing both the dog at Tristin's side and that little spark between her and Ken, "Quit hittin' on my new neighbor." It was a clever double entendre, catching everyone by surprise. He could have been talking about the dog, but also about Ken. Tristin's mouth dropped in shocked amazement, Ken shook his head and shrugged, and everyone chuckled to offset an awkward moment.

Awkward to everyone except Gil Nortze, who loved putting people in uncomfortable spots. "We have plenty of steaks, so why not join us," he offered, in a manner approaching, but not quite reaching the level of an apology for such rudeness.

"Oh, I don't think so," said Ken. He wasn't all that hungry, but also didn't want to intrude. "Thanks for asking, though, Gil." He looked straight at Tristin, saying. "I've been working on something and have to get back to it."

Nortze mumbled into the grille, "What's your game, Ken?"

Ken never consciously heard the question. Instead, he was watching as Tristin cocked her left eyebrow and touched her tongue to her lower lip, letting Ken know that he would be missing something—her specifically—if he left.

"Yo, Ken?" shouted Nortze, now turned from the grille.

That pulled Ken away from his silent interlude with Tristin. He turned with a dumbstruck look on his face that everyone around him could see had been thoughtfully zeroed in on the beautiful, young, single, and attractive woman before him. "Huh?"

This time in a manner reflecting an insight into the true nature of what had just happened between Ken and Tristin, Dan and Dave broke out laughing, followed by Carrie and Patty. Carrie saw that Ken and Tristin sure made for a cute couple, and she whipped out her digital camera and took a picture of the two of them standing together.

Now it was Ken's turn for facial flushing, and Tristin coyly averted her eyes.

Nortze repeated, "I said, 'What's your game?' What do you do?"

"Oh, I'm an acoustical engineer." That seemed to flatten the humor of the moment, but only briefly.

"Apparently a deaf one, from where I'm standing," said Nortze, and this brought a round of now-uncontrollable laughter.

Ken couldn't help but laugh aloud, too. He found himself not so unpleasantly trapped in a spontaneous, albeit painfully public romantic moment, experiencing feelings and emotions he'd not felt for a long, long time. He turned and shrugged to Tristin, suggesting to her a response along the lines of, *What can I say? I'm caught red-handed!*

"Well, suit yourself," said Nortze. "We're eating in fifteen minutes, with or without you."

"Thanks again for the offer," Ken said to Nortze and the others, and then turned his eyes back to Tristin, voice lowered slightly. "But I really have to be going. Nice meeting you. Enjoy yourselves."

"And you, too." Tristin said back.

The twins and their wives said their goodbyes, and Ken turned on his heels. He was almost to the north end of the bluff before realizing Lindy wasn't with him. He turned and saw her still sitting upright at Tristin's side, looking right at him, unmoved.

Lindy had been Valerie's dog, and as devoted to her as a dog gets. Lindy obviously still missed that unquantifiable human female presence, taking this rare opportunity with Tristin to reconnect.

"C'mon, girl," Ken coaxed. Lindy was reluctant to leave, but Tristin shooed her off in Ken's direction. "Thanks," he called, disappearing over the hill with a little wave back at Tristin. What didn't disappear, however, at least for the next hour, were thoughts of Tristin.

Geez, it's been so long, I forgot how to act around women. She probably thinks I'm an idiot ... well, since she knows I'm an engineer, maybe not a complete idiot. But a deaf one, anyway.

That memory brought an audible laugh from deep down. He turned his thoughts briefly to Gil Nortze. *Well, it has to be somebody who owns that lot. Wishin' it was me won't help now. Nortze isn't all that bad, considering alternatives.*

Passing the birdhouse, he whistled for Jake the Tern. Jake stuck his head out the hole and chirped. "Top of the afternoon to ya, little buddy. How's it hangin'?" Ken didn't make the connection that despite the shock of meeting the new owner of his next-door property, and all the negatives implied regarding his future privacy, he was in a great mood.

Back inside the house, Ken fumbled inside the fridge for something to eat. Now he was hungry. Ravenously so. He pulled out the container of Thai take-out from three nights ago, still half-full. He ate it cold. Lindy sat patiently a few feet away next to the kitchen counter, every once in awhile turning her head toward the south hallway. Standing with his back against the stove, Ken picked up the vibe. "She was nice, wasn't she, girl?" Lindy wagged her tail.

"What, you'd rather be with her than with me?" he said, shoveling down another bite of spicy chicken.

Lindy lowered her head, inching down until she had her paws out in front of her on the floor. She held her head up and looked straight at Ken.

"Thanks for the vote of confidence, Lindy. I won't forget it." He went back to the fridge and the fixings for a sandwich. He ate that with a glass of milk, and scarfed down the last six fig newtons with a second glass of milk. Finally sated, he went to his office to get some more ideas on acoustic sensor arrays, but it was no use. For the next hour, his mind drifted to one subject only—Tristin Barnes.

It was dark by 5:15, and by then Ken had bounced aimlessly around the house, getting quickly bored with, in turn, his work, the TV, and a half-finished novel. And then it was back to the computer. But even a birthday card he was creating for his sister on PhotoShop couldn't keep him from his pleasant distraction—Tristin.

Lindy sat upright and trotted out of the den with a little whine. Not a growl or a bark, like when someone was coming to the door, but something different. Ken cocked his head, realizing she hadn't done that in years. It's what Lindy did when she heard Valerie coming home.

For a moment, Ken froze. But the vision of Valerie's ghost appearing at his front door quickly dissipated, and he brought himself back to reality with a shake of his head. But when the doorbell chimed, it sent a shock through his heart, nonetheless. He convinced himself before he got to the door that it was one of Nortze's guests in need of sugar or something they hadn't brought along for the barbeque. However, Lindy waited silently by the door, something she didn't do with strangers. Deep down, Ken offered up a silent prayer to heaven that it was Tristin.

It was answered when he opened the door to find Tristin standing before him, flashlight in hand. Lindy scurried past Ken and went right up to her, looking up and waiting for a response, her tail wagging furiously. "Hi, Ken. Sorry to bother you, but I've been sent as an emissary." She bent down and rubbed Lindy's ears.

Ken tried to act nonchalant, although his heart was now racing. "Really. Run out of graham crackers for smoors, did you?"

Tristin tossed her head back and laughed. "Haven't had those in years. No, not smoors, Ken." She calmed herself before continuing. "It seems that Gil has this little ceremony, or something bizarre, all planned out. It sounds fun, and we thought—actually, I thought—and Gil and everyone else approved, that you might like to join us."

There was no amount of money in the world that would have made him say no to her request. "Well, thank you, Tristin, I'd like that a lot. Very thoughtful of you."

"Great. Go get ready then." She bent down and snuggled her face against Lindy's, a sight that sent a powerful image of Valerie to Ken's brain.

"Please, come in. And bring Lindy with you." That wasn't necessary. Ken left the door open and hurried to his bedroom to change.

Tristin stepped through the door, Lindy right at her side, and began taking in the details of Ken's house from the foyer. It was quite attractive and cozy, she thought, although not realizing at the time that it was Valerie's decorating touch that had made it so. And a housekeeper that kept it from disintegrating into a bachelor hellhole. Tristin was, like everyone else who saw it, practically floored by the view through the living room out to bluff and the rock formations and sea beyond.

Ken returned all dressed in multiple layers of warm clothes, plus a knit ski cap, to face the weather. "All set."

"Very nice house, Ken. I envy your view."

"It definitely grows on you."

Lindy wanted to go along, but Ken stroked her head and said she had to stay home this time. He'd already locked the doggy-door, and Lindy wouldn't be happy about that. Closing but not locking the door behind him, Ken led Tristin on the long, easy route.

They walked together up the driveway. "Lindy seems to have taken a liking to you," Ken said innocently, and then thought about what was left unsaid: *So have I.*

Tristin didn't miss a beat. "She's such a sweetheart, and I love dogs, but I don't have one myself."

"You can borrow her any time," he replied, again without thinking, and he regretted appearing too forward too soon.

Tristin picked up on the subtle hint but let it slide ... for now. After seeing how cute he was at their first meeting up on the bluff, Tristin's eyes had zeroed in on his left hand—no wedding ring. "What's the rent on a border collie these days?"

"Just the promise to get her back when I start missing her." *Oh, jeez, shut up, will ya? Don't be such a basket case, for crying out loud. Anyone with half a brain can spot a lonely bachelor from a mile away. Suck it up, man.*

Tristin looked straight ahead and went for what Gil Nortze might refer to as the gut-shot raise. "So, there's no one else for backup when Lindy's not around?"

"No, not for a while, I'm afraid." At least it was now getting out in the open. "My wife and son died in a car accident three years ago," and here Ken pointed down the coast, "not too far from here." Before he allowed Tristin to give in to shock and offer her sympathies, Ken quickly added, "So now it's just me and Lindy." He shook his finger in a humorous mock warning. "She's a great companion, so it's not one of those rent deals with a later buyout option."

Tristin had to chuckle in appreciation of how deftly Ken had given her the critical information but had quickly passed onto a lighter subject. She held up her right hand, still holding the flashlight, like a trial witness, "I promise." She paused a moment, and was compelled to add, "I'm sorry about your family."

"Yes, thank you," Ken said, and then he shrugged, adding, "I'm dealing with—"

Before Tristin could train the light ahead of them, she caught her left foot on a stray rock, and she began to tumble forward. Ken caught her by her coat and kept her from falling. "Whoa! You okay?"

She righted herself and stopped. "Yes, thanks. I guess using the flashlight would be real smart here." They were three-quarters up the driveway now, nearing the mailbox. "So, you were saying about dealing with something?"

"Oh, yeah. I'm dealing with it all in the best way I can. It was tough for a while, that's for sure, but time is a good healer."

"Work, too."

"What is it *you* do, Tristin?"

"Property management in Las Vegas. Gil is one of our good paying customers, so that's why I'm here ... to give him our take on this property."

Ken figured a little levity at this point wouldn't hurt. "Tell him it's a lousy investment, will ya?"

Tristin laughed aloud. "In any other circumstance, Ken, I would do just that, I swear." She recalled that moment when his face had slackened and his demeanor had rapidly changed when he found out that Gil had the property.

"I know, just kidding. It's a valuable lot. I offered the previous owner a million cash, but I didn't know the situation."

"Well, I don't know all of it, and even if I did, it wouldn't be very professional of me to talk about it, but it's all about the money with Gil. Whoever comes to the table with the most gets it, I suppose. You're looking out for a little privacy, others something else, perhaps."

"Yes, I guess that's the long and short of it."

They were now just past the mailbox and starting down the hill, and Ken stopped in his tracks. "What the heck is that?"

Down on the bluff, Gil Nortze had supervised the erection of a tepee made of those two-by-fours, and it was situated directly over the fire pit, now burning low. There was just enough room to walk in a stooped fashion inside without bursting into flames. All hands were holding and placing a large white cloth tarp around the two-by-fours, with Gil shouting orders about how it was to be placed and tied. Dan stood on his tiptoes to wrap the two-by-fours with twine at the apex.

"I have no idea, Ken. Gil said it was a surprise, some sort of ritual the Indians used to go through when they lived here."

By the time Ken and Tristin reached the tepee, Gil was folding back a section of tarp to open up the top of the tepee for the rising smoke to get out. Nortze turned and spotted Ken. "Hey, you showed up, great. Help yourself to a beer from the cooler." Ken greeted the others with a wave of the hand and went for a couple of beers for himself and Tristin.

Nortze stepped back for a look at his handwork and exclaimed, "There! Next is the cross. Where's that handsaw?"

"Right here," said Patty. She gave it to Dave, and he stepped forward. "I'll do the cutting, Gil."

"Perfect. We have one two-by-four left. Cut a third off the end, Dave."

"Will do." Dave laid the ten-foot two-by-four across his knee, and with Dan standing on one end, began to saw off about three feet. Patty and

Carrie busied themselves with sorting out stuff from a shopping bag onto the ground.

"Anything we can do?" said Tristin, meaning herself and Ken. It was not lost on Ken that she referred to the two of them as an item.

"Yes, take those shovels and start digging a hole. Right over there." Gil pointed to a spot just to the side of the tepee.

Ken chimed in with, "Um, the soil's only a foot or two deep here, Gil."

"That's fine for our purposes. We'll use rocks to make it steady."

With that, Ken and Tristin began digging an 18-inch deep hole down to bedrock. They used Tristin's flashlight to locate a few large rocks, placing them near the hole. Tristin whispered to Ken, "I have no idea what this is all about, I swear."

Also in a whisper, Ken said, "Whatever it is, it sounds interesting."

"Hey, you two—get a room!" Gil Nortze was nothing if not observant. Ken and Tristin stifled their laughter.

Dan cut through the two-by-four and placed the center of the short piece across the longer one at a right angle. Nortze was right there to wrap the two pieces together with twine to make the cross. "Okay, let's take 'er to the hole and stand 'er up."

With Nortze calling out adjustments to keep the cross perfectly vertical and facing due west, Ken and Tristin shoveled the dirt back around the bottom of the hole around the wood. Dan and

Dave supplied periodic tamping with their size-14 shoes, and in a few moments the hole was filled. Dan and Dave then placed the rocks in a pyramid around the exposed two-by-four base. With an assortment of little trinkets Carrie and Patty had arranged and displayed on the dirt, it was done.

Patty was the brave one. "Now, are you going to tell us what this is all about, Gil, or do we have to beat it out of you with those shovels?"

"Okay, okay," squealed Gil, his hands shaking above his head as if forced into a confession. "Let's all go sit down and I'll tell you."

They all sat down in their chairs and Ken pulled the cooler over to the group, sitting on the lid and next to Tristin.

"Back in the old days, the local Indians—of the *Rumsen* tribe—"

Carrie looked up from her dried flower arrangement and asked, "Rumsfeld? Did you say Rumsfeld, like in Donald, the Secretary of Defense?"

"rum-SEN," Nortze repeated. "Like in the Secretary of Jamaica." Everyone cracked up.

"Anyway, the tribe used to come to the Carmel River, where it dumps into the bay, and set up camp for fishing and hunting. Or take abalone from the rocks. Just in the spring and summer, though, as it was too cold and rainy during the fall and winter."

"Did they swim in the ocean?" asked Carrie, shivering at the thought.

It was a good question. However, the anger on Gil's face—reflected from the fire at the second interruption—suggested silence during his monologue. But it was his condescending and rapid-fire response made that mere suggestion very clear. "No, Carrie, they didn't swim in the ocean—they couldn't swim. The water was always cold—just like now—and the currents were treacherous—just like now. So, they stuck to the shoreline and the river to hunt and fish. Lot's of abalone, too."

"Sorry, go on."

Nortze sighed heavily, as if it was a major disruption. "Anyway, when the Mexican's came—Spaniards, mostly—back in the mid-1700s, they got all chummy with the Indians—"

"Is *chummy* the right word here, Gil?" said Dave, purely to aggravate the man. "I mean, didn't they want to convert them to Christianity or something?"

There were a few stifled chuckles, but Gil's was not among them. "Whatever, Dave. Anyway, they all ran around mostly naked, but they did show the newcomers some tricks about how to live off the land. And of course, being naked savages and all—"

"Oh, Gil," Patty scoffed, "they weren't savages, they were natives."

"Yeah, yeah, whatever. Anyway, these *noble creatures* were almost completely immune to infection—the men anyway—and the reason was that they built *temescals,* what we call saunas," and Gil now pointed to the tepee, "and scratched their skins with abalone shells or sharp knives before going for a sweat inside."

"You're joking," said Tristin.

"Swear to God. Got it right out of my great-great-grandmother's diary." Nortze reached inside his coat and pulled out the leather bound diary of Maria Nortze, holding it up for all to see."

"Wow, can I take a look at that?" asked Tristin.

Gil tucked it away, saying, "Not right now. I'm not done with the story yet."

Dan chimed in, whining, "We don't have to bleed like a bunch of naked savages tonight, do we, Gil?"

"Only if y'all don't shut the fuck up and let me finish!" Everyone laughed. "Okay, like I was saying, when it was really cold outside, like this evening, the men would go into the *temescal*, actually just one of their *rucs* turned into a sauna.

"Did you say 'rocks'?"

"R-u-c, ruc. It was the little hut where each family lived. A ruc took about two hours to build, and it was made of branches and thatch, not two-by-fours and a tarp. Anyway, a *temescal* was just a *ruc* with a fire inside, and they'd sit by the fire and sweat."

"Just the men?" asked Carrie. "What about the women?"

"Women were banned from *that* ceremony, Carrie. I'm thinking about that right now for *this* one if I don't get finished with this fucking story."

"Okay, okay. Just asking."

Ken and Tristin looked at each other, each of them trying unsuccessfully to stifle their laughter. Their eyes held each other's gaze for a moment, a very nice moment.

"Anyway," Gil plodded on, "the point is that the men developed immunities to infection, and the women didn't. That's pretty much it on the *ruc* and *temescal*, but now we come to the cross. It seems that Portola, the explorer, erected them so that future ships found their way safely to shore. When the Indians found it the next spring, they thought it was some sort of powerful spirit or something, and they remembered the little crosses worn by the Spaniards. So, to placate the gods, I guess, they placed meat, both raw and dried, and shells and seeds and what not all around it." Nortze stood up and motioned for everyone to follow. "C'mon, everybody grab something."

From the assortment of trinkets so carefully arranged by Carrie and Patty, Nortze handed some dried flowers to Carrie, seeds to Patty, some beef jerky to Dan that Margie had purchased at the local 7-ELEVEN, and a hunk of raw meat to Dave. Tristin and Ken were the last to arrive, and Nortze handed a cheap beaded necklace to Tristin, not part of the original offering back in the Mission Period but a bargain at 75 cents. Nortze then gave Ken an abalone shell and two mussel shells. The last item he saved for himself, a bright aluminum Zippo lighter replica, circa 1950, purchased by Nortze at the McCarran Airport in Las Vegas.

Nortze had them all stand around the cross and, one by one, place their offering either on the horizontal member of the cross or on the pyramid of rocks at its base.

"Here's to good spirits," said Tristin, hanging her beads over one cross arm and raising her beer bottle with the other.

"And to the vultures," added Dave as he placed the piece of steak on the rocks. Dan put his beef jerky nearby.

Patty placed the little bundle of dried poppies in the middle of the pyramid. "Let's not forget those who died here before us."

Patty silently sprinkled seeds all around the base of the cross. Finally, Ken placed the shells on an empty spot on the rocks. "May we all be honorable hunters in life," he added, and that got a round of approval from everyone.

Well, almost everyone. Nortze snorted and walked away toward the tepee. "Okay, next up is the *temescal*," said Nortze, "We all have to go inside."

"Oh, oh," said Dan, "I think that *cutting-the-skin-with-the-shells* part is next."

Nortze jabbed a finger in Dan's direction. "Hey, no it's not, and don't go scaring the womenfolk." Nortze removed his jacket and opened the flap. "It's going to be hot in here, so you might want to strip down a bit."

Everyone followed suit, and one by one, they stooped and entered. Nortze lingered outside a few moments, and when he came in, his face was almost completely blackened. He held up a lump of coal, saying to the astonished group, "It is the Rumsen tribe's color of welcome from their chief. It's from when Portola was here ... in 1770."

It was hot inside the *temescal*. Very hot. But when seated, at least the highest temperatures were above them. "Okay," Nortze began, "this is where the men usually did their cutting the skin thing to open the pores, but we'll pass on that one. Just close your eyes and breathe deeply, and try to imagine you're here three hundred years ago, greeting newcomers and about to leave for warmer and dryer inland areas."

It was all sort of silly, really, but everyone tried to show some good faith by getting into the mental groove. And it was a very cleansing, even spiritual moment for all. Gil Nortze had a special moment in the hot enclosure, but it related more to what was about to happen next. Something primal, from way, way down.

After only three minutes, it was unbearably hot inside the *temescal*. But no one spoke a word until Nortze finally whispered aloud, like in a trance, "Okay, everyone outside. There's one last thing."

Silently they left the *temescal*, all of them with sweat running down their cheeks. The cold night, moist with the salty air, felt soothing on their faces. Gil went over to a sack and retrieved a can of lighter fluid. He squirted a continuous stream of the stuff all over the *temescal* cloth as he walked around it, speaking in a low monotone as if he was still in some sort of trance brought on by time in the sauna. "This is what the local Indians did to their thatched *rucs* every time they moved camp. Since they sometimes used their *rucs* for *temescals*, this here will be a good substitute."

When he had emptied the can of lighter fluid onto the tarp, he held up the Zippo lighter and flicked it once. It was a big flame. He reached over and touched the flame to a wet spot on the tarp, which immediately erupted into flames. No one spoke a word as the flames reached higher and higher into the night air as more of the tarp caught fire. They even had to step back a few feet because of the heat. With the view blocked by the second bluff behind them, the fire could only be seen from the lower garden of a single house (it wasn't), or far up or far down Pacific Coast Highway (no one saw it from there, either).

It took several minutes of intense flames before the tepee collapsed onto the fire pit, and then another ten minutes before it had pretty much died down. And through it all, no one had said a single word. It was kind of spooky, in a way, each person mesmerized by the little ritual, but especially the experience inside the makeshift *temescal*.

Ken felt the heat, both temperature-wise and in his burning desire to acquire this property from Gil Nortze.

Nortze likewise felt his own heat, but it was in the form of a damaged hereditary psyche, and it was calling the shots. Fueled by the flames, Nortze's little voice was telling him who'd been good and who'd been bad, and it affected a major decision. He finally broke the silence. "Well, folks, that's it."

"What about the cross?" Carrie asked.

"It's staying, at least until I start building the house." He purposely didn't look over at Ken to check for a reaction, already knowing the guy would be crushed. *You don't have nearly enough money to buy me out now, Mr. All-American prick.*

Tristin looked over to Ken, and she watched as his chin slumped down on his chest. She knew it was a quite a blow. Ken turned and caught her stare, and there was a shared moment of sadness between them. Not only was any chance of his buying the property now gone, but also their first meeting was coming to an end. At that moment, the former seemed only slightly worse than the latter.

Nortze ended with, "I say we get packed up and back to the bed & breakfast for some martinis. Margie is supposed to be here in fifteen minutes."

Aside from the thoughts about the property, there was another common theme coursing through the minds of Ken and Tristin—being a GUP, or Geographically Undesirable Person. No matter how strong the feelings about a relationship, if apart, it's tough. They both understood that.

The old adage about absence and hearts growing fonder was a bunch of malarkey as far as Ken was concerned. He wanted her now … and tonight, tomorrow, and maybe forever. It was an intense, albeit brief thought that sailed through his brain.

Ken helped Dave load the ice chest into the back of the minivan, but that left the barbeque grille. Nortze checked his watch: 6:29. "I told her to be back at six-thirty sharp. I'm gonna be pissed if—"

On cue, headlights wound down the driveway, and Margie beeped the horn. She turned left down the steep dirt access and stopped the truck, right on money at 6:30. They loaded up the rest of the stuff into the back of the pickup, and then it was time for goodbyes.

"Very nice meeting you, too," said Ken to Carrie and Patty with a nod and a wink to Margie. She liked that. He stepped around to the passenger side of the rental van, and Tristin rolled down the window. Her smile was restricted yet somehow very provocative. Ken saw it, but looked past her for a moment. Nortze's face was still partially blackened from the coal. "Thanks, Gil. I appreciate your including me in this."

"No problem, neighbor." *See ya around the old construction site.*

Ken's eyes then fell on Tristin, who said, "I have to come back around noon tomorrow to take some pictures. Maybe I'll see you then?"

"I'll be here," Ken replied, holding that look telling her he was *very* interested.

Boyfriend my ass. More than mere suspicion now, Nortze knew for certain Tristin had lied to him, using Stu Adams to do it.

As they drove off, Ken knew his world was about to change, especially if everything went right with Tristin. He just couldn't at that time know how by how much. In addition, in not knowing the strengths and weaknesses of one particular player at the poker table, Ken Easton was about to learn a valuable lesson in human behavior, one not altogether embraced by "polite society."

That same night, on a lonely road outside Las Vegas, Robert "Sparky" Sparks parked his car off the pavement. He placed a five-page letter, addressed to his only child, Neil, on the seat, got out, and leaned against his door. He looked up to a clear night sky, Saturn shining bright high in the east. Sparks began to cry, softly at first, then fell into a continuous sob. He put the .38 revolver to his right temple and pulled the trigger.

*****

Note to John: This was supposed to be much shorter—sorry. Steven

12 Tea and Sympathy

Ken Easton finally dragged himself out of bed at 9 a.m., two hours beyond his normal rising time, even for a Sunday. It had been a fitful night, with nightmares about excessive heat that had made him sweat harder than a crack-whore drug mule stopped by K-9 alert at airport security. But it was just that he'd forgotten to turn down the thermostat.

Making their way into his dreams also were worries about his coming loss of privacy combined with excitement over meeting Tristin. A yin and yang thing there, he tried to concentrate on the yang when he awoke. He showered and shaved, even plucking some nose hairs when he saw himself close up in the mirror. Tristin had said she wouldn't be arriving to take pictures of the property until noon, so he had plenty of time, but there was a bit of housekeeping to do prior to her arrival.

His housekeeper, Connie, wasn't due until Monday, so Ken decided to at least clean the guest bathroom and the kitchen, neither exactly filthy, just in case Tristin made an appearance.

Ken fed Lindy and made Earl Grey tea, and immediately started the cleaning. By 9:30 he was done. His next project involved Jake the Tern. The feeder needed to be a little more protected from the weather, so Ken dressed and shuffled off to the garage and his work bench. He took down his Makita battery-operated reciprocating saw and went into the corner, locating a small piece of plywood. A string tied to a pencil was his protractor, and he drew a six-inch diameter semicircle. He then put the ply into the bench clamp to hold and cut the half circle. Two little hinges and a coat of quick-dry varnish later, it was ready.

Next, he went into the garden and checked for Jake the Tern, but he was already out and about. Ken removed the smaller cover over the seed dish and mounted the bigger one in its place. It was then 10:00, with two hours still to go.

Ken fussed around the house and garden for the full two hours, doing minor chores and maintenance he had let slip for a long time. He clipped the top leaves from the Bergamot plant and stored them in a baggie, ready for brewing with his Earl Grey. The winter squash was coming up nicely, as were the zucchinis. To guard against the sea gulls, he placed domed wire cages over them. It was all very invigorating, getting all these chores done at one time. While in the garage, he spotted the new hose he'd bought to extend the existing one out in the garden. He snipped off the binders and placed the washer in the female end.

Just as he finished connecting the hoses, Lindy brushed past him on her way toward the slope. He heard the voice come down from above. "Hey, stranger," Tristin called down the bank, camera in hand. She was atop the south end of the sloping rocks, technically on Ken's property but less than five feet from Nortze's northern property line. Lindy had already started up the slope to greet her.

Ken looked up and gave her a big smile and a little wave. "Good morning. Get your pictures okay?"

"Yes, I did."

"Can I interest you in a cup of tea?"

"Yes, you can." Tristin bent down and stroked Lindy's head, her tail wagging.

"Do you want to go the long way or come down this way?"

"The rental car's up here, but I think I can make this." Tristin zigzagged along the slope, Lindy right behind, and paused at the two-foot jump down to the garden. Ken offered his hand and helped her down. Eyes fixed on each other and still holding hands, Ken said, "I am so glad to see you again."

Tristin stepped in close and gave him a peck on the cheek. "Me, too."

Even though still overcast and on the chilly side, it was the start a beautiful day. Over morning tea, they talked about their lives, their interests, and anything coming to mind. Ken gave Tristin a tour of the garden, and then the house, simple in design but taking the best advantage of the view. And always, there was Lindy following Tristin. Walking down the south hallway toward the den, Ken showed her the spare bedroom and then opened the door to Tyler's room; it was as if he was still there. The toys and stuffed animals were left just as they had been for almost a year.

"I come in here once in awhile, just to remember what he was like."

Tristin didn't enter, as if it would be violating a sanctuary. "Oh, Ken, I ... I don't know what to say."

Ken closed the door and brightened up. "I've been thinking of taking down the common wall and expanding my office." Since last night, anyway.

"That's probably a good idea if you expect to move on, emotionally I mean."

"I know," he replied sadly. "I know that's what I *should* do."

With that discussion at the emotional nadir of the conversation, it went uphill from there as he opened the door to his office. "This is where I spend most of my time."

The view west out the large window included the rocky outcrops just offshore, and the view out the south window and past the garden continued the panorama. Tristin was overwhelmed. "If I had an office with that view, I doubt if I could get any work done."

"Oh, it settles down to something you get used to but never take for granted."

Tristin saw the program on Ken's computer, the nine windows and their little spiked waveforms. "What are you working on now?"

"It's a contract from FEMA." That was the Federal Emergency Management Agency. "I'm doing consulting work on acoustical sensors to help determine if a building is safe for occupancy after a major quake." Ken led her through a little computer tour of the project and mentioned how he'd done the testing out on the rocks. "It's just the first in many test projects, but I hope to be involved enough to see it through."

Tristin walked to the south window and stood, silently, staring out across the garden and up the sloping rocks to where she was standing when she had called down to Ken. "Like you said," she began with a little sigh, "he's going to be right on top of you, isn't he?"

"Unless he stays well south of the property line up there, yes. Single story would help, but it's not too wide north and south, as I'm sure you saw, and my guess is he has to go up two stories."

"Yes, I saw the general layout. Gil still insisted I take the pictures, though. Just to convince Stu Adams—that's my boss—that it's a good investment." She turned and cracked a smile. "The good news is he'll probably still live in Vegas most of the time, and come out here just during the summer. Maybe on long weekends, too."

"And what about you, Tristin? Think you might like to come out on a long weekend some time in the future?"

"Are you inviting me?"

"Yes, I am." Ken stepped in close and took her hands in his, and their eyes locked. "The sooner the better." He pulled her toward him and kissed her gently on the lips. She kissed him back. After a long moment, they moved into a very tender mutual hug. "I wish I could stay longer, Ken, but we're about ready to head back."

"Yeah, I figured that." Ken knew the answer to his next question before he asked it. He broke the hug and held her by the waist. "Christmas is coming up. Would you like to come back over the holidays?"

"I'd like that. You should call me and we'll talk about it."

"Got a card?"

Tristin fished into her jeans pocket and pulled out a business card, her home telephone number already written across the front. She held it up to her nose, her eyes peeking out over it, for Ken to see. "Sometimes a girl gets a feeling about these things."

Ken laughed and pulled out his own card, his private number also scrawled across the front. "A guy, too." They shared another hug, and then it was time for Tristin to leave. Ken walked her, hand-in-hand, back through the garden, spotting Jake the Tern at the feeder eating some of the birdseed. He stopped for a moment in front of the birdhouse. "Tristin, meet Jake the Tern. Jake, this is Tristin."

"Hello, Jake," she said softly. Jake didn't fly away, but rather sat perched, cocking his head back and forth.

"He likes you," said Ken. "And Lindy likes you … .and I like you, so it's all settled."

Tristin squeezed Ken's hand, and then her eye caught something on the ground. "Hey, nice frog." It was a ceramic garden frog squatting next to the summer squash. "I have a small collection myself."

"You know about frogs?"

Tristin's jaw dropped. "Yes! You know about them, too?"

"An old school buddy is a reptologist, and he's now in Sri Lanka. He said in his last email that every time he goes out into the rain forest, he discovers a new species."

Tristin laughed. "You never cease to amaze me. I like a man who knows about frogs."

"Well, don't get too impressed. I can't name a single one."

"Neither can I, but they're beautiful."

Ken led her up the slope to the top of the bluff, Lindy again right behind. Ken spotted the white Lincoln Continental. "I thought you had that green van."

"Gil was insistent that I have a nice car to run around in. He drives a red one—gets a new one every year, same color—and wouldn't accept anything less for me today."

"That was nice of him."

Tristin had to chuckle. "Gil is a strange guy, but the one thing he's not is cheap."

They walked past the cross and fire pit, every scrap of wood and tarp now reduced to white ashes. "That was some little ceremony last night," said Ken.

"Yes, and Gil keeps making excuses about me not looking at that diary."

Lindy trotted along beside Tristin all the way to the car. She bent down and kissed the top of Lindy's head. "Goodbye, Lindy. See you soon." She opened the door and turned to Ken. "Well, thanks for everything."

Ken went to her and kissed her on the lips one more time. "And you," he said. "I'll call you."

"You'd better," she said in mock warning.

After the Lincoln disappeared into the trees up the second bluff, Ken turned and spent a few moments looking around at Nortze's lot, while Lindy had her eyes still fixed up the driveway. Ken hoped against hope that Nortze would take his time with coming up with plans and permits, if he built at all, before starting any construction. But deep down inside, Ken knew that a new neighbor was a *fait accompli*, and only a matter of time now.

*****

Note to John: I know, more relationship stuff. After a gazillion revisions, my wife likes it, too. Steven

13 Chance Meeting

Bobby Wynette walked into the living room holding the schematic for the walkie-talkies where Sam sat on the couch watching a Sunday football game, Raiders at Broncos. "Hi, Dad, who's winning?"

"No score yet. Broncos have to punt. What's up?"

Bobby handed him the schematic, pointing to an electronic symbol Bobby had just circled in red. "Do you know what that symbol is? I thought it was a resistor, but it may be a capacitor."

Sam reached for his reading glasses on the side table, but caught the blocked punt by the Raiders out of the corner of his eye. Raiders recovered and ran it nine yards for a Raiders first and ten on the Broncos' 18.

"Yes!" Sam said. "Raiders and Rams in the Super Bowl," he predicted.

The schematic looked like alien scribbling to Sam, lines joining up with circles and squares and triangles, each containing a different symbol, but the legend explaining what was what had been smeared in the printing process. "Hmmm. Can't help you here, son. This is pretty much Greek to me."

"Oh, okay."

"Tell you what, though. Tomorrow I'll stop by the hobby shop and look in another box. Maybe it was just all smudged on that one schematic."

"Well, I'll try to work around it later, and if I can't, I'll give you the schematic to show the guys at the hobby shop." He then paused and took in a breath, hoping that Sam would cut him some slack since it wasn't his fault the diagram was all smudged. "Uh, Dad, can I go out for a walk?"

Sam thought about relaxing the strict grounding punishment as on the first play after the blocked kick, Raiders ran off left tackle for an 18-yard touchdown.

"Way to go, Raiders," Bobby called. He knew his dad was in a good mood now.

"Way to go, Raiders," echoed Sam with a smile. He knew Bobby was buttering him up, but that was okay. The kid had a point. "Yes, but be back in two hours … and no meeting your friends, okay?"

Bobby stuffed the schematic into his back pocket. "Thanks, Dad." He hurried back toward his room, stopping at Cheryl's door. He knocked and said in a loud whisper, "Hey, Cheryl, it's me. Open up."

"Come in."

Bobby opened the door and stuck his head in. "I have a two-hour reprieve. Wanna go with me for a walk?"

"Yeah, sure," she said, and was up in a flash to get her coat. "Where we going?"

Bobby shrugged. "I dunno, down towards Spindrift Road maybe."

"That's all private property."

"Yeah, but it's Sunday, so maybe we can sneak down somewhere and get a look at the ocean."

They walked together on the half-mile hillside route, down a ravine and back up, and then across the Coast Highway and down the tree-lined road. At the top of the private driveway, they paused, looking to see if anyone was watching. "C'mon, if anyone says anything, we can pretend we didn't see the sign."

At the fork with the mailbox on the far side, they could see the long rectangular house down to the right, and the dirt driveway down to the left, emptying out onto a vacant lot overlooking the ocean.

"Hey, what's that?" asked Cheryl, spotting the cross, and next to it the fire pit. "Looks like the Moonies were here and built a campfire."

"Yeah, let's check it out."

They made their way as far to the left as possible down the dirt driveway so as not to be spotted by whoever lived in the house to the north. They cautiously approached the cross, Bobby in the lead, noticing the trinkets on the rocks at its base and the beaded necklace hanging off one arm. Bobby looked around for other possible signs of life. "Wow, who do you suppose did this?"

"Like I said, maybe it was the Moonies."

Bobby laughed. "Somehow I don't think so." They walked to the edge of the bluff and looked down. "Have a seat, Cheryl." They sat side by side and watched the little waves breaking against the cliffs and the rocky outcrops just beyond.

"Wouldn't it be great to live here?" Cheryl asked.

"No kidding. Probably takes a lot of money though."

"Someday, maybe we'll have lots of money, and we could live here."

Bobby played along. "Sure, as soon as we're old enough to play the lottery."

They both heard the two consecutive barks coming from the north. "Oh-oh," said Bobby, "We've been busted."

"What should we do?"

"Just sit tight and enjoy the scenery."

Ken watched from the window as Lindy sat at the end of the garden looking up towards the top of the bluff. She barked again. He concluded that someone was up on Nortze's lot, and figured he'd better go take a look. He grabbed a jacket and headed out the back door.

With Lindy leading, Ken climbed the slope and reached the top. Lindy sat on her haunches facing the two kids, who were in turn sitting facing the ocean. Ken stuffed his hands in his jacket pockets and approached, calling out, "Hi, there." For reasons unknown to Ken at the time, Lindy stayed put.

Bobby and Cheryl turned and smiled. "Hi," said Bobby.

Stopping a few feet away and smiling, Ken said, "You know this is private property, right?"

Before Bobby could give Ken his "didn't see the sign" excuse, Cheryl chimed in. "Yes, but we figured no one would mind if we just sat here looking at the ocean."

"Oh, I don't mind at all. Just be careful, okay? The cliffs are very dangerous."

"Do you live there?" asked Bobby, pointing to Ken's house.

"Yes. Me and Lindy here."

"What is that, like, four bedrooms?"

"Three and a den."

Cheryl pointed to Lindy. "Is she friendly?"

Lindy stood with her tail motionless. "If her tail is wagging, she's friendly." He couldn't figure why Lindy hadn't come over to sniff the newcomers.

"It must be great living here," said Bobby.

Ken turned his attention back to the kids. "Yes, it is."

"How long have you lived here?"

"A long time. Grew up here."

"Wow," said Cheryl, and then she gestured back towards the empty lot, adding, "Is this yours, too?"

"No, it belongs to a new owner." He didn't mention the name.

"What's with the cross and fire pit?" asked Bobby.

Ken threw back his head with a laugh. "Oh, that's him, the new owner. It's from a little welcoming ceremony last night. He brought some of his friends as a way of breaking the place in, so to speak."

"Wow, that's great," said Bobby. "Oh, I'm Bobby Wynette, and this is my sister, Cheryl."

Cheryl smiled big. "Hi," she said.

"Nice to meet you. I'm Ken Easton." That name—Wynette—sounded vaguely familiar, but he couldn't place it.

Bobby had a long shot idea. "By any chance, Ken, do you know anything about electronics?"

Ken was taken aback. "Yes, a little. Why do you ask?"

Bobby stood up and pulled out the schematic from his back pocket, offering it to Ken. "I'm building a walkie-talkie and I can't read the instructions 'cause the printing at the bottom is all smudged."

Ken looked at the diagram and saw the red square around the familiar symbol. "It's a capacitor."

Bobby's eyes lit up. "Wow, that's great! I thought it might be, but I wasn't sure."

"Yes, the little squares are resistors, and the double lines are capacitors. The triangles with the lines are electronic switches."

"Boy, that saves my dad a trip back to the store, thanks."

"You're welcome." Ken handed the diagram back to Bobby. He had seen and heard enough to know these kids weren't trouble. "Well, kids, enjoy the view, but don't get too close to that cliff, okay?"

"Sure, thanks, Ken," said Bobby.

"Bye," called Cheryl.

After Ken had disappeared over the bluff, Bobby and Cheryl sat in silence for a few long moments. Bobby then turned and flicked his eyebrows up and down to Cheryl, whispering with a wicked little grin, "I'll bet Ken has a big enough house." It was the code word they'd used over the years when talking about current or future living arrangements.

"Bobby!" scolded Cheryl, "Mom and Dad wouldn't appreciate that."

"Yeah, whatever. Just thinking, that's all, if worse came to worse. I'd like to live in a place like that."

Thinking. Planning. Scheming. Dreaming. And negating the importance of current family attachments. Past Nortze family failures—financial and otherwise—were born out of such thoughts, but it certainly didn't appear to be anything of that sort to Bobby Nortze-Wynette.

14 The Lost Highway

Bobby and Cheryl arrived home in plenty of time so as not to be past the 2-hour deadline. Bobby found his mom and dad in the living room, Sam still watching the Oakland-Denver game while Darcy was reading a magazine. Bobby stopped and watched the TV, waiting for a pause in the action to tell his father the good news about the schematic.

With less than seven minutes to go, it was already a blowout. The Raiders were up 41-17 and poised to score again from seven yards out. On second down, Raiders went over right tackle and scored again.

"Hi, Dad. Hi Mom."

Sam turned and saw Bobby standing behind him. "Oh, hi, son. What's up?"

"Not the Broncos, that's for sure."

Sam and Darcy laughed, Sam adding, "Yeah, quite a day for Oakland."

"Guess what?" said Bobby, pulling out the schematic. "I met a guy who knows all about this stuff. He gave me the information on what was what."

"Oh, yeah? Who was that?"

"A guy named Ken Easton, down on Spindrift Road."

The name and location triggered his memory, and Sam and Darcy exchanged quick glances. "You walked all the way down there?" Darcy asked.

"Yeah, me and Cheryl. We sat on the bluff and looked at the ocean. Do you know him?"

Sam pondered whether or not to tell his son what he knew, and came up instead with a question that might cut to the chase. "Did he tell you anything about himself?"

"No," Bobby said, and Cheryl silently shook her head.

Sam figured a summary might help drive home a subtle lesson about road safety. "Well, it was a year ago this coming Christmas, but I remember it like it was yesterday. Ken's wife and son went off the cliff—or were forced off it—in their car down Highway 1. On Christmas Eve day." Sam paused, the impact of holiday cheer gone sour meant to impress. "No one knew that at the time, because she just showed up missing, and she had told no one where she was going. And because of the storms and conditions, there was no evidence of anything on the road. A month later, a woman down near Big Sur came forward with vital information, and a careful search turned up scrape marks well down the cliff. And then divers found the car—and the remains."

"Sam!" said Darcy.

Sam shrugged defensively. "Hey, I'm not going into the details." Sam turned again to Bobby, "Anyway, son, I spoke with Ken Easton on that Christmas Eve about not finding his wife and son, and the man was devastated."

Replaying the scene in his head as he envisioned it, Bobby was appropriately shocked. "Wow, that's really awful."

"Yes, it was very sad," said Darcy. She remembered it well, too. She and Sam had attended the delayed funeral, Darcy meeting Ken for the first time. He was a basket case, and her heart went out to him. Darcy could only imagine her own grief if it were her own child and husband in that car, and it was something she would never forget.

Bobby turned the conversation back to the accident. "Did you say they might have been forced off the road?"

"Can't say for sure," said Sam. "As I recall, they found a big dent on the fender behind the left front wheel, and what they suspected were faint red paint streaks, resembling a butterfly. But the car had been in the ocean at the base of that cliff for two months. Saltwater corroded the paint job—and the butterfly streaks—making a positive ID on a hit-and-run impossible to trace with any accuracy."

A cat's muffled scream made its way up from the basement, and then a different cat cried out.

Sam made a directive to Bobby. "That damned cat is a neighborhood terror! Go check on Tramp, okay?"

In the basement, the two male cats were a foot from each other, ears back and hissing in unison. They were perched atop the workbench below the access window to allow Tramp easy ingress and egress. The feral cat had, as it had done before, trespassed, and Tramp had caught him. All of Tramp's head and face scars came from fights with this one cat.

When the feral cat saw Bobby approach, it made a beeline for the open window and escaped. Bobby returned to his room, giving his father's recounting of the traffic accident and the catfight little further thought. Instead, he turned his attentions once more to the walkie-talkie schematic.

Bobby was not only unaware at this point in time that his biological father now owned the lot next to Ken Easton, but also that it was Gil Nortze who, speeding too fast north along the narrow, winding Coast Highway during the rainstorm, got a little squirrelly on that one outside curve, crossed the center line and rammed Valerie Easton's car off the cliff.

Valerie had secretly driven down the coast on that Christmas Eve day to purchase a special (and expensive) Christmas gift for Ken, a 1973 Henry Miller print entitled, *Amour Toujours*. He was also the renowned author of *Tropic of Cancer,* and had been a resident of Big Sur. The whimsical piece reminded Valerie of how she and Ken had met—on a summer horseback ride—and how their lives had been, as she said, "one big rainbow." On the $4,000 print (including frame) was also an inscription in French by Miller that read (translated): "Give me a little space; give me a little sky; give me a little love." Ken and Valerie had lived that dream.

Coast Gallery in Big Sur had the Miller print on hand, and they were holding it for her. Valerie knew a storm was coming, but she still insisted on having the framed piece carefully packaged for transport in her car trunk, but in the hour it took to do so she used up valuable time. Valerie misjudged the speed of the storm, and was caught on the treacherous highway during the afternoon downpour. She was just over a mile from Coast Gallery when it happened.

Gil Nortze had met a woman the previous weekend in Vegas who lived in Cambria, his old hometown. He drove to the coast via San Louis Obispo and paid her a weekend visit. By Sunday morning, Christmas Eve day, the poor woman had had enough and asked him to leave. He then drove north on Coast Highway heading up towards Carmel Highlands planning to take a look at his gambling winnings from Robert Sparks, what he figured would eventually be his oceanfront property on Spindrift Road. After a brief look, he had planned to drive inland past Salinas on a circuitous route back to Las Vegas. His plans for a stop at the Yankee Point property changed in the blink of an eye during the rainstorm on that outside curve.

Doing over forty on a blind curve designed for twenty-five on a dry day, Nortze's tires skidded over the midline of the road. The left front corner of his heavy Lincoln Continental hit Valerie's little white BMW just behind the left front wheel, leaving a streak of butterfly-shaped red paint. The force of the impact propelled the BMW airborne and clear over the 300-foot cliff.

Nortze had stopped, but only to peek down the steep cliff on the off chance the car had not plunged all the way into the ocean, but it was gone. He looked around for a moment to see if anyone had witnessed the event, but there was no one else on the road for miles that rainy Christmas Eve afternoon. He had then quickly picked up all but the tiniest pieces of broken glass from his left headlight, leaving the heavy rain to disperse the rest.

Never learning—or having the desire to know—what happened after he'd left the scene of the accident, it was the end of the story for Gil Nortze. Consciously, anyway. Subconsciously, at his very core, was the little voice inside that constantly fought for recognition, trying to solve a new self-awareness puzzle.

Like an eager student finally called upon to answer a hypothetical question of a favored teacher, Nortze's ego waxed eloquently, reinterpreting and thereby justifying his actions that horrible afternoon to fit into its own positive world view. The ego tries to satisfy the id (basic needs of survival), while mollifying the superego (conscience). Once he had determined that leaving the scene of the accident threatened his economic survival, it was a battle of the Titans inside Nortze's head—ego against superego—an internal battle of preferred identity versus conscience usually lasting one's lifetime.

But for Gil Nortze, the battle lasted less than two months, a month later than the discovery and dangerous recovery operation of the car, the bodies of Valerie and Tyler, and two months sooner than the close of the investigation. Six months hence, with nary a word spoken and knowing he had gotten away with it, Nortze's evil little voice had won out.

No one in Vegas even knew that Nortze had driven out to Cambria, and he had paid cash for gas, so there were no computer records. And he had dropped the car off at a repair shop in Henderson, just outside Vegas, early the next morning on Christmas Day. Leaving a note on the windshield with the car in the repair lot, Nortze took a taxi back to the condo complex. No one had seen him drive home, either.

Ken Easton had been understandably devastated at the sudden disappearance of his wife and son. After a police polygraph proved his non-involvement, the waiting for news was almost unbearable, and it didn't end until a month later when a Coast

Gallery staff member read of Valerie and Tyler Easton's month-long disappearance. News of America's War on Terror had dominated everything. The short news article had a description of them and the car. The gallery staffer recalled helping with the packaging and loading into the trunk of the white BMW that Christmas Eve afternoon, and she connected the dots.

A thorough search down the rocky faces of the outside curves with no guardrails finally turned up evidence of white paint streaks. In a dangerous search and recovery operation, divers found the BMW submerged in twenty feet of water. The front windshield was completely smashed in, allowing fish, crabs, small sharks, and other marine life to feast on the remains of the occupants. The divers recovered most of the skeletons, plus the framed and packaged Henry Miller print in the trunk.

A few months later, after recovery of the car and the remains of Valerie and Tyler Easton, a guardrail was installed on that curve. The State of California had had it on its to-do list for years, but it never got done until after Valerie's death.

*****

Note to John: The first meeting with Ken and the kids is interesting, from a dramatic point of view, because the kids were so close to finding out that their real father owned the lot. Even if they had

found out at that time, however, I don't think things would have changed all that much. You'll see for yourself later, but no peeking ahead!

As for Valerie Easton's death, most people finding themselves in Nortze's circumstances, and after knowing there was a human being who went over the cliff and probably died, would never get past the first ten seconds of guilt. The horror, the self-recrimination, the pain of it—even with immediate notions of criminal and/or financial liability—are overwhelming for most. The fear of being found out, perhaps even prosecuted, shows up immediately as a distinct possibility if that first notion of not reporting it even pops into their heads. But that's most people.

Following extensive interviewing (plus my own work in this area), much of the above is informed speculation on my part, but it holds up to scrutiny, given what we know. Steven

15 A Room with a View

That same Sunday afternoon on Thanksgiving weekend, Gil Nortze flew Tristin and the other members of his entourage back to Las Vegas. Near the end of a marathon six-hour session at the Luxor later that same night, he got on a roll with five consecutive winning hands in Texas Hold'em, and cleaned everyone out to the tune of $165,000.

On the other side of the world in Afghanistan, at the prisoner uprising in Mazar-e-Sharif, a CIA operative and former Navy SEAL, Johnny "Mike" Spann, had become the first official combat casualty of America's War on Terror. John Walker Lindh—the American Taliban—was identified in the aftermath of the rioting. Gil Nortze was one of the few Americans celebrating anything that night.

The next morning on the phone with his financial advisor, Stu Adams, Nortze opined that his winnings were more than half of what he needed to build a house out on the coast. He told Adams of his plan to rent it out when he wasn't using it. He also asked Adams to confirm local building costs and square footage considerations and get back to him, a task Nortze knew would be given to Tristin. Nortze also knew that this new tidbit of information would be, sooner more likely than later, passed along to Ken Easton. Tristin Barnes was Ken's only pipeline into the inner sanctum, and Nortze could see in his mind's eye Ken's crestfallen demeanor when he would learn that things were going to start happening faster than he'd anticipated. What Nortze didn't know was that Ken had called Tristin right around the time Nortze cashed in his many piles of chips at the Luxor. Like a love-struck puppy, Ken couldn't wait so much as a whole day before speaking with her. They talked on the phone for over an hour, planning out the Christmas holiday.

At 10 p.m., Nortze turned off the nice warm fire in the fireplace. He slept very, very soundly that night, for the first time in months.

The morning of the next day, Tuesday, Nortze called Stu Adams again, this time giving him specific instructions. First, he wanted lot survey stakes in the ground by the start of the Christmas holiday, "No if's, and's, or but's about it." And secondly, he told Adams to find him a local architect and engineer. "It's just a house, Stu, and any architect will do." Based on obtaining a surveyor's plot map, Nortze said, "Get me a preliminary design for a single-story, 3-bedroom house, also before Christmas, set 20-feet back from the north property line."

Nortze had already anticipated the future conversation. Ken would ask what the place was going to look like, and Gil would promise to have the architect mail him a sketch, "With my compliments." Of course, it wasn't going to be the house that Nortze really planned to build—a two-story behemoth—with the north wall of the actual house—white stucco and almost 20-feet high with no windows— set just five feet from the property line.

Enjoy the view, asshole!

*****

Note to John: You might be wondering under what circumstances Nortze lets his evil streak out. Basically, he has no choice in the matter.

He knows on a conscious level when he's about to go against conventional morality, but his warped ego ensures that subsequent behaviors are kept secret to the outside world. Therefore, his antisocial behavior is not traced back to him for blame. Meanwhile, he is in a constant battle of justification, a vicious cycle of internal conflict that consumes much energy and time. Steven

16 Bridget Jones' Diary

Cheryl Wynette had been eagerly awaiting gym class all day on Monday. Not because she relished getting all sweaty playing two-on-two volleyball, but rather because of her scheme on Tory, the girl who had humiliated her in front of the other girls about her menstruation. It was payback time.

It was a quick hit, planned down to the second. Tory always showered after gym, whether or not she needed to, in order to flaunt her physical maturity—larger breasts and more curvaceous than the others. As did most of the other girls, Tory left her purse below her locker and went in for a shower. Lingering in the toilet stall until the girls had headed off to the showers, Cheryl checked that the coast was clear and went into action.

With a towel wrapped around her and wearing a pair of plastic gloves, she placed a paper towel on the floor and opened Tory's purse, noticing the diary's exact position. She pulled it out and held it over the paper towel, quickly flipping through it while pouring the red nail polish on the pages as she went, careful to catch the few errant drops on the paper towel. She then slowly squeezed the diary shut and replaced it carefully back in Tory's purse the way she found it. Next, she wrapped the nail polish bottle and her gloves in the paper towel and stuffed the whole wad in her own purse for later disposal. She used the far entrance to the showers and slipped unnoticed into the last shower stall. Afterwards, while everyone was dressing, Cheryl took an occasional glance at Tory down the row of lockers, trying to imagine her reaction when she finally made the discovery.

Cheryl was among the first group of girls to leave, knowing that she would miss the privilege of Tory's actual reaction upon discovery, whenever that might be. Tory would surely feel violated, and a year's worth of careful notes and impressions—meaningless drivel to Cheryl and everyone else—would be damaged beyond repair. With no evidence and so many possible perpetrators, there was no way Cheryl could be fingered as the guilty party. It all added up to one delicious fantasy.

Menstruate on that, bitch!

For Cheryl, the fantasy was always better than the reality.

*****

Note to John: As you may have figured out by now, these two kids exhibited many signs of antisocial personalities—which I will go into later. In light of recent concepts of genetic predisposition affecting one's mental state, as opposed to purely environmental factors, the genealogy here is very, very illuminating. More on that later. BTW: Tory's parents moved her to another school after that incident. Steven

17 XX/XY

For Ken Easton, the 25 days leading up to the time when Tristin was due to arrive was nothing short of agony. He tried to immerse himself in his work, and even got quite a lot accomplished, but his mind wandered constantly between Valerie and Tristin. Slowly, the guilt passed at being emotionally involved with another woman before the unspoken one-year statute of limitations had expired. He called Tristin three times a week.

Ken made it a point *not* to inquire about Nortze and the next-door property, and Tristin, despite what Nortze figured she would do, didn't bring the subject up either, although she knew many of the details. It was a matter of professional ethics. Instead, they talked about anything and everything else coming to mind. The conversations eventually steered themselves toward physical intimacy, and the agreed upon AIDS tests. They made a game out of it, swapping code numbers by e-mails, each calling and confirming the obvious—negative. So by the time Friday, December 21 rolled around, Ken and Tristin were both primed and ready for some serious lovemaking.

Ken hadn't left the house in two days leading up to that Friday, as he forced himself to get his preliminary acoustical analysis up to date and ready for e-mailing to Greg at D&M prior to the holidays. He finished up at noon and was feeling on top of the world when he pushed the send button.

"Done!" he shouted.

A female voice down the hall responded, "Did you call me, Ken?"

"No, Connie," he called back. "Just me celebrating, that's all."

Connie walked to the open den door and stopped, leaning against the jamb. "I found the dry cleaning hanging in the garage. Did you want them hung up in your closet?"

Connie Halperin was 27 years old, with long dishwater blonde hair tied back with a clip. Her lightly freckled face showed through the tan, as she loved the outdoors. Trim and yet strong, she was a bit on the tomboyish side, and definitely a hippie throwback, into art and astrology and all sorts of things Ken found quite endearing, if not altogether scientific. She was the married mother of a five-year old son, Dag, and did housekeeping for six other families in Carmel Highlands. Her husband,

Randy, was an accomplished wood sculptor who sold his wares in Carmel, Big Sur, and Monterey.

"Oh, rats, I forgot about that. Yes, please, if you would?"

"Did you forget to eat, too?"

Ken thought about it and shrugged with guilt. "Uh, yeah."

"How about some zucchini and squash soup, fresh from your own garden?"

"That would be great."

At the kitchen counter, Ken and Connie sat next to each other eating the soup, with fresh baked bread and cheese to go along. Connie was quite a cook, and she always provided Ken with enough dinners to last him three or four days. As Connie sat admiring the Christmas tree, all decked out by Ken himself, she spotted something and reached across the counter, picking up a folded paper she'd found. "What's this, Ken? I found it in the garage on the floor."

Ken unfolded it, immediately recognized the walkie-talkie schematic. "Oh, that's Bobby's. He must have left it."

"He's been spending a lot of time here. Is he being a pest?"

"No, far from it. Smart kid. He's gotten stuck from time to time building the walkie-talkies, and I've tried to help him with the finer points of soldering, and also understanding the color-coding on the resistors." Ken folded it and stuck it in his shirt pocket. "I'll get it back to him."

After a few quiet moments, Connie asked, "So, are you excited?"

Ken played it for laughs. "Nah, she's just a friend. We'll probably spend the whole time talking acoustic wave dynamics."

Connie knew better after conversations with Ken over the past three weeks. "Sure, while rolling around on your bed." They both burst out laughing.

"Yeah, I guess we might get around to that."

"A buck says five minutes, tops."

"I'll set a timer."

Connie chuckled. "Speaking of timing, any word on the lot next door?"

"No, but I've got a feeling it's coming—maybe late spring. It takes a while to draw up plans and get permits."

"You seem resigned to it now. I guess that's good."

"It's one of those things in life one just has to put up with, I guess." Ken thought back to when he was growing up, and a house was under construction up on the next bluff toward Coast Highway. "I remember them building the house up on the corner of my driveway and Spindrift. Everyone complained—me included—about the constant noise, dust, whatever. But one day my dad reminded me that people had to put up with *our* construction, too."

"Yes, people don't think about that." She added the caveat, "But most people don't have a house like this, one that will lose a lot of privacy when the other one is built."

"Maybe the guy will have some consideration and stay single story, who knows?"

"And like you said before, he probably won't be living here all the time. Besides the summer ... and holiday weekends ... you'll have the rest of the time to yourself."

"Whoopee."

"Sorry, just trying to cheer you up."

Ken sighed, "I know, Connie. Thanks." He glanced at his watch. "Oh, oh. Gotta pick up Tristin in less than an hour. Better get dressed. Thanks for lunch, Connie—and making the other meals, too." Ken started to stack the dishes, but Connie stopped him. "I'll get these. You go get ready for that heavy discussion on acoustic dynamos ... or whatever."

Ken blushed as he left. "Thanks, Connie."

With Connie leading the way slowly up the driveway in her car, Ken was just even with Nortze's lot when he glanced over. His heart skipped a beat, and he slowed and turned right into a slanted dirt parking area used for summer guests. Around the perimeter of Nortze's lot, a dozen short wooden stakes were driven into the ground, orange ribbon dangling from the tops

Survey stakes. Boy, that was quick. Damn!

And so it began.

There was still time, so Ken drove up to Bobby Wynette's house. He knocked on the door, and

Darcy answered. "Oh, hi, Ken. Nice to see you again." Ken had made sure that Bobby's parents knew who he was, helping their son and all, and knowing Ken's past, they had welcomed him with open arms.

"Same here, Darcy." Ken retrieved the schematic and handed it to her. "Bobby left this at my house. I think he's still going to need it."

"Oh, thank you. He should be home from school soon. How's it all coming along?"

"I think he's mostly done. He said he wanted it finished by this weekend."

"I'll make sure he gets it."

Ken got to the airport a few minutes before Tristin's plane arrived.

18 Talk Radio

Over the next two days, Ken and Tristin made love constantly. In the bedroom, the shower, the spa, the kitchen, and anywhere else that was convenient or desirable. They came up for air only to eat, soak in the hot tub again, or watch one of the videos Ken had rented.

Tristin loved Meg Ryan, so there was *You've Got Mail* with Tom Hanks, and *When Harry Met Sally* on hand. However, they didn't make it past the fake orgasm scene in the cafe, as Ken stopped the DVD and insisted Tristin do her own fake version for his viewing pleasure. It turned into a real one not long after. And all the while Lindy stayed nearby, relishing the occasional cooing by Tristin or her scratching under her chin. Ken didn't mind, as both he and Lindy were very content.

By Sunday morning just after ten, Ken was ready to show Tristin the sights, particularly in Carmel-by-the-Sea, a city he knew Tristin would love. "We'll have brunch at a little cafe on Ocean Avenue," he offered, "and check out the shops and the locals."

Ken was in the shower and Tristin in the kitchen, sporting a new bathrobe purchased by Ken. With Connie's help, Ken had packed up and given all of Valerie's clothes away to the Goodwill the weekend before, along with Tyler's toys and bedroom furniture. A little remodeling in January would complete Ken with the transition—physically if not emotionally.

Tristin was putting last night's dishes into the dishwasher when the doorbell rang. She made mental note that at least it was past the appropriate time on Sunday morning for a drop-by visit. She opened the door to see Bobby Wynette holding up a walkie-talkie in one hand for her to see.

Bobby's expression, and his arm holding the walkie-talkie, dropped at the unexpected sight of this woman. "Oh, hi," he said. On the one hand he was disappointed that it wasn't Ken; on the other, however, he couldn't help but admire Tristin's natural beauty.

"Hello. Can I help you?"

"Yeah, I'm Bobby Wynette ... Ken helped me build this—"

"Oh, yes, Bobby. Ken told me all about you. C'mon in. We're just getting ready to go into Carmel."

"Thank you, ma'am." Bobby stepped inside and sized up the situation in a few seconds—Ken had a very pretty girlfriend.

"He's in the shower, but I'll go tell him you're here." She went off down the north hall towards the master bedroom.

"Thank you." *This changes everything. Just have to work around it.*

Five minutes later, Ken walked down the hall in his own bathrobe, Tristin now in the shower. "Hi, Bobby, what's up?"

"This!" he said proudly, holding up the completed walkie-talkie.

"Hey, right on time."

Bobby shrugged and smiled. "Yeah, I'm not grounded anymore." He handed it to Ken, saying, "Check it out. Press the switch."

Ken looked it over and pressed the long, spring-loaded switch on the edge. It hissed for a moment, and he released it. A soft female voice said, "Hi, Ken. Can you hear me?"

He knew how to operate one, and he pressed to talk and released to listen. "Hey, is that you, Cheryl?"

"Sure is. Pretty cool, huh?"

"Where are you?" Ken expected Cheryl to be outside, perhaps around the side of the garage.

"At home."

"Wow," he said to Bobby. "Nice range."

"Yeah, that's about the limit though."

"Okay, Cheryl, thanks. I've got to be going now, but I'll see you later."

"Over and out," she said.

"Well, Bobby, that's quite an accomplishment. I bet your dad is impressed, too."

"Yeah, sort of, I guess. He really didn't understand how complicated it was."

"I do, and you are to be commended." He put his arm around Bobby's shoulder and led him toward the door, whispering, "Man to man, Bobby, I need a little privacy with Tristin. We'll talk later, okay?"

"She's pretty. Is she your girlfriend?"

Ken nodded. "Yeah."

"Are you going to marry her?"

That stunned Ken, not because of the impertinence of the question, but because he had been thinking about it. "Well, just between you and me, it's a possibility, okay?"

"Your secret is safe with me." *Well, me and Cheryl anyway.*

"Thanks, I appreciate it." He sent Bobby out and closed the door, retreating back to the bedroom to get dressed.

Outside, Bobby walked up the driveway, waiting until he was a quarter the way up to the mailbox before clicking the switch twice. "You still there?"

"I'm here," said Cheryl.

"We have a problem."

For reasons related both to adolescent fantasies and a childhood ripped away by unfortunate events outside his control, Bobby had embarked on a plan to ensure his and his sister's survival should the need arise. At first, it had been passing thoughts of Sam being killed in a road stop shootout with a felon on the lam, or Darcy dying of heart failure. The problem at that moment was not in the conscious act of pre-planning against unforeseen circumstances, but rather in the way Bobby and Cheryl were, day by day, letting slip usually very strong paternal and maternal bonds.

In their minds, the importance of Sam and Darcy in their lives began to wane. They had begun to allow themselves, with proper justification to Cheryl, to emotionally detach from Sam and Darcy, and then quickly attach themselves, at least superficially, to Ken Easton. For most kids, such a transition could easily take many years; for Bobby and Cheryl, it had taken a month. One might suspect that such an attachment was not based so much on a solid foundational pillar of trust, but rather upon the shaky foundation of expediency.

With Tristin now in the picture, it complicated matters for Bobby and Cheryl, but not to the point of abandoning their plan altogether. It just needed a bit of tweaking. The ever-diminishing roles of Sam and Darcy in the twisted fantasy lives of Bobby and Cheryl Nortze-Wynette made it all the easier to think about how to get rid of them—per-manently—in order to get to the preferred substitution.

*****

Note to John: One might fairly ask where the mindset of Bobby and Cheryl came from—origins, if you will. Considering the family history, however, it is not all that much of a leap. Using psychometric testing techniques here at the prison, some volunteer inmates have confirmed such personality disorders arising at an early age. Steven

19 Kermit the Frog

It was Christmas Eve, 2001. The soul of America still reeled from the attacks on the World Trade Center. Fear of more attacks fueled the media frenzy, and few people felt truly safe. Osama bin-Laden had not been killed or captured, but it came out only later that the mere vision of body bags on the news made sending special forces up into the mountains of Tora Bora politically disastrous, and the warlord we paid to kill Osama promptly let him escape out the back door.

Even in Carmel-by-the Sea, rumors abounded about terrorists contaminating the whole city with anthrax spores. But out on Spindrift Road, things were somewhat calmer.

Ken's living room was decked out in holiday trim. A 7-ft Douglas fir sat in the corner, twinkling lights setting off the tinsel and decorations. Several wrapped presents sat under the tree, and a fire burned hot in the fireplace to offset a cold, windy evening. Ken and Tristin sat on the couch, sipping hot toddies and listening to Nat King Cole Christmas songs.

Walking over to the Christmas tree, Ken pulled up a wrapped present the size of a small hatbox. He returned to the couch and sat down. "Here, this is for you. Merry Christmas."

"Oooh, thank you." It was a heavy package. She unwrapped it and pulled out a beautiful, highly polished wood sculpture of a frog. "Oh my God, it's beautiful. Where did you get this?"

"Let's just say I know someone in the trade." Connie's husband had sculpted it on special order for $200.

Tristin leaned over and kissed Ken on the lips. "Thank you." She then placed the frog on the coffee table facing them both. "Okay, your turn." Tristin also got up and walked over to the tree, picking up and bringing to him a six-inch-square box.

Ken tore off the wrapping and opened the box, staring at the cement frog inside. He lifted it out and held it up. "It looks like my frog in the garden, only smaller."

"And female," Tristin said. "He looked like he needed a soul mate."

Ken then turned to Tristin and leaned over towards her, holding his face a few inches from hers, and uttered in his deepest voice, "Ribbit." He stroked her hair and looked her straight in the eye. "That's frog for *I love you.*"

Tristin's eyes moistened. "Ribbit," she said back.

20 Lady in Red

Despite the festive atmosphere inside the High Rollers room at the MGM grand, Gil Nortze was not a happy camper. He barely noticed the soft background Christmas music, and hadn't touched the free appetizers and free drinks. More exceptionally, he hadn't flirted with any of Santa's Helpers, waitresses in their red and white—and very skimpy—costumes who came by to ask if he wanted anything. He seemed distracted.

Nortze had been playing Texas Hold'em for two hours, and he was down about ten grand. That wouldn't have been so bad had he not begun the night with high expectations. He had walked into the MGM Grand feeling like a winner, telling himself that tonight was a big night for him and the $25,000 on which he planned to turn a handsome profit.

Such bravado was, however, a cover against the sneaking suspicion that Tristin Barnes and Ken Easton were screwing each other unconscious out in Carmel Highlands. Nortze still couldn't rid his mind of her lie about having a boyfriend just to get him off her scent. And then she promptly hitched up with Mr. Hunk.

What am I? Some sort of cretin?

Even knowing that by now Ken had seen the survey stakes didn't quite satisfy; transferring his animosity to Tristin's lover had not yielded the intended satisfaction.

Before the next hand was dealt, he decided that this would be the last hand for him that night. He just wanted to go home and sit by the fire, perhaps even go on-line and play a little anonymous draw poker on AOL.

Five men and a woman, named Laura, a nice looking brunette of about 40 wearing a low-cut satin red dress, all sat at the $1,000/$2,000 limit table. For this hand, Nortze was in 3rd position, just behind Big Blind in the order.

As required, the game started off with Little Blind (Laura) betting a thousand, and Big Blind two thousand. The dealer dealt the two pocket cards face down, clockwise one at a time to each player, ending with the Button, or dealer's position. To the Button's left, Laura (Little Blind), had Jack-7 suited in hearts; Big Blind had Jack-4 unsuited; Nortze took a peek and saw Ace-Queen suited in spades, a great start. Probability theory put him in Group 2, second only to Group 1 containing mostly matched face cards or aces. Position 4 drew 3-2 suited in diamonds; Position 5 drew Queen-5 unsuited; and the Button had 8-6 unsuited.

For the pre-Flop bets, Nortze called two thousand, knowing that with a set of pocket spades, he had minimal strength. Position 4 (with suited diamonds) called. Positions 5 and 6 (the Button) both folded, and Laura called, leaving $8,000 on the table.

Out came the Flop—2 of spades, 5 of hearts, and 4 of spades. Nortze saw visions of a flush, beat only by four of a kind or a straight flush. The odds were against anyone else having pocket spades. Laura, however, now had three hearts, also a possible flush, but lower than Nortze's.

Laura bet the minimum of a thousand. Big Blind folded. Nortze raised a thousand. Position 4 folded, leaving just Nortze and Laura still in the game, and another four thousand in the pot. It was now $12,000. Laura called.

The Turn card was a 6 of hearts, no help to Nortze but looking better for Laura. With one card to go, the River card, each had four suited cards, Nortze in spades and Laura in hearts. Nortze was confident that the next card would be a spade, providing evidence of his earlier feeling that this was his night. With the minimum bet now two grand, Laura bet two grand, and Nortze raised two grand, knowing now that Laura either had two hearts in the pocket, or else she was bluffing. It was show-down time. Laura didn't hesitate in calling his raise. The pot stood at $20,000.

With everyone in the room now standing around the table, it was now down to the last card, the River. The dealer put an 8 of hearts face up on the table.

Nortze looked to Laura for a reaction, and he caught something in a single blink of her eye and a miniscule drop in expression suggesting to him she didn't make her flush. He had caught her *tell*. The others caught it, too.

Laura bet two thousand and looked to Nortze for a response. He smirked and called, then raised her two thousand. She re-raised him two thousand, but Nortze didn't blink, re-raising Laura another two thousand. She looked worried now, lighting a cigarette, but she raised another two thousand. Nortze stared at Laura a long moment, thinking, *You are mine tonight, bitch.* He called and raised her for his 3-raise limit, looking to her for reaction.

Laura arched her eyebrows and called with a final two grand, giving Nortze a little smirk that told him he'd just been had. She laid her cards on the table, showing Nortze, and everyone in the room, that she had the flush after all.

The room erupted in applause and shouts of, "Way to go, girl!" and "Did you see what she did?" Someone at the table put it most succinctly, "She bluffed a bluff."

Nortze had misread the bluff tell hook, line, and sinker, and inside he was beside himself with anger. Laura raked in the $40,000—$11,000 of it his—in chips and stood up. "That's it for me, guys," she said, and then looked at Nortze with just a hint of attitude, adding, "Merry Christmas."

Nortze said nothing. It was like a dream. His head was abuzz, the heat of the moment transferred to something akin to a hot flash. Sounds were muffled, and what his eyes saw were a blur of people and lights and motion around him. A pat on the shoulder and, "Better luck next time, man," finally brought him around. Nortze stood up and left the table, getting almost to the door before someone from the table shouted, "Hey, Mr. Nortze, you forgot your chips!" Nortze heard but did not turn back, leaving $7,000 dollars on the table. *Management will make sure I get it.*

Nortze took a taxi home, replaying over and over in his mind how it was that the woman had suckered him. The blink, the cigarette, the subtle nervousness—all played perfectly. He had always picked up on the *tell*, except this once. *By a woman, dammit!*

By the time he was back inside his condo, the little demons had done their work inside his brain. He went right to the computer and sat down, booted up, and was on-line at AOL in just a few moments. He went right to the High Stakes poker rooms—25-200 token bet/raise limits—where he had over a million tokens credit spread amongst several screen names. It wasn't real money, just tokens accumulated over the past year.

This being Christmas Eve, there were plenty of unfilled 4-player rooms. He entered "Ante Up," and searched the screen names for players with female-sounding names. And there they were: Prissy1, eve2064, and junelovesbob, with a spot open. He pressed the "play" icon on the empty seat and joined.

Joining in the midst of a hand, he typed in, "hi girls" into the chat box and hit return. A moment later, eve2064 folded, and then responded, "hi luckylady gl2u," chat room shorthand for "good luck to you."

The screen name "Luckylady" was Nortze's means of duping players into thinking he was a she, and perhaps not all that good at poker. He had two other female names, which he changed every session. He kept a log of players and his persona at the time, and with hundreds of players in 25 rooms, he never got outed by someone remembering his name or past conversations. But it went far, far deeper than that.

When the "ante" icon showed up, he clicked it and began playing. Each player's token count was displayed on the screen. Prissy1 had 362,712 tokens; eve2064 had 92,005; junelovesbob had 17,787; and Luckylady had 248,988.

Gil said nothing the first few hands except for the occasional "nh" or "n1" (for nice hand or nice one) to the winner, and a "ty" (for thank you) when someone else wrote "nh" on his hand. It didn't take long before he saw the message hoped for— junelovesbob writing, "where u frm LL?"

In between bets, Nortze typed and entered, "Phoenix, and u?"

"Mobile." With her limited number of tokens, junelovesbob was obviously a novice at the game.

In between bets and folds and raises and even 30-second intermissions, the chat started off casual and friendly, sometimes even funny. "lol" (for laughing out loud) was used a lot for self-deprecation over lousy hands, and grammar ranged from complete sentences to misspelled words.

junelovesbob: aack I hate 2 pr
Luckylady: I know! 3 3s and u r sunk
Prissy1: gotta ck on kids at inter
eve2064: got any kids LL"
Luckylady: 2 teen grls — not eeeezy
eve2064: girl 2 boy 7 here
junelovesbob: 1 in HS
Lucklady: found smthg in drawr of 16 yr old
junelovesbob: do tell
Luckylady: u no
junelovesbob: oh, one of THOSE
Luckylady: yes
Prissy1: did u try it out lol
Luckylady: no. mayb should hve
eve2064: girls, this is poker!
eve2064: I have 2 myself lol
Luckylady: Y 2?
eve 2064: 1 for each hand
Prissy1: lol
junelovesbob: lol

Luckylady: lol never done that
Prissy1: girl, u r missing out

And so it went, Nortze pretending that he was a woman with two teenaged girls and inexperienced in matters involving sex toys. Nortze carried on a conversation with the three women for almost an hour. He played like a loose aggressive, keeping the pots high and rarely folding until the last minute, even with poor hands.

His chat depended on his mood and the response from the other players. It had ranged from a woman with a straying husband who was thinking of having an affair with her boss, to a college girl with sex fantasies about her hunk teacher. He always played it cool, getting players to think he was holding back personal information and to volunteer their opinions—and experiences—on what "she" should do. With regularity, he also masturbated to the titillating discussions, sometimes even climaxing during the middle of a hand.

It was pretty sick by any standard of adult behavior. Masquerading as a woman, Nortze felt as though he were peeking inside the minds of women, unlocking secrets normally left unsaid in male company. He had come to the conclusion that women were just as horny as men, only much more devious in keeping it a secret. They were, in effect, consummate liars. And whores, ready to jump the bones of a stranger if given the opportunity, or at least to encourage strangers into immoral behavior.

Gil Nortze ejaculated onto a lap towel and called it a night. He typed in "gn all Mry Xms" and logged off, heading for a hot shower. It cleaned him up physically, and the game had cleaned him up mentally. Back in control following his victory, he made a single cryptic entry on his log sheet, the closest he ever got to writing a diary: "Pulled one over on the bitches—again! They didn't know what hit 'em." Somehow he forgot to mention his $11,000 loss to Laura, the lady in red.

Before closing his eyes, he thought about how he could best put his free time to good use the next time he went to the Highlands. Margie Swanson had screwed his brains out the last time he was there. She just hadn't got the joke when he had suggested she put a bag over her head. Not snidely to a common acquaintance, but to her face. He had insisted it was all in fun, but it was just another way of humiliating a woman who he felt was beneath him. Which was every female on the planet. Finally he fell asleep on the living room couch, and the cement logs glowed red in the fireplace all night.

*****

Note to John: One can't really place Gil Nortze's behavior in the category of paraphilias (sexual deviance), in the criminal sense of the word, as there were no physical consequences of his fantasies outside his own sexual gratification

during his online voyeurism. Since there is evidence, however minimal, that paraphilias run in families, it may well be that other "behavioral deviances" are genetically inherited. With his passive hostility toward women, Nortze's unspecified behavioral deviance is closer to the mark. So, whatever the outward manifestation, the source might still be PPE.

Although the various Nortze family diary entries are very cryptic and inferential, they reveal a lot about the man whose ancestral record is rather spotty. FYI: I had to take two weeks off-project to supervise a study on aberrant sexual behavior at Soledad, extra time required because many inmates outside the sex offender program were understandably reticent to come forth with truthful responses the first time asked.

I wish Nortze were around to clarify a few things, as interviews with MGM Grand casino employees present at that game were, as you can imagine, fraught with time-consuming obstacles prior to stealthily (and successfully) extracting certain critical information. Ditto that for an AOL security contact in providing redacted transcripts from that night. Nortze could have laid it all out in five minutes. It ran about $2,000 extra in out of pocket expenses. But as my collaborator, you will undoubtedly have your own expenses, too. United We Stand. Steven

21 Stakeout

After a week of constant companionship, Ken and Tristin had fallen in love. Promising herself every hour it seemed that she would fess up about her past relationship with Gil Nortze, Tristin just couldn't bring herself to admit it to Ken. And then, standing on the bluff overlooking the ocean, Ken proposed marriage and Tristin accepted.

It was a love borne not just of mutual attraction, and sexual compatibility, but also of shared interests. They both wanted children, and their independent careers were more asset than liability in working together to achieve personal goals. Tristin could get a job in property management anywhere, and many opportunities in the Monterey Peninsula area were listed in the want ads and online. Corporate headhunters were always looking for people like Tristin Barnes. It was agreed that she would move into the house with Ken and look for work in the region, starting in early February.

On the Saturday before New Year's, Tristin packed her bags and headed back to Las Vegas. *Next time I see Ken, I'm definitely telling him about that night with Gil Nortze.*

According to the news, New Year's Eve celebrations were, due to post-9/11 fears, going to be muted, if not cancelled in many cities, so she and Ken had agreed that they would not really be missing anything. Besides, Tristin needed the time to start making arrangements for the move, and to give Stu Adams a month's notice so he could find a replacement. She also felt absolute relief that her conflict of interest issue would finally be resolved. A short conversation with Stu, and even Gil Nortze, was now justified. Unbeknownst to Tristin or Stu, Gil Nortze had planned to fly out for a one-day visit on Sunday to raise the ante in his mental poker game with Ken Easton.

By the time Tristin left, Bobby Wynette had extracted—in little pieces at a time—enough vital information from Ken to plan his next few moves. He would have a whole month with Ken all to himself prior to Tristin's return. And Bobby knew that Cheryl would play an important role, too. In his mind, he constantly fantasized, albeit irrationally, about what great parents Ken and Tristin would make for both he and Cheryl.

It all began with what Bobby perceived as a mere prank, or at least what he felt Ken would find bold, hopefully humorous. Knowing how concerned Ken was about the house to be built next door, the prank was meant to show Ken how he, Bobby, could be an ally against whoever was going to intrude on Ken's privacy. Only Bobby didn't plan on telling Ken until he had tested Ken's reaction.

Late Saturday afternoon, just before dark, Bobby knocked quietly on Cheryl's door. "Cheryl, it's me."

"Come in."

With his hands behind his back and a devilish grin, Bobby entered.

"Whatcha got behind your back, Bobby."

"Oh, just a little something to throw off the construction schedule next door to Ken."

"What is it?"

Bobby drew his hands out from behind his back, holding out a dozen small survey stakes, little orange ribbons dangling from each. "This oughta slow them down."

"What are those?"

"Survey stakes from the property next to Ken's."

Cheryl didn't understand the import. "Why'd you do that?"

"I pulled 'em out and covered up the stake holes, so they'll have to start all over. Ken will appreciate it, believe you me, at least when I get around to telling him it was me who did it." Bobby actually thought he was doing Ken a favor. Like an ally against a common enemy, Bobby wanted Ken to know at some point who was on whose side. He had no real understanding of all the repercussions.

It was Cheryl who understood Ken's possible culpability. "Bobby, everyone knows that Ken wanted that property, so isn't he going to be the first one everyone suspects?" It was a rhetorical question.

"Ken, the all-American guy?" Bobby scoffed, "Who's gonna suspect him?"

Cheryl vented her frustration. "Bobby, *everyone* is going to suspect him, whether or not he did it."

Bobby caught the rebuke but shrugged it off. "They can't prove anything."

"That's not the point, Bobby."

"What is, then?"

Cheryl turned sullen. "I don't think Ken is going to be all that happy, that's all."

"Well, we'll see."

Cheryl was right on all counts. And with a little bad timing thrown in for good measure, the prank almost backfired. At 9 am the next morning when Ken answered the door in his bathrobe, the last person he expected to see standing on the front porch, plans rolled up in hand, was Gil Nortze. "Gil?"

Ken's shock revealed itself to Nortze. "You don't seem happy to see me, Ken."

Fighting off the surprise, Ken chuckled. "Sorry, I just wasn't expecting company, you in particular." Noticing the red Lincoln Continental rental car behind Nortze, Ken stepped aside and motioned inside. "Come on in, Gil."

Nortze didn't waste any time on idle chitchat. "Know what happened to my survey stakes?" Like reading a poker opponent, Nortze looked for the tell of guilt.

"What?"

"They're gone. Not just pulled out, but the holes cleverly filled in. Know anyone with an interest in sabotaging and delaying my project?" His meaning was obvious, and he wanted to catch Ken in the lie.

Ken shook his head. "Jeez, Gil, I know what you're thinking," and now he looked Nortze straight in the eyes, and was very firm, "but it wasn't me, I swear. I would never dream of doing that kind of thing. I've resigned myself to the fact that you're building a house, and that's all there is to it. As a matter of fact, the sooner the better."

Nortze accurately read the lack of deception and concluded that Ken had nothing to do with it. "I'll take your word on that. Probably some kids then."

A quick vision of Bobby Wynette passed through Ken's mind, but he was not about to openly accuse the boy without evidence. Subconsciously, he even made a physical comparison between Gil and Bobby, but quickly dismissed the close resemblance. "I'll keep an eye out." Ken motioned Nortze towards the kitchen. "Like some coffee?"

"Yeah, sure. Black."

"Comin' right up. Have a seat at the counter." While retrieving cups, Ken asked, "So, how's it coming … I mean, besides the survey stakes."

Nortze held up the single rolled sheet, secured with a rubber band. "Preliminary sketch, right here. Just picked it up from the architect."

"Can I take a look?"

"Be my guest." Nortze rolled out the single page on the counter. It was an overhead view, or plot plan, showing the boundaries and shape of the house. "It's single story with three bedrooms, and as you can see, I've set it back about twenty feet from my north property line."

Ken breathed a sigh of relief. "Hey, thanks, I appreciate that."

"See this?" Nortze said, pointing to a spot on the middle of the bluff.

Ken could make out the sketchy details of a spa and a surrounding deck overlooking the ocean that specified "Clear Redwood," the best of the best. More importantly, it was set far enough from his property line that he wouldn't be able to see it, nor could anyone look down into his garden.

"Hey, nice. That view grows on you, especially when the waves are big."

"I'm looking forward to it."

It didn't take long for the conversation to drift around to Tristin, Ken sheepishly telling Nortze she had spent Christmas there, and that they were engaged to be married in June.

"You're a fast worker, Ken." Nortze saw the future. "I guess my financial advisors are going to be losing a valuable asset." *And you will pay dearly for that, my friend.*

Ken demurred. "Well, she's planning on telling her boss the first chance she gets. Maybe she's called him already, I don't know. Just don't say anything to her, or Stu, until then, okay?

"Sure, Ken. No problemo. When's she coming out again?"

"In early February, if everything works out."

"Hey, just in time for Valentine's Day." *I'll have to plan a little something special for you two lovebirds.* "Oh, and by the way, you can have this copy of the plan ... with my compliments. I have another in the car."

"Thanks, Gil." *Hey, this guy's not so bad after all.*

After coffee and a brief tour of Ken's house, Gil Nortze decided he'd accomplished everything he'd set out to do—except for calling the surveyor—and he said his goodbyes. Back up on his lot, he placed the call to the surveyor's office, leaving a message about the missing survey markers and authorizing him to come out and replant the stakes and bill him through Stu Adams.

Back in his house, Ken fumed at the thought of Bobby Wynette pulling out those stakes. "That little bastard, I know it was him," he said aloud. He placed the call to Bobby's house, and Sam answered. "Hi, Sam, this is Ken Easton."

"Oh, hello, Ken. How are you?"

"Just fine, thanks. Is Bobby around? I need him to bring his walkie-talkie set over here. I have an idea that may help him get more range out of them."

"He's upstairs. I'll send him down to your place. He'll appreciate that."

"Thanks, Sam. Say hi to Darcy for me."

An hour later, Bobby and Cheryl showed up at the door, each holding a walkie-talkie. After sitting them down at the kitchen counter, Ken was polite, but firm. "Bobby, I'm not going to ask if one or both of you pulled up those survey stakes on the lot next door, because I know it couldn't have been anyone else. The question is why?"

Bobby confessed, "Yeah, it was me, but not Cheryl. It was just a prank. I thought it would be funny."

"Well, it's not," said Ken.

Cheryl turned and weighed in. "See, I told you."

"And Gil Nortze didn't think it was funny, either."

Two adolescent minds reeled, and both asked, in unison, "Who?"

"The owner of the property. He flew out from Las Vegas this morning, discovered the stakes missing, and raised hell with *me,* thinking at first that *I* had done it. He's on his way back home by now. I didn't tell him what I thought—or knew, for that matter."

Bobby and Cheryl were both in a state of shock, but Ken figured the dilated pupils and blanched skin were just the results of being found out. He went to the coffee maker and began preparing a new pot. "You would be in a heap of trouble right now if I had told him … or your parents."

"Sorry, Ken," said Bobby, so consumed with other thoughts that he could barely speak. He turned to Cheryl, and by her expression, he knew that she knew: Their biological father, who had abandoned them, was the one who was building a house right next door to Ken. Bobby shook his head quickly as a sign for Cheryl not to say anything, and she nodded.

"I told your dad I was going to do something to those walkie-talkies to increase their range." He came back to a stool and sat down. "Tell him I tweaked something inside, okay?"

Despite her shock, Cheryl recovered enough to help execute the plan. She slipped off her stool and went between Ken's knees, throwing her arms around Ken's waist. She hugged him with her face on his lower chest. "Thank you, Ken. You're going to make a great dad someday."

Ken was a little taken aback, but he responded naturally and hugged her warmly in return. "I hope so." So disarmed, he gently warned Bobby, "But if you ever do anything like that again, I *will* tell your dad, got it?"

Bobby nodded. "Don't worry, it won't happen again." The thought of stargazing hours on end was thankfully a short one.

Ken broke Cheryl's hug and asked her, "Want a ride home?" I'm going into Carmel for groceries and stuff."

"No, thanks," she said with a cute smile and briefly squeezing his forearm. "We'll walk."

The walk up the driveway for Bobby and Cheryl was a very long, silent one, as time seemed to expand while thoughts of what they had just learned began to sink in.

Cheryl broke the silence near Ken's mailbox. "It has to be him, doesn't it?"

"Oh, yeah, it's him alright."

"So, what do we do?"

"*You* sure made a great start, I'll say that. Ken likes you."

Cheryl sucked up the flattery. "You think so?"

"As for our, um, real father, there's nothing *to* do, really. Except we can't say a word to anyone, at least not right now, okay? I need time to think."

"Yeah, me, too."

*****

Note to John: Like I said in a previous note, it doesn't appear that subsequent events would have been significantly altered had Bobby and Cheryl known earlier. Minor timing changes, perhaps, or even Bobby not pulling out the survey stakes. But since no one besides Ken knew, that incident seems to have had little effect on anyone's motives or opportunities. Once again, I know we didn't agree on this narrative form, but the little bits and pieces seem sterile out of context. I couldn't help myself. Makes for good drama so far, though, don't you think? Maybe it will give you some ideas for your screenplay. Steven

22 Lolita

Saturday, January 5th of the New Year found Ken at his desk, compiling a statistical summary of his acoustic model. It was all coming together, helped by his experiments out on the cliffs. Connie had fired up the Jacuzzi and left an hour before, and things were quiet. The stereo was turned low to a soft R&B station pumped throughout the house, and he was deep in concentration for half an hour before he stood up and stretched.

Ken walked the length of the house, stretching his arms and twisting his body to get the kinks out. He was ready for a quick soak in the Jacuzzi.

With the temperature hovering in the low 60s and a slight breeze, the wind chill factor was in the mid-50s. Ken undressed and donned his short terrycloth bathrobe, opened the sliding glass door, and stepped out in front of the redwood privacy lattice. Glancing through the large square holes, he spotted the face of someone in the spa. He stepped closer to the lattice and peered through.

Even with her auburn hair slicked back, Ken recognized Cheryl. She then stood up facing Ken, the water level to her navel, and before Ken could even blink, she walked forward, climbed up onto the submerged seat and began wringing the water out of her hair, all the while facing Ken stark naked. For a 13-year-old, she was remarkably well-developed, with fullish breasts and very womanly curves.

Ken averted his eyes and decided to go back inside without saying a word. He was a little angry that she would take such liberties without asking, and figured a gentle talking to was in order, but not now.

"Ken, is that you?"

Ken stopped while facing the sliding glass door, a little embarrassed that he'd been seen. "Yes," he shouted to the glass. "What are you doing, Cheryl?"

"Taking a Jacuzzi. I didn't think you were home. Do you mind?" From the bluff above, she and Bobby had seen Connie turn on the spa. Bobby had instructed her what to do. Not until Connie's car was well up the driveway had Cheryl made her way furtively down the hill and around to the north patio area. She waited over an hour in the hot water for Ken to show up "unexpectedly," and she was pruning rapidly.

"Well, as a matter of fact ... " Ken couldn't decide whether to be harsh and scolding or gentle and scolding, but a scolding was going to be part of the conversation. But before he could complete the thought, and the sentence, Cheryl sauntered completely naked around the lattice, holding her clothes by her side, and stopped beside him. "Well?" she said with a little fake shiver, "are you going to let me freeze out here or invite me in?" Holding his gaze with hers, Cheryl acted as though she didn't have a modest bone in her body. She found the power her body had over this grown man quite stimulating.

Ken was floored. He looked away, speechless for a moment. "Oh, uh, sorry," he finally blurted out, sliding open the door and looking to the ground as she passed inside. He counted to ten— slowly. Stepping inside and expecting her to be in the bathroom, he saw her from behind, still nude, standing in front of the closet mirror. "Do you think I'm too fat?" she asked, turning.

Multiple visions sped through his head in quick succession. First there was Sam Wynette, in full uniform, standing at the open bedroom door, arms folded with a billy club in one hand and with a look on his face suggesting a painful thrashing;

after that, he saw himself standing in front of the honchos at D&M, his consulting contract terminated; next was an insider's view of vertical jail cell bars in a tortured explanation to Tristin; and only finally, a vision of an obese teenage girl for comparison with Cheryl. He once again turned his head to the sliding glass door, knowing this was trouble on all fronts. "No, you're not fat, Cheryl. But you must get dressed … now!"

"Oh, Ken, don't be such a prude." Cheryl walked over and stood in front of him at parade rest, feet apart and cupping her breasts in her palms. "I'm not ashamed of my body." She made an effort to raise an eyebrow in appreciation of Ken's legs beneath his bathrobe.

Before averting his eyes, Ken spotted several parallel lines on her inner thigh. He didn't give it any more thought until much later. "It's not about that, Cheryl, nor is it about being a prude. You should have a talk—"

Ken was about to add, *with your mother,* but that showed up immediately as not the thing to say at this point, afraid that she actually would. *Hey, Mom, I was stark naked in front of Ken in his bedroom, and he told me I wasn't fat.*

"Oh, man!" Ken said, closing his eyes and taking in a deep breath. He let it out slowly as he tried to think of the best way to handle this awkward situation. Looking Cheryl in the eyes, and nowhere else, he said, "You've got to promise me that you will *not* do this again. And if you tell your mom, I'll be off to jail within an hour, got that?"

Cheryl stepped up just off to his side and threw her arms around Ken waist, nestling her bare crotch up against his bare lower thigh and gave a little push. "I wouldn't do that to you, Ken," she cooed softly.

Ken pushed her back and held her upper arms firm, stark terror now in his eyes. "Don't do that!" he shouted. Again, that vision of Sam Wynette with the Billy club—and worse—was too much to bear. "Now get dressed."

"Oh, alright," Cheryl said, "I'm sorry. I was just trying to be friendly." She was being more than that. She mistook the neural stimulations and hormone production with true feeling and a basis for attachment. She could have been forgiven had she not known from her own experience that the two feelings were distinctly different. But when one looks to people other than one's parents to fulfill basic and yet unspoken needs, *something* usually gets mucked up in the works.

Ken walked the length of the house and sat down at his computer, but he could not focus. The option of calling Darcy and explaining what had happened loomed large; it would at least be preemptive, just in case Cheryl mentioned it to her mom. Ken didn't want to get the girl in trouble, as she was not coming on to him sexually—technically—but it was right on the margin.

Cheryl stood in the doorway, fully dressed now, drying her still-damp hair with a towel. "I'm sorry,

Ken. I didn't mean to embarrass you." She walked over and stood next to him, putting her hand on his shoulder. "Do you forgive me?"

Ken nodded at least a dozen times before finally replying, "Yes, Cheryl, I forgive you." He turned and looked up at her. "But you can't be doing that. It raises all kinds of very serious problems that you don't understand yet."

She bent over quickly and pecked him on the cheek. "I guess you're right. You're always right. Like I said, you're going to make a great dad." She turned for the door with, "I'll be a good girl from now on, promise. And I won't say anything to anyone. Love you, bye."

Those words seemed to settle the matter in favor of Ken not picking up the phone and spilling everything to Darcy before Cheryl got home, a judgment call that he wondered if he would ever come to regret.

For her part, Cheryl was elated at the power her body conferred on her. In the shower stall incident with Trevor, *he* had had all the power, but today, *she* had definitely been calling the shots as she saw it.

23 Love Thy Neighbor

It became like a tag team match the entire month of January, as Bobby and Cheryl alternated shows of affection and admiration towards Ken. It was all very subtle, and all very well scripted by Bobby Wynette.

Since they were both in school, afternoons would pass without a visit by either one or both, and even an entire weekend during the middle of January. Ken was focused either on his work or thoughts of Tristin, and as the time for her arrival drew near, they talked more frequently and at length on the phone. At no time did Ken realize how much time the kids were actually spending at or near his house, and he certainly never suspected that he was being set up. If Lindy could have spoken, she would have warned him; whenever the two kids were in the house, she would be out the doggie door in a flash.

For Cheryl, her role was to endear herself to Ken, lavishing him with attention and brief shows of affection at opportune moments. She would hold his hand, or give him a hug, or whatever seemed appropriate to the situation. Ken suspected that Cheryl had an adolescent crush on him, but he kept his actions strictly paternal. For her part, Cheryl still savored the effect her naked body had had on him.

Cheryl even struck up a relationship with his housekeeper, Connie, who described it to Ken as an "older sister" connection. On two different Saturdays, Connie and Cheryl talked about girl stuff in Ken's kitchen, Cheryl being careful not to be a distraction. Connie taught Cheryl how to make coffee and heat up pastries, which she practiced on Ken on two occasions with fine results, from both culinary and emotional point-scoring perspectives.

As for Bobby, he told Ken in early January that he had decided he wanted to grow up to be an engineer, just like Ken. Ken was flattered, but wisely asked the key questions: How are your grades in math and science? Are you ready to endure the torment of organic chemistry, molecular cell biology, calculus, and physics, all at the same time?

Bobby's answers were calculated to be more impressive than accurate, fooling Ken into believing that Bobby was being straight up with him. Having put off for the time being any remodeling work, Ken even went so far as to set up a spare computer in Tyler's bedroom just so Bobby could use Ken's engineering program to crunch numbers. Ken copied the raw experimental acoustical data, taken out on the bluff, from his computer onto a CD and had Bobby perform basic statistical comparisons.

Bobby got to be quite the number cruncher, but it was all just a ploy to establish closer and closer emotional ties with Ken. Cheryl would use the excuse of "helping" Bobby on the computer, but it was just to be close to Ken, too. And it was working. Ken felt a strong bond with the two kids, and they always obeyed instructions, if not to the letter then at least in spirit.

Everything was going according to plan for Bobby and Cheryl Wynette up until the morning of the last Sunday in January, the 27th. It started with a phone call from Sam Wynette, asking to speak privately with Ken. Sam made mention of the fact that Darcy had taken the kids to the aquarium in Monterey and wouldn't be back for several hours, and if Ken had a few moments, he would like to drop over.

"Of course, Sam. I'll put on a fresh pot of coffee."

"Much appreciated," he said.

Unlike Ken's previous vision of Sam Wynette standing at his bedroom door in full battle array ready to taser him for untoward behavior involving Sam's 13-year old daughter, when Ken opened the door he saw a mild-mannered guy in civilian clothes a little embarrassed by a perceived intrusion.

"Come on in, Sam. How do you take your coffee?"

"A little cream and sugar, thanks."

Ken led Sam to a kitchen counter stool and went to the cupboard for cups, Sam staring out the living room window to the churning sea. "Wow, that's some view."

"Yes, it is."

"I can see why the kids like it here."

Ken put the cups on the counter and returned with the cream and sugar. "Yeah, they're both great kids, Sam."

Sam cleared his throat. "That's what I need to talk to you about, Ken."

"Is there a problem?" Ken poured the cups almost full and set the pot on a counter trivet. He sat down, a worried look on his face. "They're not in trouble, are they?"

Sam scoffed, "No, nothing like that." He poured a cup and added cream and sugar. "It's just that both Darcy and I have noticed they've spent a lot of time down here this past month. We aren't sure if they're bugging you, or generally making a nuisance of themselves, or what." He sipped his coffee.

Ken shook his head. "No, they're great kids. I figure that at their age, they just need an adult friend who is *not* a parent to hang out with once in a while."

Sam chuckled. "That's what I figured, too, at least at first."

"What do you mean?"

"Well, this is difficult for me to say, Ken, so bear with me while I go into a little background here." He took another sip, nervous about Ken's reaction. "Darcy and I adopted Bobby and Cheryl less than a year ago."

"I didn't know that."

"They didn't mention it, huh?"

"Not a peep."

Sam shrugged, knowing Ken was being forthright. "Well, anyway, it was a tough decision for both me and Darcy, as we originally intended adopting one child—a baby, actually. What with Darcy's heart and all, we figured she could slowly adapt to motherhood. The notion of adopting two kids about to enter puberty wasn't exactly high on our list, let me tell you."

"Well, they seem pretty mature for kids their age. I haven't seen anything suggesting wild obnoxious behavior. Is Darcy getting stressed about something?"

Sam lowered his eyes. "Yeah, she is, and this is the tough part, Ken." Sam picked up his head and spoke directly to him. "With the kids always talking about you, and all the stuff you've done with them, she's feeling like they're slipping away—Cheryl especially. Emotionally I mean."

Ken knew by Sam's demeanor that Darcy wasn't the only one feeling transferred out. It then hit Ken like a wave smacking against his cliff. The time spent with the kids, both quantity and quality, was as if he were their father, replacing Sam. The *appearance* of emotional bonds had formed, but at the expense of increased distance from their adoptive parents who obviously loved them very much. "Wow, I see it all now. I don't know why I didn't see it before." Ken did not see it all then, and he could not, without much study, have seen it all before.

"Oh, hell, Ken, it isn't your fault. You're a great guy—smart, too, according to Bobby—and have this great place here. Hey, if I were a kid, I'd want to hang around here, too. But I need to ask a favor."

"I know already what it is, Sam. And you will have my full cooperation."

Sam nodded in silent appreciation, and then said meekly, "Thanks, I had a feeling you'd understand the situation. Darcy did, too."

"So, how do you want to work it? Cut 'em off completely for a certain period of time, or limit visitation rights to the weekend, something like that?"

"Well, I don't want to traumatize the kids—a clean break might do more harm than good. Maybe if we limit it to a Saturday or Sunday once a week for now, that would help. Meanwhile, Darcy will try to take up some of the slack with Cheryl—she has a few ideas—and I'll try and do the same with Bobby." Sam shook his head and bit his lip. "But I don't know that much about engineering, his favorite subject these days."

Ken had a thought. "Well, you could spend some time with him asking questions about what he's working on. I said to him recently that the best way to learn something is to explain it to someone else. Who better than you?"

"Yeah, that might work."

"Got an idea!" Ken shouted, and hurried off toward Tyler's old room. "Be right back," he said. Ken returned carrying the computer mini-tower Bobby was using and placed it on the counter. "This computer is loaded with my software, the one he uses to crunch the numbers on. Have him set it up in his room—he already has a monitor and keyboard—and let him have at it. Maybe get him some more programs, too."

"I'll set it up for him. I can do *that* much. Make it a surprise when they get back from the aquarium."

"There ya go." Ken had another thought. "As far as the weaning is concerned, I think we need to double-team them here, Sam. You and Darcy broach the subject and set the ground rules, and I'll back you up when they ask about it, which I'm sure they will."

The relief on Sam's face was palpable. "We think alike, you and I. That's what I had in mind, too." He not only had the cooperation of the very person he needed, but the man had provided a tool by which parental bonds might be tightened. "I can't thank you enough, Ken. And Darcy will appreciate it, too."

After half a cup of coffee each, Sam took the computer, and Ken opened the front door and the trunk to Sam's Honda Civic. "By the way," Sam mentioned in passing, "I saw the lot next door with all the survey stakes. Looks like you're going to have a neighbor. Bobby said you weren't too happy about it."

"Well, it was a problem with me for a long time, but I'm resigned to it now. Besides, ol' Gil Nortze ain't such a bad guy after all."

Sam was about to close the trunk when he did a double-take. "Did you say 'Gil Nortze'? Please don't tell me he's from Las Vegas." He was truly begging.

"Yes, he's the new owner. He's living in Vegas now, but—"

Sam leaned against the trunk, covering his face with his palms.

"What is it, Sam, are you okay?"

"Oh, shit," he mumbled, "I don't believe it."

"Believe what?"

Sam turned to Ken, shaking his head in shocked disbelief. "Son of a bitch, there *can't* be two guys from Las Vegas with that name."

"Do you know him?"

"I know his two kids, Ken." He took in a breath and looked into Ken's eyes. "Bobby and Cheryl. He's their biological father."

Now it was Ken's turn to go into shock. "What?" he asked quietly, and then he shouted, "WHAT?" *No wonder they look so much alike.*

Sam had to walk it off. He preferred not to go into details about Nortze's complete abandonment, or the awkward conversation with Bobby and Cheryl a year before about the few parents who do. But an explanation was justified. Sam summarized the situation. After, with hands on hips and still shaking his head in disbelief, he muttered, "I can't believe this." Sam then threw up his hands. "What are the God damned odds? This is bad ... very bad. Darcy is going to have a fucking coronary, I know it."

"It gets worse, I'm afraid."

Sam turned to face Ken, thinking him joking. "What?"

Ken unconsciously scratched his head in apology. "They know it's him, Sam."

"How do they know that?"

"Because I mentioned his name almost a month ago to both Cheryl and Bobby, that's why. I thought their reaction was from, um … "

Ken briefly considered telling Sam about Bobby and the survey stakes, but that seemed trivial now, " … something else, I can't recall, but I can see now they recognized the name but didn't say anything."

"Jee-zus," Sam said, slipping into a mental funk getting deeper by the second. "A whole month? They didn't say a word to me or Darcy."

"I don't know what to say, Sam. This all comes as a big shock to me, too."

"Well, I don't know what to say, either. I'll have to put some thought into it, that's for sure, before I go shooting my mouth off to Darcy."

"That sounds like a good idea, at least in the short run. But she's got to know sooner or later, don't you think?"

Sam's shock had turned to consequences. "I'm thinking later, but I know she's going to sense something wrong. She knows all my tells."

Ken had to chuckle at that, thinking back to Valerie. "I know what you mean. It's like they're psychic or something."

"Well, Ken, it's been quite a morning. I'd better get home, as some of the guys are coming over for the Super Bowl this afternoon." He walked over and shook Ken's hand. "Thanks for everything."

"You're welcome. I have a feeling the Raiders are going to take it."

"Me, too," Sam said, making his exit, "I got fifty bucks with Darcy says they do, anyway."

"Okay, we'll talk later."

"As soon as I have the ground rules laid out, I'll call you."

And so it was on that Super Bowl Sunday in 2002, in an increasingly complex world made more so by terrorists and madmen, the little drama out on Spindrift Road was just getting started.

*****

Note to John: One has to appreciate the many levels of internal chaos generated in so many people in so short a time to fully comprehend motives leading up to specific actions that followed. If Sam and Darcy had known about the serious problems with attachment battling for recognition in the minds of Bobby and Cheryl, they might have acted to prevent several tragedies. But their desire to have children had completely overwhelmed any notions of pre- or post-adoption psychometric testing,

I also find it noteworthy for comparison that just as surely as there are Neighbors from Heaven, there are also Neighbors from Hell; one lives directly across the street from me. It helps for a person's frame of reference. Please excuse my indulgence with a few extra words on the subject. With our deadline approaching I am, however, trying to be calendar conscious. Steven

24 Life with Father

Sam turned on the dishwasher and sat at the kitchen table. "Honey, there's something we have to talk about." It was a rainy Friday evening, February 1st, and the kids were upstairs. Sam couldn't keep silent any longer.

Darcy finished wiping off the countertops and sat down. "What is it?" The previous Sunday, after the Super Bowl where the Patriots beat the Rams, Sam and Darcy had talked about the kids spending so much time down at Ken's. They had agreed that at most two hours once a week—on either Saturday or Sunday—were the limits to be imposed on Bobby and Cheryl. Sam had not broached the subject of Gil Nortze, needing more time to think.

"Maybe I should have told you on Sunday, but this is a separate subject altogether, and I didn't know quite how to handle it." Sam took in a breath. "You know that lot next door to Ken?"

Not knowing what to expect, Darcy held her breath. "Yes."

"Gil Nortze owns it."

Darcy's vacant stare lasted a good ten seconds. She finally expelled a shocked breath of air, saying almost in a whisper. "Wha-a-a-t?"

"Yeah, and he's building a vacation home or something on it. He's still living in Vegas, but he'll be out here at some point. He just got his permit application approved."

"Did you see him?"

"No, but I'm sure it's the same Gil Nortze. I went over to the County Building and Safety at lunch today and looked up the permit application to check the spelling. One of the plan checkers remembered Nortze because he was here earlier this week. He and the architect and engineer were all there, it seems, and Nortze caused quite a stir in pushing the plans through plan check. After a lot of bluster and shouting and insistence that he get started right away, they made a few plan corrections and he got his permit."

"And you're sure it's the same Gil Nortze?"

"I asked the plan checker for a description of Nortze, and it was as if the guy was describing Bobby—hair, physique, everything. I know it's him."

Darcy was still in mild shock. "He's going to be living right here in the Highlands? What do we tell the children?"

"They already know, I'm afraid."

Darcy's eyes bugged out. "They know? How did they find out?"

"It was about a month ago. Ken mentioned the name, and he remembered their reaction, but he thought it was related to something else."

"Oh, my God! And they never said anything."

"No, they didn't. Maybe they want the whole thing forgotten."

Darcy turned silent and stared out the window. "Do you think we should move, Sam, just in case?"

Sam leaned forward, resting his elbows on the table and his chin on his balled up hands. "I've thought about that. I'm not sure which is worse, though—pulling them out of school and having them start all over in another school, or just waiting to see what happens."

"We should at least ask the children what they think about it before deciding."

"Let's do that now. I'll go get them." Sam walked upstairs, knocking on Cheryl's door first. "Cheryl, can you come downstairs for a minute?"

"Sure, Dad," she answered, "Be right down."

Bobby opened his door and looked to see what was going on. Sam motioned for him to follow. "C'mon on downstairs, Bobby. Your mother and I need to talk to you and Cheryl about something."

"Okay. Be right down."

"How's that computer working out?"

"Fine, Dad, it's great, thanks. I called Ken and left a 'thank you' message on his machine."

"Good for you, son." While Sam went back downstairs, Bobby waited for Cheryl. When she came out, Bobby whispered, "Okay, something's up. Remember what I said if they found out, okay?"

"I remember," Cheryl whispered back.

With all four seated around the kitchen table, Sam began. "Well, kids, we have a little dilemma here. It seems that your biological father, Gil Nortze, is going to be building a house next to Ken Easton." He looked for surprised reactions, but there were none. "And we know now that you are aware of this."

"Yes," Darcy chimed in, "And we just want to know what you think of it?"

Bobby shrugged. "It was a little weird at first, but I don't see a problem."

"Yeah, me neither," Cheryl said with assurance. She pointed in turn to Sam and Darcy and smiled. "*You* are my Dad, and *you* are my Mom." Cheryl shrugged. "What's left to say?"

Sam leaned in closer to Bobby. "How do you think *he* would feel if he found out?"

"Well, considering what he did, pretty shitty, I guess."

Cheryl stifled a laugh with her hand over her mouth.

"Bobby!" Darcy said in mild shock, "Please don't use that language."

"Oh, sorry, Mom."

Sam chuckled, knowing that Bobby had hit that nail squarely on its head. "You're probably right, son. But I guess I'm concerned—and your mother is, too—about some sort of confrontation. That wouldn't be very productive, would it?"

Cheryl asked, "You mean, like, us asking him why he abandoned us?"

Sam looked to Darcy, eyebrows raised, and let her answer. "Yes, something like that, Cheryl," Darcy said. "He could say anything, honey—true or untrue—but the question is, does any of it really matter now?"

"Not for me," said Bobby, "I don't really care *why* he did it. Just that he did it is enough for me."

"Yeah, me too," Cheryl said.

Sam didn't see the need to beat the subject to death. "Well, you two are sure taking a very mature attitude about all this. I'm proud of you."

"And so am I," Darcy said. She looked at Sam, but the words were addressed to Bobby and Cheryl. "There's something else, too, now that we're all here."

Sam took the cue. "Yes, it's about all the time you've been spending down at Ken's house."

Cheryl broke character and squealed, "What's wrong with that?"

"Did Ken say something?" Bobby asked.

Sam stiffened. "No, *I* said something. And your mother, too. I know how much you both like Ken—he's a great guy. But we need to spend a little more time together, and there's only so much time in the world. So, here are the ground rules. You can see Ken, but weekends only. On Saturday or Sunday, but not both. And for two hours, that's the limit."

"Dad," whined Cheryl, "is this, like, a punishment or something?"

Darcy intervened. "No, Cheryl, it's not a punishment. We want you home sometimes, with us."

Bobby turned to Sam. "This is about Gil Nortze, isn't it?"

"No, Bobby, it's not. But now that he's in the picture, your mother and I think that it might be

for the best if you don't run into him accidentally."
He looked to Darcy for backup.

"Your father is right," Darcy said, "You've got
to call Ken before going down—no surprise visits—and if he says that Mr. Nortze is there, you
stay away, okay?"

Bobby glanced over to Cheryl and shrugged.
"Okay, if you say so."

"Cheryl?" said Darcy.

Cheryl lowered her head. "Okay, Mom."

Back in Cheryl's room, Bobby sat on the edge
of Cheryl's bed and mindlessly picked at his fin-
gernails. "Well, I don't see how we can get around
this, Cheryl."

Cheryl was agitated. "I know. it's frustrating.
Do you think Ken said something to Mom or Dad?
I thought he was our friend."

"I don't know," Bobby said, staring down at
his lap.

"So, what do we do now?"

"I have to think about it." Bobby stood up
and walked towards the door, and then he
stopped and turned back to Cheryl. "I would
love to see the expression on our real father if
we told him face-to-face that we were his kids."
Bobby went into a little pantomime. "Hey,
where ya been all these years, Dad? Ever go
visit Mom's grave? I need some money for college. Got any?" Bobby laughed, but it was a
laughter that masked the pain of it all, a pain
shared by Cheryl.

"Bobby, don't do that." An idea popped into Cheryl's head. "And you know what? We know, but he doesn't. I say that gives us power."

Bobby thought about that and nodded. "Yes, it does. We'll just have to figure a way to use it to our advantage." He had been thinking about dyeing his hair for starters.

Sam put in a call to Ken and summarized the meeting with the kids, remarking on how well they handled the questions and the restrictions. He saved the building project for last. "I checked with building and safety, Ken. He got his permit and can start any time." What Sam didn't notice on the permit application was the fine print in the small boxes and rectangles: 2-story, 3,500 square feet—plus garage space.

"You're kidding me. How'd he get it through it so quickly?" Ken was so shocked by the news that things were moving so quickly he didn't even think to ask about building particulars. "He's going to be starting foundations before the end of the rainy season."

"Yeah, fast-track approval, I guess." Sam didn't think it necessary to go into the hearsay details about the ruckus inside the permit office.

Ken was resigned to the fact that his life was about to change. Looking out his office window to the stormy night, he said, "Well, I guess the sooner it starts, the sooner it's over."

After ringing off with Sam, Ken sat at his desk staring blankly out the window into his garden.

He heard the waves as they pounded against the cliff, and felt the vibration. Taped to his desk was a short passage from writer Stuti Garg: "Sometimes … we need to find solace in the raging waves of the ocean pounding on the rocks."

Rereading the passage, such violent natural activity did seem to soothe Ken's troubled mind. He realized at that moment that it was the *not knowing when* aspect that had driven him to distraction, but now at least that issue was settled once and for all.

Ken caught a glimpse of Jake the Tern swooping by the window and out onto his now-protected perch at the birdhouse. "Don't worry, Jake," Ken said aloud, smiling just a little now, "It'll all be over before we know it." Ken turned his attention to Tristin, as she would be arriving the next day, Saturday, with the moving van right behind her.

25 The Gift

Ken opened the front door to find Bobby and Cheryl standing on the porch. They had not called to let him know they were coming down. "Hi, guys, what's up?"

Cheryl was all smiles. "We just wanted to give Tristin something—a housewarming surprise. Is she here yet?"

"Yes, she got in this morning. Come on in," Ken said politely, adding in a whisper to both, "You should have called first, though."

"Sorry," Cheryl said with a little sheepish grin. She and Bobby followed Ken to the kitchen.

"Look who we have here, hon?"

Tristin was crouched down putting away kitchenware in a drawer, with Lindy the dog hovering close by. "Oh, hi there."

"Welcome to Carmel Highlands," Cheryl said.

"Thank you, Cheryl." Tristin stood up and walked over to Cheryl, giving her a hug. "Nice to see you again. And you too, Bobby." Lindy made a silent retreat out the kitchen doggie door.

"Same here," Cheryl cooed while Bobby merely nodded. Cheryl then beamed, adding, "We have a housewarming present for you."

"How thoughtful of you," Tristin said.

Cheryl opened her purse and pulled out something wrapped in newspaper. "I didn't have time to wrap it," she said, holding out the present to Tristin.

Tristin unfolded the newspaper wrapping and smiled. "Oh, how beautiful!" she exclaimed, inspecting the abalone shell up close and holding it out for Ken to see.

"I found it on the rocks at the beach this morning," Cheryl said, "Must have washed up from the storm last night. I don't know why, but it just reminded me of you."

Bobby watched Tristin's reaction closely. It had worked on Darcy, so he figured it might have the same effect on Tristin. It was close. "Thank you, Cheryl. That's very lovely, and very thoughtful." She gave Cheryl another hug, but this one with much more feeling.

Bobby looked at his watch. "Well, I guess we'd better be going, Cheryl. They probably have a lot of stuff to do."

Tristin took the bait, and asked Cheryl, "Oh, you don't have to go so soon, do you? How about some hot cocoa?"

Cheryl pleaded with her eyes to Bobby, then said softly, "Come on, Bobby. Just for a few minutes, okay?"

"Oh, alright, why not?"

After cocoa and an hour's visit, Ken drove the kids home, but Sam and Darcy were away for a few hours. Safely inside Bobby's room, both Bobby and Cheryl couldn't believe how well it went.

"Talk about perfect execution. Did you see her eyes?" Bobby asked, "She was almost in tears."

"Yes, I saw. After that," Cheryl said proudly, "she couldn't keep her hands off me the whole time."

In between stroking Cheryl's hair, telling her how cute she looked, asking about how she was doing in school, and all the rest, Cheryl was becoming a believer in Bobby's hidden talents. "How did you know she would react that way, Bobby?"

Bobby shrugged. "Just did, that's all. Mom reacted that way on the beach in Carmel, so I figured Tristin would, too."

"Maybe that's just what moms do. She'll make a great mom for us. And you spent time with Ken in the garage, so how'd that go?"

"Like clockwork. We talked about the walkie-talkie, but I got around pretty quick to how bad I felt about his not wanting us around so much."

"You said that?"

"Just to get a reaction, that's all."

"What did he say?"

"Oh, just what I expected. He protested up and down that it wasn't it at all, saying he liked me very much. And then he started talking, like, about how family life is very complex. He said we needed to spend more time with Mom and Dad—do things with them, you know."

"Did you mention anything about our real father?"

"He did. He said that if we ever met him by accident, we shouldn't say anything."

"Would you say something to him?"

"Yeah, I would." He pointed to his head, and with a wink, said, "I've got it all up here." *Up here* was also in the process of convincing Bobby of two key factors: First, that his father didn't (and could never) make enough money being a highway patrol officer to get Bobby all he was entitled to in life; and second, that his mother's heart could go at any minute, leaving him (but mostly Cheryl) without a mother—again. Very imperfect parents. Once Bobby had decided that Ken and Tristin would be perfect as their parents, everything else was icing. Both children had fallen in love with what to them represented ideal parents.

Back at the busy little house on Spindrift Road, Ken and Tristin began to sort out the fundamentals of living together, both of them deliriously happy. They had no clue as to the torture about to ensue. But instead of a few large blows, it would come rather like small drops of water hitting one's forehead, one at a time, for hours and days and weeks on end. For Ken Easton and Tristin Barnes, eternity would be defined as what was to be endured over the next three months.

*****

Note to John: The plan checker at building and safety confirmed everything here (and more later), so we're on solid ground with what followed. BTW: Just read your post card. Cannes looks like a nice place to be in mid-May for the film festival—hope you are making some good contacts (and keeping track of expenses). Sorry I missed your call (and our 'soft' deadline) when you were in L.A., but I needed some time alone up in the mountains to get moving on this. Speaking of getting away, I'm hoping to wrap this up in about a dozen more sections because my wife just informed me that she found a great 10-day vacation package for us and our two-year-old in Puerto Vallarta, Mexico. We booked it for May 30, so I better get cracking here to meet our new 'hard' deadline. I've been on this

thing since March 4, and it's true what they say—time flies when you're having fun. Steven

26 Smiley's People

It was on Monday, the fourth day of February 2002 when the crew showed up to lay out the foundations for Nortze's house. In his office, Ken was watching the TV news report that John Walker Lindh, the so-called "American Taliban" had been indicted by a federal grand jury on ten counts of terrorist-related activities. Some pundits were after the guy's head, saying he should receive the death penalty for his treasonous acts. Ken turned off the TV and booted up his computer, trying to decide what he would do if it were up to him to decide Lindh's fate. And that's when Lindy began to bark.

Ken cranked open the window and stuck his head out, spotting Lindy up on top of the sloping bluff. He watched and waited until she barked again. "Lindy, come 'ere!"

Lindy turned and walked down the slope to the garden, and Ken started to work on his acoustic parameters for the earthquake study. With the window open, he heard hammers pounding the wooden stakes into the ground and setting up batter boards for the string lines, but he didn't go to pay a visit. *I'll keep a low profile, and I won't butt in,* he reminded himself. *I've got my own work to do.* Tristin had driven over the hill into Monterrey to check on a work lead, a housing/condo development company with vacation rental packages throughout the region. With no one home, Ken turned up the stereo with some soft jazz as background and cranked the window closed.

He worked all day in his office, taking a few breaks including lunch. Mid-afternoon he even jumped in the spa on the far side of the house to work out some kinks in his back. He had a seven p.m. flight up to San Jose that night, and wouldn't be coming back until late Wednesday evening. But before his trip, he had a few more pages of calculations to wrap up, and poured on the coals.

By four o'clock he was finished for the day and decided to go check the mail. He also wanted to take a peek at the project from above. He was just out the front door when he saw Tristin's car pull up in front of the garage. She alit from the car and waved a few envelopes. "Hi, there. Picked up the mail on my way down."

"Thanks, hon."

Once inside, all thoughts of Nortze's project disappeared. Instead, he and Tristin discussed her day job hunting. The development company, Mitchell Properties, had offered her a job on the spot, but she put them off saying she had to look around a little more. The phone rang and Ken answered, responding, "Yes, she's right here."

It was Sharon Meyers, the Vice President of Personnel at Mitchell Properties, upping her already substantial offer, including a signing bonus as if Tristin was a star athlete. Sharon practically begged Tristin to come to work for them. "I'll discuss it with my fiancé," Tristin told Meyers with a wink to Ken, "and get back to you tomorrow, okay?"

After she rang off, Tristin and Ken discussed the pros and cons, Tristin ending with, "If I take the job at Mitchell, I can start next Monday. I'd like that."

"Sounds good to me," Ken said.

It was dark when Tristin drove Ken up the driveway. Ken tried to see what was going on with the project next door, but a thick cloud cover blocked the light of a half-moon, and all he saw was a dark expanse of bluff. At the Monterey Peninsula Airport, they hugged and said their fond goodbyes, Ken joking as they parted, "Keep an eye on the project and make sure he's not building a skyscraper, okay?"

On arrival in San Jose, he took a taxi to the Marriott. He had already eaten dinner before leaving, so he went straight to his room. He put in a quick phone call to Greg's office and left a message confirming his arrival and the meeting time at D&M the next day. Then he called Tristin to tell her everything was fine, and after the requisite, "I love you—no, I love you more—no, I love *you* more," he drifted off to sleep.

It was a great day for the acoustic sensor project, technical progress beyond expectations and ahead of schedule. When Ken returned to his hotel room after dinner, he was all but bouncing off the walls. He called Tristin to give her the good news and to find out how the conversation went with Mitchell Properties.

"Hey, babe, what's cookin'?"

Tristin didn't seem nearly as excited as Ken. "Well, they insisted on throwing in a leased Volvo for me to drive—all expenses paid—and I start on Monday."

"Wow, hon, that's great!"

"But there's something else, Ken. I don't know what it means, but something next door just doesn't look right."

"What do you mean?"

"They started trenching the footings today, and I couldn't help noticing that the one on the north side was only ten feet from your property line."

"Ten feet? The plan I saw had it set back more than twenty."

"That was the preliminary design sketch, though, right?"

It was at that moment when Ken's heart skipped a beat. "Nortze wouldn't do something like that," he said more out of fear than conviction. "And you're sure you were looking at the outside wall footing?"

"Pretty sure, but I can't say for certain. There was another one parallel to it, but set about twenty feet inside of it. Could be an inside wall or an outside wall, I'm not sure."

"Hmmm," Ken said, "I'll have to see it when I get back tomorrow."

"Everything go alright up there?"

"Yes, it did," Ken said, and he briefed her on the meeting and what was to come. "They bumped up my fee to cover the extra work already done and what was agreed to for later, and tomorrow we get into the specifics."

"That's good news." They talked for another few minutes, and Ken slept restlessly that night, as he couldn't get the gnawing suspicion out of his head that maybe Nortze's house project wasn't exactly shaping up as originally planned. By the time Tristin picked him up at the airport Wednesday evening, Ken couldn't wait to have a look for himself.

"There's a chain link fence now, Ken, covered with that thick green plastic all around."

"Yes, I've seen those. Not very pretty, but it does keep out the casual thieves."

At the mailbox, Ken directed Tristin to take the left fork down the lot. "Leave your lights on," he said as he jumped out. He tried to peek through the fence at the northwest corner, but he couldn't see a thing. With the plastic covering six feet high on the outside of the chain link, he also couldn't easily climb the fence for a look. So, since it was so dark anyway, he figured he'd have to wait until the next day to take a look.

At 6:45 the next morning while sitting at his computer, Ken heard the first crew truck arrive. He figured he'd give them until eight a.m. to get going, then walk up and introduce himself and take a look. It was a very long 75 minutes.

Promptly at eight, Ken stood at the open bedroom door and heard Tristin humming in the shower. Lindy lay in front of the bathroom door, her chin on her front paw. "C'mon, girl, want to go for a walk?" No dice. Ken laughed. "Found a great woman—lost a great dog," he said aloud.

Outside the house and walking toward his garden, Ken heard a generator start up, and shortly thereafter the distinctive metallic clatter of a jackhammer on bedrock. He climbed the slope and walked west along the hundred-foot fence, noting it was at least on Nortze's side of the property line. He was still unable to see inside. He covered his ears as he passed the noisy jackhammer just on the other side of the fence.

It wasn't until he reached the open double gate that he got his first look. Panning the lot from left to right, inspecting from afar the footings and wood stem wall forms under construction, he made a quick assessment: The footings had probably been inspected and approved yesterday. Six men on the foundation crew were busy cutting and placing rebar.

As the jackhammer chattered away on a rocky outcrop near the southeast corner, but away from the footings, Ken wondered if he was on the right lot, maybe not even the right planet.

I don't believe it! What happened to the two thousand square foot floor plan? And are those fifteen-inch footings? They should be twelve inches for single story.

Looking to the north side of the lot adjoining his property, Ken calculated that the foundation for the exterior wall ran a good fifty feet east-to-west. It was intersected at ninety degrees by two interior footings. The northwest section caught Ken's eye. Twenty feet square, it looked to Ken like it was made for a large interior room—and so close to the property line that even a single story structure would be visible from his garden-view window. He also noticed that the cross—used in the celebration-ritual that had been in place since late November—was gone now.

"Can I help you?" The sub-woofer voice started from way, way down deep and made Ken turn to find the source. It came from a six-foot seven-inch behemoth with a red beard and mustache coming out of the small construction trailer. With his dark blue jeans and heavy red plaid shirt, he reminded Ken of a short Paul Bunyan.

Geez, I wonder if he brought along his blue ox, Babe. "Hello, I'm Ken Easton." Ken's right hand disappeared in the man's firm but tempered grip. Ken pointed, saying, "I live next door."

"Brad Smiley," he said with a smile. "I'm the general contractor. What can I do for you?"

"Gil showed me the preliminary drawings, but I haven't had a chance to see the real thing yet, so

I just thought I'd come up and take a look. How's it coming?"

"Coming along fine."

"Are those two-story footings?"

"Yeah, but just on the north side. It's single story to the south."

The north side? If he's going two-story, why not put that on the south side? "How many square feet, total?"

"About thirty-five hundred, plus the garages," Smiley said.

It was as if Ken's life flashed before his eyes. *Nearly four thousand square feet? That bastard Nortze lied to me.* Shrinking by about an inch, Ken realized at that moment that the preliminary sketch Nortze showed him had been just for show. Had Ken known the true scope of the house—and it's proximity to his property line—he would have immediately filed a complaint with the building department prior to any permit approval. As he stood there on the site, Ken felt like kicking himself for being such a patsy as to allow Nortze to pull one over on him at such a critical juncture. He pulled himself up half an inch and gathered his strength to ask about the exterior wall closest to the property line. "So that north wall is two-story all the way back?"

"Yeah," Smiley said, pointing, "The three-car garage is on the right side there."

Ken pictured in his mind the view from the second floor down onto his garden, and then from his garden up to Nortze's house. *There goes walking naked out to the birdhouse.* "I guess it's not going to be wood siding, either, is it?"

Smiley shook his head. "No, white stucco with a slick-trowel finish." And here Smiley gave himself away, knowing what that meant for Ken Easton. Lowering his voice and approaching an apology, he said, "At least it's on the north side and won't reflect direct sunlight—until late afternoon."

Ken nodded and let out a faint, "Yeah." Even the momentary vision of having to wear sunglasses to look up at that smooth, highly reflective wall on a sunny summer afternoon was enough to put Ken into a mild state of shock.

Ken thanked Smiley for the information and walked in a daze up the driveway. He stood by his mailbox for a long look down at the house-to-be. He visualized the monster, with the thought still gnawing at his gut that he had probably blown any chance of making Nortze scale back; or at least move the whole house further south and away from the lot line. And he could still see in his mind's eye that white slick-trowel finish, with the expanse broken up by a few windows.

Deciding right then to call a lawyer, Ken's hopes were high, but his expectations were low. "*Gil Nortze,*" Ken said, looking down on the project, "*You are one lousy bastard.*"

Intentionally and subconsciously, Gil Nortze was just getting warmed up.

*****

Note to John: Five minutes on the phone with a lawyer in Carmel later that same morning reinforced Ken's belief that because he hadn't filed any objections to the project prior to permit approval, if he now tried to force any changes, or caused any project delays, he was opening himself up for an immediate (and probably successful) lawsuit by Nortze. I confirmed the general conversation with Brad Smiley and the lawyer who Ken spoke to. Steven

27 Switch

By Friday, February 8, everything was set and ready to go for the foundation pour scheduled for the next day. Brad Smiley had personally checked all the dimensions to ensure square, plumb, and level throughout the foundation area. The building inspector had just an hour ago signed off for the pour. It was one o'clock, and Smiley was in the trailer, about to let everyone go home early, when he heard a screeching of tires.

It was Gil Nortze in his rented Lincoln Continental, red of course. Nortze jumped out with plans in hand and walked briskly into the trailer. Inside, the little office contained a single large desk, three chairs, and plans were pinned to the walls. Behind the door, Smiley startled at Nortze's sudden and unannounced appearance and almost knocked the coffee maker off the little refrigerator.

"Glad I caught you, Brad. We have to make a change."

"A change? In what?"

"The profile of the house. I want it all a foot higher for better drainage around the side yards."

"What?" Smiley asked in shock, quickly starting to crunch numbers in his head for the logistics of such a change in elevation at this late date. "Everything's inspected, Gil, and ready to pour tomorrow morning. The first cement trucks are scheduled for seven o'clock."

"I know, I know," Nortze said in frustration, "But I was talking with the architect, and he said that if we don't do it now, it will never happen."

Smiley was incredulous. "What's wrong with the grading as is?"

"It's too shallow. I don't want a lot of flat spots for the rainwater runoff to puddle."

"Did you get a change approval from building and safety?"

"No, but I'm sure they'll give it to me." Nortze stiffened. "I've made up my mind, Brad, so let's call off the pour and get to it, okay?"

"You know it's going to cost more money, right?"

Nortze shrugged as if it were a minor inconvenience, "Yeah, sure, how much?"

Smiley was now resigned to the task. "It's going to take an entire day at least, so I'm thinking five grand, but I'm not sure, so we'll have to do it on time and materials. We'll get the extra lumber here sometime tomorrow and start first thing Monday morn—"

"No way!" Nortze fired back. "I want that lumber here this afternoon, and I want to see the entire crew here tomorrow."

Smiley's jaw dropped. "Gil, you're not serious."

"Dead serious."

Smiley chuckled and scoffed with a shake of his head. "Gil, I'm sorry, but the subcontractor is starting another foundation tomorrow, so he won't be—"

"Stop!" Nortze shouted, holding his hand up like a stop sign. He reached into his pocket and pulled out his checkbook, writing furiously. He tore out the check and handed it to Smiley.

Smiley was floored. "Ten thousand dollars, Gil?"

"That's right, Brad. Ten grand if you get on it right now."

Leaning back in his chair, Smiley rubbed his face with both hands, letting it all sink in. He let out a huge breath into his palms, grumbling, "My wife is going to kill me." Finally, he stood up and went for the door. "I'll check with Franco, but I can't promise anything." Nortze started to follow, but Smiley stopped him. "No, Gil, you wait here. I'll handle this."

The sun had already set and the temperature was dropping fast as Brad Smiley waited alone for the lumber delivery. The foundation crew had already made good headway on carefully deconstructing the forms. But Brad was worried. He knew how to make things happen if need be, but the one thing he couldn't control was the weather. He hadn't seen any predictions of rain for the next several days, but that was no guarantee in the middle of the rainy season. It was the one thing that could wreak havoc on the whole project schedule if the foundations weren't poured in time.

Ken turned left at the mailbox and headed down to Nortze's lot. Leaving the headlights on, Ken alit with preliminary design drawings in hand and spotted Smiley. "Hey, Brad. Got a minute?"

"Sure, what's up?"

"Step over in front of the headlights. I just want you to take a look at something." Ken unfurled the single sheet so Smiley could see.

"What the hell is that?" Smiley asked.

"This is what Gil said it was going to look like." Ken pointed to the north property line. "He said he was keeping his *little single-story cottage on the bluff* twenty feet back from the property line.

Smiley shook his head. "I've never seen that. All I saw were the plans for what's there now. What did you do to piss him off?"

"Beats me." Ken rolled up the plan and they stood. "But he sure pulled a fast one, making me think he was doing something much smaller and away from the property line. And now it's too late to protest." Ken was dejected. "My privacy is all but gone now."

Smiley showed some compassion. "I'm sorry, man. Watch out for Nortze—he's slick."

"On you, too?" Ken didn't really expect an exposé, as Nortze paid the man's salary.

Smiley hesitated a moment, then figured *what the hell*. "Well, it's an old trick, and I didn't fall for it, but he tried it anyway."

"What was that?"

"Nortze showed me an unapproved version of the plans, asking for a firm bid. Said I couldn't take them out of his little temporary office in the architect's building unless I gave him a two hundred dollar deposit. So, when he left and I was doing the take-off, I whipped out my digital camera and took pictures of the plans. And sure enough, when I got a look at the stamped and approved set and compared them with my photos, there were a lot of changes—much more complicated than what I was shown."

"Did Nortze know you had photos?"

"No, but when I went through the plans with Nortze and I said stuff like, 'This rec room on the south side is twice as big now; Where did this welded I-beam moment-frame come from? This wasn't here before, there's five extra piers here,' that sort of thing. He tried to play dumb, but I knew he was scamming to get me to do twenty-five or thirty grand more than I had agreed to. Like I said, watch him like a hawk."

"Yes, well, it appears this hawk has already swooped down and taken most of my scalp."

Smiley tried to restrain a laugh, but it burst through his pursed lips. "I'm sorry, Ken, I don't mean to laugh, but that was funny."

Ken chuckled, too. "Well, if you lose your sense of humor about these things … hey, I gotta run. Thanks for the chat, Brad," Ken said as he got back into his car.

"No problem, Ken," Smiley said, waving.

It was dark when the truck showed up, and Smiley had the driver roll the metal-strapped form lumber off the back end right where the truck had stopped. Smiley then tipped the man a hundred dollars for his efforts, with another hundred folded up for Stan at the lumberyard. Stan had gone the extra mile and made all the arrangements.

The next morning, Smiley pitched in to help the foundation crew raise and reinforce the stem walls and south patio footings. He had even hired four extra men to help with the work. It was dusk when they finished, and everyone was beat. Once again, Smiley made sure everything was level, plumb, and square, ready for re-inspection on Monday afternoon. With Nortze back in Las Vegas, the architect was scheduled to walk the changes through plan check Monday morning, and the pour would be on Tuesday.

At home that night watching the TV news, Brad Smiley saw the weather map and heard the prediction of rain for the coming week. A premonition of disaster swept over him, and Smiley closed his eyes. *Please, please God don't let it rain on Tuesday.*

Brad Smiley's prayer was answered, but he had forgotten an important addendum.

On Monday morning at eleven o'clock, Marvin Tulley, the 37-year old project architect, showed up at the door to Smiley's trailer, plans in hand but with a defeated look on his face.

"You okay, Marv?"

"No," Tulley said, "My stomach is so churned up with acid, I'm afraid I'm going to puke."

"What's the problem?"

"They wouldn't give Nortze the approval for the extra height. Said he needed a variance, and that means notification of neighbors and a week's delay at least." Tulley had been dealing with Nortze's intimidating ways for two months, and he had come to accept the man's innate dishonesty. He, too, felt sorry for Ken Easton. "Brad, do you think for one minute Ken Easton is going to sign off on that?"

Smiley shook his head, saying, "Not in a million years."

"That's what I figured, too." Tulley sighed heavily. "I haven't called Gil yet. Thought I'd talk it over with you first."

Smiley saw the future, and it was not good. "We're probably thinking the same thing, Marv."

"I'm afraid so. Everything's got to be changed back to its original elevation, and if we get hit with a lot of rain, we're screwed."

"Exactly," Smiley said, the anger building inside. Smiley made a good living, but he didn't feel the need to cheat people in the process. Teach Nortze a lesson, maybe. "I'm going to charge him twenty grand to put it all back where it was before. If he don't like it, tough."

"Can I call him from here, so we can get it straightened out now?"

Smiley reached over and speed-dialed Nortze's cell phone number and switched over to speakerphone.

"Yes, Brad," Nortze said cheerfully, "How's it going?"

Smiley gestured to Tulley that it was his show.

"This is Marv Tully, Gil. I'm here at the site with Brad right now."

There was a pregnant pause. "And?" Nortze asked impatiently.

"The peak of the roof is already at maximum allowable without a variance. In order to get the height profile changed, you're going to need that variance, Gil."

"So, get the fucking variance!" Nortze shouted.

"Not as simple as that. You need to notify all the neighbors in writing—including Mr. Easton—and they will have an opportunity to oppose it. It'll take at least a week, definitely more if Mr. Easton or anyone else fights it."

A long silence followed from Nortze's end. "So, you're telling me that we should change everything back to the way it was."

"That's right, Gil, or else apply for the variance and maybe not get it approved anyway."

Another long pause was followed by, "Well then, Marv, I guess you'll just have to change it back."

Smiley leaned closer to the speakerphone. "Twenty grand, Gil."

"What? That's highway robbery, Brad. It only cost ten grand to change it."

"Everyone's schedule is really thrown off now, Gil. And there's rain coming, hopefully not before Wednesday. If that happens, you're looking at a lot more than twenty grand. So, that's the price." Smiley secretly wanted Nortze to fire him on the spot and hire a new general contractor.

Nortze had no wiggle room. It was either pay the money now, or pay a steeper price if they got hit with the rains. He asked only one question: "Can you do it in one day?"

"Yes," Smiley replied, "if you fax me the change order right now so I can start greasing the skids." Smiley knew that he would have to play Santa Clause, handing out hundred dollar bills like candy to the subs and the suppliers, plus ten grand for his own troubles.

"Okay, start greasing. I'll be out Tuesday afternoon," Nortze said, and he hung up without thanking the two men for their efforts or even saying goodbye.

By late Tuesday afternoon, no one on the Nortze job site was in anything close to a good humor. It was never about the money, but rather about how everyone's lives had to revolve around the whims of a man who really didn't give a damn about them. But with teeth clenched, they got the job done with an hour to spare before sunset.

For the third time, Smiley made sure all the stem walls were level, plumb, and square within an eighth of an inch over a hundred feet. His last task of the day was to call and confirm the arrival of the concrete pumper and the first two concrete trucks, the rest scheduled thirty minutes apart.

28 Crime and Punishment

Gil Nortze arrived at Margie's Bed and Breakfast at eight o'clock on Tuesday night. "Same room as last time," Nortze said.

Margie gave Nortze a come-hither look. "Any room you want is fine, Gil." Even though he had humiliated her in their previous sexual encounter, Margie was ready for seconds.

"Ever cash in that poker chip, Margie? You definitely seem to have the temperament." The hundred-dollar chip that Nortze had left her for as a "tip" for getting all the gear organized for the bonfire ritual was more like payment for other services rendered.

Margie smiled. "Yes, Gil, I still have the chip. You want to play a few hands and see if you can win it back?"

"Sure, I'm game." Nortze figured it would take about half an hour for Margie to lose it all back to him.

Margie turned the registration card around and handed Nortze a pen, saying, "Five card draw, deuces wild, five dollar ante, two-raise limit of ten dollars each." She glanced at the clock. "Be back here at eight-fifteen, Gil. I only got until nine." She had already made up her mind that she would either win or lose by then, and she wanted a time limit.

"Like I said, Margie, whatever you say."

At eight-fifteen sharp, Nortze returned with a sealed deck of cards and $200 of real $5 poker chips from the Mirage casino in Las Vegas. He always carried them for opportunities such as this. "Where shall we play?"

"Over by the fireplace," Margie said, pointing. "At that table." A bottle of scotch and two glasses sat on the table.

"Mind if I have a cigar?"

"No, as long as you don't mind if I smoke, too."

Nortze won the first two hands and $20 with a pair of kings and trip sevens. He downed his glass and filled it up. On the next hand, Margie took it all back, and $10 extra, on an inside straight. She drained her glass and refilled. Nortze folded the next two hands after it appeared to Nortze that Margie had winners. He was getting nervous, and decided to bluff. When Margie called it, it cost Nortze $40.

By nine o'clock, Nortze was getting desperate, and a little drunk. Margie didn't have the *tells* of most beginners, and she played winning and losing hands with the same deadpan expression. She was also up $120. Margie called, "Last hand, Gil," and dealt the cards. They both anted up $5.

Nortze took a peek at his cards. Draining half a glass of scotch, he bet $10. Margie called and raised him ten, and he re-raised her another ten. She called, and the pot stood at $60. "I'm good," Nortze said.

"Dealer takes two," Margie said, and she dealt herself the cards.

Nortze put out two $5 chips, and Margie called and raised two chips. Nortze re-raised Margie two chips, and she re-raised again. Nortze called, and the pot was $110.

"King-high flush," Nortze said proudly, laying down his hand.

"Ace-high straight," Margie said with a furrowed brow, adding, "Nice hand." She was about to stand when she saw something. She leaned over and spread out Nortze's cards, where a ten of spades sat where a ten of clubs should have been. "What the hell is that?" Margie said, pointing.

Nortze's eyes widened. "Oh, Jesus!" he said in a loud whisper.

Margie stood hunched over the table and raked in the pile of chips, staring Nortze between the eyes. "You trying to cheat me, Gil?"

Nortze was completely flummoxed. "No, Margie, I swear. I only peeked once, and I thought

I had a pat flush." He held up his right hand in earnest. "I swear to God, Margie."

Margie shrugged it off, knowing that Nortze was a few sheets to the wind. "Yeah, okay, I guess it happens." She swept her chips into her purse, saying, "Sorry, but I've got to go now. Thanks for the game."

"Same here," Nortze said. "Maybe we can do this again sometime when my eyes aren't playing tricks on me."

Margie smiled genuinely, convinced that Nortze had not tried to cheat. "Sure, I'd like that." She took the scotch and glasses and went off to the kitchen. Nortze sat staring at the fire. He, too, was on a slow burn, castigating himself not only about his loss to this novice yet very good poker player, but also about being caught trying to pass off a bum hand. Nortze had known at first glance that he didn't have the flush, and that he was going to bluff it anyway. He cheated people whenever he thought he could get away with it, but to be caught by a neophyte gambler made him furious at his own negligence.

For the first time in a long while, that little voice didn't shift the blame onto someone else; it blamed Gil Nortze. Not for cheating, but for getting caught. And Gil Nortze paid the piper that night, trying to prove to Margie that he hadn't tried to cheat her. During sex with her, he even made sure she came before he did. And he didn't mention putting a bag over her face, either.

Later in his room, Nortze sat down in front of the fire and opened up Maria Nortze's leather-bound diary. From the hand-written notes, and little sketches and narrative entries going back ninety years, he immediately felt the connection to his roots. Within a few minutes it became clear to him that he had done nothing wrong in attempting to maximize his opportunity to win. He had merely gotten caught, and he felt quite comfortable in the belief that he had paid the appropriate penalty.

29 The Perfect Storm

In accordance with Smiley's prayer, God didn't let it rain on Tuesday. But at one o'clock the next morning, it began to drizzle. And then drizzle harder. By three a.m. it had turned into a light rain that came harder and harder even as the first two cement trucks arrived, each with ten yards of concrete ready for pumping into the footings. By the time the pump man had set out and connected the thick hoses, it was a solid and very cold downpour.

Brad Smiley stood just inside the open door to his trailer shaking his head. Even with three sump pumps going, he felt disaster looming. He turned and nodded repeatedly, little snorts of air coming from his nostrils. "We are so screwed."

Gil Nortze was bundled against the weather and seated on a chair, coffee cup in hand. At that moment the phone rang, and Smiley pressed the speakerphone button. "Smiley here."

"Brad, this is Jim Banks, and Marv's in my office," said the disembodied voice of the structural engineer up in Monterrey. With Banks was the architect, Marv Tulley. "You getting rain down there?"

"Lots and lots, Jim. The trucks are here and we're ready to go, but we haven't started yet."

"I'm looking right now at the Weather Channel Doppler radar image, and it looks like a big one comin' down from Alaska."

Smiley recalled the words of the Borg spokesman on *Star Trek*: "Resistance is futile!" Unspoken were the thoughts of three men who knew they would have to answer to their own version of the Borg queen—Gil Nortze.

But this was reality for Brad Smiley, not fantasy. "Gil's here, too. I say we call it off, Jim."

Nortze jumped out of his chair, fuming mad— but thankfully silent in his resignation—and caught up in a tight, circular walk, almost in place where he stood.

Smiley looked over to Nortze, eyebrows arched. Nortze stopped pacing, thought about it, and grudgingly gave the okay.

"And so does Gil."

"Well, that makes four of us," Banks said, and they rang off.

Smiley began the mental preparation necessary to deal with having to inform the man before him who paid the bills that he'd best arrive quickly at the mental version of a Brinks armored truck dumping a load of money onto the site.

Smiley sent the cement trucks back to the yard and cancelled the remaining trucks. The concrete dispatcher said two more trucks were already loaded, but there were no other jobs to put them on because of the rain. So, with concrete, three trucks, concrete pumpers, and extra manpower gone to waste, Nortze would be stuck with a bill for over $1,500.

"Yeah, well," Smiley said to the dispatcher, "Life does suck sometimes." Smiley rang off and started to make preparations to go home.

"Brad, let's get some more pumps and hoses in those footings," Nortze said, "so the guys can keep ahead of the rain."

Smiley turned slowly, not quite believing what he was hearing. "It's over, Gil. I'm not going to ask Franco or his guys to man those pumps and catch pneumonia for nothing."

Without blinking, Nortze responded. "Well, then, Brad, I guess since you have refused my reasonable request, you're fired. You've been paid up to date, but expect to hear from my attorney." With that, Nortze left in his Lincoln and sped up the road.

Brad Smiley knew what had to be done, but it wasn't he who was going to do it. He called the architect, told him about his being fired, and laid out the bad news. And he did not allow any interruption, giving it to Tulley in one fell swoop. "If this storm lasts more than a day, it's all got to come out, Marv—every form, stake, and piece of rebar. The trenches will have to be dug out, and possibly dug deeper, depending on what the inspector says. My guess is he is not going to sign off without approval from the soils engineer, so he'll have to be brought out, too, after the trenches are clear. It's going to take a week to dry out after that, so to prepare for the worst, I'd count on that being a thirty thousand dollar storm, above and beyond what's already been spent. And I'm outa here."

Brad Smiley had one stop to make before heading home. In his rain slicker and hat, Smiley rang Ken Easton's doorbell, and waited a few moments before Tristin opened the door. At first taken aback by the huge man standing before her, she quickly matched Ken's description with the man standing on the porch.

"I hope I'm not calling at a bad time, Mrs. Easton."

Tristin flushed slightly at the premature address. "No, not at all. I'm Tristin, Ken's fiancée, and you must be Mr. Smiley." Tristin had a great memory for names and conversations.

"Yes, ma'am—Brad."

"Please, Brad, come in out of the rain. Ken's in his office."

Smiley stepped inside, dripping wet. "Thanks." He removed his hat and mindlessly folded and unfolded it while Tristin walked down towards Ken's office.

Ken recognized Smiley from down the hallway. "Hey, Brad, what's up?"

"I just wanted to stop by and give you the happy news … for me, anyway."

"Oh, yeah, what's that?" Ken said, stopping far enough away to speak to the large man without having to strain his neck.

"Nortze just fired me," Smiley said with a grin.

"You don't seem very displeased."

"I'm not. I have better things to do with my life than put up with people like him."

"I wish I had a choice," Ken said sarcastically. "What happened, if you don't mind me asking?"

"Well, it's a long story, but the short of it is, I'm not about to run the subs into the ground, especially in this weather. I was thinking of quitting, but it's better this way. Anyway, I just wanted to let you know, 'cause after the storm blows over, which could take a while, there's going to be a new general contractor up there. I hope everything turns out for the best."

"Me, too, but I hate to lose a good ally against evil."

Smiley chuckled and nodded, saying, "Maybe you'll want to remodel someday."

He reached under his rain slicker and pulled out a business card he'd stuck in his pocket on his way down the hill. "That's also my home number."

"Great, thanks, Brad."

They shook hands and Smiley departed into the ever-increasing rain, thunder and lightning starting to roll in from the sea.

Gil Nortze spent the rest of the day holed up in his room at Margie's B&B, most of it in a trance in front of the fireplace as the storm raged outside. He read and re-read passages from the family diaries, gathering strength for what he knew lay ahead. He even turned down a poker game with Margie, knowing she'd want to take him back to her room and screw their brains out. In a sulk, Nortze left just after dark and flew home to Las Vegas, in his mind still blaming everyone but himself for things gone awry on the jobsite.

30 Backdraft

Glancing over every now and then to the TV, Bobby Wynette sat at his computer tweaking Ken's acoustic software program into all sorts of interesting graphs and charts. He didn't even hear the pounding rain outside. With headphones on and watching the 1974 movie, *Towering Inferno,* with Steve McQueen, Bobby was lost in a world of disaster engineering. And suddenly, his mind switching to his current dilemma, Bobby had a thought: *Maybe it doesn't have to be an explosion at all. It could just as easily be a big fire.*

Once he'd settled on the methodology, Bobby removed his headphones and went down the hall, sticking his head inside the open door. Cheryl was seated at her desk, cutting a piece of heavy red paper.

"Whatcha doin', Cheryl?"

"Making Valentines. Ken, Tristin, and Mom and Dad."

Bobby closed the door behind him and lowered his voice. "Well, as for the last two, it might be their last from us."

"Oh, yeah?" Cheryl said calmly. "What did you come up with?"

Bobby straightened up real proud and tall, and he began to lay out his plan to Cheryl. "Well, with all the probabilities of shit happening in our dangerous little world, sometimes shit happens … "

It rained heavily in Carmel Highlands all that day, and all night, and all of Thursday. By Friday it was down to a light rain lasting all day, and then it rained heavily on and off all weekend. When the skies finally cleared on Monday afternoon, the footings of Nortze's house were almost completely filled in with thick, dark-brown mud from the surrounding areas, and all of the lower rebar and steel ties were buried solid. The lower third of the 2x6 lumber forms were also buried, so with the steel rebar, steel hold-downs bolts, ties and supports still in place, it made the job of digging out the trenches without first removing the lumber and rebar all but impossible, just like Brad Smiley had predicted. The pit for the welded steel I-beam frame was also half filled in with mud. Instead of a solid concrete foundation well cured by the rain and ready to build on (if Nortze hadn't made the changes), it was instead a muddy morass.

Marv Tulley, the architect, went out to the site and performed a damage assessment. He then called Nortze with the limited options available. Nortze immediately rode right up Brad Smiley's tail. "Fucking general contractor should have stopped me. I'm thinking of filing a suit against him for negligence."

As if it was all Smiley's fault for not grabbing Nortze by the throat and making him change his mind. It was actually Marv Tulley who had, in fact, warned Nortze that such late changes could be problematic, although he hadn't been specific as to driving rain ruining the footings. Tulley felt pretty awful about the whole mess, but not to the point of trying to blame Smiley or feeling responsible himself for the final decision. It was Nortze's half-baked idea in the first place, and all Marv Tulley had said was that if the change in elevation was going to happen at all, it had to happen quickly.

Marv Tulley didn't take the bait on Nortze's ramblings about the now ex-general contractor. Instead, he stuck to his plan of attack. "Gil, it's time to fish or cut bait here. What do you want to do about the foundation work?"

"What else can I do? I'll go to the poker game tonight, and you hire someone to tear it out tomorrow. I'm flying out on Wednesday and check things out for myself."

"Okay, see you then."

Wednesday would be the 13th, the day before Valentine's Day.

*****

Note to John: As this was a major turning point in Nortze's building project, I thought it prudent to put in as many pertinent facts as I could. The specific dialogue is mine, although it does reflect—accurately, I believe, and based on interviews with the principals—the real events as they unfolded. Before I forget, we had a little factional strife at Soledad today. Ended up having to separate out the Muslimists from the Islamists, and then the Islamists from the Nation of Islam followers. Seems that religion starts more fights than it prevents. Steven

31 Rocky and Bullwinkle

"So, do you get the day off tomorrow?" Ken asked, Chinese take-out and a bottle of quickly diminishing Merlot on the kitchen counter. It was miserable outside, as the moist sea breeze had begun swirling in around the entire Monterey Bay, and the deep waters further chilled the air. There was no rain, but when the system passed over the hill and down to the Highlands, it made for bitterly cold conditions. It was almost dark by three o'clock in the afternoon on Wednesday, and with the new moon two days old, the nights ahead promised near-invisibility. Ten-foot waves battered the cliffs, and both Ken and Tristin felt the shaking under foot.

Tristin had already told her boss at Mitchell Properties she needed the day off, and he had happily obliged. She also knew that tomorrow was Valentine's Day, and Ken had a big surprise for her. Tristin blushed and looked over with adoring eyes, and whispered, "I do if you do?" They hadn't set a marriage date yet, so she was teasing with the vows.

Now it was Ken's turn to blush, although half of it was because he'd had two glasses of wine, but he could give as good as he got. "I *will*. That's all I have in me right now, babe."

"Can't quite spit those words out yet, huh, Ken?" Tristin said, pressing the tease even harder. She held up the bottle. "Perhaps a little more wine to loosen up the tongue?" She was feeling giddy and splashed the glass half full. She still felt the guilt of not having disclosed to Ken her little secret about Gil, but they were having such a good time, so why spoil it?

Ken toasted her and gulped it down in three swallows. Paraphrasing Roy Scheider in the movie, *Jaws,* Ken said, "I'm going to need a bigger glass."

Tristin burst out laughing and almost peed her pants. Once she had calmed down, he said, "The reason I asked if you had any plans is because my plan requires you to be ready to go early."

"How early?" she asked warily, knowing it was a surprise.

"Oh, ten o'clock."

She relaxed and put her arms around Ken's neck, still a little tipsy from the wine. "That I can make."

They both were in good humor, ready to watch the DVD movie, *Rocky and Bullwinkle.* They had both enjoyed watching episodes from the original cartoon serial compiled on VHS. Woozily helping to clear the dishes, Ken said, "With De Niro, Rene Russo, and Jason Alexander, it *sounds* terrific."

With some sounds, even acoustical engineers can be wrong.

32 The Arrangement

Nortze had been shivering on his cell phone for an hour making arrangements to get laborers to the site, and going over site requirements by the soils engineer and the structural engineer. Banks and Tulley were awaiting the trenches to be dug out prior to them coming out and having a look, followed by a test by the soils engineer. The few moments of waiting on hold seemed to Nortze an eternity. Inside the job trailer with the electric heater cranked up trying to fight the cold, he was trying to locate a tractor-backhoe to start cleaning out the footing trenches.

Gil Nortze had decided to take on the role of general contractor on his own house as owner-builder. He figured it wasn't that big a deal. Banks and Tulley both advised against it, warning Nortze that he was going to run into all sorts of situations about which he knew little or nothing.

Banks and Tulley had even conspired to make him change his mind. They each said that Nortze had ten free phone calls. After that, it would be chargeable at three hundred dollars an hour, firm. After the first three site visits, extra visits were going for five hundred a day. Nortze had still held firm.

The dispatcher at the rental yard came back on the phone. "We can have it out by seven tomorrow."

"Great!" Nortze shouted, a minor victory at hand. "We'll be here." After ringing off, he called Tulley and left a message on his machine, then called the structural engineer, Banks, to let him know, too. Banks answered.

"The laborers and the backhoe will be here at seven sharp," Nortze said proudly, as if it were a great leadership accomplishment. "What time are you guys coming out?"

"I already talked to Marv, and we figure by three o'clock we'll be able to tell for sure. If we think it's all okay, we'll get the soils engineer out to confirm it. By the way, Gil, are you sure your workers can do the job in these conditions?"

"That's why they call them workers. See you both at three."

Gil Nortze promptly left the trailer and hopped into his car. In a great mood now, he drove with purpose to Margie's B&B, where he also promptly lost another $200 to Margie in deuces wild draw poker.

In his room and sullen after his second defeat in as many outings, Nortze said aloud, "I'm going to have to teach that woman Texas Hold'em." One-on-one Texas Hold'em was for the pros, and it was also Nortze's best hope of winning back his money. The fact that he didn't use the term *bitch* was promising, as he was coming around to actually admire Margie's poker talent, and her sexy body, if not her looks.

Nortze's primary concern was more practical. Now the owner-builder and expecting to spend a great deal of time in the Highlands, Nortze needed a cheaper place to stay than in Margie's $200 per day B&B. She would just have to be made to understand the situation. This *temporary arrangement*, he figured, would last a week at most while he searched for a cheap rental house in the Highlands close to the job site.

Nortze did not plan on the wide range of his term *temporary,* or on the upper range of *cheap.*

*****

Note to John: I don't know where Gil Nortze got the idea that he could run a big project like that—hubris certainly was involved—so I didn't even speculate. BTW: The Muslimist inmates settled for Walkmans with earphones so they could hear their own music and Imam lectures. It is not exactly Guantanamo Bay at the training facility at Soledad, and besides, most are not dangerous felons, just regular crooks who got caught like everyone else. I wish I could get some of this material in the story, but I can't find a spot for it … yet. Steven

33 Castles in the Sky

"Where do you want to start?" shouted Ruben, the backhoe operator, over the loud engine idle. The air was moist and cold, and Ruben had layered himself in rain gear and warm clothes. It was just past seven o'clock as he stood next to the tractor, ready to climb aboard and start moving mud. The five Hispanic laborers were not so well dressed.

"At the south end," Nortze shouted, pointing toward the single-story footings and rec-room area.

"Where is the mud going?" Ruben asked.

"In front of the garage," Nortze replied, this time pointing to the northeast corner. Nortze hadn't calculated how much mud there would be, but he figured the area in front of the garage would handle it. Feeling the cold biting his fingers, he rubbed his hands together. He was bundled up against the elements, but could still felt the cold on his head and a draft down his neck, and his ungloved hands were especially cold.

And so it began. With the laborers shoveling out the deep mud from the perimeter footings into the front scoop of the backhoe, and the tractor inching its way along, it was slow going. Only one of the laborers had rubber boots on, while the others were quickly covered in mud up to their knees.

By ten o'clock, three hours into the task, Nortze could see that his estimate of progress had been a long way off the mark. That was because each time the scoop was filled, the tractor had to make its way around the perimeter footings and over to the garage area, dump its load, and return. And the mud didn't stack up like dry dirt, but rather slumped and ran flat due to the high water content. The area in front of the garage quickly filling up and was began oozing towards the fence on the north side of the lot. The laborers were cold and exhausted, but Nortze pushed them hard, allowing only one ten-minute break every hour. He didn't offer them coffee.

Nortze came up with an idea all by himself. When Ruben came by with his next load, Nortze stopped him. "No more mud here!" he shouted, "Dump it over the cliff," he said, and he pointed back to the south end of the property, close to where they were working. Ruben nodded and spun around, heading back around to the south side.

"That should save some time," Nortze said aloud, proud of his analytical capabilities. His eye caught movement, and he turned to see Ken Easton's white Ford Bronco heading up the driveway, Ken and Tristin inside. Nortze didn't wave, but rather followed the Bronco with his eyes as it disappeared up the driveway.

I wonder where those two little lovebirds are off to on Valentine's Day? Nortze concluded that Tristin had not yet told Ken about the encounter one year before. Remembering his promise, he decided on a little something special for them both.

Ken turned right on Coast Highway and headed south, and Tristin turned to him, saying, "Well, I see we're not going to San Francisco."

"Nope. Someplace a little quieter."

It took less than twenty minutes to get to Bixby Bridge, a coastal landmark and one of the most photographed man-made structures on the west coast. Ken pulled over so they could get out and take a look. Build in the early 1930s, the Bixby is a concrete bridge with a main span of more than 300 feet, centered almost 250 feet above the ravine floor and close to the sea. Ken pointed out to Tristin that the view she was looking at had probably been used in a hundred car commercials.

"It does look familiar," she said. "It's gorgeous."

The next stop was breakfast in Big Sur, where they ate next to a huge stone fireplace at a roadside inn. After breakfast, Ken led Tristin on a walk through the redwoods. Tristin had never been to Big Sur, and like most first-timers she was duly impressed.

They continued south on Highway 1 for half an hour, stopping at a turnout on the flatter section of coast, where two huge rocks stood a few hundred yards offshore. "Keep an eye on the big rock out there," he said, adding, "and you might want to get your camera after you see it."

The larger offshore rock, perhaps thirty feet high and seventy feet wide, stood like a sentry against the sea, fairly calm now, with waves splashing several feet up the sides. Suddenly, a huge spray of water shot up from behind the rock and spilled over the top and around the sides. For a moment, the rock was invisible.

"Wow! Where did that come from?" Tristin asked in awe.

"On the other side of the rock, the base is slanted and goes down under the water. When a wave comes along, the submerged slope funnels the wave into a triangle. The force of the entire wave is transferred and concentrated into a small area, and it explodes like that, and the only way to go is up. The waves sometimes do that just west of my diving perch."

"Oooh," Tristin said, fetching her camera from the Bronco. "I've got to get a picture of that."

The next stop, at the southern end of Ken's planned excursion was Hearst Castle in San

Simeon. On the tram up to the castle, Ken said, "I just want you to see the style to which you deserve to become accustomed." They spent three hours gawking at the lap of luxury set in the Santa Lucia Mountains overlooking the sea.

When they arrived back in Big Sur at six o'clock, Ken made like he didn't know where he was going in the dark as he turned off the main highway. It was a surprise for Tristin to pull up the Big Sur Lodge.

"A little dinner, my dear?" Ken said

At the table, he retrieved an envelope and handed it to Tristin. "Happy Valentine's Day."

Tristin pulled out the card inside and laughed in surprise when she saw the picture. "Where did you get this?"

"I got it in the mail two weeks ago. Carrie Snowden found my address and sent it to me"

It was the photograph Carrie had taken of Ken and Tristin on the night they met, up on Nortze's property before the ritual ceremony. Ken had made the card on his computer.

"Oh, Ken, this is really wonderful. How many couples have a picture of themselves right when they met?"

"Not many, I suspect. I guess that makes us special."

Tristin leaned over and kissed Ken on the cheek. "You're special, Ken. And I love you."

"I love you, too, Tristin." They kissed tenderly. He then reached into his inside coat pocket and retrieved a long narrow jewelry box. "And this is something I thought you would enjoy."

"A present? For me?" she swooned. She opened the box and saw the gold tennis bracelet, little charms dangling. "Oh, Ken, it's beautiful," she said, holding it up and clasping it around her left wrist.

"See what the charms are?"

Tristin looked closer. One was a sea otter on its back, eating an abalone. The second was a pair of little gold shovels tied together at the handles, small replicas of the ones they used to dig the hole for the cross that night they met. And the third was a frog.

Tristin got out of her seat and sat on Ken's lap, her arms around his neck. "Your Valentine presents are back at the house, and only one of them is a card, too."

On the road home, Ken called home on his hands-free cell phone to check messages. There was only one—from Gil Nortze—coming through loud and clear on the speaker. "Hey, Ken. Sorry I had to leave things in such a mess. But don't worry—everything will be straightened out tomorrow. Oh, by the by, wish Tristin a Happy Valentine's Day. Maybe she'll give you what she gave me last Valentine's Day."

With a quizzical look on his face, Ken turned to Tristin. Her hands were already over her face, mumbling, "Oh, God!"

Having to tell Ken the story of how, in a moment of financial desperation, she had succumbed to

Nortze's quid pro quo advances prior to him putting in a word to Stu Adams for an opening in his property management firm, Tristin was consumed with guilt. She even had to turn her face to the window when she blurted out, "Just a hand job."

For both of them, it more or less ruined the romance of the moment.

They drove in silence for the next ten minutes. Tristin felt unclean and guilty as hell. Instead of being able to confess, on her own terms and in her own time, she had been made to look deceitful and whorish.

As for Ken, the thought of Tristin jerking off Gil Nortze was almost unbearable. He would not, and could not, imagine the circumstances justifying that act. He was angry at Tristin for hiding something important.

Two imaginations began to spiral into respective abysses of doom and gloom, with thoughts of a common future losing heretofore firm footings.

It was Ken who finally realized that things could quickly get out of control here. He pulled the car over to a wide dirt turnaround, stopped and turned off the ignition and the headlights. It was nearly pitch black inside the car.

"We have to talk, Tristin."

Tristin thought about what she could possibly say to lessen the gravity of the moment, but she couldn't come up with a reply that came close to satisfaction. She said, simply, "I was going to tell you."

Softly, Ken asked, "Then why didn't you?"

She took in a deep breath and blew it out her nostrils. "The time never seemed right."

"So, this was better?"

"No. As a matter of fact, I can't conceive of anything worse." Tristin stared through the windshield into the blackness of the night.

"Well, let's hear it."

Tristin felt her soul being pried out from under her skin. "I was desperate, I suppose. I'd gone through half my savings, and I saw that great job with Stu Adams as something that would bail me out. But from what Gil told me, there was a lot of competition, and all of them female."

Ken wasn't sympathetic. "So whoever gives the best hand job gets the job? Gee, I missed seeing that on your resume."

Tristin didn't rise to the bait. "It wasn't about anyone else, Ken. He wanted me, and only me. It was a power trip. He first wanted to fuck me, but I said no way."

"So you negotiated down to a hand job."

"In so many words, yes. I had two choices. Passing up a golden opportunity, or doing something personally offensive lasting at most three minutes. It took a few drinks to loosen me up, but I made the decision."

"And how do you feel about that decision now?"

"Like a prostitute, of course. Anything for a buck, damn the integrity."

"My dad once said to me, 'Son, you can build a dog house, but it don't make you a carpenter. You can steer a plane, but it don't make you a pilot. But if you suck just one cock, by God you're a cocksucker."

"So, you think I'm a whore?"

"No, just a liar for not telling me. When do you think would have been the right time to tell me you sold out for a job interview?"

Tristin thought about the question—really thought about it. Her eyes began to mist over, and then tears Ken could not see trickled down her cheek. "Realistically? Now that it's out in the open? Probably never. There never would have been a good time."

Prepared for a cop-out answer, the truth was disarming. "That's what I thought, too. At least you're honest enough to admit it."

"I wanted you to think I was a good person, Ken."

"You are."

"I mean ... that I'm not the kind of person who does that all the time."

"You're not."

Tristin's nose began to run, and she sniffled. "How do you know? I could be a serial masturbator or something."

Ken chuckled. "I know because I love you, Tristin. And the woman I know and love did something she knew at the time was wrong but did it anyway. And a year later, she gets busted flat on Valentine's Day of all times. Headline News: Fiancé Feels Let Down—Bye-bye Perfection."

He turned to her, seeing only her silhouette against the window. "Gil Nortze has probably ruined a lot of lives, Tristin, but he's not going to ruin ours, unless we let him. At least if we love each other as much as we say we do."

Tristin reached through the darkness and touched Ken's arm. "I love you so much, Ken."

Ken covered her hand with his, squeezing it firmly. "Let's get some air." He opened his door and stood outside the Bronco, spotting Tristin standing on her side. He walked around the back and joined her near the door. They leaned against it, and Ken took her hand. Offshore, a large rock stood out against the sky. "See that rock?" Ken said, pointing through the side windows.

Tristin turned and saw the dark form. "Uh, huh."

"Well, you and me have to be just like that rock—steadfast against the relentless waves of Gil Nortze. If we crack and split, he wins. If we stand as one, we win. It is our choice." In his best Kung Fu master voice, Ken said, "Choose wisely, grass-hopper."

Tristin threw her arms around Ken's neck and pressed up against him. She kissed him tenderly on the lips, and then she said, "I've made my choice, master. We're going to do this together. And to seal the deal, I'm going to jump your bones right here and right now."

Hey, thanks, Gil. Nice Valentine's Day present.

34 Goldrush

Nortze stared at Margie across the table, an hour into their first game together playing Texas Hold'em. Margie hadn't needed much instruction and was already up $20 in chips. Nortze turned over the River card, a seven of spades.

"I don't think you have it," Nortze said with confidence. He tossed in two $5 chips on the $65 pile. "Raise you ten."

Margie called and laid out her two pocket cards—two sevens.

Nortze tossed his cards in the air in front of him, and the two sixes landed face up on the pile of chips. "Damn, woman. How much are you up now, overall?"

Raking the chips to her side of the table, Margie did the math. "Six hundred and change, Gil."

"Jesus. I should take you back to Vegas with me and stake you a hundred grand. We could split the profits fifty-fifty.

"Seventy-five twenty-five," Margie shot back without thinking.

"Sixty-forty and you've got a deal," Nortze replied. "You really are good at this, Margie."

"Thanks, Gil. Just lucky, I guess."

"No, Margie, it's more than that. I've seen some of the best players in the world, and I know talent when I see it. If you ever learned the actual odds, and betting strategy, you could clean up. You have a natural talent."

Margie shrugged. "Yeah, maybe someday." She glanced at her watch. "We have to make this the last hand, Gil. I've got some people coming over from Salinas Valley."

Nortze lost another $45 on the last hand and called it a night. He drove into Carmel for dinner, most of the time thinking about how he could convince Margie to go partners with him in Las Vegas.

That woman is a fucking gold mine!

*****

Note to John: Just thought I'd fill in some details—especially about Margie—that come into play later. Steven

35 Like Water for Chocolate

The next morning, Friday, at seven o'clock, Ken and Tristin were having coffee at the counter. Ken opened up the Valentine's card from Cheryl. "Hey, take a look at this."

Tristin read card in the shape of a red valentine, handwritten by Cheryl, and she smiled. "How darling." She read aloud the inscription. "To the nicest two people we know and love. Happy Valentine's Day. Love, Cheryl and Bobby."

"She's a sweet kid."

"I guess they've settled into their new surroundings pretty well," Tristin said.

"With Sam and Darcy at the helm, how could they go wrong?" Ken had another thought. "I should give Cheryl a call later when she's home from school."

"Say thanks for me, too."

Tristin showered and dressed and was out of the house by seven-thirty, a long day ahead to catch up on work since she had taken off the day before. Ken kissed her at the door and went for a shower himself.

Ken had been sitting at his computer for an hour when he stood up to stretch. He walked over to the garden window and stared out, hoping to catch a glimpse of Jake the Tern. What he saw instead almost floored him.

Not bothering to don a jacket, Ken ran out the side door and slowed to a jog when he got to his garden, finally stopping at the foot of the slope, eyes panning the scene. "What the fuck?"

The entire slope of rock was covered with up to a foot of chocolate colored mud, its water content now drained into a big puddle at the base of the small brick retaining wall. His herb garden was buried under two feet of muck. Like so many desert sand dunes, a dozen piles of mud stretched all along Ken's side of the green vinyl-coated fence above and back towards Nortze's future garage. The fence was heavily splattered with mud. The piles had slumped down the rocky bank, and water puddles along the base of the bank were six inches deep in places, covering the ice plant and red apple vegetation. His ceramic garden frog was also buried somewhere under the ooze. It was one unholy mess.

Jake the Tern stuck his head out briefly, somehow sensed the hostility in the air, and dove back inside. Ken was beside himself with anger, realizing only now what the call the previous day from Nortze was all about. "Nortze, you sonofabitch!" He turned on his heels and went into the house to put on his warm clothes.

Standing in front of the site trailer with the gate closed and locked, Ken waited impatiently for someone to arrive on the jobsite. He didn't know who had dumped all the mud on his side of the fence, but he knew that Nortze was ultimately responsible, no matter who did it.

The red Lincoln Continental headed slowly down the dirt driveway, now deeply rutted by the rains. It came to a stop and Nortze jumped out, his hands in the air as if he was ready to be handcuffed. "I know, I know, Ken. I tried to warn you. It looks bad, and I'm sorry. Fucking backhoe operator took it upon himself to dump it there. Don't worry, I'll have it all cleaned up in no time."

That little display disarmed Ken temporarily. "What the hell happened, Gil?"

"I had to leave the backhoe guy and laborers here while I went off on some errands, but I told him to keep piling the mud in front of my garage. By that time I got back, he was finished up and already gone." Gil shook his head in mock apology. "I saw what he did, but you weren't home, so I figured I'd catch you this morning and explain."

Ken didn't know whether to believe Nortze or not. "So the guy just took it upon himself to dump all that mud on my side of the fence? Did you see where it all spilled over the slope and down into my garden?"

Feigning ignorance of the damage, Nortze's eyebrows shot up. "Really? How much mud?"

"A lot, Gil. Come and see for yourself."

They walked around the perimeter fence, and Ken said, sarcastically, "And thanks for the heads-up about making it two stories on this side and almost four thousand square feet, not the *little cottage on the bluff* as you called it. It's going to ruin my privacy down there," he added, pointing dismissively.

"Hey, I won't be lookin', if that's what you're worried about. And besides, it was the architect who did that, not me, Ken. He said that the land was too valuable to go with so little square footage. And the bedrock underneath was shallower on this side."

Ken didn't buy any of it.

Nortze reacted with faux alarm at the low piles of mud set ten feet apart next to the fence and all the way to the cliff. "Man, what a mess!"

"No shit, Gil. And look down there," Ken said, pointing down the bluff and into his garden.

Nortze shook his head repeatedly. "What can I say, Ken?"

"I say you call that backhoe company and have them send someone out to clean it up."

Nortze nodded. "I'll see what I can do."

"Yeah, see what you can do." Ken didn't want a confrontation, but he was mad enough to punch Nortze's lights out. Instead, he made his way down the slope perilously close to the drop off into the ocean.

At noon, it began to rain again. A storm swept in from the northwest, and then stalled, circling clockwise around the whole Monterey Bay Peninsula area. In just three hours, the thick outer rain bands dumped ten inches of water on Carmel Highlands—and Nortze's job site, most of it seeming to collect in the newly dug footing trenches..

By 3:30, the skies began to clear. Ken stood at his office window watching the mud from above oozing down the slope and into his garden. He was in a state of despair.

A few minutes later the phone rang, and Ken picked up. "Hello," he said, his thoughts still tuned to the disaster in his back yard.

"Hi, Ken. This is Cheryl."

Ken brightened a bit. "Oh, hi, honey. Hey, Tristin and I were away all day yesterday, so we didn't read your Valentine's card until this morning. Very thoughtful of you, thanks."

"You're welcome. I just got home from school, and I thought about you. Haven't seen you for a while, and I thought that with the storm over, maybe Bobby and I could come down for a quick visit. Bobby should be home soon. We won't stay long because we have to study for tests on Monday."

Ken was about to put her off, but then he figured he could use a little sunshine in his life right about then, and with Nortze gone, at least an accidental meeting wasn't possible. "Yeah, sure, come on down. Tell your mom or dad, though, okay?"

"Okay, we'll be right down."

At the top of Ken's driveway at Spindrift Road, Cheryl tested Bobby's modification to the walkie-talkie. "Okay, Bobby, I'm turning down the volume to its lowest setting."

"Okay, do it," said the voice coming from the speaker.

Cheryl turned the potentiometer button until just before it clicked over to turn off the power. She set the unit on the ground, a makeshift cord and plug attached, along with an in-line transformer, and stepped back about ten feet, keeping her eyes on the red indicator light until she saw it flash three times. "Can you still hear me?" she asked in a normal voice.

The little red light flashed five times, Bobby's pre-arranged affirmative response.

He had bypassed the talk-listen switch so that the second unit remained on listen-only, as in one of those baby monitors parents use when they're elsewhere in the house. He'd figured that out all on his own. He'd also installed a fresh set of special heavy-duty lithium batteries, with enough power to last a couple of hours in listen-only mode if there was no power. "Put it behind that screen in the corner of Ken's office," Bobby had instructed. "There's a wall plug concealed by the screen."

Cheryl had wanted it in the master bedroom—for eavesdropping on potentially intimate moments—but Bobby had wisely scotched that idea, knowing the house layout. There was no place to conceal it in their bedroom, and Connie, the housekeeper, could easily find it if Ken or Tristin didn't stumble on it.

Cheryl scooped up the walkie-talkie and slipped it into the inside pocket of her jacket and headed down to Ken's house.

Before Cheryl arrived, Ken got another call, this time from Greg in San Jose. "You know those sensors you sent up? Well, some of them don't work, I'm afraid. We're trying to isolate the problem, but I may need to talk again if we can't find it."

"I'll be here, Greg. Any time—day or night. Keep me posted." He rang off, but before his mind could get wrapped around what might be the problem with the acoustic sensors, the doorbell rang.

All smiles and full of hugs, Cheryl greeted Ken when he opened the door. She explained that Bobby's absence was due to his not getting home on time. Ken brewed up some hot chocolate, and they talked about what she was doing at school, what he and Tristin had done on Valentine's Day, and other small talk. He mentioned the mess in his garden, and Cheryl insisted she get a look from his office.

With Cheryl staring out into the garden, she commiserated about the damage, and then asked for a second cup of cocoa. When Ken disappeared around the hallway corner, Cheryl seized the opportunity. She went to the southwest corner and pulled back the far right section of decorative Japanese screen, then stooped down and placed the walkie-talkie unit in an upright position on the floor just behind an inward fold. She plugged the cord into the outlet on the south wall, and made sure, as instructed by Bobby, that the unit was against the screen and facing into the room so its microphone could pick up any conversations. She pushed the screen back into place and returned to the garden window, awaiting Ken's return.

After downing her second cup of cocoa, Cheryl said she should be getting back home. She hugged Ken goodbye, even pulling him down for a quick peck on the cheek. "Love ya, bye," she said in earnest, "Say hi to Tristin for me."

Back in his room, Bobby didn't have to wait long for the first real confirmation that his covert spy operation had proven successful. Bobby saw the spikes jump on his computer screen and heard the sound of a ringing telephone in his earphones. The computer's internal link engaged at the first sound coming in, and the hard drive began recording the voice in .wav file format.

"Hi, Connie, it's Ken … .I'm afraid there's been a little mud disaster in my back yard, and I seem to have tracked it all through the house. I've mopped most of it up, but I just wanted to confirm that you're coming tomorrow?" A pause followed, and then, "Thanks, see you at nine."

Cheryl returned twenty minutes later, and she knocked quietly two times on Bobby's door. "Come on in. The coast is clear," Bobby said.

"We got our first hit," Bobby said proudly, slipping off the earphones. "Clear as a bell, though not very interesting stuff. Just Ken talking to Connie about some mud."

"Oh, you should've seen it. It was coming down from the lot above and made a mess of the garden."

Bobby shrugged. "I'm sure there will be more interesting stuff later." He pointed the cursor to the beginning and double-clicked, letting Cheryl hear what Ken had said to Connie.

A second storm that evening pushed its way over the peninsula and down into Carmel Highlands, dumping another four inches of rain. Tristin was delayed in getting home by an hour, as there were several small rockslides partially blocking the Coast Highway.

The rain came in torrents until midnight, but it tapered off throughout the rest of the dark early morning hours. By sunrise the next morning, Friday, it was clear and sunny. When Ken inspected the damage to his garden, he could only shake his head in disbelief. Looking up to the top of the slope, Ken saw that the mud piles had been washed almost completely away by the rain. Not back onto Nortze's lot, but down onto his. A deep cut through the earlier, and somewhat drier mud looked like a mini-Grand Canyon meandering its way down slope, into his garden, and off toward the cliff. Some of the mud had oozed around the east side of Ken's house, blocking access to the garden from that side.

Ken hadn't heard from Nortze yet, and since Ken didn't have his cell phone number (Nortze blocked his own caller ID), Ken couldn't call him. He walked up his driveway and down Nortze's lot to ask the first person showing up to give him Nortze's phone number. Ken didn't know at this point that Nortze had appointed himself the general contractor, nor that Nortze was holed up in Margie's B&B.

It was Nortze himself who arrived in his red Lincoln at 7:30 sharp, a pickup truck full of laborers right behind. Nortze didn't even acknowledge Ken's presence, but rather went back to the pickup truck and started barking orders for the men to men to man the pumps and hoses and get the footings cleaned out ... again.

Scurrying by Ken with not so much as a howdy-do, Ken tried to stop him. "Hey, Gil, I've got a real problem down on my slope."

Nortze held up his hand like a stop sign. "Later, Ken," he said dismissively, "I've got serious problems of my own to deal with right now." He opened the gate and walked quickly toward the utility shed where the pumps and hoses were stashed.

"What's your phone number up here," Ken shouted.

"Can't remember," Nortze called back over his shoulder. "I'll get it for you later."

Ken stood with his hands on his hips, completely frustrated. When he walked past the open gate and looked around, Ken could see Nortze's problem—the rains had filled the footing trenches once again, and the sides of the trenches were now more V-shaped than vertical, meaning a lot more concrete, or side forms, or most likely both before the concrete pour. While Ken didn't exactly feel sorry for Nortze, he knew the man would have his hands full getting rid of all that water and reconstructing the forms.

Sticking around just long enough to ensure that the hoses dumped the water over the cliff and not onto his property, Ken then walked back up the dirt drive and down to his house, not having had the conversation he wanted with Nortze about what was going to be done to clean up his slope and his garden.

When Connie arrived at nine, Ken was in a sour mood. He closed the door to his office and sat staring at his computer screen, but his mind was elsewhere. He finally decided to wait a day or two until Nortze could pull things together up on the site before approaching the man again.

Thinking that he wanted that mess cleared out before it dried solid, Ken decided to hire a few laborers and send Nortze the bill. He then got to thinking about all the time Nortze was spending on the job site, and Ken hadn't seen anyone who remotely resembled a contractor, much less a general.

And that's when it hit him hard: *Gil Nortze is now owner-builder—his own general contractor.* Ken slumped forward in his chair, his elbows banging on the desk with his chin planting itself firmly into his palms. *Oh, man, what have I done to deserve this?*

Since he couldn't concentrate on work anyway, Ken called the lumberyard in Carmel and asked if there were any laborers outside the gate waiting for work. "At least ten," said the man. Ken grabbed his jacket and told Connie he was off to pick up a few laborers to help clean out the mess in his yard, and also that the floors could be even worse by tomorrow, Saturday. "I may need you tomorrow, too, Connie. Golden time."

Connie shouted, "You got it, mister!" With two people now living in the house, there was much more work to be done. She realized it would take tomorrow to finish up. And the extra money would come in handy. Twenty minutes later, Connie took a break. She poured herself a cup of coffee and went into Ken's office and sat down to make a phone call. Spotting Cheryl's valentine card on Ken's desk, she picked it up and read it.

Like little bells going off inside her head, Connie saw something in her mind's eye that others had only speculated about: Cheryl had a deep crush on Ken Easton. For most young teenage girls, it wasn't that extraordinary.

Connie had been informed weeks before by Ken of Bobby and Cheryl's adoption situation and the ground rules agreed to by all parties, asking her to let him know if either one of the kids showed up unannounced while he was out. Connie didn't need a hammer to her head to understand everyone's concern, especially about Cheryl's relationship with Ken. Connie also understood very well that these things in a young girl's head didn't disappear overnight, and she noticed how much time and effort had gone into the Valentine card. She pushed the speakerphone button and dialed the number for her friend, Stacy, a stay-at-home mom.

"Hello?"

"Hey, Stace, what's up?"

"Kids, kids, kids," she said happily. "What's up with you?"

"Oh, just taking a little break here at Ken Easton's house. And looking at a Valentine card from a neighbor who has a crush on him."

"She's not the only one. God, is that man gorgeous, or what?"

"You got that right. If he wasn't engaged to Tristin, and if I wasn't married ... "

Stacy's laughter was quickly followed by, "Not if I get to him first."

"Well, fortunately, he has me around to run interference for him. Little Cheryl is going to have to learn at some point that she should stick to boys her own age. It looks like I'm going to be the one who has to get that through her head."

"Yes, Lucy was stuck on the older boy next door, but she has *a little friend now.* The two are practically inseparable."

Connie and Stacy got off onto other subjects, ending with Stacy inviting Connie and her husband, Randy, over for dinner the next night, Saturday. "Looks like I may have to come back here tomorrow, but it won't take all day. Sure, around seven?"

"See you both at seven," said Stacy, and they rang off.

When Ken returned home with the laborers in tow, he set them to clearing out the mud with shovels and brooms. "Over the cliff, right there," he instructed, as close to the south slope as possible and away from his diving perch.

Back inside his office, Ken saw the red light flashing on his answering machine. He pressed play and listened to the message.

"Ken, Greg here. We have a problem, buddy. There's still some kind of glitch in six of the ten acoustic pickups from DynoElectric, and the big cheese from FEMA who's overseeing the project is coming first thing Monday for that conference. Can you get your butt up here ASAP so we can get them working? Call me as soon as you get this message."

Ken speed-dialed Greg's number. "Hey, Ken," Greg said.

"No go, huh? Dyno sent them FedEx from back east, and I checked them out myself before mailing them up. It has to be something pretty basic."

"Only you would know what that means, Ken. Maybe something got damaged in shipping. Can you *ple-a-s-e* fly up tomorrow and take a look?"

"Boy, does this come at a bad time. I've got workers here cleaning up the mud around my house, and I can see already I'm going to have to have them back. I was hoping tomorrow."

"I'm really sorry, Ken, but maybe the mud can wait until Monday."

"Guess it'll have to."

Ken had no other options, but he was disappointed at having to make the trip, even if it was for just a day. "I'll be up on the first flight out tomorrow morning, Greg, and take a cab to your office."

"Thanks, Ken. We all appreciate that. Hey, why don't you bring Tristin? We can all have lunch—on me."

Ken thought about it and liked the idea of showing Tristin around San Jose once the problem with the acoustic devices, obvious to Ken a minor one, was solved. "I'm sure she'd love it. I'll call her and see if she can make it."

Ken rang off with Greg and called Tristin on her cell phone, asking if she would like to go up to San Jose for the day on Saturday. "Sure, sounds fun. I'll be home by five this afternoon at the latest. Want me to pick something up?"

"No, Connie made some great meatless stew. It'll stick to your ribs."

"Mmmm. Looking forward to it."

The four Hispanic laborers worked all day on clearing the mud—and locating his ceramic frog—but there was so much of it that Ken had them stop work at three o'clock, asking in makeshift Spanish if they could come back on Monday. They all agreed. He paid them and agreed to pick them up at the lumberyard at seven o'clock Monday morning.

36 The Bitch

Later that evening after dinner, Bobby poked his head past Cheryl's open door, and whispered loudly, "You gotta come and hear this!"

Cheryl put aside her homework and followed Bobby into his room, where he closed the door behind them. "I was playing back the conversations in Ken's office, and Connie's onto you, Cheryl."

"What do you mean? I like Connie, and we get along great."

Bobby shrugged. "You'd better listen for yourself then." He handed her the headset and clicked the playback icon.

Cheryl didn't seem to think much of it for a brief moment, but as the conversation between Connie and Stacy progressed, she opened her eyes wide, then wider and wider, and finally her mouth dropped open. "That bitch!" she said in an angered whisper, switching 180-degrees in her attitude towards Connie. "Who does she think she is?"

Bobby motioned for her to give back the headset, and Cheryl removed and handed them back. "She's going to be a problem, Cheryl, but I think that with Ken and Tristin away tomorrow, I can come up with something."

Based on all the conversations picked up by the walkie-talkie and recorded onto his 40-gigabyte hard drive, Bobby sat for two hours thinking up a plan. He didn't know at what point in time it would be executed—days or weeks, perhaps. But knowing that Connie would probably be alone in the house the next day, Bobby tried to make that work into the schedule.

Later that evening, Bobby was at the dinner table when his parents decided on a late-morning movie date—the first *Pink Panther* with Peter Sellers. Sam wouldn't be going on duty until three p.m. the next day, Saturday, and he said he'd go pick it up from Blockbuster when it opened at ten.

And that was it—sooner rather than later. Depending on his parents' schedule, Bobby finally settled on the idea of showing up at Ken's sometime around noon.

*****

Note to John: I didn't realize how long it takes to write things out like this, as opposed to a more formal report detailing little pieces of evidence scattered all over the map. I see already I'm not going to make the earlier "dozen more sections" estimate, but there's so much more to tell. A dozen more, tops. Sorry it's taking so long. But I'm using up my accrued vacation time to work on this, so it is, like they say, on my dime. Steven

37 Natural Born Killers

Ken and Tristin left the house at six a.m. Saturday morning for the flight out of Carmel to San Jose. Connie showed up at ten and started with laundry. She had at least three hours of work to do, but she decided on leaving the floors as the last task before she left.

At noon, Connie was in the master bedroom making up the bed and heard the doorbell over the stereo music. She walked down the hall and opened the front door, seeing both Bobby and Cheryl Wynette on the porch. "Hi, kids. What's up?" She noticed Bobby's now-dark brown hair. "Did you dye your hair, Bobby?"

"Yeah," Bobby said matter-of-factly. "I needed a change."

"Looks nice," she said, adding, "Oh, Ken and Tristin aren't home."

Bobby stepped forward in his old jeans and faded red and white flannel shirt, backpack on his back and holding up an electronic capacitor with wires dangling off it. "Yeah, I know. Ken said I could come down and use his soldering gun in the garage while he and Tristin are up in San Jose today."

"Oh," Connie said, convinced by the specificity of it all. She pulled down her navy blue sweatshirt over her beltline against the chilly air swirling in through the door. "Okay, I'll open the garage. But you can't come in the house and track any more mud in, sorry."

"No problem," Cheryl beamed. "We'll stay in the garage."

Bobby set both his backpack and the capacitor on the workbench and pulled open a drawer, taking out Ken's soldering gun and a roll of flux-core solder. He plugged the gun into the outlet and leaned against the bench. "We wait."

"How long?" Cheryl asked.

"Oh, a few minutes."

With the soldering gun warmed up, Bobby soldered a third, and totally unnecessary wire onto the two lead-wire capacitor. "That should about do it," he said with a grin, holding it up for Cheryl's inspection.

Connie came through the door into the garage, an empty laundry basket in hand. "How's it coming?" she asked.

Bobby showed her the capacitor. "Almost done, thanks."

"You sure are good with that electronic stuff, aren't you? Ken says so, anyway."

Bobby shrugged with mock embarrassment. "Yeah, I guess." He turned his back so Connie couldn't see his face, and he winked at Cheryl, giving her the signal."

"Connie?" Cheryl began, "Can we go out front and look at the ocean before we go."

"Sure, but stay away from the edge. With all the rains and mud, it's slippery out there."

With a little more confidence than usual, Bobby replied, "Yeah, we know."

Connie set the laundry basket down and went back into the hallway, closing the door behind her. Bobby put the soldering equipment back into the drawer and closed it. Leaving the backpack on the workbench, Bobby then motioned for Cheryl to follow. "Let's go around by way of the Jacuzzi."

Out front near the cliffs, they walked slowly toward the south end, keeping well back from the cliff. The waves were coming in sets of five, the biggest ones ten to twelve feet high and breaking just a hundred feet offshore at the start of the funnel-shaped submarine canyon. Bobby stole furtive glances back towards the house, finally spotting Connie in the kitchen at the sink. He kept his eyes fixed until she lifted her head and spotted him. Bobby waved, and Connie waved back.

Connie stood at the sink rinsing off silverware to put in the dishwasher as Cheryl burst through the kitchen door, screaming and crying at the top of her lungs, "Connie, come quick!" Cheryl grabbed Connie by the wrist and pulled her toward the door. "It's Bobby ... he slipped down the cliff and can't get back up." She was in near hysteria.

Outside the kitchen door, Cheryl sobbed and pointed to the south end of the bluff. "Over there." Connie bolted across the cement porch, out onto the path of crushed rock and stones, and ran full speed, Cheryl right behind. Lindy's ears perked up and she followed, too.

Connie slowed down when she got to the end of the path. The laborers had hosed away all the mud in that area the day before, and the rocky ground was still wet. Connie stepped lightly up to the first incline, a 45-degree slope about three feet long. Bobby was leaning flat against the rocks below it, his head and shoulders visible, and one side of his face smeared by contact with the rocks. He was panic-stricken. "Help," he cried weakly, "I can't—" He slipped a few inches down and stopped.

"Don't move, Bobby," Connie called out, inching closer to the edge of the cliff. She kneeled down at the start of the incline and reached her left hand out, just inches from Bobby's. "Take my hand, Bobby."

"I can't let go," he cried.

Cheryl cried out weakly from behind, "Bobby, don't fall."

Connie inched down the cliff on her knees as far as she could go, and she extended her left hand.

She was almost at the tipping point. "You've got to take my hand, Bobby. It's the only way."

At that point, Bobby was standing on a ledge with his knees bent and leaning quite comfortably against the inward sloping rock. He quickly straightened his legs a good six inches higher, grabbed Connie firmly by the left wrist with both hands, and pulled hard. Connie lunged forward, gasping, and when she was clearly past the point of no return, he let go his grip, Connie flying over him.

Connie tumbled forward in mid-air. She squealed but did not scream. From forty feet above the water, her forward and downward momentum caused her to do a half-somersault, and she hit the swirling, foaming water on her back. The surface tension of the swirling water was low, so she landed more with a plop than a splat, but it still knocked the wind out of her. The 57° water must have been quite a shock to her system, too. With no air in her lungs, she sank and disappeared below the surface for a few long moments.

Bobby and Cheryl watched for ten seconds until Connie's head finally bobbed up. She gasped for breath, only to have the next wave's four-foot high wall of whitewater roll over her. When she came up the second time, she was further from the cliff than when she first went in, and fighting to catch her breath against the cold water.

There was only one way out. Having watched Ken bodysurf on two occasions, Connie tried in vain to swim away from the cliff and around the headland to the north but she was already weakened by the fall that knocked the wind out of her lungs. With her jeans and sweatshirt soaked and heavy, the time underwater with no air, and a near-freezing ocean sapping her strength, her arms were not pulling hard enough to make headway against the strong current. The strong undertow leading down to the offshore submarine canyon sucked her toward the oncoming waves. She was facing the cliff and didn't see—maybe didn't even hear—the five-foot wall of whitewater that rolled over her.

Bobby and Cheryl kept their eyes on Connie's last position, and they waited for her to surface. After five minutes, they both knew that she was gone.

Leaning against the inward-sloped rock face, Bobby was standing firm on the rock ledge. He began his climb up to the top by first moving up to the right along a six-inch wide ledge, and used the same firm handholds and footholds going up as in climbing down.

Once safely at the top of the bluff, Bobby turned to Cheryl and saw her tear-streaked face, quickly drying. "Well, sis," he said, only slightly out of breath, "it looks like you won't have to find *a little friend* your own age after all."

The pair then made their way back along the path and around the Jacuzzi towards the garage, leaving Lindy seated on her haunches and staring down into the ocean. Inside the garage, Bobby unhooked the backpack straps and pulled out a clean shirt, jeans, and sneakers. He made Cheryl turn around while he dressed and tied his shoes.

"Wait outside the garage," Bobby ordered, and Cheryl complied. He pushed the button on the inside wall and ran out under sectional door as it closed, making the little hop over the safety sensor beam, that if broken would stop the door from closing.

On the walk up the driveway, Bobby checked his watch: 12:30. They had been in and out in less than half an hour. Keeping to the far left of the driveway, the two kids walked stooped over for a short time near the mailbox so as not to be spotted by two Hispanic workers busily shoveling mud inside the steel I-beam pit in the middle of the foundation. The two laborers had been working in the pit since Bobby and Cheryl had hurried past that exposed part of Ken's driveway thirty minutes before. Even if the two kids had been spotted—then or later—Bobby already had his answers ready for anyone who might inquire.

Bobby and Cheryl reached the top of Spindrift Road and hurried to the far side of the Coast Highway, continuing up the road on the far side. No cars had come by. They then took the long route home through the hilly backstreets towards the north, having to cross only one ravine in the process.

At the bottom of the ravine, Bobby opened his backpack and removed his dirty jeans and flannel shirt, and lastly his oldest pair of sneakers. With his hands, he dug a hole and put the clothes and shoes into it, covering it all with dirt and mud. He found a heavy rock and placed a rock on top.

Walking up the other side of the ravine, Bobby turned to Cheryl, saying, "I hope Mom made something for lunch. I'm starving."

38 Without a Trace

Ken and Tristin arrived home just after sunset, and Ken was surprised to see Connie's car in front of the closed garage. "She must be working overtime," he said to Tristin. He opened the garaged door with the remote and drove inside.

Inside the hallway, Ken first noticed that the stereo was on and playing classic rock, Connie's favorite. He called Connie's name repeatedly as he walked towards the master bedroom. Tristin headed towards the kitchen, wondering why Lindy had not been at the door to the garage to greet her.

After checking the master bathroom, Ken stood at the sliding glass door, searching the spa area through the glass and past the privacy lattice.

As Ken came back into the kitchen, Tristin pointed to the open kitchen door. "She left the door wide open, and the water is still running in the sink." Ken walked to the sink and noticed a knife and fork sticking up above the rubber protector of the garbage disposal.

"Oh, look, Ken," Tristin said, pointing to the stool tucked under the countertop. "There's her purse, too, so she has to be around somewhere." Ken turned off the faucet and removed the silverware from the garbage disposal. He saw no marks on them, as would have been the case if the disposal had been running at the time.

Walking down the hallway and checking both rooms, Ken entered his office. He checked his answering machine, showing a single call had come in, and pressed the playback button. After the date and time stamp, "Saturday, 1:16 p.m.," there followed a cryptic, muffled message. "Habla Espanol?" There was a two-second pause, then, "Trabajo manana?" This was followed by another pause, and then the dial tone sounded.

Ken recalled his talk with the workers, but they had all agreed to come back Monday, not Sunday. Also, he hadn't given them his phone number. Having no clue as to what the message was about, he walked back towards the kitchen very perplexed.

It was really very simple. The call had been made at the pay phone at the lumberyard—by a normal looking teenaged boy with dark brown hair on a busy afternoon following a rainstorm, when everyone was too preoccupied to taken any notice. Hispanic laborers at the yard had numbered more than a dozen. Darcy had driven Bobby to the lumberyard on the pretext of buying a pre-fab shelf for his CDs and DVDs, staying in the car and waiting for the weather report at 1:15 on the radio.

Inside, Bobby had the small shelf in his hand as he made the call to Ken's answering machine, using his fingers over the mouthpiece to muffle his lowered and near-whispered voice. Bobby had used only four Spanish words: "Habla Espanol" and "Trabajo manana." Bobby figured his little misdirection would throw anyone off his own scent. He then walked calmly over to the register, paid cash for the wood shelf and was back in the car in minutes. "Thanks, Mom," he said. "This should work out great."

Back home, Bobby had monitored his listening device in Ken's office for the rest of the afternoon. He even heard his own Spanish words on Ken's answering machine when Ken played it back.

Ken walked back to the kitchen and out through the door to the porch, where Tristin stood scanning the bluff. "I'll check around," Ken said.

"By the looks of that roach on her purse, she could be sitting somewhere stoned out of her mind."

Ken turned with a puzzled look on his face. "What?"

Tristin led Ken back inside and pointed to the open leather purse on the stool, a marijuana joint sitting on top of the fold.

With surprise, Ken said, "I didn't know she got loaded."

"Well, some people do try to keep it a secret from their employers, Ken."

"Yeah, I guess so." Ken then suggested that Tristin search every room in the house, including the closets, while he did a thorough search outside.

Once outside on the lawn, he listened to the waves breaking against the cliffs. "Connie!" he called loudly. He walked to the north end of the bluff calling her name, and then turned around and walked toward he south end, again shouting, "Connie! Connie, where the hell are you?"

At the far southern end of the bluff, Ken spotted Lindy on her haunches, staring down to the ocean below. Ken felt a strong, eerie feeling sweep over him. It gripped him by the gut, and his head got lighter as some of the blood rushed down toward his heart. He stopped and petted Lindy's head, staring down over the cliff into the pounding surf and still-churning sea.

"You see something down there, girl?" he asked, still gripped by that eerie feeling. "Connie!" he shouted, "Can you hear me?" Hearing nothing, Ken stepped back and shook off the light-headedness but not his suspicion that Connie had met some sort of untimely death at or near this very spot.

He wanted a better look down the cliff, so he picked his way carefully across the sloping rock face that curved around to the south towards his property line, twenty feet away. Making sure of his footing, he went as far as he could safely go in the quickly diminishing light, and searched down the rocks, hoping to spot something that would offer up a clue. He saw only the exposed cliff face and the whitewater crashing hard against it. He could feel the vibration under foot every time a wave hit the cliff.

Ken spotted Tristin jogging towards him on the grass, a phone in her hand, and she gestured that he had a phone call. He made his way carefully back along the rocks, hoping all the way that it was Connie with a simple story of how she had walked home because her car wouldn't start, or someone had picked her up and she'd forgotten her purse. As Tristin got closer, however, the concerned look on her face turned his fervent hope into a prayer.

Lindy was still sitting in the same spot but now looking up to Tristin. "It's Connie's husband, Randy." Tristin covered the microphone with her hand, saying softly, "Connie was supposed to be home hours ago—they are going to a dinner party in less than an hour." She handed Ken the phone and reached down and petted Lindy's head.

Ken stiffened as he took the phone. "Hi, Randy. No, I'm sorry, I can't find her anywhere. Her purse is here, and so is her car … I can't imagine where she would go … yes, I just checked outside, but I'm going to do a thorough search before it gets dark … Did you call your friend where you two were going for dinner? … Uh huh … Uh huh … Yeah, c'mon down if you want."

The look on Ken's face when he handed the phone back to Tristin told her something was very wrong. Ken shook his head, thinking, and didn't utter a word for a long time. Finally, he said, "Lindy's been staring down into the water the whole time we've been here." Looking down over the cliff, Ken added, "I have a bad feeling about this."

By the time Randy arrived, Ken had checked every inch of the property, spending a lot of time where Lindy had sat at the southern end of the bluff and where that eerie feeling had come over him. Tristin had taken the phone with her and re-checked every room and closet in the house.

Randy was visibly upset, as Connie had not done anything close to this before. Ken sat Randy down on a stool at the counter with a cup of cof-fee and asked all the obvious questions again. After, he then reached down and picked up Connie's open purse, pointing out to Randy the roach on the folded leather.

Randy stared at the roach. "Well, she told me she never gets high when she's at your house, afraid you'll smell the smoke and fire her. Maybe today she made an exception."

"Jesus, I wouldn't fire her for that," Ken re-sponded defensively. He hadn't smelled anything funny when he came in the house.

"Yeah, I know that." Randy stared out the liv-ing room window towards the ocean, coming to grips for the first time that Connie had somehow fallen over the cliff. His voice wavered with emotion. "But she never gets crazy high, you know. Just a toke or two sometimes."

Ken saw where Randy's moist eyes were fixed, and empathizing with the emotion behind them, he recalled his own sick feeling earlier out on the bluff. The memory of Lindy staring down over the cliff then locked in his brain. Ken took in a deep breath, forcing himself to broach the subject. "Randy, I think we should call the police."

The Monterey County Sheriff dispatcher was, as with most missing person reports, reticent about sending an officer to investigate this early in the timeline. But after Ken summarized the situation—in his office and with the door closed—the dispatcher said he would try to get someone down, but he didn't say when. After hanging up, Ken dialed up Sam Wynette. Darcy answered the phone, and Ken asked to speak with Sam.

"Hey, Ken. What's up?"

"Got a missing person down here, Sam. It's my housekeeper, Connie. I called nine-one-one, but the sheriff may take awhile in getting here. I know this isn't your area of expertise, but we can't for the life of us figure out what happened to her." Ken then summarized once again the situation as he saw it, ending with, "I was wondering if maybe you could come down—if you're not busy—and at least ask the right questions."

"Sit tight, and don't touch or move anything. Be down in ten minutes," Sam replied.

Bobby Wynette sat at his computer, headset in place, having heard the one-way conversation in Ken's office. It was all going according to plan. He removed the headphones but left the program running and ready to record any and all future conversations.

*****

Note to John: Some of the above is my own speculation, but it all makes sense, even considering the limited information available to Sam and the two sheriff's investigators at the time. Of course, when the clothes were finally discovered, it was too late to put in any meaningful report. Instead of pasting their report verbatim into this work, I took the liberty of spreading it out in dramatic form. Steven

39 Dog Day Afternoon

By ten o'clock Sunday morning, the Easton property was abuzz with activity, both inside and outside the house. Inside, sheriff's investigators were busy dusting for fingerprints, having already taken exemplars, or reference prints, from Ken, Tristin, and Randy. And since Sam had been in the house, too, his prints were taken.

It was Sam who, on his own, drove home to bring Bobby and Cheryl down to have their fingerprints taken by the man from the crime lab. On the short trip down to Ken's house, Sam briefed the kids on what to expect, and warned them about touching anything or getting in the way of the investigation.

Bobby and Cheryl both said they hadn't seen Connie in a couple of weeks, and Cheryl offered that she had stopped down at Ken's house on Friday afternoon, at Ken's invitation, to thank her for the Valentine's Day card and talk briefly "about regular stuff," as she phrased it.

Immediately after the kids' exemplar prints were taken, Sam whisked the kids off and dropped them at home. Sam turned the car around and returned to Ken's house. At Ken's mailbox, Sam spotted the search and rescue helicopter just at bluff height to the north the headland, a hundred yards from the cliff, making its way slowly to the south. Two helmeted crewmembers sat cross-legged at the open portside bay door and searched the sea and the base of the cliff below Ken's property.

At noon, the two-man investigative team—Detectives Tony Sanchez and Carey Waxman, both in their mid-thirties—told Ken they were going into his office for a private conference. Randy, Ken and Tristin all sat in the living room, silent.

Sanchez was tall and lanky and of Hispanic descent; Waxman was shorter but almost barrel-chested, mainly due to the fact that he worked out in the gym every day and lifted weights. Waxman closed the door behind them and they took up seats in Ken's office, Sanchez in Ken's desk chair, and Waxman on the easy chair next to the floor lamp.

"So, whaddya think so far, Carey?" Sanchez was the senior man and usually was the one to ask for his junior partner's analysis before providing an opinion of his own. They shot out ideas, possible connections, and questions to check validity.

"It's a puzzler, Tony, that's for sure," Waxman began. "As far as the timeline goes, she left her house around a quarter to ten, arriving here about ten. She did all the laundry but not the floors. She was in the kitchen cleaning up. Since her husband said she expected to be home by two o'clock at the latest, and with the work left to be done, that limits it to between noon and one, maybe a little later. No signs of forced entry, no obvious struggle, nothing stolen. She left the music on, the water running, and the dishwasher door open. A marijuana roach on the top of, rather than inside, her purse—like she could have taken a few hits. A kitchen door to the bluff side of the house left open. No detectable footprints on the rock path or on the rocky bluff to give away the number or size of potential perpetrators. And finally, a cryptic phone message in Spanish left on Easton's answering machine."

Sanchez thought for a moment. "And don't forget the dog staring down at the ocean." It was not said in jest.

"Yeah, that, too." Waxman thought about it a moment. "The dog didn't run inside to greet them as usual when they got home, but stayed out on the bluff."

Sanchez nodded. "That's what I thought, too. It looks like something—or someone—got Connie to go outside in a hurry, and she may have gotten too close to the cliff and gone over."

"Like someone calling her from outside? Someone calling for help?"

"Not from the south end of the bluff, no. They would have had to shout pretty loud for Connie to hear anything from that far away and over those crashing waves. Unless the kitchen door was already wide open. Or someone shouted loud enough through the windows that Connie heard and responded."

"The wind was blowing in off the ocean, but from the northwest," Waxman offered, and he stood up and began to pace, "That would have been a pretty cold, stiff breeze coming through the kitchen door. I sure wouldn't be leaving it open, especially if I'm cleaning up."

"Yep, that's true," Sanchez said, "But a cry for help—or some of it, anyway—could have carried back towards the house, even from the south end of the bluff."

Waxman stared out the west window, thinking out loud. "A boat blowing its horn? Maybe blowing it repeatedly, like an SOS or something. A boat lost an engine, got too close to the cliff, or someone had gone overboard. But from her view out the kitchen window, Connie couldn't have seen

anything within a hundred yards from the cliff."
Waxman paced some more while he threw out
ideas. "Connie saw or heard something or someone on the bluff. She ran down to the south end,
got too close to the edge, and slipped over."

"As for a boat in distress, no word of any Coast
Guard activity. If the boat had broken up, the guys
in the rescue helicopter would have seen that by
now." Sanchez then echoed Waxman, also thinking out loud. "Slipped over? Maybe there's blood
or tissue on the rocks. Have the lab man, um ...
what's his name again?"

"Stoeffer. Alex Stoeffer—he's new."

"Right—Alex," Sanchez said. "Ask Alex if he
can go over the edge down at the south end where
the dog was and see if he can find anything."

"He's going to need a harness."

"So, let's locate a harness and rig him up,"
Sanchez concluded, "It's about all we have to go
on at this point."

Alex Stoeffer wasn't so sure about rappelling
even a few feet down that forty-foot cliff. He
wasn't one afraid of heights, per se, just of falling
into that churning ocean below. "I can't swim,"
he said as Sam Wynette, Sanchez and Waxman
tested and retested his harness.

"Don't worry," Sanchez chided, "The fall alone
will probably kill you."

"That's a comfort," Stoeffer replied, deadpan.

Joe Sanborn from the Monterrey County
Sheriff's Rescue Team had hammered the three-

point piton belay securely into the cracks of the solid rock. Sanborn and Sam Wynette held the climbing rope hooked at one end to a common rope between the pitons, and the other to Stoeffer's seat harness. A plastic spray bottle dangled on his right side, and a battery-powered fluorescent light on his right side.

The 27-year old crime lab technician and father of two young boys bravely stepped backward down the rocks well to the south and away from the area Sanchez and Waxman had agreed was the logical place for Connie to have slipped or fallen. They referred to the two-foot by three-foot area of 45-degree sloped rock as "the slip and fall area." The solid rock was moist but not wet, as it had mostly dried out now. Ken had told the investigators that he had personally hosed off the rocks 43 hours before, after the laborers had already gotten rid of most of the mud.

Keeping well to the south of the slip-and-fall area, there were several good footholds on Stoeffer's slow descent—the same ones Bobby had used. Once situated, Stoeffer held up his fist to stop letting out the rope. He then carefully moved across to his left, again standing on the same ledge Bobby had stood on. The rock sloped inward at this point, and it was easy to stand with his knees propping him up against the rock face without rope assistance. Stoeffer combed every inch of rock with his eyes.

Ken had done a good job washing almost all of the mud off the rock surface down the rock about

six feet from the top. Stoeffer removed a hand magnifying glass from his right breast pocked and
scanned the rocks carefully from the top down, looking for an obvious smear of blood or a chunk of skin.

He took the spray bottle—filled with fluores-
cein dye to detect specific blood proteins—and
pumped the sprayer repeatedly. He covered a two-
foot wide by four-foot long area of the rock to his
left, half below the start of the 45-degree slope up
to the top, the other half more steeply sloped below it. If there were so much as a single tiny drop
of dried blood on the rock surface in the slip-and-
fall area, the fluorescent light would make it
visible. He shined the light on the area, panning
slowly and then zigzagging down. Nothing.

After five minutes of checking closely, Stoeffer
blinked his eyes and shook his head, saying,
"Don't see a thing yet, guys." Continuing on,
Stoeffer then spotted something. He positioned the
magnifier to get the most he could out of it, and
peered closely. Removing his sterile package of
tweezers from his left breast pocket, he unwrapped
them and carefully picked off several fibers
clumped together on a tiny piece of protruding
rock. When Bobby had feigned slipping a few
inches down the cliff, that little rock had hooked
a few white fibers from his flannel shirt.

"What is it?" Sanchez shouted down against the
sound of the waves.

"Maybe nothing," Stoeffer shouted back up. "A
few light colored fibers hung up on the rock." He

reached back into the same breast pocket and pulled out a small sterile plastic bag, slipping the fibers inside it from the end of the tweezers. He placed the tweezers into the bag with the points up and stuck the bag in his breast left pocked. Stoeffer then resumed his search with the magnifying glass, going further down the cliff in the same fall line until it dropped off to near vertical. "Okay, that's it," he shouted up.

"Haul him up," Sanchez ordered.

At the top, Stoeffer pulled out the plastic bag and held it up to the light. Sam stepped in closer, looking but saying nothing. He was there to provide assistance, not to butt in. To Sam Wynette, the tiny fibers were barely visible inside the little bag.

Joe Sanborn stepped forward. "You need to go back down for any reason?"

Shaking his head vigorously, Stoeffer said, "No, you can pack up your gear."

Stoeffer then opined to Sanchez that the fibers could be white or off white. "I'll take a look at them under the microscope when I get back to the lab." He turned to Sanchez. "Do we know what she was wearing?"

"Blue jeans … an old navy blue sweatshirt." The helicopter search and rescue team also had that information.

Stoeffer held the bag close up for inspection, and used his magnifying glass. "These fibers aren't blue, I can see that."

"Maybe a white or cream-colored sock?" Waxman offered.

Stoeffer shrugged. "Yeah, maybe. But for someone slipping down the cliff, it was pretty light contact with the rocks. I expected to see more fibers, even a sole streak from a shoe, if not some actual skin or blood."

Waxman looked out to sea. "Let's take a walk," he said to his partner. The two detectives ambled slowly north together along the bluff, Waxman the first to offer his thoughts. "The divers will be here soon to take a look down around the base of the cliff. Damn, maybe she just leaned out too far while looking down, and she fell forward instead of backwards."

"Could be," Sanchez said, "Although, once someone realizes they're going over, it's instinctive to get to ground in a hurry and try to grab something—anything."

Waxman shrugged. "Unless she dived off on purpose."

"Say what? Why the hell would she do that?" Sanchez asked, "Her husband said she wasn't that good a swimmer."

"Someone down below in the water," said Waxman, still looking out the window. "A kid maybe."

Sanchez scoffed at the idea. "You're a good swimmer, Carey. Would you dive forty feet off that cliff to save anyone but your own kid?"

"No, I guess not. So we can eliminate her going over on purpose."

Sanchez scratched his head, reviewing aloud what they had so far. "Connie's at the kitchen sink doing dishes, music playing on the stereo. She goes outside and takes a few hits off the joint and comes back in, closing the door behind her against the cold wind. She places the roach on her purse, thinking she'll have another hit or two later. While doing the dishes, she sees or hears someone—or something—so startling that she drops the silverware, two pieces going down through the rubber into the garbage disposal. She leaves the water running and runs out the door, leaving the door open. She runs down to the south end of the bluff, the dog behind her. Someone is just over the edge of the cliff, needing help. She tries to help, but she somehow lunges over the cliff without slipping on the rocks."

"I see only one problem with that, Tony." Waxman stopped and put his fingers to his lips for silence. A moment later, he said, "I can barely hear myself think out here with those waves crashing and beating against the cliff. I sincerely doubt if anyone's voice down below that ledge could carry up and over, all the way to the kitchen and through the closed kitchen door."

"A high-pitch scream ... maybe that would carry. A kid or a woman."

"It's just too damned far, Carey, and the ocean waves are too loud." Sanchez glanced back toward the house. "She had to have run out that door with some clue as to some emergency unfolding.

Otherwise, why drop the silverware and leave the water running."

"Maybe someone was stuck down just over the edge of the cliff where Alex found the fibers. Of course, that would mean two people—a second person to bring assistance to the one stuck down over the edge."

"Those fibers could have been from one of the laborers," Sanchez said, "washed over the edge and hung up on the rock. If Stoeffer finds dirt or mud on it, that's probably the explanation. If it's clean, though, that could be something." Sanchez couldn't get the notion of a single person in trouble summoning help by merely calling out, at least from that far away. He then had an idea based on Waxman's last comment. "Okay, you go back to the slip-and-fall area, and crouch down low and call for help back this way. Scream like a girl. I'll go in the kitchen and stand in front of the sink. I can't see you from there, so I'll signal from the kitchen door."

"Sounds like it's worth a try," Waxman said. He began warming up the high-end range of his vocal cords. "And get Mr. Easton to turn on the stereo station and approximate the volume when he came into the house."

"Will do," Sanchez called back. He entered the house told Ken and the others in the living room about the little test he and Sanchez were going to conduct. He asked Ken, "Would you mind turning it on and approximating the same volume?"

Ken went to his office and turned on the stereo, already tuned to the classical station. He adjusted the volume to what he heard when he came home, and then returned to the living room with Sam, Tristin, and Randy.

When Waxman reached the south end of the bluff and looked down, he saw the Sheriff's dive boat just off the cliffs fighting both the waves and the currents, with two scuba divers already in the water. Waxman picked up the hand signal from Sanchez and crouched down close to the edge of the cliff, waiting a moment before shrieking at the top of his lungs towards the house, "Help, help!"

With his eyes focused on the bottom of the sink, and the faucet running, Sanchez heard nothing but the music station and an occasional rumbling of a wave breaking against the cliff. He felt it underfoot, too. Looking up and to the south, Sanchez could not see Waxman, and he strained to hear his voice. Nothing. He then stepped outside and spotted Waxman, giving him hand signals to continue yelling. With the door open, he again took up his position at the sink, water still running, and listened. Still nothing but the background music.

Sanchez turned off the water and walked outside onto the grass, signaling Waxman to join him.

"I couldn't hear you at all, Carey. The music, even at that low volume, pretty much masked everything else but the sound of the waves. Besides, you were shouting from on top of the cliff.

If someone was down over the edge, any sounds would have been even fainter."

"So, Tony, where does that leave us?" Waxman asked hoarsely, his voice a little trashed.

"Well, looks like we have a conundrum here. It certainly wasn't someone stuck on that cliff with a megaphone, shouting 'Help ... Help' loud enough to get Connie's attention. *Someone* got her attention, though. It wasn't a phone call, and it wasn't something out in the ocean. Whatever it was, it happened in or just outside the kitchen, and she followed someone—or was physically taken—out to the slip-and-fall area."

Waxman couldn't think of anything else. "A disgruntled ex-lover shows up, throws Connie over his shoulder, and walks to the south end of the bluff and dives off."

Sanchez chuckled. "At least that scenario fits with the facts." As the two men walked back towards the kitchen, Sanchez added, "Either the divers find something, or else we should check with the guy building the house next door. If there were any laborers on the site, maybe they saw or heard something. Whoever's in charge up there would know."

When they got word that the divers had found absolutely nothing, Sanchez and Waxman called it a day. With Stoeffer's fiber analysis not expected until Monday at the earliest, they closed down the operation, stopped by the office to make a few phone calls, and spent the rest of Sunday afternoon with their families. They were still on call for any emergencies.

Sam arrived home, met by Bobby in the kitchen. "Any news?" he asked his father.

"Not really. The divers found nothing, but they managed to find a few fibers of something on the cliff. Won't know until next week if it's anything."

There was only one priority in Bobby's mind, something he realized could now be disastrous. He was already scheming how to retrieve his converted walkie-talkie before a new housekeeper found it.

*****

Note to John: I guess it's a mixed blessing that Bobby recorded all of this for posterity, although I'm sure it wasn't his intention to have anyone but him—and maybe Cheryl—listen to it later. It's also interesting that both of the investigators were within a few feet of that Japanese screen in Ken's office with the monitor on the floor behind it. If only they had discovered it then. If only. Steven

40 The Accidental Tourist

At 6:45 the next morning, Ken sat in his Bronco with the engine warming up. He stared straight ahead at the garage cabinets, heartbroken at the almost certain death of Connie. He had a gut feeling she had gone over cliff, and knowing the waters beyond, Ken could visualize what might have happened. With no swim fins to go against a strong and very cold current, and probably getting pushed down into the start of the undertow leading down into the submarine canyon, the sharks would surely have come calling, followed by every other scavenger in the area. Ken hoped she had drowned quickly, without too much suffering.

Ken backed out and turned around, heading up the driveway to pick up the laborers. The detectives didn't see any reason to keep the cliff face cordoned off, so he planned on a full day's work for the laborers to finish up the mud clearance. Just past the mailbox, he slowed by habit to check for anyone coming around the next uphill corner. He saw the front end of a car and hit the brakes, stopping immediately. He leaned on the horn.

Gil Nortze didn't see it all coming until it was too late. Driving too fast for the blind curve, he saw too late the white Bronco stopped just ahead, its horn blasting. Nortze slammed on the brakes and tried to veer right, but skidded twenty feet down the pavement and slammed into the left front end of Ken's previously immaculate Bronco.

Ken started a slow burn, and by the time he opened the door and stepped out, he was fuming mad. He checked the crushed bumper and crumpled fender, but the crash had not affected the tire. By the time Ken had walked up to Nortze's closed window, he was furious. "God damn it, Gil!" he shouted through the glass. "What the hell you doing driving so fast down this driveway?"

Inside his car, Nortze heard and opened the door, stepping out to confront Ken. "You were on my side of the driveway," he shot back. "If you had been where you should have, I could have passed you easily."

"No way, Gil. You know these curves by now. You were going too fast for the conditions, pure and simple."

Nortze threw up his hands. "Well, that's why we have insurance, isn't it? We'll let them sort it out."

Ken calmed down, ready to do the paperwork and get on to picking up the laborers at the lumberyard. They exchanged insurance cards and other basic information officiously, if not exactly in an overly friendly manner. Ken finally got Nortze's cell phone number and that he was staying at Margie's B&B.

Slowing at the entrance to the lumberyard, Ken noticed the absence of workers by the side of the road. There were usually at least three or four, more on weekends. He turned into the driveway, and that's when he spotted the sheriff's patrol car and two late model sedans. Two men in suits were talking to the sheriff's deputy, and behind them, standing against the wall to the office, were six Hispanic men.

Ken parked the car and got out, searching for his laborers. He then recognized Sanchez and Waxman standing together. He called out a hello and waved. Sanchez called back, "Morning, Mr. Easton," and both he and Waxman came over.

Sanchez said, "I just called and left a message on your machine. I guess you were already on your way here. Waxman and I came down early to talk to the laborers—to check if they knew anyone who'd been up to your house or the guy next door. What's his name?"

"Gil Nortze," Ken said flatly, not wanting to disturb his current mental calm.

"Nortze—right." Sanchez stopped there, not telling Ken any more at this point. "I need you to tell me if any of those guys over there are your four laborers."

Ken walked over with Sanchez and immediately recognized the two sets of brothers. "The last four," Ken said. "I came to pick them up to finish clearing out the mud around the east side of my house and garden."

Sanchez and Waxman had previously talked to them, and they had solid alibis for their whereabouts all day Saturday. The other two men had said they worked for Gil Nortze, and the detectives had been trying to reach Nortze, so far without success.

"Have you seen Gil Nortze around?" Sanchez asked.

Ken let out a big breath. "Yes, as a matter of fact, I just ran into him—or I should say, he ran into me—literally." Ken pointed out the crushed front end on his Bronco. "He's down at his lot right now watching the mud dry."

Waxman didn't react to the dig. "Do you have his number?"

"Yes, I just got it." Ken pulled out the paper with the accident info on it, and Waxman copied it down.

"Well, thanks, Mr. Easton. You've been a big help. Go on over and get your guys. We'll keep you posted if we turn up anything."

After Ken had departed with his laborers in tow, Waxman turned to his partner. "If someone like a laborer saw something happen at Easton's house—or did something to aggravate a situation—it's doubtful he would be out front here looking for work right now. He would have either reported it, which these guys often do if it's serious, but more likely he'd be far, far away if he had any culpability."

"You're probably right about that," said Sanchez, "But let's call Nortze and take these two down there so he can confirm."

Waxman then whispered sarcastically, "Did you ask them if they heard that bullhorn you were talking about?"

*****

Note to John: Don't you think this section reads better than a dry, lifeless investigative report running two single-spaced typewritten pages?

It's attached for comparison. I thought you would agree. Steven

41 Blind Man's Bluff

On Friday afternoon, March 1 of 2002, a little after two o'clock, Gil Nortze finally poured his foundation. In line with what his former general contractor, Brad Smiley, had predicted, the extra work cost Nortze about thirty grand. The architect and engineer had exceeded their limits on free telephone calls and site visits the weekend before.

Nortze had no clue how to prepare for the foundation, other than to call for bids, and he did not coordinate the plumbing and electrical subcontractors for their groundwork prior to the pour. At the last minute, he hired a foundation contractor who took on the job only because of the extra five grand Nortze tossed in to get the pour done before the next rain.

In the mean time, Nortze had all but given up finding laborers who would work for him more than once. He was so hard on them that they quickly, and collectively, refused to come to his job site. No one wanted to be treated like a slave, or be paid like one. Nortze routinely insisted on both … and word soon spread in the small community.

Nortze was so preoccupied with the foundation pour that he neglected to do the one thing necessary at that time—order the windows and doors. With a six-week window between ordering and delivery, usually about right for most new residential construction, it was the general contractor's job to know that and to have all the windows selected and measured. Nortze was the general now, but without a clue as to the order of battle.

On that same Friday afternoon, after picking up his mail at three o'clock, Ken Easton opened a notice from his insurance company which said that since there were two conflicting stories—and no corroborating witnesses—about what had happened ten days before on the common driveway, both Ken and Nortze were going to be charged with 50% fault. The written notice ended with, "This incident may result in higher rates on your next renewal."

"May—my ass," Ken scoffed aloud, tossing the notice on his desk, thinking: *When was the last time an insurance company didn't raise someone's rates after an accident?*

The phone rang and Ken switched to speakerphone. "Ken Easton," he said, still smoldering about Nortze.

"Hi, Ken. It's Randy Halperin." His voice was low and subdued.

"Hey, Randy. How's it going?"

Randy let out a whoosh of air, and his voice wavered. "They found something, Ken."

With Connie's body—or any part of it—not yet discovered, despite daily scuba searches along three miles of rugged coast, Randy had been trapped in a netherworld of hope and despair. To Ken, Randy's words meant only one thing—body part. "What was it?" he asked softly.

"Part of her arm, and a piece of her sweatshirt. One of the sheriff's divers ... somewhere down that submarine canyon between some rocks. The lab results just came back, and Detective Sanchez called me. He offered to call you, but I said I wanted to tell you myself."

"I'm glad you did. I'm so sorry, Randy." It had been a daily ritual for Ken to walk out to the bluff around noon, watching for a few minutes—sometimes with binoculars—as the sheriff's divers continued searching. In cold water and under treacherous conditions, their only goal was to put closure on a family's ordeal. It appeared they had finally achieved that goal without losing one of their own in the process.

Randy's voice wavered again, and Ken could hear the sniffle. "Yeah, thanks. Anyway, Mr. Sanchez said the divers spent a lot of time searching in the area, but there was nothing else."

Between sharks and scavengers, Ken knew it usually didn't take long. "Is there going to be a service?"

"Yes, that's partly why I called. I was thinking a week from Sunday, the tenth. I'll get back to you with details as soon as I've worked them out."

"I'd like to say a few words, if that's appropriate."

"I would like that, Ken."

"Okay, man, hang in there. I know it was tough to make this call. If you need anything, I'm here, okay?"

"Thanks, Ken."

After ringing off with Randy, the problems with Nortze and an insurance rate increase seemed to pale in comparison.

Twenty minutes later, Tristin showed up early from work, entering from the garage. She walked down the hallway, Cheryl and Bobby Wynette following behind. Bobby had on his backpack and Cheryl carried a single book in her hand. "Look who I brought with me," she called down the hallway. "Bobby needs help with something."

Ken sat back and saw the three of them through his open door, calling with minimal emotion, "Hi Cheryl. Hi Bobby."

"Hi, Ken," the kids said in unison.

Tristin came into the office, bent down and gave Ken a kiss. She reacted to his lack of passion. "Anything wrong?"

Ken looked past her to Bobby and Cheryl. "Come on in," he said gravely, "I have something to tell you."

Tristin suspected it was something about Connie, and she steeled herself against the news. Bobby and Cheryl stood together, and it was Cheryl who said, "Is it about Connie?"

"Yes, it is. The sheriff's divers found some of her remains off the cliffs here. It wasn't much, but it was enough for a positive ID. Her husband called to tell me himself, and there's going to be a service for her, probably next Sunday. Will you tell your dad for me?"

Bobby leaned forward. "I'll tell him. He's been wondering what happened."

"Randy must be feeling awful," Cheryl said.

"Yes," Ken said, a bit confused by Cheryl's apparent familiarity, but also by Bobby's disassociative statement as well, as if it was only Sam, and not Bobby, wondering what had happened to Connie. "I didn't know you knew him," he said to Cheryl.

Cheryl's face paled, and Ken caught it. "Actually, that's what Connie called him. I've never met him."

"Me, neither," Bobby added, more as backup to Cheryl than for imparting an important piece of information. Ken also caught the defensive nature of an otherwise voluntary statement, but he consciously dismissed both Bobby's and Cheryl's responses.

Subconsciously, however, Ken's gray matter began to churn away. There was a distinct disconnect in the logic, and it needed resolution. Neither of the kids showed any sign of shock, or real sadness, nor did they ask the usual impertinent questions at a time like this, such as, "Ooh, what did they find, her head? Had the sharks gotten to her?" Instead, their responses were too distant and dispassionate— too measured, somehow— for two young kids faced with such a disturbing announcement.

It was Cheryl who apparently picked up the strange vibe coming from Ken. As if she had read his thoughts, she walked to the garden window, sullen now. Staring out into the garden, she said, softly, "She taught me how to make coffee," and then began to sob. She covered her face with her hands and shook as she cried.

Tristin felt a little uneasy, but didn't at first understand why. Recalling her own sad reaction to hearing Ken's telling of finding Connie's remains, she thought Cheryl's coffee remark to be more of a performance than a fond memory recalled of someone lost forever. But she also noted that this young girl had had a hard life in her emotionally formative years, and that perhaps it was something she had done on the spur of the moment because it was somehow expected.

Tristin came up from behind Cheryl and placed her hand on her shoulder. Cheryl turned and placed her face on Tristin's chest. "It's okay, honey," Tristin said, and stepped back while turning up Cheryl's chin, revealing to Tristin Cheryl's moist eyes and a few streaked tears. Despite an outwardly sorrowful look, Cheryl's tear volume didn't quite match the previous outward display.

"Go on into the kitchen with Bobby. I have to talk to Ken for a few minutes, and then I'll be out to make some cocoa. You can help, Cheryl."

That seemed to brighten both of them up, but not for the reasons one would normally expect. Bobby just wanted out of that room. All this fake emotion was killing him, and he saw how Cheryl's performance had done little to convert the masses, so to speak.

As for Cheryl, she wanted a change of scenery if only to change subjects, as their original mission in coming down to the house was to retrieve the converted walkie-talkie, not get into some emotional scene over Connie. She hadn't prepared for that, and it had forced her into an improv performance—not a good one by her own standards, judging from Ken and Tristin's reactions. Cheryl wanted only to snatch the walkie-talkie and move on with the plan.

Back in game mode now, Cheryl casually placed her school book down on the table next to Ken's easy chair and walked off toward the kitchen, Bobby right behind. Once in the kitchen, Cheryl whispered an apology to Bobby for her performance, explaining that she had been totally unprepared. He commiserated, also caught by surprise and knowing his own performance lacked any true emotion as well.

"At least you planted the book," Bobby said softly with a wink. "When Tristin comes back, you help her make the cocoa. Talk about how you've never known anyone who died like that before. It's true, so you can ask all the questions. Meanwhile, I'll get Ken back into the garage to help me fix the other unit, and you excuse yourself to go back for your book. Hurry, though—you don't want her coming in and catching you."

"Yeah, okay."

And that's exactly how it came down, everyone playing roles as scripted. In the garage, Bobby pulled the second walkie-talkie out of his backpack and handed it to Ken. "It keeps going in and out," he said, "and I can't find anything wrong."

"Well, let's take a look." Ken opened up the back panel, and it took about two seconds for him to spot the problem. He pulled on a tiny silver wire, and both the wire and the solder popped up from the circuit board. "Bum connection here. It needs re-soldering."

"Can I do it?" Bobby asked eagerly.

"Yeah, sure. Go for it." Bobby then pulled open the drawer and removed the gun and solder, plugging it into the wall. His countenance changed, and he lowered his voice. "I never knew anyone who died like that before."

"Most people don't until they get older," Ken replied. "It's a tough thing. One moment they're here, smiling and carrying on … and the next minute they're gone. It gives you an appreciation of people while they're still around."

"How do you think she died?"

Maybe the kid was just being polite when I told him the news. "I'm not sure, Bobby. She probably drowned first. The rest is probably something one shouldn't think about before going to sleep at night."

"Is that an awful way to die? Drowning, I mean?"

"Actually, it's one of the least painful. You just quit struggling, give in, and take a gulp of water instead of air. It's over quickly and painlessly."

Bobby nodded but said nothing. He touched the solder to the thin silver wire and circuit connection simultaneously, just long enough for the solder to melt over the connection.

Ken looked over to check the boy's handiwork. "Perfect job, Bobby." Ken wondered why Bobby hadn't figured it out on his own. It was a pretty obvious problem for someone with Bobby's talents.

They both heard Tristin calling from the kitchen, "Ken, Bobby. Cocoa's on."

Bobby started to pack away the walkie-talkie, and Ken asked, "Aren't you going to test it out?"

Bobby hesitated too long. "Oh," he finally said, "Cheryl forgot the other one at home. I'm sure it's okay, though. But I'll test it when I get back, just to be sure." He returned the equipment back to the drawer, closed the backpack and tossed it over one shoulder, walking away from the workbench and Ken towards the door into the hallway.

In the moment, the kids forgetting the other unit didn't come off quite right to Ken, either. But he dismissed it for the moment as nothing more than a lapse of memory, although perhaps not on Cheryl's part. He switched off the light as he left and closed the door behind him.

Back in the kitchen, Bobby caught Cheryl's wink and a quick smile. She had the walkie-talkie and was ready to go home anytime Bobby was ready. After relating to Ken and Tristin what they'd been doing at school, it was obvious—at least to Ken—Bobby had some sort of schedule to keep. After the third time catching Bobby stealing glances at his watch, Ken stood up and grabbed his keys off the counter. "Come on, guys. I'll take you home."

When he stopped the Bronco in front of the Wynette house, Ken turned to Bobby in the passenger seat next to him. "Ask your dad to give me a call. And say hi to your mom."

"Okay, and thanks, Ken. For the help with the walkie-talkie and the ride."

"No problem."

Cheryl leaned over from the back seat and planted a very tender kiss on Ken's right cheek. "You're the best, Ken," she said after, and then added, "Love ya, bye."

When Ken arrived back at his house, Tristin was seated in the living room with a glass of wine in her hand, an empty glass on the coffee table, and an open wine bottle on the table. He sat down beside her and poured himself a glass. He raised it, saying, "Here's to Connie."

"To Connie," Tristin said, clinking glasses.

"The kids seemed to take it in stride," Tristin began. "Although it came off kind of weird."

Ken nodded. "I know. They must have had a rough life before settling in with Sam and Darcy. Stunted emotionally or something, that's my feeling."

"Mine, too. Although Cheryl did bring up the fact that she had never known anyone who had died like that."

"So did Bobby," Ken said without thinking about the coincidence, adding, "but he did ask how she might have died."

"So did Cheryl."

"When I told him Connie probably drowned first, Bobby asked if drowning was an awful way to die."

"That's odd," Tristin said. "I also said Connie probably drowned, like we talked about in your office after they had gone to the kitchen, and Cheryl asked if I thought Connie had suffered long."

Both Ken and Tristin then sat in silence, thinking about the conversational coincidence. Ken then shrugged it off. "Well, you and I think alike. Maybe they do, too."

Tristin moved close to Ken, touching her breast to his arm. "Want to go in the bedroom and think alike together?"

Ken took a gulp of wine, and then placed the glass on the table. "What, like watch TV?"

Tristin gulped down the last of her wine, too, saying, "Life is short, Mr. Easton, but if that's all you want to do, I'm up for it."

42 Chances Are

From the top of the carpeted stairs, Bobby heard his father come in the front door. He reached the landing and was about to continue down when he heard Sam say to Darcy, "They found some of Connie's remains in the ocean off Ken's property. The DNA tests were positive."

"Oh, Sam," Darcy said plaintively, and then paused to reflect a moment. "I guess her husband is better off knowing, though."

"Yes, he apparently took it hard, but you're right. And there's something else. Have you seen Bobby wearing that red and white flannel shirt we gave him for his birthday a couple of years back, the one from Sears?"

Up on the landing, Bobby's heart skipped a beat. He listened closely as Darcy responded, "No, not that I recall, why?"

"The lab report also came back on the fibers found at Ken's place, and when Sanchez said, 'red and white flannel,' it took a while, but after I hung up, I thought of that shirt. It's probably nothing, but I just want to rule it out. Is he upstairs?"

With that, Bobby stepped gingerly back up the stairs and hurried to his room, trying to calm himself down and come up with something. A few moments later, Sam knocked on the door. "Bobby, you in there?"

Seated at the computer, Bobby said, "Yeah, Dad, it's open."

"Need to talk for a minute, son."

"Sure, Dad," he said cheerfully, swiveling around in his chair and pointing to the bed. "Have a seat." It was crunch time.

"Thanks." Sam sat down with a puzzled look on his face. "Do you still have that flannel shirt—the red and white one we got you from Sears?"

Bobby's brow furrowed and he went to the closet, saying, "I don't think so. It got ripped or something a long time ago." He opened the sliding door and picked through the hanging shirts. "I think I remember Mom sending it off to the Goodwill." He finished checking. "Nope, not here." He closed the door. "Why?"

"Just a few loose ends I have to be absolutely clear on. You weren't down at Ken's house, for any reason, on the Saturday Connie went missing, were you?"

Bobby shook his head, thinking. "No, Dad. Cheryl and I were home all morning doing homework. I remember 'cause we both had tests the next Monday. And then Mom fixed lunch and you guys went up to your room and watched that goofy movie."

Sam chuckled, "Yeah, well, your mother and I like those *goofy movies.*"

Concluding his recollection, Bobby said, "We ate our lunch down in the basement while you guys were upstairs. I was working on some speakers for my room, but I didn't have any needle-nosed pliers for the wiring." Bobby shrugged his shoulders, adding with finality, "And then you went to work in the afternoon."

"And when I came home, you'd changed your hair color."

Bobby's shrug and sheepish grin were genuine. "Yeah, like I said before, Cheryl teased me about needing a new look. I didn't want Mr. Nortze recognizing me if we ever met. So far, so good."

"So, you didn't leave the house at all that day for any reason?"

Bobby thought about it. "Well, after you left, Mom did take me to the hardware store in the afternoon to get those needle-nosed pliers. Cheryl came along to get out of the house for a while. When we got home, we got back to doing homework."

He felt the heat of his father's stare, not knowing whether Sam believed his alibi around the critical noontime window of opportunity. But since he and Cheryl hadn't been spotted, he didn't have to worry about his prepared explanation: Stayed in the garage; closed down the door when they left; Connie wouldn't let them into the house because of the mud. Bobby decided to change subjects. "Did you know they found some remains or something of Connie?"

"Where'd you hear that?" Sam had only just heard of it himself, but through official channels.

"Ken told me. I went down with Cheryl to ask him to help fix my walkie-talkie, and he gave us a ride home after. He didn't say too much about it—

I don't think he wanted to go into the details. But he wanted you to call him."

Sam guessed correctly that Randy had called Ken personally. "Oh, thanks." He stood up and left the room. Bobby heard his dad in the master bedroom on the phone with Ken, and he weighed the possibilities of having just dodged a significant bullet. Bobby knew he was now quite proficient at lying through his teeth, and even a pro like his cop father probably couldn't see through him now. In the final analysis, however, Bobby Wynette just couldn't take that chance.

*****

Note to John: This pretty much lays out most of the foundation—psychologically and evidence-wise—for the carnage to come. Again, I know it's taken a long time to get this far, but you of all people should appreciate how important a solid foundation is to a story (and a house, too.) BTW: I got your post-card from Rio today. It sounds like there's going to be true international interest in your screenplay, but I hope you're not just running around the world chalking up expenses to be charged to our project. I should have my part done by the time you get back to L.A. so you can get started. Steven

43 Little Monsters

The next day, Saturday, March 2, would prove to be one of the longest days in Ken Easton's life. It began at seven a.m. and ended in the wee hours of Sunday morning.

After not getting to bed until after midnight on Friday, Ken and Tristin were both still asleep when a long, loud car horn blared close enough to wake them both. "What the hell?" he asked sleepily, wanting only to sleep in for a change.

A few minutes before, just above Nortze's lot, a lumber truck had spun its dual rear tires, the driver trying to back up the deeply rutted dirt driveway. One of the ruts had steered the truck right into the side of the hill, and the right rear traction tires had strained, and repeatedly failed, to get up and over another deep rut behind. The driver had gotten out of the truck, saw his hopeless situation, and walked down to the lot looking for someone with a phone to call the yard. He knew it would take a big tow truck to pull his rig back up the hill enough to get straightened out.

And that's when Nortze had arrived—late—to take delivery of the lumber. Not knowing the situation, or caring about the early hour, Nortze found his way blocked and leaned on the horn of his Lincoln. And now, with no response, and seeing no one down on his lot, he leaned on the horn again. It was enough to wake the dead.

When the driver finally appeared, Nortze parked in front of Ken's mailbox and stepped out. "What the hell's going on?" he shouted down to the man walking up his driveway.

It took two hours for a big tow rig to show up and solve the problem, and Nortze found himself caught in a maelstrom of logistics.

In the interim, a conga line of work trucks had backed up on the narrow driveway well beyond the curve where Nortze had run into Ken's Bronco. There was the foundation crew waiting to strip the forms; behind them, framers ready to start cutting and installing pressure-treated plate stock; and behind them, trucks carrying crews to dig the trenches to lay in the plumbing and electrical groundwork. With no other place to park and to let the tow truck pass, Nortze had directed the work trucks down Ken's driveway and onto his little auxiliary parking area above Ken's garden.

Ken and Tristin slept in until 9 a.m. Cup of coffee in hand, Ken stepped out the front door to get the newspaper. He stopped cold when he saw all the trucks in his parking area above, and Nortze's red Lincoln parked in front of his mailbox. He turned on his heels and went back into the house to get dressed.

As Ken walked up the driveway and past the trucks, he noticed that the workmen men had walked up to Nortze's lot right through the ice plant on Ken's far slope, leaving a trail of minor destruction in their wake.

When he reached his mailbox, Ken spotted Nortze's new mailbox next to it. It was the worst looking job of installing a mailbox that Ken had ever seen. A hole had been dug and the dirt left piled up against Ken's mailbox support. Concrete had been splashed into the hole, splattering the driveway and surrounding dirt. A 4x4 wood post, of the cheapest construction grade stood out of plumb by half an inch over its three foot height. The mailbox, the cheapest one imaginable, was secured directly onto the top of the post, but when Ken shook it with his hand, it was loose and wobbly, the thin metal crunching against wood.

Ken reached into his shirt pocket and removed a folded invoice. He contemplated sticking it inside the box, but decided instead to walk it down and hand it to Nortze himself.

Ken started down Nortze's driveway and had to keep to one side of the rutted and partially washed out dirt surface. He concluded that Nortze could probably not get his car down without bottoming out, but he couldn't figure out why the other trucks, with greater clearance, had not gone down and parked below.

Knocking on the site trailer door, Ken waited a moment before Nortze opened it and stuck his head out. "Hey, Ken." He left the door open and backed inside, adding, "Come on in. It's been one fucked up morning."

"Why are all those trucks parked down in my lot?"

Nortze practically fell into his chair, throwing his hands up in the air, responding gruffly, "Because my goddamned driveway is fucked up and the lumber truck got stuck. Took a tow truck to get it out. And the other trucks had to be moved so the tow truck could get by, so I had the guys park down there. It's only temporary, for Christ's sake, and I didn't think you'd get your panties in a twist about it."

"I don't have a problem with that," Ken said, now realizing the situation. "But instead of walking up and around, the men took a shortcut right up through my ice plant."

"Oh, Jesus, Ken," Nortze said dismissively, "I got so many problems to deal with right now. What do you want, a check for the damage?"

That infuriated Ken. "Yes, Gil, but not for that." Ken handed Nortze the invoice.

"What's this?"

"An invoice for the laborers I hired to clear away all the mud from my lot."

"Oh, let's take a look." He went right to the bottom line. "What? Five hundred and twenty dollars? What did you do, hire a whole battalion?"

"Four guys, Gil. It took them thirteen hours. I didn't charge you for the extra shovels I had to buy."

"Ten bucks an hour? I get them for eight, sometimes seven-fifty."

"I guess I just like to pay people a living wage. And I got tired of waiting for you to send people down to do it."

Nortze shook his head, reaching for his checkbook. "Okay, but next time, I'll send the people down to do any work that needs to be done."

"Well, send 'em down and have them restore the ice plant."

"I'll have 'em catch it before they go home." Nortze thought of something. "Speaking of workers, have they found your maid yet?"

"Housekeeper," Ken corrected him, "No, not yet."

"Oh, I didn't know there was a difference," Nortze replied, showing his total lack of sensitivity.

"There is to me. She's like family around here."

It was as if Nortze didn't even hear, already off into his own thoughts. "I just got off the phone with a grader, but he can't be out here to fix my driveway until Monday. Can you give me a break until then? I mean with parking the trucks on your lot?"

Ken Easton was a generous man. And considerate, too. He didn't want a running confrontation with Nortze, although he had already predicted Nortze was the prototypical Neighbor From Hell. "Yeah, okay, Gil. Just until Monday, though."

Making an excuse to get out of the trailer and away from Ken, Nortze stood up and headed for the door. "I've got to make sure those guys aren't sleeping on the job out there."

It was just after sunset and when Ken was at the birdfeeder adding seeds for Jake the Tern. The sound of the waves crashing off shore and against the cliffs was very loud. He looked off toward the ocean, a few clouds just above the northwestern horizon. More rain was expected by Sunday. The swells had already increased, some of the wave sets ten or twelve feet high, and Ken expected they would be even higher by the time the storm arrived.

After filling the dish with seed, Ken set the bag down and walked to his diving perch, checking out the waves. Down in the water to his left, his eye caught something floating in the water. He stared down, and it took but a few seconds to see what it was—a three-foot long piece of plywood with jagged edges. And at the base of the cliff in front of Nortze's property, he saw a cluster of broken plywood and 2x lumber—2x4s and 2x8s— mostly in short pieces and broken on the ends.

Ken walked to the south end of the bluff and climbed out onto the west-facing slope beyond where Connie had gone over. All along the base of the cliffs, form lumber was in the process of either breaking up or getting sucked out to sea.

"That pig!" Ken said aloud, thinking to himself: *Who would do such a thing?* For Ken, the violation ran much deeper than any city, state or federal codes on waste disposal. It was about violating a personal code of conduct. He envisioned the ends of the two-by-fours crushing shells and anemones wherever they bashed into the rocks. Later when the wood had splintered, shards could disrupt the lifecycles of many marine organisms, if not injure or kill them outright.

Ken knew that the toxicity of plywood—more specifically the adhesives used to bind the layers together—made for one very poisonous substance. *Could the man possibly not know the consequences of his actions?* Ken concluded that if Nortze thought he could get away with something, he would do it. It showed bad character. And as he watched the pieces of lumber down in the sea below, Ken remembered an old adage: Character is all about who you are when no one is looking.

Heading back inside the kitchen, Ken dialed 9-1-1.

"Nine-one-one emergency," said the female operator. "Please state your emergency?"

"Yes, my name is Ken Easton, out on Spindrift Road in Carmel Highlands. Someone has thrown a bunch of lumber off a cliff into the ocean."

"Did you see someone throwing it off, sir?"

"Um, no, but I'm pretty sure I know who did it."

"So, you didn't witness who did it." It was a rhetorical question. "Were there any people in the water?"

"No, just lumber from the house under construction next door, but its got all that toxic—"

"Well, sir, it's getting dark, and unless there's someone in trouble, it will have to wait until morning. I'll give you the number of the Carmel Police Department."

Ken sighed, thinking: *Where's the Coastal Commission Swat Team when you need them?* "Yes, give it to me." He took down the number, knowing already that by the time anyone came out for a look tomorrow, most if not all of that lumber would be sawdust by then.

Tristin entered the kitchen to make a cup of tea, and when Ken rang off, she asked, "Hey, how about dinner and a movie tonight—in town. I think you need to get out, Ken."

"You're right about that, babe." He summarized the situation with the wood tossed off the cliff. After cooling down, he asked about the movie, "What's playing?"

"*Time Machine,* with Guy Pearce. Just came out yesterday."

"Video."

"Okay, there's *Dragonfly.* A suspense thriller with Kevin Costner."

"Possibility. What else?"

"Well, there's *Monster's Ball*, with Billy Bob and Halle Berry. I hear there's some great sex scenes."

Ken teased her. "What, like I need to work on my technique?"

"I'm always looking for pointers myself."

"Then point the way, my dear."

It felt good to get out for a night on the town, and Ken was in fine spirits. They started with wine and cheesebread at the Hog's Breath Tavern, Clint Eastwood's place on San Carlos Avenue in Carmel-by-the-Sea. Then they moved on to the Aw Shucks oyster bar on Ocean Avenue, followed by a nine o'clock showing of *Monster's Ball* at a mall outside Monterey. They both loved it.

After the movie, they drove back over the hill and down to the beach at the south end of Ocean Avenue, and sat in the car watching the waves. They even necked for a while and, following that, they were eager to get home and into bed.

It was after 11:30 when Ken slowed to a stop on Highway 1, just a mile from Spindrift Road. A highway patrol officer directed two ambulances, in tandem, lights flashing, out onto the highway and toward Carmel, passing a fire truck sitting off the highway with its lights flashing, too.

Up the hill to Ken's left, he saw more flashing lights, smoke rising through searchlights, and his heart skipped a beat. All the emergency activity was centered at the Wynette house. Ken rolled down the window and got the patrolman's attention. "Excuse me, what's going on up at Sam Wynette's house."

At the reference, the patrolman came over to the window. "You know Sam?"

"Yes, and Darcy and the kids, too. We live down on Spindrift. Is everyone all right?"

"No, sir, I'm afraid not. There was a big fire, and a lot of smoke." He sighed heavily and paused for a moment. "Darcy died and Sam was badly burned."

Tristin put her hands to her mouth. "Oh, my God, no!" She started to cry.

Ken went into slight shock, tears forming in his eyes.

"The two kids managed to get out safe, though," said the officer.

Ken closed his eyes and lowered his chin, shaking his head back and forth. He thought about what Bobby and Cheryl must be going through right now, and he pulled himself together by force of will. "I'd like to go up there, officer. We know the kids pretty well. Maybe there's something we can do to help."

"Let me check. What is your name, sir?" He spoke into his remote microphone strapped to his shoulder and called up the hill.

Ken turned to Tristin, and she was sobbing into her hands. He reached over and held her shoulder, saying nothing.

"You can go up Mr. Easton. Talk to Captain Davies—he's been trying to reach you at home."

Driving slowly up the road, powerful floodlights lit up the Wynette residence, or what was left of it, which was not much. Emergency vehicles were everywhere. Fire hoses were strung out around the property, and water shot through the nozzles onto the still-smoldering ruins. Only part of the garage remained, the roof having collapsed and rested at a steep angle on top of Sam's smashed Honda.

Ken passed neighbors on the street in groups of two's and three's outside watching and talking. A group of police and firemen congregated on the Wynette's driveway next to Darcy's car, and a policeman waved the Bronco through, directing him where to park near the Wynette residence.

Ken turned to Tristin. "You want to wait here for a while, or come with me?"

"I'll go with you," she said, fighting back the sniffles.

With his eyes trained on the group of uniformed policemen and firemen on the driveway, Ken led Tristin up to speak with them and see if there was anything they could do, especially for Bobby and Cheryl.

"Mr. Easton?" called a man who looked to Ken to be a senior fire official.

Ken raised his free hand, but before he could join them, a plaintive wail came from his left. "Ken!" said the sobbing voice, and he turned to see Cheryl breaking away from a female police officer and running towards him, crying. Wearing a coat meant for a grown man, Cheryl ran headlong into his arms, grabbing him around the waist.

"It's okay now, honey," he said, tears forming once again and pulling her close. He looked up to see Bobby walking slowly towards him, head down, also wearing an oversized coat.

Cheryl wailed, "It was terrible ... terrible."

"I know, hon. I know." Ken held her tight against him, rubbing her back. He then looked to Bobby and reached out his hand, Bobby taking it and coming in for a hug, too. "You okay, Bobby."

Head still lowered, he said softly, "Yeah, I'm okay."

Turning his eyes to the man who called him, and then to Tristin, he indicated to her to take over with Cheryl. Cheryl made the transfer into the arms of Tristin quite smoothly.

"Everyone wait here," Ken said, "I've got to go talk to those men for a few minutes. I'll be right back, though, okay?"

"Okay," sobbed Cheryl.

Stopping in front of the man in the uniform of an officer, Ken wiped his eyes, ready for the bad news ahead. "Mr. Easton, I'm Captain Mike Davies, with the Carmel Highlands Fire Department." The fifty years old Davies had short gray hair and a stocky build. He and his engine company were officially assigned to the California Department of Forestry, the state organization taking over responsibility for some local fire duties starting in 2002. It was just much easier to say he was from the fire department. He was also a fire investigator with 20 years experience. Ken offered his hand, nodding in sober silence. "I'm afraid there's been a tragedy here, Mr. Easton."

"Yes," said Ken, softly, "I understand from the patrolman that Darcy died and Sam was badly burned."

"Third degree burns over sixty percent, I'm sorry to say. He could recover, but it's too early to tell yet. I was just informed that the family cat didn't make it, either."

"I'll tell the kids myself, if you don't mind." Ken stared at the ruins of the Wynette house, asking, "What happened here?"

"Well, I'd rather not go into that right now, because I'm more concerned about the children—"

"Yes, of course," Ken said, interrupting and stealing a glance back at Bobby and Cheryl. "That's why I came up."

"The kids say they have an aunt over in Monterey—Sam's sister, I believe—but the kids didn't want to go there. The little girl said the three dogs are always trying to bite her or something like that, and it's apparently pretty crowded there already. Anyway, both the kids wanted to contact you, so I called your house."

Davies could see with his own eyes the bond between the kids and the neighbor couple standing before him. It dovetailed with the girl's emotional state and her request. He was going to call for the people at child protective custody to take them, but he figured they needed someone close, if not exactly family.

"Yes, we were out for the evening. They can stay with us until things get sorted out, if that's okay." Thoughts of either one or both of the kids somehow running into Gil Nortze were very low on his priority list now. The kids needed a place to stay, and that was that.

"Sure. Let me take your number and address, and I'll give you my card. I'm on call until Monday morning, Mr. Easton, so I'm available at that number twenty-four/seven if you need anything, or if the kids need anything." He handed Ken his business card and wrote down Ken's information in a small notebook. "I probably won't call you until tomorrow morning. By then, the kids will have calmed down and we can talk to them about what happened. Also by then, I should have something on Sam's condition."

"Yes, I understand. Thank you."

Ken went back to where Tristin, Bobby and Cheryl were gathered, and he told the two kids they were coming home with him and Tristin.

"Oh," said Bobby, turning to Ken, "I have my backpack in Mom's car. It's all I have left. Can we go and get it?"

"Yeah, sure," Ken said, and they walked together to the car, where Bobby opened the rear passenger door, reached in, and pulled out his backpack.

On the short drive home, Ken turned and asked, "Are you guys hungry?"

"No, thank you," Cheryl said weakly.

"Me, neither," Bobby added.

Tristin turned to the kids. "I'll fix up the spare bedroom next to Ken's office. There's a small bed in there, and a fold-up in the closet. You two can sleep there together until we can get the other bedroom in shape, okay?" Both Cheryl and Bobby nodded silently.

Ken pulled into the garage, he and Tristin facing front. In the back seat, Bobby reached over and gently squeezed Cheryl's leg. She picked up his wink as Bobby said, sadly, and just loud enough for all to hear, "Don't worry, Cheryl. Everything's gonna be okay."

Bobby was very proud of himself. With the exception of his father surviving the fire, everything had gone off without a hitch.

Once Bobby had formulated his plan, it had all gone rather like clockwork. Sam and Darcy had gone to bed early around ten and fell quickly asleep. That was because Bobby had slipped the contents of two sleeping pills from Darcy's medicine chest into each of their wine glasses at nine-thirty. By 9:45 they were both yawning, and by 10:15 fast asleep. Bobby had crept into the room and placed the corked and half empty bottle of wine on Sam's bedside table, along with their two wine glasses plucked from the sink top. Next Bobby had gone downstairs, his backpack slung over one shoulder. Inside the backpack were the walkie-talkies and computer disks. At the kitchen sink, he'd turned on the hot water faucet, draining the first of the hot water from the basement water heater. He then snuck out the side door and around to Darcy's car, where he used her keys to open the door. After placing his backpack on the floor in front of the rear seats, he gently closed the door but did not lock the car back up. Darcy didn't lock it up half the time, anyway, and never set the car alarm. He checked to make sure he had not been seen and went back in the house, returning Darcy's keys to her purse.

Bobby then went to the garage and returned with a six-foot stepladder. He'd quickly unsnapped the 9-volt battery from the basement smoke detector, and slid a completely discharged battery back along the plastic holder, sliding it along and snapping it forward into the contacts. With partially discharged batteries, the alarm would chirp until new ones were installed, so Bobby had discharged all the energy from that and five other batteries, his prearranged answer to any questions already firmly in mind: "*I guess I got confused and put old ones in instead of new ones.*" Once he had rigged the basement smoke detector with the drained battery, Bobby did the same with the other two detectors downstairs and the three upstairs. He then returned the ladder to the garage where only his father's car, a late-model Honda Civic, was parked.

Next, Bobby had gone down to the basement and looked on the bench. The cat, Tramp, with the contents of three adult human sleeping pills added to his supper at seven, was now barely breathing and near death. Bobby picked up Tramp and placed him on the bench next to the closed window.

Earlier, at seven o'clock that evening, once Bobby had lured Tramp through the window and onto the bench top, Bobby had closed the window and made sure Tramp ate all of his dinner—including the sleeping pills in powder from inside their capsules—before Bobby had left the basement.

Bobby had then climbed up onto the bench and searched through the dirty window, but there was nothing to see outside but thin bushes and a dark hillside beyond. The neighbors didn't have a view to this window. He re-opened the window just enough for Tramp to slip through, or make it appear that he had.

After climbing back down, Bobby then pulled out a small sheet of plywood from the back of the bench, and placed it next to the open basement window. He used a block of wood under the center of the plywood to act as a fulcrum. He rocked the plywood back and forth like a teeter-totter.

Once he was convinced the simple contraption was functional, he pulled over a one-gallon gas can, three-quarters full and used for the lawn-mower, placing the can carefully onto the back edge of the teeter-totter. He loosened the gas cap until it was secured by only a fraction of a thread of the spout.

He then picked up Tramp's near-lifeless body and, holding the cat as high as he could reach above the bench where Tramp would normally jump down, dropped the twenty-pound dead weight onto the front edge of the plywood.

The gas can shot up in the air and backwards a few inches, landing at an angle on its bottom edge. It fell over onto the bench, and the cap came off, gas spilling out all over the wooden work bench and dripping over the edge and onto the plywood.

He had placed several small pieces of plywood in front of the bench as a makeshift standing platform against the cold concrete floor, and the one directly under the dripping gas began soaking up some of it. Cardboard boxes filled with all sorts of old household items had already been moved closer to the bench, making for a narrow path between.

The gas fumes were heavy but not dangerous—yet. Bobby then went over to the water heater and stooped down, removing the outer access door at the bottom so he could see the flame. Having already turned on the hot water faucet upstairs, much of the hot water had already left, and the heater had kicked in. The flame was burning at full volume behind the inner access cover. He tucked the outer cover inside the opening, something he'd seen his father do.

And that was it for the basement. Bobby went up the basement stairs, leaving the door ajar a few inches, and then ran upstairs to his room where Cheryl was waiting impatiently, clutching her purse.

"Put it back!" Bobby had said angrily, slightly out of breath. "Don't take anything. Everything's got to go."

Except, that is, for the walkie-talkies and certain critical contents of Bobby's computer's hard drive. He had already transferred all of his game programs and sound files—including recorded conversations from Ken's office and the software program to play it back—onto a dozen high density CDs, and had those stashed in his backpack, too.

"How come you get to keep stuff, and I don't?" Cheryl whined softly.

"Because that's how it is, Cheryl. I've already got the backpack in Mom's car."

Bobby had a good idea what to expect later, and he and Cheryl had rehearsed repeatedly how to react, what to say, and what not to say.

Going it over now one more time, Bobby had said, "You can get away with a lot of silence if they think you are in some kind of shock or something."

"Should I cry a lot?"

"Yes, even for no reason. And hug people if they look like they think you need it. I can't be around every second telling you what to do, so you're going to be on your own sometimes. Especially later when they start asking questions about what happened. They'll talk to us separate for that."

Bobby could smell the smoke now. He flicked his thumb over his shoulder, saying, "You get undressed and get into bed. I'll be right back."

Downstairs at the basement door, Bobby saw black smoke was already streaming out under the top of the jamb and around the top of the door, and he could see the reflection off the staircase wall as flames spread in the basement.

Standing poised to run upstairs, he'd watched patiently as the thick smoke swirled into the kitchen, dining room, and hallway back to Sam's private office. It hung down two feet from the ceilings. Soon the smoke began to find its way up the staircase, and into Bobby's eyes and throat.

The whole lower floor was quickly filling with smoke. He knew it wouldn't be long before the flames coming from the basement would start in on the ceiling above the basement door. Above that was the master bedroom, the door now closed. The last thing he saw before dashing upstairs were the flames blowing through the open basement door in search of oxygen, finding a fresh supply in the house.

As he walked by Cheryl's room, he knocked gently three times, and then opened up the bathroom door to allow better flame ventilation. He'd already opened the bathroom window.

The fire had spread faster than Bobby imagined, but he and Cheryl were prepared. By standing next to the window at the end of hallway, all they had to do was pull back the thick window drapes, lift up the lower section of the double hung window and climb out. He'd tested it out several times. It was a four-foot drop to the lower ridgeline over the garage. He wanted the drapes to cover the windows for as long as possible so no one outside could see the flames until it was too late.

As the smoke thickened, it also came further down from the ceiling. Finally, when crouched down on their knees and Bobby seeing the massive flames shooting up the stairwell, he drew back the window drapes, opened the window, and he and Cheryl climbed out and dropped to the top of the attached garage. Their faces covered with soot, he smudged her face and rubbed his own face with his hands.

From that vantage point, Bobby had a good view of the street and of the surrounding houses. With all the pine trees, it was difficult for anyone to see the house. He scanned with his eyes, looking for anyone coming outside. And they waited.

When the flames finally reached the window some five long minutes later, Bobby spotted Mr. Avery, from the house across the street, run into his front yard.

It was show time. On demand, Cheryl screamed at the top of her lungs, and shortly after, Bobby shouted, "Help, Mr. Avery ... up here!" He coughed loudly and repeatedly. "We can't get down!" he cried.

Scott Avery, in his pajamas and robe, ran across the street and to the far side of the garage where the roof sloped down his way. "Come on down, kids," shouted up, waving his arms. "This way, hurry!" When Bobby and Cheryl reached the edge of the roof, Avery saw little Cheryl's smoke and tear-streaked face. He called up. "Jump down, Cheryl. I'll catch you."

Without protest, she jumped into his arms. Avery, in his mid-40s, caught her a little off balance, but he didn't fall, and Cheryl landed safely. Bobby jumped next, and Avery's chest caught the full brunt of the downward force. He fell backwards, clutching Bobby to his chest and protecting the boy from the fall.

Avery quickly ushered Bobby and Cheryl back towards his house, shouting to his wife, outside on the porch, "Marcie, call nine-one-one … hurry!" Marcie and Darcy had been best of friends, sharing almost everything about their lives and those around them.

Heroes do things on instinct, and Bobby had just found the perfect one in Scott Avery for his little drama. Bobby didn't know that a few seconds before, his father had fallen out the second story window, and was still alive, made possible by the true hero of the night—Darcy Wynette.

More accustomed to the effects of her sleeping pills than Sam, Darcy had coughed and coughed again before finally being aroused by the smoke. For Sam, the combination of wine and sleeping pills had knocked him out cold.

The swirling black clouds of smoke were already thick in the room, and flames had made it through the floor over the basement door below and up the inside wall, blocking any exit into the hall. Coughing repeatedly and still woozy, Darcy shook Sam, trying to wake him, but he didn't stir. She yelled in his ear, shaking him as hard as she could. Sam finally opened his eyes, his brain groggy. "Come on, Sam," she cried, "Wake up. There's a fire!"

Darcy strained to push him out of the bed onto the floor, but Sam was all but a dead weight. She crawled over the top of him and plopped onto the floor on his side of the bed, using the edge of the bed for purchase as she dragged him over the side by his arm. He landed with a thud, and that shocked him into a semi-conscious state. He looked her in the eyes, but he couldn't focus.

"There's a fire, Sam. We have to get out!" The flames were close enough for Darcy to feel the intense heat, and she began dragging Sam by the arm towards the window overlooking the back yard. She was becoming quickly exhausted. "Please, please help, Sam," she cried, inching towards the window.

"Huh?" he replied, aroused by the pull on his arm, his brain not anywhere close to being in gear. He felt the heat on his back, and that stimulated him to move forward with Darcy pulling him.

Once at the window, invisible above them in the thick smoke, Darcy stood up, feeling with her hands to find the double hung window latch while holding her breath. In her panic, Darcy found but could not open the latch, as she was pushing up on the lower window with her left hand, forcing the two sections together. The heat in the room was now intense. She dropped back down and tried to get another breath of air near the floor before another attempt, and noticed that the back of Sam's t-shirt and pajama bottoms were on fire. She lunged across him and tried to smother the flames with the front of her body.

The extra weight on Sam stirred him to further consciousness, and he struggled to free himself. Darcy then made the second attempt at the window latch, with eyes closed and again holding her breath. Precious seconds ticked away while the flames and intense heat closed in. She finally cleared the latch and pulled up on the lower section. It opened. She again dropped to the floor gasping for breath. She reached over and helped Sam to his knees. She pulled him up to a semistanding position, his knees against the wall, smelling the burned flesh on his back. She then pushed his head out the window. He lay bent over the windowsill, half in and half out.

Almost totally exhausted now, Darcy collapsed to the floor, taking in more smoke as she gasped. In a final effort, she strained hard to push Sam up and over the sill and out the window. He wouldn't budge, despite several attempts. Finally, Darcy collapsed to the floor for the last time, her heart now in fibrillation. She clutched her quickly failing heart and slumped over onto her side, where the flames closed in on her sleeping gown. She died of cardiac arrest before the flames got to her.

With his head out the window and able to breath fresh air, Sam came to life a little. He felt the intense heat on his backside and legs. On fire, he struggled to wiggle himself out the window. He dropped from the second story window, with only a few scraggly bushes to break his fall. He managed to roll around enough to extinguish the flames before crawling about ten feet away from the building. Sam searched for Darcy, but she wasn't around. He finally passed out, smoke from his clothes and burned flesh pungent in the air.

After that, chaos had ensued. Several neighbors saw the flames from their front windows and dialed 9-1-1. Neighbors came outside, and with Bobby and Cheryl both screaming that their parents were still inside, several neighbors ran over to the Wynette house, now engulfed in flames inside and out. Neighbors then ran around the house shouting Sam's and Darcy's names and looking to find if there was a safe way in without literally running through the flames. There was not. The house was totally engulfed.

Both Bobby and Cheryl used the adrenaline rush of the moment to augment their performances with Avery, and he bought them hook, line, and sinker.

After a few moments, a man came running around from the back of the house, pointing back and waving to the neighbors nearby. "Sam made it out!" the man cried, in near hysteria. "God, he's burned awfully bad. Get some blankets or something." The sight and smell of Sam, all his clothes burned off revealing a charred body, was just too much too quickly for the man. He bent over, now weeping, and vomited.

Bobby flinched, and then responded coolly, "It's Dad. I've got to go see him."

Avery grabbed Bobby by the arm and held firm. "No, Bobby. You stay right here." Avery didn't want Bobby having a close-up look at his badly burned father. He led Bobby and Cheryl, both weeping uncontrollably, back into his own house, and instructed Marcie to keep them inside.

Their main performance over, only the curtain calls remained. "Just don't forget to keep mentioning how Mr. Avery saved us," Bobby whispered secretively to Cheryl through his sniffles, adding, "Everyone loves a hero, even if it's a bit of a stretch."

Bobby and Cheryl went to their separate twin beds at the Easton house, both exhausted from the ordeal. It was nearly two o'clock in the morning. Bobby turned over to face Cheryl, saying softly, "I think I'm going to get used to this real fast."

"Me, too, Bobby. I hope they let us stay forever."

Neither Bobby nor Cheryl gave much further thought on what may have happened to their parents. They certainly felt no remorse for what they had done. They were, in fact, oblivious to how Darcy had suffered, and how Sam was going to when he regained consciousness. And, in addition to his physical trauma, Sam had lost the woman he loved.

But to Bobby and Cheryl, it meant only that they now had a new family … and one of their choosing. Someone to love and take care of them, providing the things that money could buy. In the final analysis, it wasn't the parents themselves who provided the lure for Bobby and Cheryl, but rather the idealized image of the parents—a handsome couple with strong financial prospects.

*****

Note to John: Once again, the official reports were a bit dry on the results of the fire investigation. I hope you find the dramatic license appropriate. Steven

44 The Crying Game

Ken Easton reached over and picked up the phone, glancing at the clock, reading 10:15 a.m. "Hello," he said sleepily, rubbing his eyes. Tristin turned to him and was now awake, too, wondering about the call.

"Mr. Easton?"

"Yes."

"Good morning, sir. This is Captain Mike Davies—from the fire department. We spoke last night. Sorry to wake you."

Ken sat up and tried to clear the fog from his head. "No, that's okay, Mr. Davies." Glancing outside, he first saw then heard it raining heavily outside. The rain had been coming down since just after sunrise.

"I know it must have been quite a night for you and the missus. How are the kids?"

Ken knew not to correct the mistake about Tristin, as he suspected a divulgence of their unmarried status might somehow throw a monkey wrench into the works. "It was pretty rough for them, I'm sure, but we put 'em to bed and they fell asleep immediately. Tristin and I checked on them a couple of times, and they seem fine."

"That's good. I would like to speak with Bobby and Cheryl today and was wondering if I could come by around noon. There really is no *good time* to speak with youngsters after something like this, but experts agree the sooner the better. Is that a problem?"

"No, I'm sure it won't be. We'll make sure they're up and ready."

"Thank you, Mr. Easton."

After showering and dressing, Ken walked down the hall and opened the door. Both Bobby and Cheryl were awake, laying facing each other on the twin beds. "Hi, everything okay?" Ken asked.

"Yeah," Bobby said.

"Me, too," Cheryl said, adding, "But I'm hungry."

That was a good sign to Ken. "No problem, sweetheart. We'll rustle up some breakfast. You like bacon and eggs, right?" Cheryl nodded and so did Bobby. "And sourdough toast?" Ken added. Again, two heads nodded. A sudden thunderclap off to the west startled them, but each smiled when they realized it was just thunder.

At the dining table, and once the kids had polished off all their plates, Ken said, "The man from the fire department needs to talk to both of you. Are you guys up to it?"

Tristin chimed in with, "If you're not, that's okay, but we should know as soon as possible, because he's coming in less than an hour."

"It's okay," Bobby said without emotion. Cheryl lowered her chin and nodded.

Promptly at noon, Mike Davies showed up at the house. While having a cup of coffee with Ken and Tristin, Davies briefed them on Sam's condition. "He's got extensive burns, and even under the best medical care, it's 50:50 at best. He's fighting for his life right now, but I don't want the kids to know that."

Ken ushered Davies down the hall and into his office where Bobby and Cheryl waited. After introducing the kids to Davies, Ken left, closing the door behind him and joined Tristin in the kitchen. "Grab your coffee cup. Let's bundle up and go for a walk on the bluff."

In contradiction to Bobby's firm belief that they would be separated during some form of "interrogation," Davies actually wanted the kids together for mutual support. If there were any discrepancies, Davies could deal with that later. He began by telling them that their father was in intensive care at the burn ward, under heavy sedation and very seriously injured.

"Can we go see him?" Cheryl asked, wiping tears from her face.

"No, not right now, honey. He wouldn't know you were there, but maybe in a few days he'll be awake."

"Is he going to die, Mr. Davies?" Bobby asked, his eyes welling with tears. He looked out the garden window, watching the rain come down.

"He's under the best medical care in the world, Bobby. People with burns like that have a good chance at recovery." Davies was being very optimistic, and he didn't go into the grim actuarial details, or the aftermath of recovery, physical and psychological, that lasted a lifetime.

Next, Davies turned to events of the previous night, asking them what had occurred. Bobby and Cheryl told Davies about dinner, and that Sam and Darcy had drank wine, and then polished it off after dinner in the living room. Bobby said he went upstairs to his room with Cheryl to play computer games, and Cheryl concurred. No, they said, neither had been in the basement. Davies asked about the cat and the open window, and Cheryl started crying, "Poor Tramp ... I hope he didn't suffer."

Bobby took over and told Davies that's how Tramp got in the house, adding, "He was chased there sometimes by this wild cat that roams the neighborhood."

In their telling Davies what happened during and after the fire, both of them became emotional at various parts of the story. Cheryl sniffled and even cried in all the right places, and Bobby maintained—for the most part—a stiff upper lip and in support of his younger sister.

When Davies got around to the smoke detectors, he asked, "Did you hear any alarms go off?" Davies asked.

"No," Cheryl said. "Alarms from what?"

Davies looked to Bobby, a petrified look coming quickly on the young boy's face. He stared unblinking at Davies, who later put in his report, *"Bobby was not looking past me—he was looking through me, like he had something to say but was afraid to say it."*

"What is it, Bobby?" Davies asked.

Bobby lowered his chin and squeezed his eyes shut, shaking his head side to side.

"Bobby, did you hear an alarm, and maybe not respond right away?"

"No," Bobby said, starting to sob. "I didn't hear any alarm. And I knew last night that it was all my fault, but I didn't want to say anything."

"What do you mean? What was all your fault?" Cheryl demanded.

Davies glanced to an appropriately shocked young girl.

Tentatively, Bobby asked, "When you test one of those things—by pushing the button—and you don't hear anything, does that mean they're okay?"

Davies shook his head. "No, they're supposed to chirp a few times, why?"

"I was afraid of that." Through tears and sniffles, Bobby related the story. "On Valentine's Day ... I saw my dad with the stepladder and asked him what he was doing ... he said he was going to change the smoke detector batteries ... I offered to do it as a sort of extra Valentine's Day present, and he let me change them all. He said that after I closed the cover to be sure and press the button to make sure the battery was okay … but he didn't say what would happen. He told me the new batteries were in the kitchen drawer. When I opened up a drawer and saw some batteries, I thought they were the new ones. But they weren't wrapped or anything. They must have been the old ones. Mom didn't like to throw them in the trash because of the environment."

The tears started to flow, but Bobby slogged through the rest of the story, building to a crescendo of emotion. "Anyway, when I pressed the first one, nothing happened, and I figured it was okay, so I did the same thing with the other five." At this point, Bobby broke down, weeping. Through his sobs, he finally managed to say, "They were run down and didn't work … I just know it."

At that point, Cheryl started to wail, "Bobby, how could you?"

It was quite a performance. Davies left his chair and put his hand on Bobby's shoulder, speaking to Bobby but indicating through facial gestures to Cheryl to not castigate Bobby any further. "It's okay, son. These things happen."

As if to underscore the moment, a close rumbling of thunder rattled the windows.

Davies left the kids in the office to calm down while he spoke with Ken and Tristin, both waiting in the kitchen. Davies began by summarizing Bobby's confession about the smoke detectors. Ken and Tristin were understandably shocked, but they also felt great empathy for Bobby.

Tristin wiped a tear from her eye. "They've already had a tough life, Mr. Davies. And now this."

"They are both probably going to need professional counseling, Mrs. Easton."

Tristin looked askance at Ken but didn't wait for his chance to say or not say anything. "Yes, we can see that, um ... actually, Mr. Davies, Ken and I are engaged, but not married yet."

Ken knew it would come out sooner or later. He hoped for the best.

"Oh, I see." Davies scratched his head in mild embarrassment. "Actually, I got some heat on letting the kids stay with you, not being family and all. But it was my call at the time, and I still say this is where they should be." He thought for a moment and chuckled. "Last night I just assumed you were married, and that's still my assumption, if you don't mind?"

Ken appreciated Davies' assessment of their character. "Thank you, Mr. Davies. We won't let you down."

Tristin held up her left hand, showing Davies her simple gold engagement band. "If anyone asks, I'll just say my husband is a tightwad."

*****

Note to John: Davies was apparently devastated later when he learned of the kids' involvement, especially after personally interviewing them the day after the fire. He told me that, as a

seasoned fire investigator, he'd never seen such a convincing performance by an adult, let alone two teenage kids. Steven

45 Taxi Driver

The rain stopped mid-afternoon and the skies cleared all along the central coast. For the next week, the weather was cool and breezy, but otherwise ideal for construction activities up on Nortze's lot. The entire first floor got framed up, and the framing crew was in good spirits, perhaps due to the fact that Gil Nortze wasn't poking his nose into everything. He couldn't. On Monday morning, while walking and looking up at the framing, he had stepped in a hole that trapped his left foot while he continued forward, breaking his ankle. He was on crutches with his foot in a fiberglass boot cast, not good for leaping around a building site.

Nortze hadn't shown up on the site until Wednesday, eager to push the framing crew to new heights of productivity, although they were about as efficient as could be. "More lumber!" he shouted to a man carrying a heavy load of two-by-fours on his shoulder, "You can carry more than that." Only he couldn't get past the gate, as it was stacked side to side with lumber. The crew managed easily enough, jumping up and walking back and forth across the lumber, but Nortze couldn't make it on his crutches.

The framing contractor, Al Jenkins, had "stacked him out," purposely making it impossible for Nortze to get past the gate. "The man's a menace," Jenkins had told his crew. "And today, when I asked him when the windows and doors were coming, Nortze gave me this blank stare, like they suddenly drop out of the sky or something on the day when we need to start installing them."

Nortze spent the entire week in the trailer gnashing his teeth and arguing with window and door suppliers, trying to get them quicker. He paid an extra $7,500—on top of the $32,000 bill—for rushed production and delivery. It wasn't until Saturday that Nortze finally demanded that Jenkins clear away the blocked entrance so he could see what the hell was going on.

Also during that same week, the Easton household began to settle into a routine. Ken had worked at home in relative seclusion for so long that he had to fight off the feeling of being intruded upon. But with his life now changed, he concluded, he was simply going to have to make the best of it; not just for himself, but for Tristin and the kids, as well.

Both he and Tristin had worked tirelessly to clean out the guest bedroom, Ken's sister Laura's old bedroom, and set up a bed and some furniture for Cheryl. Bobby had Tyler's old room to himself now, and he and Cheryl shared the bathroom between. The arrangement provided for privacy when they wanted to be alone, but they were close enough talk when the mood struck. And because of the common heater vent supplying both Bobby's room and the bathroom, Cheryl sometimes kept up a running conversation with Bobby while she was in the bathroom and he in his room.

The kids had new wardrobes, too, Tristin having insisted on paying half as her contribution. There was money coming from insurance policies to the children for such essentials, but it hadn't arrived yet. Tristin had taken Cheryl and Bobby to the mall on a little shopping spree on Sunday, and Cheryl especially had shown Tristin how much she appreciated her efforts.

Ken was an early riser, so he made sure the kids were up and dressed for school, while Tristin cooked breakfast and talked to the kids about their activities for the day. Ken then made and packed lunch for them, and Tristin drove them to school before heading off to work. Ken picked them up from school at 3:15, and the kids had to do their homework until around six when Tristin got home.

By then, Ken had defrosted whatever they were going to have for dinner, sometimes cooking it himself, while the kids helped set the table. After dinner, the kids helped rinse and stack the dishes in the dishwasher. And then it was time either for talking, or watching a video together in the living room, or playing games in their rooms.

There were also regular updates from the burn ward. Ken called three times that week, and each time the nurse said there had been little change. "We're going to reduce his sedation on Friday," said the nurse, "so he may be coming around this weekend."

The kids didn't pester Ken with constant requests for their father's current condition, mostly because Ken had said, rather firmly to press home the point, "It's a very slow process, and if there is any change—good or bad—I'll know about it, and then I'll tell you."

With the kids in school and Tristin working, Ken had plenty of solitude to work on his acoustic sensor project. Even the construction noise, bad as it was, did not keep him from plowing ahead, often with headphones on and listening to music. By Friday afternoon, he'd gotten a lot accomplished, and eagerly awaited the shipment of the revised prototypes of the sensors. The package arrived by FedEx just before it was time to go and pick up the kids.

Going up the driveway, he saw that the ice plant damage on the slope still had not been fixed, reminding himself to say something to Nortze when he next saw him. Coming back down the driveway with the kids in the Bronco, Ken stopped to pick up the mail. As he was just reaching in to retrieve the mail, Nortze drove up his newly graded driveway and stopped, leaning partly out the window. "Howdy, neighbor," he said cheerfully.

"Oh, hi, Gil," Ken said politely, his brain in high gear wondering what the kids were thinking right now.

"Anything for me in my box?" he asked.

Ken opened Nortze's unstable mailbox and pulled out a couple of pieces of mail, walking over and handing them to him. "Here ya go."

"Thanks," he said, taking the mail. "Managed to go and bust up my ankle, so I'm a bit lame these days."

Ken saw the crutches over the front seat. "Sorry to hear that."

Nortze pointed to the Bronco. "I didn't know you and Tristin had kids so fast."

Dismissing Nortze's inappropriate attempt at humor, Ken stepped up close and leaned down, hands on his knees. "Theirs was the house that burned down last Saturday night. Their mother was killed, and their father was badly burned. Tristin and I are looking after them."

"Oh, I heard about that. And I've seen the kids come and go from your place, so I was just wondering." The man had no grasp of the painful circumstances.

Not wanting to make formal introductions at this point in time, Ken begged off, saying, "Hey, gotta go, okay?" He had understandably forgotten all about the ice plant damage.

Back in the Bronco and heading down the lower driveway, Ken waited for one of the kids to say something. There was only silence. Finally, in the garage and with the engine shut down, Ken broached the subject. "So, how did you react when you saw him?"

Bobby shrugged. "Seems okay to me." Bobby looked to Cheryl, ready for her prepared answer. "He does look a lot like Bobby, that's for sure."

"Yeah, I noticed that, too," Ken offered, and then changed the subject. "Everything okay at school?"

"Yes, everyone is being so nice," Cheryl said, softly.

"And the school gave us all new books and stuff," Bobby added.

"That's great," Ken replied. "You guys got homework to do this weekend?"

"An hour or so," Cheryl said.

"None for me," Bobby added. "We just had a test today."

"Oh, yeah, what on?"

"Math."

"How'd you do?"

"Aced it." Bobby said proudly.

"Good for you. How about if I call Tristin and have her stop by the video store? Any movie you want … on the house."

From the back seat, Cheryl stifled a little laugh. "Oh, Ken, it's *always* on the house."

"That's true," Ken said. He looked in the rear-view mirror and caught Cheryl's sparkling eyes and her smile. He hadn't seen her like that in weeks. "But this is something special—for Bobby." With Darcy's funeral coming up the next day, Ken wanted them to enjoy themselves a little that night. Ken also had Connie's Memorial Service to attend on Sunday, so it was looking to be an emotionally tough weekend ahead for him.

"No, I'm okay," Bobby said, "Me and a couple of friends are going to network tonight on our computers. But thanks anyway."

"How 'bout you, Cheryl? Got any big plans for tonight?"

She smiled again, this time a little embarrassed. "No, I just want to be with you and Tristin."

That touched Ken. "You got it. After dinner, we'll look through my video collection and see if there's anything you want to watch."

"That would be great." Cheryl wanted to see Jody Foster in *"Taxi Driver,"* part of Ken's collection, but she figured she had better wait a while to make that request. The watched *"My Mother the Car"* instead.

The following afternoon, Ken was still in his dark suit and tie, and he had his back against the pillows of their bed. "Well, that was pretty awful. At least it puts me in shape for Connie's service tomorrow." After the attempt at gallows humor, he rubbed his eyes now drained of tears, then turned to Tristin lying next to him, also still fully dressed but with her shoes off. "You okay?"

"Uh huh," Tristin said, tired from the emotional ordeal. "I think the kids took it better than we did."

With their father not doing well at all after the doctors reduced his heavy sedation, the mood at the funeral was even more somber than Ken or Tristin had expected. All of Sam's ChiP buddies had shown up, and all of Darcy's friends. She had no brothers or sisters. It was a closed-casket funeral, and every time Ken had looked at Darcy's coffin, the image of what lay inside haunted him.

"Yeah, well, they're tough little hombres," Ken replied, "I'll say that for them."

It was as if Bobby and Cheryl had networked the cemetery chapel full of mourners. To every single person who offered their condolences, Bobby and Cheryl had made sure to say something about how grateful they were to Ken and Tristin for taking them in. Or that they were doing fine, thanks to Ken and Tristin, or that Ken and Tristin were being very supportive of their emotional needs. Knowing the stakes were high, Bobby and Cheryl had shot for unanimous consent that they were in the right home environment at the Easton household.

"After they've had some time in their rooms," Tristin suggested, "with maybe a nap or something, what say we take them on 17-Mile Drive out on the peninsula. We could walk on the beach and maybe stop and all have something to eat at one of the nice restaurants out there near Pebble Beach."

Not feeling like cooking, and suspecting that Tristin felt the same way, Ken said, "I'm up for it if you are."

46 The Good Son

It was just after one o'clock on Sunday afternoon, and Ken had already left for Connie's funeral service. Tristin was washing Cheryl's hair in the master bathroom, and they were chatting away about girl stuff. Bobby shouted from the hallway that he was going for a walk. Tristin's voice echoed from the bathroom, "Just be back by three, okay?" That's when Ken was expected back home.

"Okay." In the garden on the south side, Bobby saw Jake the Tern fly out of his birdhouse and head out over the cliff to the north, that problem with his wing still affecting his flight. Bobby pulled an invisible rifle to his right shoulder, closed his left eye, and followed Jake for a moment. "Pow!" he said aloud, and then jerked back a bit, mimicking recoil to his shoulder.

He walked up the south slope, stopping at the fence and then walked east the length of the fence. He was crossing the level ground just beneath Nortze's dirt driveway when something caught his eye. Stopping and staring at a man trying to remove a screen from the site trailer window, Bobby quickly realized it was Gil Nortze. And he was on crutches, cursing under his breath and struggling with the window screen. Bobby walked over and stopped a few feet away. "Can I help you with something, sir?"

Nortze startled and turned to Bobby, then sank onto his crutches, winded from the effort thus far.

"Locked my fucking keys in the trailer just after I got here," he began. "I'm trying to get this window open."

"Let me see if I can get it." Bobby offered.

"Yeah, sure, thanks." Nortze stepped back and watched the youngster with the dark hair and stocky build first remove the screen and then pull out a penknife from his pocket. Like a seasoned second-story man, Bobby easily pried up the bottom of the cheap aluminum window, and then pulled it out and away from the track. He placed the window down against the trailer, and in one hop, jumped up and pulled himself over the sill and inside the office.

"Wow, that was fast!" Nortze exclaimed, and he began to hobble around to the front door. It was open by the time he got to it, Bobby inside and bowing like a butler as he held up a Nortze's keys.

Nortze smiled. "Well, thank you, son."

Nortze ascended the stairs awkwardly, struggling up the last step. What's your name?" he asked panting, stopping just inside the door for a rest.

"Bob. Bob Wynette."

Nortze extended his hand and Bobby shook it. "Gil Nortze. Thanks for savin' my bacon here, Bob. Don't know what I would have done if you hadn't come along."

"No problem, Mr. Nortze. Glad I could help."

Still winded from all the activity, Nortze plopped down in his chair, placing his crutches on the floor. "So, you're staying with Ken and Tristin, huh?"

"Yes, sir. At least until my dad gets better."

"Sorry to hear about that. And your mother, too."

"Thank you," Bobby said softly, eyes turned down.

"Your dad's a cop or something, right?"

"Highway Patrol."

"Haven't run into any of those yet, thank God."

"Just don't speed between the top of Spindrift and Point Lobos. They hide in the trees."

"Hey, thanks, I didn't know that." Something popped into Nortze's head, and he picked up a tape measure off the desk. "Damn, I've got to go and re-measure that front entrance. I think the framers got it a foot too narrow for the side panels on the front door assembly." He glanced at his watch. "Shit, I told the door guy I'd call him at home half an hour ago."

Without so much as asking, Bobby walked over a few steps and reached out his hand for the tape measure, insisting, "Give it to me. I'll go do it."

"You sure?" Nortze said, handing Bobby the tape.

"No problem, Mr. Nortze. I'll have it to within an eighth of an inch."

"You're my man," Nortze said, smiling. "I'll come to the door, and you can shout it over to me."

"Sure thing." With that, Bobby practically skipped out the door and across the dirt. When he was at the framed entrance, he stuck the tape down at the base of the inside stud, let it out and made sure it was straight and flat as he pulled it to the opposing stud. He stared at it a moment, pushed the lock down, and let it sit on the floor while he stood up. "Eight feet, one quarter inch—exactly!" he called to Nortze.

"You sure!" Nortze shouted back.

Without rechecking, Bobby shouted. "Exactly!"

Nortze waved Bobby back. "Okay, if you say so."

Bobby returned to the trailer, and Nortze was already on the phone. "No, no changes—that's the right width. Framers must have screwed up and got something right for a change," he said, and he rang off.

"Gotta keep a close eye on things around here. People are always getting stuff mixed up."

Bobby smiled. "If you want it done right, gotta do it yourself."

"You are so right. Hey, want some coffee?" Nortze pointed to the coffee pot.

"Sure, thanks," Bobby replied. Not a coffee drinker, Bobby nonetheless wanted to stick around for a while longer. He felt very comfortable in Nortze's presence, wondering if it was because the man was, in fact, his own real father. Bobby went to the coffee pot and poured the hot coffee into a paper cup, adding plenty of sugar and dry creamer.

"What do you do on weekends?" Nortze asked.

"Just hang out, I guess," Bobby replied, not knowing where that was going.

"Well, I was just thinking that maybe with you living so close and all, you might want to come up and help me out up here once in a while. You know—pick up nails, sweep the place down once a week—stuff like that. There's probably other stuff, too, things I can't even think of now, but what with me in this damned cast for six weeks, it might be easier with you around."

At the prospect of earning extra spending money, Bobby's eyes practically bugged out of their sockets. Computer games and accessories were expensive, and he felt uncomfortable asking Ken for money, at least this early in the game. "You mean you want to hire me?"

"Sure, why not?"

"Wow, that would be great."

"Five bucks an hour," Nortze said, waving his pointed finger at Bobby, "but not a penny more. Just on weekends, though."

That seemed like a small fortune to Bobby, and as for the schedule, he was already committed to homework during the week. "Sounds great, Mr. Nortze. I'll have to ask Ken, though."

Nortze was a little disappointed that he couldn't strike a firm deal while the fire was hot and the labor dirt-cheap. "Oh, sure. Just let me know as soon as possible."

Walking back to the house, Bobby was in a dilemma. Not only had he gone off on his own and met Gil Nortze, but the man had offered him a paying job. It would put him in frequent contact with Nortze, something perhaps not so agreeable with Ken and/or Tristin. He needed time to think about how to make it all work out.

By the time he reached the front door, Bobby already had a solution in mind. It involved only two key conversational components, both meant to wear down any defenses: "keeping busy" and "financial independence." Bobby was quickly developing the ability to achieve a desired goal, first by formulating a sound overall strategy, and then employing whatever tactics, and at any cost, necessary to achieve it. He was at least true to his bloodline.

47 Trading Places

Ken arrived home trying to break out of his sullen and mildly depressed mood. Two funeral services in two days had taken its toll. Inside the garage, he switched off the engine and sat for a moment in the Bronco. An image from the memorial service stuck in his mind: Little Dag, Connie's five-year old son, asked his father how it was that "all of Mommy was in that little jar," containing the ashes of her remains.

Ken picked up the typed sheet off the passenger seat and read the opening sentence of his brief statement at Connie's service:

"This day brings home to all of us the special nature of life itself—a complicated series of personal relationships and memories now coming together at one place, and at one time, to help soothe the pain."

Words didn't come close to encompassing the true nature of the pain that Ken still felt over Connie's death. But at least he had said something, and Randy had appreciated it. When he got older, Dag might appreciate it, too.

Inside the house, Ken took Tristin aside in the bedroom and summarized the service. Tristin told Ken what the kids had been doing, ending with, "And there's something Bobby did that you should know about." Tristin took in a big breath of air and expelled it. "He was on a walk, and he found himself up near Gil's lot. Gil was there and on crutches trying to break into his own trailer to get his keys. Anyway, Bobby could see the guy needed help, so he helped Gil get his keys."

As Tristin related the rest of the story, Ken went from a state of shock about the possible consequences to one of reluctant admiration for Bobby. Even when Tristin brought up Nortze offering Bobby a job helping out up there, Ken could only shake his head in amazement. He had always feared the worst—some major confrontation ending with Bobby and/or Cheryl feeling awful, and

Gil Nortze in a state of deep resentment, if not high panic.

But now, it seemed, the worst was over. He agreed with Tristin that Bobby could actually benefit by the association—it would give the boy something productive to do on the weekends, and he could "pay some of his own way," as Tristin put it, rebuilding his self-esteem. Bobby had been successful in planting the ideas.

Ken was seeing things from a new perspective now. "So what if Nortze finds out," he said. "Things like that don't stay secret forever."

"That's true, too," Tristin replied, "And Bobby said that at some point, when the time is right, he's going to tell him—face to face. He said he didn't want Gil finding out from anyone else but him."

"Well, that's pretty damned brave of him."

"I know. But I think he's mature enough now to handle it. And with Bobby right here, and Gil up there, maybe it was meant to be."

Without thinking about it, Ken blurted out, "Yeah, maybe there'll be a Nortze family reconciliation or something." It was only after the words left his mouth that Ken thought about the ramifications of that possibility.

Tristin elaborated on Ken's statement. "If Sam were to die, or be so disabled that he couldn't take care of them, their only legal relative is Sam's sister."

"And their only blood relative is Gil," Ken said. "Please tell me I'm crazy to think that Gil Nortze might even consider taking his kids back."

"If we don't adopt them, then yes."

Ken slumped down a good two inches. "Man, life is complicated sometimes."

Not for Bobby Wynette, though. Knowing that Ken's probable immediate response to Bobby's newfound relationship with his real father would be negative, once he'd planted the seeds with Tristin in a flanking maneuver to bypass that reaction, Bobby had wisely butted out, leaving it up to Ken and Tristin to do the watering.

As for Ken and Tristin, they were helping to lay the emotional groundwork for what neither of them could possibly see coming—a valuable lesson about the universal, and immutable, Law of Unintended Consequences.

*****

Note to John: At this point, you may think you know where things are headed, and you might be right. I sincerely doubt, however, that even a man with your dramatic talents could accurately predict the roller coaster ride to come. Steven

48 Back to the Future

"The man abandoned us, Bobby, and our mother, too. How could you even think of working for him?"

Bobby swiveled in his chair, trying to make his sister understand. "For several reasons, Cheryl. The extra money will come in handy—that's the obvious one. But there's a bigger picture here you're not seeing." He stopped swiveling and leaned forward, elbows resting on his knees. "What if Dad recovers?"

"Do you think he might?"

"Yesterday I overheard Ken say to Tristin it was still fifty-fifty—so he could."

Cheryl thought for a moment. "Then we go and live with him, I guess."

"That's right," Bobby said. "And after that, it's back to square one. Ken and Tristin get married in June, she gets pregnant, and it's over for us."

"They're getting married in June? How do you know that?"

"It's supposed to be a big secret between them, but I wormed it out of her. Anyway, after she gets pregnant, we're out of the picture."

"Why is that?"

"Because if we're with Dad, and they start thinking about their own family, they'll drop us like hot potatoes."

"I guess you're right."

"Of course I'm right. Now, what if Dad *doesn't* make it? I didn't burn down our house so we could be taken back to the pound—or live at a real one at Aunt Mary's. I did it so we could live here, with Ken and Tristin as our new mom and dad."

"Then we stay here, right?"

"Maybe, maybe not. The government people may say we *have* to go live at Aunt Mary's and those mongrel dogs. Or they might say we have to go back to foster care."

Cheryl was taken aback. "They wouldn't do that, would they?"

"That's the problem—we don't know."

"What's all this have to do with Mr. Nortze?"

"He's our backup in case things don't work out here."

Cheryl was aghast. "You mean live with him?"

"Don't be so impractical, Cheryl. The guy is loaded, and he has that great big house going up right next door."

"But he doesn't want us, Bobby."

"Maybe not before." Bobby's brain had been working overtime. "But if push comes to shove, he might *have to* take us back."

"What do you mean, *have to*?"

"Well, like I said, the man's loaded now. I don't mean putting a gun to his head or anything … just make him decide it's the lesser of two evils. Like it would be better to take us in than keep us out."

"How do you do that?" Cheryl asked.

"Ever heard of lawyers?"

49 Battery Park

It was the next Saturday, the 16th, before the doctors would allow Bobby and Cheryl to see their father. He had been fighting pneumonia in his lungs and septicemia in his bloodstream, caused by bacteria from the burn areas, with chills and a high fever. And he had to be under heavy sedation for the dressing changes on his back and legs, front and back.

The doctors purposely had not changed the dressing on Saturday, or given him more painkillers, as they wanted him as alert as he could be to see his children. Ken and Tristin drove Bobby and Cheryl to the hospital in Monterey, and Ken warned the kids what to expect and not to expect.

"The doctors say he can't talk yet," Ken began, "And he might be in some pain, too." Ken didn't say why. "Also, you're going to have to put on surgical gowns, gloves, and masks so you don't bring in any germs from outside."

At the door into the burn ward, the nurse took Ken and Tristin aside and whispered, "They can go in for just a few minutes to say hello. It's more for Sam's spirits than anything else. Seeing the kids may give him the strength to fight this thing. I'll come and get you when the time is up. If there's a problem before that, bring them back out right away. "

Sam was on his right side, and his eyes were closed as they moved up close to his bedside. Heart monitor wires and intravenous needles were hidden beneath a blanket draped over his upper body. The only thing visible was the set of oxygen tubes up his nostrils.

"Dad?" Cheryl said weakly. "Dad, can you hear me?"

Sam opened his eyes and slowly picked up his head. He saw Cheryl, blinked twice and nodded his head very slightly, and he made a little grunting noise.

Bobby now stepped forward. "We just came to see you, Dad. We're praying for you."

Sam blinked his eyes, and they began to fill up with tears.

Cheryl stepped a few inches closer. "Ken and Tristin are taking good care of us, Dad, until you get better."

Sam now looked first to Ken and then Tristin, nodding his head and closing his eyes.

Cheryl then said, "We'll come back when you're feeling a little better."

The nurse entered and motioned to Tristin that the time was up for the kids. She ushered the kids back towards the door.

"Can I spend a minute with Sam?" Ken asked the nurse. She nodded and closed the door behind her. Ken turned and leaned in close to Sam. "You hang in there, Sam."

Sam's eyes now flashed and he grunted something that sounded to Ken like, "matterly."

"What, Sam?"

Sam blinked and forced his eyes open. He cleared a little of his throat, and with a hoarse whisper forcing the word from his lips and tongue, he said, "Batteries."

"Batteries? What about batteries?"

"The fire … Bobby."

Ken could see that Sam was straining with the words. And he knew about Bobby confessing to not replacing the batteries with new ones. "We know all about that, Sam. Bobby told us that he must have taken the old ones out of the drawer by mistake."

Sam closed his eyes and shook his head side-to-side. "No," he said weakly, "I gave him … the new ones … put in his … pocket." Sam then opened his eyes and looked directly at Sam with a penetrating gaze, saying as best he could, "Be … care … ful."

A chill went down the spine of Ken Easton as his eyes locked with Sam's. "I will, Sam," he said. "I will."

Driving back home, Ken kept mostly silent, thinking about Sam's words. *Maybe he was delirious … who would be thinking about batteries at a time like that? Sam was just confused about what happened.* He said nothing to Tristin about his conversation with Sam, wanting to think about it.

*****

Note to John: My math seems to be a little off. Only ten more sections, promise. Steven

50 See No Evil

On Sunday morning at seven o'clock, the phone rang on Ken's bedside table. It startled both Ken and Tristin awake. Ken answered expectantly, "Hello?"

"Mr. Easton?"

"Speaking."

"This is Dr. Hovington—at the burn center. I'm afraid I have some bad news. Mr. Wynette passed away about an hour ago."

"Oh, dear God, no."

"I'm very sorry. We did everything we could, and Sam was trying to battle back, but it was all too much for his system."

Tristin put her hand on Ken's arm, and he turned to her. He closed his eyes to fight back the tears, and he briefly and shook his head, saying into the phone, "Did he say anything before?"

"No, I'm sorry, he didn't. He just passed quietly in his sleep this morning. You'll be getting a call tomorrow from the administration office tomorrow, hopefully first thing. Will you be home?"

"Yes, I will. I'll be here all day."

"Fine. They'll be going over the procedural matters. Again, I'm very sorry, Mr. Easton. I'm sure you and your wife will know best how to handle telling the children."

"Yes, we can handle that." Ken saw Tristin's tears.

"They're also fully covered under Mr. Wynette's insurance policy, including psychology. I've already spoken with the administrators, and they will be assigning one for the children in the next few days. They should be calling you soon as well."

Ken and Tristin waited until after breakfast to tell the children their father had just passed way. Both Cheryl and Bobby cried and otherwise responded as if they were genuinely crushed by the news. By then, however, Ken had already convinced himself that Sam had it all wrong.

For one thing, Ken knew from old friends that drugs and a good memory were usually incompatible. When he added that to abject horror at the scene of the fire, with a range of emotions during and after, plus Bobby's admitted guilt, it all added up to very natural reactions and responses by the children, with one exception.

For those few brief moments while helping fixing Bobby's "malfunctioning" walkie-talkie, Ken had been given a clue. But Ken Easton was an engineer—a problem solver—and not a psychologist or a criminal investigator. Even after Tristin had reported within minutes the nearly identical conversation with Cheryl, Ken still did not act on an obvious disconnect.

*****

Note to John: After the news of Sam Wynette's death, and rather than try to solve the mystery himself during a new whirlwind of activity and emotion around him, Ken elected to bury it all,

**along with Sam's last two words: "Be careful."
By the time of the funeral service on Wednesday, Ken was consumed with other priorities
involving the kids. It would be less than a month
before he dug them back up and had to face a
horrible reality, so I skipped ahead to where
things start to get really complicated. Steven**

51 Marathon Man

"I want this house wrapped by May first," Nortze
had said to Bobby in mid-March, "so they can install
all the plumbing and mechanical. I miss my Jacuzzi
in Vegas, and I want to get the gas on and set up
something temporary before the real spa goes in."

Gil Nortze was quickly tiring of the work involved in his marathon project. It was costing
much more than he had planned, mostly due to
his own lack of experience. And he was still on
crutches, making every task an onerous one.

Nortze also seriously considered setting up a
bed in his unfinished house. He had all but given
up finding a house for rent in Carmel Highlands,
and he was also tired of paying Margie's steep
B&B rates (and down more than $2,000 in poker
losses). He wanted the house finished, and he
would take up residence … if that's what it took.

Nortze had used every trick in his book to ca-
jole, harass, and speed up the construction

operation, often at the expense of mistakes and time-consuming delays, mostly his. Plus outright fraud. As was the case with Brad Smoley, Nortze had conned the major subcontractors—framing, plumbing, and electrical—by switching plans after they had already made their bids and then grinding them down on the price, even though there was substantially more work involved. The subs actually lost money on Gil Nortze's project.

And through it all, Gil Nortze forged on, his only ray of sunshine being that mental picture of his spa out on the bluff.

At the end of March, Bobby finally introduced Nortze to his sister, "Sherry." Cheryl stopped by the job site frequently on the weekends Bobby worked there, and Nortze hadn't recognized either of his own kids.

But a bond began developing between the three Nortzes, an unspoken familiarity and way of being that made them extremely comfortable in each other's presence. Nortze even showed a certain minimal fatherly concern about their lives, feeling sorry that they had been orphaned—exceptionally ironic considering the circumstances.

Nortze understood their situation only from what Bobby told him, in bits and pieces. Ken and Tristin were going to be married in June, and they loved the kids and wanted them at their house, but there were no firm plans yet for adoption. It was a big decision for Ken and Tristin, but they promised a decision by late May.

Bobby and Cheryl had both undergone grief counseling following Sam's funeral, the psychologist remarking to Ken and Tristin only a week later, "The children have responded so well and recovered so rapidly that further scheduled sessions are no longer warranted." As Sam Wynette would have said: "Duh."

Ken once again chalked it up to their hardscrabble lives, not considering that an insurance policy on Sam and Darcy established a $2 million trust fund for the surviving children. It was set to help them in the years up to the age of 21, after which the balance (including interest) would be paid out in full. Sam's brother, Chuck, as trust executor, was already making arrangements to cover the children's living expenses.

It was now May 1, and Gil Nortze was out of his fiberglass cast and walking without a limp. Bobby had spent most weekends working on Nortze's job site. In that time Bobby had not only helped Nortze with general cleanup and maintenance, but they had often talked in the site trailer, usually during a rain shower.

In between rains—some heavier than others—the house had been framed, the windows installed, a composition shingle roof put on, and it had been "wrapped" with black paper and wire lath.

After the wood-frame windows had been installed, Nortze did not, despite clear instructions in large letters glued to the side of the frame, "Seal Immediately!" After three rains, each followed by sunny days, the west facing sash windows had all but delaminated in the weather. It cost Nortze an extra three grand to have them refinished on-site. He, of course, blamed the manufacturer for defective products, but got nowhere on that front, despite the threat of a lawsuit.

Insulation had been installed throughout the house, and it was now ready for drywall. With the gas furnace operational (illegally, thanks to an unscrupulous but well-paid handyman), the house could be kept warm and was impervious to any more rain. The building inspector had no idea that Nortze was using it. Since giving an okay to cover the interior walls, he wasn't due back until the drywall was up to check the screws. The drywall never went up.

After coming to the job site directly from school, Bobby stood with Nortze as the delivery truck used a forklift to put the pre-fab spa and gas-fired heater in front of the newly installed sectional doors of the garage. Nortze had picked it up cheap for a thousand dollars. "I don't care if the house is unfinished, I just want that damned spa," Nortze said.

"It's big," Bobby said. The entire spa unit measured almost seven feet on a side, with the inner tub nestled inside the redwood frame.

"Holds two hundred and fifty gallons and three people," Nortze said, "Or, me and five women." He gave Bobby a sly wink. "I've got a new girl-friend—Trudy—in Vegas."

Bobby's face flushed as he smiled through his mild embarrassment, and he changed subjects. "Where's it going?"

"Oh, I have just the spot," Nortze said, as if it were a secret yet to be revealed.

52 Casino

Back "home" with Marge in the living room of Margie's B&B, Nortze was sipping on a scotch and water, the two of them having just finished playing an hour of Texas Hold'em. It had become practically a ritual at that point. Nortze was down another three hundred to Margie.

"When are you going to take me to Vegas, Gil?" Margie asked.

"Oh, I don't know if you're ready for the big time yet, Margie. You might want to try something a little less intimidating at this point."

"Yeah, like what?"

"Ever play poker on-line?"

"No," she replied, "but I play blackjack. Think I should switch over?"

"I think so." Nortze had an idea, sounding so good at the time that he grinned wide like a Cheshire cat. "Tell you what, Margie. I'm going to do a little test—set you up with credit card account at the gaming site I use. I know the people there, and they know me, so I'm going to stake you to ten grand." The gaming site was an off-shore entity in the Cayman Islands, and Nortze had been a customer ever since they had opened two years before.

"Really?" Margie asked, wide-eyed.

"Sure, I consider it an investment." And here he cocked his head like he couldn't remember the agreement. "We talked about a fifty-fifty split, right?"

"Talked about it," Margie shot back. "And forgot about it. I said seventy-five twenty-five, Gil."

"Ah, that's right. Well, whaddya say we compromise at sixty-forty."

"I also want the account in my name. You'll have to trust me on that."

"Deal," Nortze replied, holding out his right hand. Margie shook it. "Deal."

Using Margie's computer and 56K dial-up modem—a dinosaur by Nortze's high-speed DSL standards—Nortze contacted the on-duty gaming administrator and personally vouched for Margie. She would have $10,000 to play with, but if that ran out, she was on her own. Once the details and transfers were arranged, Margie used her password and entered the game room.

"It's all up to you now, Margie. You have one hour—go for it." With Nortze watching but saying nothing, Margie spent an hour at the Texas Hold'em table. She lost a few hundred dollars in the first fifteen minutes, murmuring apologies to Nortze when she folded.

"Hang tough, Margie," Nortze said, "It all comes around."

By the end of the hour, she had won $12,000, mostly from a single hand calling bets and raises, and then getting a flush on the River. "I had a hunch that puppy would show up," Margie beamed.

At the end of the hour, Margie left the game and sat transfixed at the computer screen, staring at her account balance. "Did I just do that?"

"You sure did, Margie. Your take comes to seventy-two hundred bucks—not bad for your first time." Nortze was so impressed that he immediately e-mailed the gaming administrator to increase Margie's credit line to $50,000, using his password and account numbers to make the transfer between accounts.

"I'm tired and going to my room, Margie. I wouldn't go back on until tomorrow, though. Enjoy your winnings and think about strategy."

"Thanks, Gil," Margie said, a cigarette dangling from her lips. "I may not think about strategy, though. I'm already thinking about a new truck."

Nortze laughed and went back to his room and showered, dreaming of his spa. Under the hot water he could think only about how his new girlfriend, Trudy. He'd just met her in Vegas the weekend before, and she saw him as her sugar daddy. He, on the other hand, saw her as a trophy to be worn at the tables and a provider of "services."

The problem was Marge, and that she would be upset knowing that Nortze was "seeing" someone else. Nortze knew he would have to give some thought about the solution to that little dilemma, especially as they would probably meet for the occasion of the grand opening of the temporary spa the next weekend.

Dismissing that problem, his thoughts turned to screwing Trudy's brains out in the hot swirling waters while overlooking the ocean. Nortze was headed back to Vegas to see Trudy on Friday for a whole weekend away from construction, looking forward to the lifestyle to which he had grown accustomed.

53 Illusions

Ken Easton was one happy camper as he stood on his diving perch overlooking the ocean. It was on Monday afternoon, May 6, and he had just received word from Greg at D&M in San Jose that the "demonstration of concept" had soared through the higher reaches of both the company and government sponsors. The project was set for a real world demonstration by early June the next year, as soon as an appropriate building project, currently in the initial design stage, could incorporate the sensor arrays.

"Your stock just went up a thousand percent around here," Greg had said. "Whatever you have to sell, they're buying."

"So, what's next on the agenda," Ken had asked.

"You need to get your butt up here this week. We'll need several days to locate and get approvals for the demo project."

Ken knew that the kids would manage fine on their own while he was away, and Tristin liked taking care of them. "Good practice for our own someday," she had said.

"How's about I fly up on Wednesday morning," Ken said to Greg, "and stay until we get it done?"

"Sounds good to me, Ken. I'll see you Wednesday."

Feeling empowered and full of energy, Ken had donned his wetsuit, hood, and gloves, and walked out to the bluff with swim fins in hand checking out the surf. It was a fairly small day, with five-foot wave sets the maximum.

From his diving perch, he leaned out and sprung off into the air. He rode five waves, each longer and more technically challenging than the last. By the time he had reached his resting ledge around the north side of the headland, he was exhausted but feeling great. With all that had happened over the past months, it was the first time he had had the desire to go bodysurfing. He was glad to have found the time and energy to do something he liked very much.

54 The Weight of Water

Gil Nortze had gone right from the airport to his construction site Monday morning a new man. Refreshed and full of piss and vinegar, he was ready for the final push. But he was between phases now, the rough inspection completed but still awaiting a signed contract from the drywall subcontractor prior to covering the interior walls. While standing in front of the garage and staring at the spa, he knew what had to be done next.

He went back into the trailer and began making phone calls, finally reaching a carpenter who said he would come out around three o'clock to take a look at what Nortze wanted. Just off the phone with the carpenter, he heard a vehicle come down the driveway. He stepped outside and recognized Margie's beat up truck. But when she got out and walked towards him, he could tell something was wrong. "I lost it," Margie said, head hanging and practically in tears.

Nortze didn't have to ask what she was talking about. "All of it, Margie? Fifty grand?"

"Yeah," she said with a deep sigh, "I'm afraid so. I was going to tell you when you got to the B&B, as I thought you were going there first."

"What happened?"

Margie shrugged and shook her head. "Every time I thought I had a winning hand, someone had a better one. Or when I did have a good hand, everyone had already folded. I couldn't read them on the computer, you know?" She looked devastated.

"Hey, don't be so hard on yourself, Margie. This stuff happens in poker."

Margie was greatly relieved that Gil hadn't gotten angry with her. "But fifty grand is a lot of money, Gil."

"Sure it is, but you gotta stick it out. Over the long haul, you'll win it back—and more."

"Where am I going to get it?"

"Where you got the last stake." Nortze could see that she was crestfallen, but he still believed strongly in her abilities. "Look, Margie. I just checked with my financial people in Vegas, and there are some investments coming due. But I won't have access to the cash until the end of this week. So on Thursday or Friday, you'll have another fifty grand in your account to work with."

"Really, Gil? My, that's very generous. I thought you'd dump me like an old rag after losing that much money."

Nortze put his hand on her shoulder. "The cards will come, Margie. The cards will come." *And so will my money.*

Margie left the job site feeling a little better than when she had arrived. She wanted to show Nortze that she was worthy of his investment, both in time and money. Over the next several nights playing poker with Nortze, she lost about a hundred dollars overall, and wondered if it was the guilt playing her hands and not her. But throughout the week, she kept a stiff upper lip with Nortze, but remained silent about her covert activities.

She had opened up a separate account with another offshore gambling site, using her personal bank debit card with a $10,000 limit. "The cards will turn," she reminded herself, justifying her actions. By the time Thursday rolled around, she had $9,000 in account debits. The gambling sites took their money from her bank account on the spot, as they didn't believe in people voluntarily paying their gambling debts later. It was a practice that kept them in business.

In a state of high panic, Margie had gone to the bank on Thursday afternoon and taken out an immediate line of credit on her B&B for $50,000, saying it was for remodeling. With her business valued at more than ten times the amount, and as a longtime resident, she signed the second trust deed documents, and the amount was quickly approved and tied into her debit/credit card. She went back home, sat down at her computer, and began trying to make up for her losses, knowing that she had an additional fifty grand coming from Nortze by the next day.

Nortze told Margie that night everything was set, except that her account wouldn't be funded until the following Monday. With a poker face, Margie let nothing slip about her losses, saying only that she would be ready to roll on Monday.

Also with a poker face, not wanting to reveal anything about his latest girlfriend, Nortze said,

"Also, I'm flying to Vegas tonight and coming back Saturday," Nortze said. "I'm having birthday party on Saturday for a friend, and some other people are flying out for the party. You're invited, Margie, so bring your sexiest swimsuit for the hot tub. It's going to be up and running."

Margie felt honored. "Sure, I'll be there." It would be Margie's chance to shine amongst Nortze's friends, to show them she had more than just a great body.

Ken Easton arrived home late Thursday evening, tired but satisfied with how well things had gone up in San Jose. Everything was set to incorporate his acoustic sensors into a FEMA-sponsored building just outside the city limits. It was working out better that he could have possibly imagined.

In his office, he heard the pounding surf outside and felt the strong vibrations underfoot. He'd seen the surf reports while up in San Jose—a huge storm to the northwest was pushing monster waves onto the coastline. After a few minutes in his office, he quietly walked down the hall and past the kids' bedrooms, but he heard a door open behind him and he stopped and turned around. It was Bobby, sticking his head into the hallway. "Hi, Ken," he said in a whisper.

"Hi, Bobby," Ken replied, and walked back to talk to him quietly so as not to disturb Cheryl. "It's late. How come you're not asleep?"

Bobby shrugged and whispered back, "Those big waves, I guess. Hey, can ask you something."

"What's that?"

"Gil is having a big surprise birthday party for his girlfriend. He's in Vegas now, but he's bringing her back with him sometime Saturday. Can we go?"

Ken thought about it for a moment, but he could see nothing wrong with it.

"Sure, why not."

"Great!" Bobby said, still in a whisper. "We get to try out his new spa."

Ken didn't remember seeing it, recalling that the last time he'd looked, nothing had been done. "Do you have swimming trunks?"

"Tristin bought some for me and Cheryl yesterday."

"Sounds fun. Go back to bed and I'll see you in the morning. Good night."

"G'nite, Ken."

The next morning, Friday, Ken kissed Tristin as she left early for work, and he drove the kids to school. Coming back down the common upper driveway, he was looking past the mailboxes and to the north, over his house and out to sea, the surf twenty feet high and expected to get even bigger. News reports said it was going to be the biggest surf in years. He never even glanced in the direction of Nortze's lot.

Once inside the house, Ken was itching to go out to the bluff and take a look at the waves. He donned a sweater and jacket over his jeans, poured himself a cup of coffee, and went out the kitchen door, heading for the spot just behind his diving perch.

Would you look at that! The outside waves must be twenty-five feet already.

The waves were coming in sets of eight and ten, and with high tide expected later that morning, Ken knew they would be breaking right against the cliff. *No bodysurfing today!*

He began a slow stroll along the south along the bluff, and that's when he saw something up on the bluff ahead that made him stop in his tracks.

"What the hell is that!" Ken said aloud, so shocked by what he saw that he unconsciously dropped both arms to his sides, spilling his coffee on the ground. Just on the other side of the fence line that stopped at the edge of Nortze's property, Ken saw a wooden deck, with hand railings on three sides, jutting out into the air, supported on the western edge by a single 4x4 wooden post, ten feet tall and perched on the western-sloping cliff a few feet before it became a vertical drop. And a huge spa was set on top of the deck planks.

One word came into Ken's mind: *Deathtrap!* He walked briskly to the south end of the bluff and stepped over the rocks and around the south side. He could feel some of the spray coming up from below, and felt the vibration every time one of the waves struck the cliff. He crouched and leaned against a rock and held firm, staring at the monstrosity up above him.

Only then did he have a passing thought that it would be an eyesore from his house and yard. What concerned him the most was how poorly the deck appeared to have been constructed.

As an engineer, Ken knew enough about structural integrity to see this didn't come close. A single 4x6 on edge lay across the top of the 4x4 post, toe-nailed together as opposed to being strapped and bolted, supporting the 2x6 joists and 2x4 planking above. The joists ran back to the start of the deck, sitting on 4x4 in direct contact with the mostly level area of rock. None of the lumber was fastened together with proper straps and hangers.

The only thing Ken saw that was right about the job was that the 4x4 post was sunk in a concrete-filled hole in the rocks. However, not knowing the depth, he suspected that was done improperly, too. Using only his eyes as a guide, the post was not quite vertical, either.

"No way!" Ken said aloud, shaking his head. The thought of Tristin and the kids on that deck sent shivers down his spine.

Ken's next thought was to call the building department and have Nortze's obviously bootlegged deck inspected and condemned. But that would take time, probably not before Monday. His only option was to tell the kids they couldn't go to the party, or if they did, they couldn't go anywhere near that spa.

And then it struck him. *What about everyone else? Don't I have some responsibility to them as well?* Ken was in no mood for argument when it came to safety, but he could already see in his mind's eye the results of any confrontation with Nortze.

The more Ken thought about it, the more he came to the realization that by making some kind of scene with Nortze before or during the party, his concerns would not be taken seriously. It was obvious to Ken that whoever built that deck had minimal skills in that area, but Nortze had obviously approved it. Ken was one hundred percent certain the building inspector had not seen it. Ken figured that Nortze had rigged it up just for the party, and that he would later try to hide it from the inspector with a tarp or something.

I should take a sledgehammer and knock the sonofabitch down myself!

He made his way around and up his own slope and took a good look from the end of the fence line. The job site was empty of workers, so he climbed around the end of the fence and along the rocks for a better look. Up close now, he saw that the spa was about the same as his own, built to seat four or five people inside.

But what really floored Ken was the use of plastic PVC pipe to run natural gas to the heater unit. It lay on the ground covered with a few inches of dirt here and there along the fence and ran 75 feet back to the garage, where it went across the side yard setback and through the metal wire lath on the outside wall. Taped to it every so often was a plastic-coated electrical wire used for interior-only wiring, as it degraded in sunlight. Nortze was using that to run his spa motor and pump. The PVC and Romex separated at the start of the deck, the PVC running to the heater and the Romex to the spa motor.

Wait 'till the building inspector sees this! Ken decided right then and there to go back to his office and call him. Sitting at his desk at 8:30 and staring out the garden window, Ken placed the call to building and safety, but it took a few moments for them to match Nortze's name with his permit, and then to match that to the name of the inspector. "Tom Ervin—extension 328. He's probably out on rounds by now, but I can put you through."

"Yes, please," Ken said with anticipation. Ken ended up leaving a message on Ervin's voicemail. "My name is Ken Easton, and you are apparently the inspector on the house being built by my neighbor, Gil Nortze, at 3940 Spindrift Road. He has just put up a bootleg deck and spa on the top of the cliffs, and I'd like you to come out today and take a look." Ken rang off, hoping the man would come out that very day. He did not know that Ervin had only four inspections that morning, and that he would go directly home from the last job inspection. Ervin wouldn't get the message until the following Monday.

The waves came like a slow and steady drumbeat against the cliffs as Ken gathered his thoughts. He could see the spa behind the railing, the whole contraption sticking above the rocks, and he went over and over in his mind what he might be able to do before the building inspector showed up. And then it came to him in a flash—video evidence!

Ken located his little Sony video camera, put in new batteries and checked to make sure he had enough tape. He walked out to the bluff and, from his diving perch, began shooting. Starting with an overall shot of the spa and deck, he zoomed in on the post, keeping a sharp eye on the waves below. He saw a big one coming in and stepped away from the edge of the cliff back toward the lawn. It hit the based of the cliff and shot up a spray of water that came up almost to the top of the cliff.

I should probably transfer this to VHS and add my own commentary to it, Ken thought. He pushed the rocker switch on the top of the camera to turn off the sound. Next, he climbed the slope and made his way carefully around the end of the fence for a good close-up on the spa. In transferring the camera from one hand to the other, his fingers passed over the rocker switch and turned the sound back on. Ken aimed the camera and began panning and zooming on the structural connections, the PVC, and the Romex wiring.. He also began a running commentary, venting his frustration, believing that the sound was turned off.

"So, what do you think of this, Mr. Inspector? Indoor Romex wiring, stapled to the deck. Not a metal hanger or strap to be found. Nice toe-nailing, though, don't you think? Not only has the sonofabitch built a deathtrap, but also located it so overlooks my fucking garden. That's right, the man *is* an asshole!"

Ken got a zoom on the lumber connections, or lack thereof. "And if you don't do anything about it, I will. It wouldn't take much but a few saw cuts on that post to send this fucking monstrosity into the ocean, I'll tell you that."

When Ken returned to his office, he checked for a message from the building inspector, but there was none. He gave thought as to provide as much evidence to the inspector—a way to nail this thing down so there would be absolutely no wiggle-room. Ken also wanted to make sure his own visual structural analysis was sound, so he placed a call to his colleague, Greg McAferty. Ken picked up the video camera and began shooting out his garden window and up the slope.

"Yo, what's up, Ken?" Greg said through the speakerphone.

"Need you to break out your codebook for a load calculation."

"Fire away."

"What's the absolute maximum load on the top of a 4x4 vertical wooden post—number two Doug fir?"

"How tall without bracing?"

"About ten feet."

"I'll check. What's this about?"

Ken zoomed in to the top of the exposed spa. "Oh, my asshole neighbor just put up this monstrosity deck and spa that looks right down into my yard. As a structural engineer, you'd be appalled at the way this thing was built." Ken backed off on the zoom, joking, "If it doesn't collapse on its own, I'm going to make sure of it."

Greg chuckled, saying, "Hold on a sec. Let me go grab the codebook.

Ken turned off the camera, shaking his head. "I can't believe the man would do that. What did I ever do to him?"

When Greg returned, he said, "Thirty-eight hundred pounds—give or take."

"Hey, thanks, man. Appreciate it."

"No problem."

After they rang off, Ken pulled out his hand calculator and started the addition. It was a small tub enclosure. Two hundred and fifty gallons of water at 8.3 pounds per gallon came to 2075 pounds. Ken added 300 pounds minimum for the spa, wood surround, and gas heater. Ken's spa held three people comfortably—five people max—so he multiplied that by the weight of five adults—150 pounds average for men and women combined. That came to 750 pounds. Finally he added his guess at the weight of the all the lumber above the 4x4 post—another 400 pounds minimum. The total came to 3,425 pounds, only 275 pounds short of the critical load on the top of the 4x4 post. If more than two or three people were on the deck at the same time, or if the lumber and spa weighed more than he had guessed, Ken knew that deck was going down like the Titanic.

With the inspector not having called back, Ken concluded it was a possibility that his phone call would not be returned that day. And also that on Fridays, people took off early sometimes. That meant he would have to take his chances over the weekend before reaching the inspector. By then, Ken realized, it might be too late.

And that's when he began to think about sabotage—how to make the spa and deck disappear without anyone knowing he did it, yet before the party the next night that could put a lot of people in jeopardy. The next rumbling underfoot from the waves crashing against the cliff solved that question.

Ken checked his watch, reading 9:30. He went to the garage and found his handsaw and sprayed some WD-40 on the blade to minimize friction and resistance. Walking back out to the bluff, he didn't give another thought to getting caught, but rather was busily calculating in his head the best angle for the saw cut.

A 45-degree angle was too much, as the top of the post could slip off and crush him underneath the deck, or just carry him down off the cliff. Half that amount, or about 22½ degrees, seemed about right—not too steep, but not too shallow. He knew that the vibration from the waves would walk the upper part of the post down the sloping cut and eventually shear it, taking everything into the sea.

Making his way carefully back out across the rocks and under the deck, Ken began his cut on the backside of the 4x4, three feet above the concrete footing. He sawed with slow and even strokes. He had cut almost halfway through when he pulled the saw out and lined up, by eye, the start of the next saw cut on the opposite side.

The closer he got to breaking through to the opposite saw cut, the more he became convinced this was the proper cut angle. He stopped just short of breaking through to the other side of the cut. His mind was so concentrated on the task at hand, he didn't see the rogue 25-foot swell rising and bearing down on the cliff.

He turned his head towards the sloping cliff and reviewed his path of quick egress back across the rocks should things start to go south on him. And there he saw Lindy seated on her haunches, in the same spot where he saw her staring down into the ocean on the day Connie had gone over the cliff.

It was an eerie *déjà vu* feeling. Ken shook it off and stepped as far away from the post as he could while still finishing the cut with his right hand. The tip of the saw was just an inch or so inside the post when he felt it pinch as he broke through. A smaller wave crashed against the cliffs and shot up spray, but Ken was used to the sound now.

Holding the saw with a tight grip, Ken wiggled it back and forth to extract it from the downward force of the upper section of post. And that's when the crest of the huge wave hit the cliff with tremendous force just twenty feet below.

The crashing sound startled Ken, and in an instant he was enveloped inside a thick wall of seawater shooting up and over the cliff. He closed his eyes and held fast to the handhold of the saw. The spray subsided, leaving him drenched and clinging onto the saw for dear life. Had he not been holding it, he was sure he would have lost his balance and gone down the cliff into the ocean. And there was no way anyone, himself included, would have survived that.

Ken's heart raced as he carefully made his way back over the slick rocks to the safety of the bluff. He didn't realize until he was back on firm ground that he had held his breath the whole way. Turning around, he wiped away the water in his eyes and on his face. After settling down, he squinted his eyes to see if there was any offset on the post yet, but there wasn't. With all day to wait if necessary for the waves to do their thing, he was not impatient. He went back into the house to put the saw on the workbench, and changed clothes.

He knew he couldn't keep constant watch, but he expected that when he came out of the house the next time to check on the situation, the whole deck and spa would be gone. His satisfaction was in knowing how these things worked, so he really didn't need to see it happen first hand.

Once the force of the repeated shocks had caused the upper part of the post to creep down the incline past the halfway point, eventually somewhere near the west face of the post the wood grain would shear off. The whole deck above, filled spa and all, would then drop about three feet.

With its downward momentum, the deck and everything on it would continue down the slope, taking the lower part of the post with it. It would all end up in the ocean, crushed to splinters, and that would be that. With the tide so high on the rocks, he figured there would be few if any little creatures in harm's way. He apologized to God for any collateral damage.

It was 10:15 when he went from his office to his diving perch and looked through a set of binoculars at the 4x4 post. It was offset only by about half an inch, not nearly as much as he had expected.

By two o'clock, he was really worried. Despite the pounding surf, the offset was not even to the halfway point, and he knew he had to pick up the kids from school in less than an hour. For the next 45 minutes, he kept a close eye on it, but it didn't move any further. The tide had been receding since noon, so the ocean level was dropping, but the next high tide was due in just after midnight.

Thinking about all the possible scenarios, including one with him out on that treacherous slope with a sledgehammer, pounding away on the upper section of post trying to make things go more quickly, he finally succumbed to reality. He would be risking his life out there, and it just wasn't worth it. He stuck to his firm belief that with the waves at their highest just after midnight's high tide, he would come out Saturday morning and find everything swept away.

Margie Swanson sat at her computer, staring blankly into the screen. In just 24 hours, she had lost nearly $24,000 of her credit line. With each series of losses, spread amongst a few winning hands, she kept telling herself that her luck just had to change at some point. She repeated like a mantra Nortze's words: "The cards will come." But instead of stopping, or even waiting until she could get some advice from Nortze, she plowed on ahead. Margie wanted desperately to show Nortze that she was a winner. Yet with every loss, the little voice in her head told her: *The cards will come.* Margie knew she had only until Nortze's return on Saturday to spring the good news that she was on the road to winning the money back.

55 Butterflies Are Free

Ken pulled the Bronco into the garage and shut off the engine. He warned Bobby and Cheryl against going anywhere near the bluffs during the high surf, and also not to go up to Nortze's lot.

"Sure, Ken, " Bobby said, and he got out on the front passenger's side. Seeing the hand saw and WD-40 bottle on the workbench, he asked, "Hey, Ken, whatcha makin'?"

Ken's heart pounded while he thought up a quick answer. "Oh, it's just something for the birdhouse." His heart continued to pound up until they were in the house and the subject forgotten.

Later that evening in the living room with the fireplace roaring, Ken and Bobby were together on the couch watching the movie *Bullit*, with Steve McQueen, on DVD. All during the movie, however, Ken was understandably distracted by thoughts of how Nortze's deck was doing. With every wave crashing against the cliffs, and the accompanying vibration, Ken imaged the deck collapsing into the sea.

During the movie's final chase sequence down the steep streets of San Francisco, Bobby was all excited, mimicking McQueen's driving skills and adding his own verbal sound effects. At the end, when the credits started to roll, Bobby turned to Ken, saying with excitement, "I can't wait 'till I drive. I like going fast, but I like curves better, just like Gil."

"Oh, yeah? Well, they can be dangerous, ya know."

Bobby leaned back against the sofa. "I was talking with Gil the other day, and he says he loves to drive his Lincoln on the Coast Highway with all the curves." Bobby's face then dropped almost imperceptibly. "Except," he said with a shrug, "for the Christmas before last when he ran that car ... off ... " Bobby trailed off when he saw Ken suddenly sit up and take notice.

Ken's mind quickly came into sharp focus and he began to feel faint, with images and tragic memories of Christmas 2000 flooding back into his head. A streak of butterfly-shaped red paint on Valerie's BMW—from Nortze's red Lincoln, was the most prominent. "Gil Nortze told you he ran a car off the road?" Ken asked weakly. His mouth had suddenly gone dry, and his heart raced.

Bobby quickly pieced together what his father, Sam, had told him about Ken's wife with what Gil Nortze had said. "Yeah," Bobby answered softly, rightly concerned that he'd given away a big se-cret—a secret Bobby might have been able to exploit someday. Now, the cat was out of the bag.

Not wanting to get his new pal, Gil Nortze, in trouble, Bobby began to backpedal. But Bobby also didn't want Ken thinking that he knew any-thing about Valerie's death, adding quickly, "He said he wasn't proud of it or anything, but it was raining and he didn't see the car. He told me not to drive fast when it's raining, especially not around curves." Bobby desperately wanted to change the subject.

Ken struggled for air, but through his pain, he could still see that Bobby was for some unknown reason uncomfortable discussing the subject. This was huge for Ken, though, and he pressed on. "Did he say what happened to the other car?" Ken asked, forcing himself to sound casual, and trying to bring the conversation back into focus.

Bobby was forced into replying, "No, just that the other guy was okay." He said it so convinc-ingly that Ken knew immediately that that's what

Nortze had told him. Changing expression like a chameleon, Bobby's face lit up. "He sure likes his Lincolns. I'm going to get one when I get enough money." Bobby stood up, stretched, and said, "Thanks for the movie, Ken. I'm going back to my room now."

Ken felt like he was going to vomit. He told Bobby he was tired, too, and was going to bed. They both went off toward their respective bedrooms.

As Bobby walked down the hall, he knew in his heart that Nortze had run Valerie's car off the road, despite Nortze telling him that no one was hurt. Knowing that Gil might get in trouble over it, Bobby's loyalties were torn … for about a nanosecond. Before he reached his room, Bobby had decided to slip Gil Nortze the word at the birthday party that Ken Easton was onto him. One had to keep one's options open.

Ken closed the bedroom door behind him and walked right past Tristin without saying a word. At the bathroom sink, leaning on his elbows over the countertop, Ken's hands trembled. His whole body trembled. He rubbed his hands together trying to stop it, but it was no use. Tears welled up in his eyes, and he ran the cold water and splashed water onto his face.

"Are you okay, Ken?" Tristin said, coming in to check on him.

"Close the door," he said, choking up with tears. Tristin closed the door and he buried his face in his hands. Ken told Tristin what Bobby had just told him, and how he just knew in his gut that Nortze was talking about Valerie's car. He broke down and cried.

It was a long, fitful night for Ken Easton. Despite all the right things going on in his little world out on Spindrift Road at that point in time, there had also been the bad things, too. Very bad things. And as Ken lay awake in the dark listening to the thunderous roar of the waves crashing against the cliffs, he concluded that everything bad that had happened in his life began, and now continued, with the presence of Gil Nortze.

Before falling asleep, Ken Easton promised himself to notify the police investigator who had handled Valerie's case. But he wanted to wait until he had calmed down enough to speak rationally, and perhaps even confront Nortze to be sure of his course of action. *Maybe when I talk to him about how his deck might have collapsed into the ocean, I'll spring it on him without warning and see how he reacts.*

56 Sudden Impact

By eight o'clock Saturday morning, the waves were still in the 20-foot range and pounding the cliffs at 20-second intervals. Every so often, the last wave of the set approached 25 feet. As Ken showered and dressed, he prayed that the deck and spa had gone down overnight. With Tristin and the kids still asleep, he donned a pullover rain slicker against the spray and grabbed his binoculars. .

He walked out onto the bluff, not looking at first towards the south, as if he couldn't bear to discover the deck still standing. Finally, he looked over, and it was still there. "Sonofabitch," he cursed under his breath. He pulled up the binoculars, peering intently at the post. It was offset by more than two-thirds now.

He knew it was getting critical, but it was like slow torture for him. With so many fears racing around in his head, and coming to the realization it might not fall in time, he was in a quandary, and had to think.

Walking over to the birdhouse, he spotted Jake the Tern perched on the opening to his birdhouse. "How's it going, Jake?" he said. Jake fluttered his bad wing. "You think you got problems, little buddy, wait 'till you hear mine."

"Hey, Ken!" the voice shouted.

Ken paled as he turned his eyes up above the birdhouse and saw Gil Nortze holding his hand high. Nortze was leaning back against the railing on the west side of the deck. Ken went into mild shock, not knowing how to react: *Warn him? Say nothing?*

With a feeling of dread in his gut, Ken held up his hand but said nothing. Another huge wave crashed against the cliff, shooting up spray above the bluff. Ken was now ready and willing to let Gil Nortze go down with his deck, if it happened quickly.

"Party tonight's cancelled," Nortze shouted gruffly. "Tell the kids, okay?"

The momentary relief that people would not be in jeopardy was quickly offset. Nortze turned and said something to someone nearby who Ken could not see.

His girlfriend is up there, too! Change of plans. Ken held up a finger and shouted, "I need to talk to you." He walked towards the slope and climbed to the top, knowing it was time to get everyone away from that deck, and then maybe see if it was Nortze who ran his wife and son off the road.

Making his way around the end of the fence, and with the surf pounding below against the cliff, Ken stopped and looked over. There he saw Margie Swanson seated on a makeshift bench on the south side of the deck, five feet away from the gas-fired heating unit. Ken knew her from their infrequent meetings in local market. The spa pumps were not running, and no steam was rising from the water.

"Morning, Margie." Ken said.

"Morning, Ken," she replied, not one of the happiest moments in her life. She had finally confessed all to Nortze about her gambling losses. Without emotion, he had cut her off from any more money, telling her she was on her own until she straightened up her financial house. Margie had promised to reverse the $50,000 transfer to become effective on Monday. Margie now sat on the spa bench, beside herself with guilt and self-loathing.

"The birthday girl is sick," Gil said with a shrug, his waxy face now drooping. "So the party's off." Trudy wasn't sick. She'd hooked up with a better-heeled sugar daddy, dumping Nortze and leaving him high and dry.

Ken didn't know quite how to begin in Margie's presence, but time was running out. He forced himself to pull it together. "I'm sorry about your party, Gil, but the deck you're standing on is very dangerous. That little post underneath is way overloaded, and it's my professional opinion that it could collapse at any moment. And don't even try to tell me the building inspector signed off on it." A shot of spray came up from behind Gil, framing him against the white mist.

Margie's eyes widened, and she looked to Nortze for a response, asking, "Is that true, Gil?"

Nortze scoffed, "Hey, don't worry about it." He pounded the top of the railing with his fist. "See? And I'll have it all fired up and working fine by this afternoon."

Taking that to infer that the gas and electrical weren't hooked up, meaning there was still time to make his case, Ken now showed his anger. "No, it's not fine, Gil. I just got off the phone with my friend who's a structural engineer. He gave me some basic numbers and I calculated the load, and it's so close to the limit of collapse that you'd better get off it—now! I've already put a call into the building inspector's office, so everyone's on notice, including you."

Nortze was incredulous. "You called the man down on me, Ken? That was pretty un-neighborly of you."

With those words coming from *that* man, Ken stepped around the fence and approached Nortze. His face reddened with fury, saying, "You have the balls to say that to me, Gil?" Through clenched teeth, Ken shouted past him to Margie. "Excuse my French, Margie, but I'd get off that deck right now if I were you. It's totally unsafe." He turned his focus back to Nortze. "And if I ever see the kids on this thing," Ken pointed and shouted, "I'll throw you right off that fucking cliff, do you hear me?" Ken felt the weight of the world crushing down on him.

Nortze stared and said nothing as he fidgeted with his sapphire ring.

Margie was caught between a conversation about poker losses with Nortze and an enraged neighbor. She shrugged her shoulders and stood up, saying, "I'm going back to my truck for some cigarettes, Gil. You guys hash it out between you."

As she rose and started to walk across the wood deck, a 30-foot wave, the biggest of the morning, crashed against the cliff. Ken felt the vibration and saw the spray shoot up ten feet above the deck railing. An instant later, he heard a loud cracking sound, and watched in horror as the seaward end of deck dropped three feet.

Margie gasped and lunged for the end of the deck on the bluff side, landing prostrate on the steeply sloped deck and barely managing to grab and hold onto the edge of the easternmost plank with her fingers. During that same brief moment, Nortze had grabbed onto the west railing for dear life as 250 gallons of cold spa water splashed over him. The heating unit, not anchored to the deck, strained against the PVC gas pipe. The deck had only minimal contact with the rocks and tension on the Romex electrical line— with two staples into the wood 2x6 planking.

In one quick move, Ken literally threw himself to the ground in front of the east end of the deck, reaching out to grab hold of Margie's left wrist with both his hands. He could see the terror in her eyes. "I've got you, Margie."

Nortze sat awkwardly with his back against the railing uprights, legs pointing up the sloping deck, now slick from all the water. With a mystified expression, he held out his right hand. "Help, Ken," he said weakly. "I can't get up."

Ken ignored his plea, concentrating instead on his death grip on Margie's wrist. Ken saw as Margie went into shock right before his eyes, and as he struggled to pull her up, he pleaded, "Margie, you've got to help."

Ken struggled to his knees for better purchase, and began pulling her dead weight slowly up the incline. Her waist was just over the top of the deck planks when Ken gave a final pull, dragging her onto the safety of the rocks. She had been so neglectful of her health for the past six years that in an emergency her body had quickly gone into a deep defensive posture. She rolled onto her back and promptly fainted away.

The deck slipped down an inch, popping out the Romex staples and straining even more against the Romex/PVC connections, now Nortze's only lifeline. Nortze screamed, "Ken!"

Seeing the desperation on the Nortze's face, Ken felt no compassion, no urge to provide assistance. He looked down at the man on the threshold of death, and with ice running through his veins, said, "You killed my wife and son, you miserable fuck!" And a bolt of lightning struck inside Ken's head, and he shouted down, "You are going to die, and I'm going to watch it happen."

Nortze was almost in tears now, and he yelled up, "What are you talking about?" Nortze heard the creaking of lumber. "Help me, please. Get a rope or something."

Ken didn't budge. "That Beamer you ran off the road?" Ken yelled over the sound of the pounding waves, "Christmas of 2000? Inside were my wife and son, Gil. Bobby told me."

Nortze knew now that he had been finally found out, and he was close to tears, but he still tried to evade responsibility by changing the focus. "Who?"

"Your son, Gil. You call him Bob and you call his sister Sherry. But his name is really Bobby and hers is Cheryl. He changed his hair color just so you wouldn't recognize him." He was toying with the man now. "Recognize the names, Gil?"

Gil sat frozen against the railing, distant memories flooding back to him.

"That's right, Gil. Bobby and Cheryl *Nortze*— your own flesh and blood—the kids you abandoned, along with their mother, who died soon after." Ken had no compassion left, and he pressed Nortze, "You know it's them, don't you, you sonofabitch?"

Nortze dropped all pretenses, and began to sob. That lasted only long enough to come to the realization that that Ken would not help him. He tried to get his feet under him, but another downward creep of the deck and sounds of straining lumber froze him.

"Come on, Gil," Ken taunted, "You can make it on your own. Maybe I should call Tristin to give you a hand. Or maybe I should say *hand job*. I think about how you missed out on a real nice piece of ass there."

Nortze's anger now pushed through his fear, and he pulled himself up to a standing position, bracing himself against the back railing for support. He looked to see which way he should climb up, and fell forward onto his knees against the wet and sloping deck, and he began a sliding a move to his left.

Inside the garage, where the 75-foot PVC gas line made its first and only ninety-degree bend, the elbow finally snapped at the few extra pounds of downward force provided by the knees of Gil Nortze against the sloping deck. The live line began spewing gas. The plug was already straining 90-degrees against the Romex wire, and the little extra tug yanked the prongs out of the socket; it and the PVC gas line made a hasty retreat out the garage wall.

Ken watched as the spa, followed by the heating unit, lurched down slope across the wood planks. Nortze screamed and stood up just before the spa struck him full force and pushed him through the railing and uprights. He went over the cliff with the spa stuck to his chest, the heating unit right behind, and a 75-foot long run of white PVC pipe and Romex trailing behind like a streamer.

The entire deck then fell away, following Nortze down into the churning ocean. A moment later, another 30-foot wave smacked against the cliffs, shooting up spray well above the top and over the cliff edge, soaking Ken and Margie. She stirred and coughed, wiping her hand across her eyes at the sting of the salt water.

Ken got to his feet and looked down onto the rocks below. Just as he had predicted, there was no post left. It had been uprooted, even popping the shallow concrete plug out of the hole and going down into the ocean below with everything else. It was as if the deck and spa had never existed. *Tabula rasa.*

Margie looked up at Ken, blinking her eyes and still in a daze. Even in her current state, however, Margie noticed the expression on Ken's face as he stared unblinking down the cliff, an expression she could never really explain to anyone later, but one she would always remember.

"Ken?" Margie called up weakly. "Ken?"

Ken came out of his trance and helped Margie to her feet, and he kept his arm around to steady her frayed nerves as he walked her to her truck. They were both soaking wet. "I'll take you down to my house in your truck, Margie. We'll call the police from there."

As they walked slowly back towards Margie's truck, Ken didn't notice that there was no longer a PVC gas line from the garage to the deck. Nor did he hear the gas flowing out the broken ¾-inch pipe inside the garage. He did notice Nortze's red Lincoln parked in front of the closed garage. Once again, the red paint brought home to him the virtual certainty about just who had killed Valerie and Tyler. He felt no remorse over the loss of the miserable human being formerly known as Gil Nortze.

At Margie's truck, she almost fainted against the door, and Ken let her down gently onto the ground. He kneeled down next to her the whole five minutes it took for her to recover.

After she'd regained her strength, he helped her up into the passenger's seat of her truck, and went over her lap into the driver's seat. It took a few more minutes to get up and around the driveways and down to the front of his garage.

Inside his house, Ken was concerned about Margie, and he and an astonished but coolheaded Tristin help put her in their bed. Tristin looked after her while Ken went down the hall and into his office. He made the 9-1-1 call 26 minutes after the deck had collapsed.

Four minutes later, Nortze's house exploded. Bobby and Cheryl ran out into the garden and saw the flames and smoke shooting up from above the bluff.

"You don't think he was in there, do you?" Cheryl asked.

Bobby shook his head. "I hope not. Gil said he wasn't coming back until this afternoon." Bobby had an assignment for school that was due on Monday, and he had wanted to get it done before the party that night. This changed everything.

The police and fire departments were late in arriving. The heavy rains earlier had undermined the roots of a large, leaning Monterey Pine tree on the east side of the Coast Highway, and it had fallen and blocked the road. The road crew had just started cutting up the branches when the fire trucks arrived at the blockage. The crew quickly cleared away just enough so the trucks could make their way around the west side.

Upon the arrival of the fire trucks at Nortze's property, it was clear to the fire captain that the delay was of no matter—the house was already a total loss. When he later saw for himself its state of construction—no drywall, and wrapped and sealed on the outside but with exposed wood framing inside—he could see why it had gone up so quickly. By the time they arrived on-scene, the roof had already collapsed, just like Nortze's ceremonial *temescal*.

An ambulance took Margie to the hospital for observation. In a fog of disbelief, Ken then spoke to one of the fire officials, detailing how he had witnessed Nortze's death, and the role the bootlegged deck had played, although he did not divulge his own role in the incident. He also thought it prudent at that point not to mention the fact that he had a video showing why the deck had collapsed.

*****

Note to John: This brings us up to where my report first starts. The rest is a lesson to all. Steven

57 Identity

Both Bobby and Cheryl took the death of their biological father very hard, but not because they were just beginning to form a strong emotional bond. Their back-up ace-in-the-hole was now gone, and if Ken and Tristin did not officially adopt them, they knew it was "back to the pound" for the both of them. The prospect of even a single hour in another foster care home made a call-to-action a high priority. That same Saturday afternoon, May 11, while the two of them sat on the bed in Bobby's room, Bobby became very insistent. "We've got to start working on them, Cheryl, before it's too late."

The next morning, Sunday, Ken and Bobby were home while Tristin took Cheryl shopping for food. Ken was in the spa, trying to soak away his considerable load of troubles.

Bobby came out of his room and walked down the hallway, sticking his head into Ken's office, wanting to ask Ken if he could borrow the video camera. He was doing a project at school on the coastal marine environment, and he'd already bragged to his friends about how big the waves were, stating that his contribution would be video of the waves and how they caused slow but steady erosion of the rocks and cliffs. He was supposed to have something to show his teacher by the next day.

Bobby spotted the Sony video camera on Ken's desk, thinking Ken wouldn't mind if he shot a few feet of video out on the bluff. He grabbed the camera and trotted off.

Out on the bluff, Bobby heard the spa running and figured that's where Ken was. Reckoning the man wanted to be by himself, Bobby went to the south end of the property and videotaped the waves from several angles and at different zoom lengths.

The waves were still big, but diminishing in size now that the storm system was moving inland.

After five minutes of shooting video, Bobby went back to his room and set up his VCR and standard video jacks to copy the footage. Listening all the while for Ken to come back down the hallway, he rewound the tape, stopping well before his own footage. He then pressed the playback button on the Sony and kept his finger poised over the record button on the remote control for his own VCR. Bobby watched the monitor as it showed Nortze's deck, but he also heard Ken's unintentionally recorded words on the videotape. He sat watching and listening in a state of mild shock.

At the end of his footage, Bobby shut down everything and quickly returned the camera to Ken's desk—exactly how he had found it. He couldn't wait for Cheryl to come home and let her in on his little secret.

Tristin and Cheryl arrived home around one o'clock, having been gone longer than expected. They had not only gone grocery shopping, but had window-shopped and ate lunch at a delicatessen.

After helping put away the groceries, Cheryl went off to her room and Tristin went to the master bedroom where Ken was just coming in from the spa.

"Hi, hon," he said with a smile. "How'd it go?"

Tristin plopped down on the bed, almost giddy with joy. "Oh, Ken, we had a wonderful time. Cheryl is so sweet and loving, and I just couldn't help thinking how it would be if we adopted her and Bobby."

"Are you ready to make that decision now?" Ken asked. "You've still got a couple of weeks to decide."

"I know," Tristin said firmly. "But I was thinking that even with Bobby and Cheryl here, we could still have a baby of our own—maybe more than one." She smiled and winked, saying, "At least we don't have to change *their* diapers anymore."

Ken smiled and sat on the edge of the bed. He reached out and took her by the hand, squeezing it gently. "Well, you know my feelings on the subject. If it's okay with you, it's okay with me. But let's talk about it over the next few days, just to be sure, okay?"

"Okay," she said, and she turned and planted a kiss on Ken's lips. "I love you, and the kids." She parted lips and cooed, "and I want *our* baby, too."

Tristin rose from the bed and hurried to a plastic bag she had brought in with her. "I bought a little something for Cheryl, but it's a surprise." Tristin reached in the bag and pulled out a box, holding it out for Ken to see. "It's perfume. We were at the cosmetics counter and she liked the smell, so while she was looking around the store, I bought it."

"She'll appreciate that, I'm sure."

"I'm going to slip it onto her bathroom counter for her to find."

58 The Conversation

In Bobby's room, he stopped the VCR and Cheryl sat transfixed at the screen. "He killed Gil, didn't he?" Cheryl said quietly.

"Well, the deck collapsed with him on it, that's for sure. When Ken told us the story, he said he was so busy helping Margie that the deck fell away before he could do anything."

"And you're sure that Ken used that handsaw you saw in the garage?"

Bobby scoffed, "What do you think, Cheryl?"

"I just can't believe Ken would do something like that." At that comment, Bobby merely stared at Cheryl, eyebrows raised. Cheryl knew what Nortze had put Ken through during construction, and she shrugged, offering a weak, "Yeah, I guess so."

"Cheryl, this is big. *Huge!*" Bobby said with excitement. He forced himself to calm down. "Look, Cheryl, *everything* is changed now. With Gil gone, we haven't got that much time left for Ken and Tristin to make a decision. You say you made good headway on Tristin today, and I'm working on Ken. But what if they say no?"

"They can't say no."

"Well, maybe before," Bobby said, pointing to the TV set, "but not now, not with that in reserve to use as a sledgehammer against them." Bobby stood up and began to pace. "If they say *no*, then we have it to use as leverage. Remember, they want kids of their own, and they don't need any more trouble right now." And here, Bobby stiffened, his eyes squinting. "Remember what I said before? I didn't pull Connie off the cliff or burn down our own house just so we could end up back in the pound."

Bobby went to the window and stared out at the sea. "This is serious shit now, and we are committed—both of us—to making this adoption thing happen. We should both be thinking about the next seven or eight years until our trust fund comes through." Bobby reflected a moment on his past covert activities, and he smiled, adding, "It's like that detective said while he and the other one were locked away in Ken's office on the day after Connie went over the cliff: 'It's about all we have to go on at this point.'"

"Okay, I'll get to work on Tristin some more."

Bobby turned and said, "Bring up the subject of adoption yourself, Cheryl. Tell her you're feeling *insecure*. Tell her you want her to be your mother and that you want Ken to be your father. And tell her I feel the same way. But remember, we don't have much time left."

In the kids' bathroom, leaning on the sink, Tristin Barnes had heard enough. In fact, she had heard *everything*—as clear as a bell—through the common heater duct that teed off at the top of the wall supplying heat to both the bathroom and Tyler's—now Bobby's—bedroom. Tristin picked up the bottle of perfume from the counter and tiptoed out into the hallway, trying to calm herself for what she knew had to be done.

Back inside the master bedroom, she made her way straight to the little desk in the corner, pulled out a pad of paper and a pen, and she began to make notes, starting with the first thing she remembered: "Cheryl, this is huge ... "

Ken came out of the bathroom and saw the perfume bottle on the desk next to Tristin. "Didn't you give Cheryl her present?" Ken asked, totally oblivious.

Cold disdain now masked Tristin's usually sweet demeanor, and she turned and caught Ken's eye. With a look of fierce determination, she said to Ken, "Houston, we have a problem."

59 The Usual Suspects

On Monday morning, after Tristin had dropped the kids at school and gone to work, Ken Easton downed his second cup of coffee and got busy. He didn't know exactly what he was looking for in Bobby's room, but he knew where to start looking. Sitting down at Bobby's computer, Ken booted it up and waited for the desktop to come up onto the screen.

Ken could at first not believe what Tristin had told him, but as he began putting the disparate pieces together in his mind, it all began to fall into place: Bobby and Cheryl were not who they pretended to be. At best, they were the product of sad and unfortunate childhoods. At worst, they were cold-blooded killers. Ken wondered if they got any of that from their real father, Gil Nortze.

The desktop appeared, and Ken began perusing carefully up and down the columns of icons. He stopped when recognized one—the icon for his acoustic software program.

When Tristin had repeated what Bobby had said about the supposedly secret discussion between the detectives, Ken remembered that at that time Sam had already driven Bobby and Cheryl back home. That meant some sort of listening device. Which meant a recording. What better place to store all that sound data than onto a computer hard drive using Ken's acoustic software program?

Bobby had hidden it as best he could, but Ken knew what to look for. Buried within six levels of computer file folders was the file folder name, "kenoffice." Ken double clicked , and up popped 32 sound files totaling 24 megabytes of disk space. Bobby had even marked the date and time for each of the surreptitiously recorded conversations.

For the next two hours, Ken listened—and re-listened—to conversations not only between the detectives, but his own personal phone calls—on speakerphone and otherwise. He realized quite quickly that any search of his office would be fruitless at this late date, as he knew that Bobby was smart enough, and had had plenty of time and opportunity, to remove whatever it was he used. He began to suspect, however, that the walkie-talkie had somehow been rigged, and his brain set to locating the logical time and place that might have occurred. He sat and stared at the monitor, thinking.

Finally he recalled the time Bobby had asked him to help him repair the walkie-talkie. Such a simple problem, Ken remembered, plus Bobby had conveniently "forgot" to bring the matching one. That was the one used to record all these files, Ken concluded. *I wonder if they're still around somewhere?*

It took five minutes to carefully search Bobby's closet, making sure not to disturb anything, before he found them in a bag in the corner behind a cardboard box. He first noticed the electrical cord for long-term use without batteries. After opening up the back with a Phillips screwdriver, Ken inspected Bobby's handiwork. *Very impressive, young man.*

Ken then put the unit back together and replaced everything in the exact same place he had found them. His head was swimming now, and he needed to think. At the kitchen counter with a cup of coffee, he went over in his mind just how desperately screwed up these kids had become to do these horrible things. His thoughts drifted back to Bobby's words told to him by Tristin:

"I didn't pull Connie off the cliff or burn down our own house just so we could end up back in the pound."

Tristin was the Rock of Gibraltar now. She had insisted on writing down every word she could remember from the overheard conversation. Ken had been merely her sounding board, sometimes triggering something she had forgotten. She had been furious with herself for being so gullible, but she turned that fury into action—writing down the logical progression of recently remembered conversation.

The day before, they had left the kids all afternoon and evening to their own devices, except for fixing meals, while secretly reviewing every scrap of memory, starting from when the kids had first come onto the scene. Tristin had written fast and furiously, and she had writer's cramp before they finished up close to ten o'clock.

Alone at the kitchen counter now, he stared down into the blackness of his coffee. The tears began to well up in his eyes as he recalled Randy's emotional response over the phone telling him they had located a piece of Connie's arm.

The next vision in Ken's mind was Sam Wynette, burned and in insufferable pain, mumbling something about the batteries, and to *be careful*. Ken now realized that Sam had been trying to give him an important message, but he had written it off to the man's drugged state of mind. Ken also suspected that only after Sam had fought to stay alive, finally having the strength to tell Ken, that he had died shortly after. Ken concluded that it had been Sam's his final mission in life to warn him. And all the while, Bobby and Cheryl had played everyone for patsies.

Ken wept openly. "I'm sorry, Sam," he said through his tears, "I'm so sorry I didn't see it before now." For a man not usually given over to such emotion, Ken Easton had been forced to tears more in the last two months than in his whole life previous. His emotions were wearing thin.

After splashing water on his face at the kitchen sink and pulling himself mostly together, Ken used several hi-density CDs to copy the incriminating evidence from Bobby's computer. Once that was done, he went to his own bedroom and stashed the CDs high on the back of the closet shelf. He then fell on the bed, physically and mentally exhausted, and was asleep in less than a minute. He had never thought to check Bobby's VCR.

What Ken didn't know by the time he fell asleep was that Bobby had evidence, too. And it was enough to make Ken's and Tristin's lives even more miserable if they did not go along with Bobby's program.

60 The Final Confrontation

Ken picked up the kids from school and drove home, not revealing anything he knew or suspected. They went off to their rooms to do homework, and Ken sat at his desk, thinking. With his stomach tied in knots, it quickly became more than he could bear to think about any more. He got up to take a walk out of the bluff to clear his head.

Walking along the cliff towards the south end and looking out to the now six-foot swells, Ken knew he had to go to the police. He thought about waiting until Tristin got home, and they would make the call together.

Standing where Connie had gone over the cliff, Ken knew the evidence was strong, but he wanted absolute confirmation. The only way to get that, however, was a direct confrontation with the kids. Would they try to run away? Not likely. Besides, how far could they get? When confronted with the evidence, would they even confess their sins? Probably not to him, but later to the police? Yes.

Looking out of the window, Bobby saw Ken standing alone looking out to sea, and figured it might be just the time to go have a little "father-son chat."

Bobby stopped by Cheryl's room and poked his head inside. "I'm going out on the bluff to talk to *Dad*," he said with a twinkle in his eye. Wish me luck."

"Ooh, I'll keep an eye out."

Walking outside through the kitchen door, Bobby approached, hands in his jeans pockets. "Hi, Ken" he shouted from 30 feet away. Ken's startled reaction made Bobby even more confident that the man was lost in his thoughts, and that that timing may be perfect. "I need to ask you something."

"Sure, what is it?" Ken responded, now trying to act nonchalant after almost jumping out of his skin.

Bobby stepped up alongside and also looked out to sea, saying, "I need to talk about Cheryl. She's pretty much on edge these days waiting for some decision on the adoption thing. Have you guys talked about it any more?"

Ken nodded. "Yes, we have. We thought it might work out okay for everyone if we went ahead and started the paperwork." That was true—yesterday.

"Really?" Bobby said, his hopes soaring now. "Wow, Cheryl is going to be happy to hear that."

"Yeah, but that was yesterday." Ken said. He just couldn't help himself. Knowing what he knew, and what he knew that Bobby knew, the impulse to speak out could not be overruled.

"What do you mean?" Bobby asked.

"Well, let's start with the fact that it was Gil Nortze who ran my wife's BMW off the highway, killing her and my son, Tyler."

Bobby appeared flabbergasted. "Are you sure?"

"I am now. He told you in an unguarded moment, Bobby, and you told me. You know your father pretty well now. And you know he was just the kind of man who would do that."

Bobby dropped his head. "But what does that have to do with me and Cheryl?"

"Because you are his son, Bobby, and like him, you have no conscience." Ken sighed heavily. "I know what you did, Bobby."

Bobby's face paled a full shade. "What are you talking about?"

Ken turned to face Bobby, his game face on now. "I know about Connie, and I know about the fire that killed your mother and father."

The only emotion Bobby felt was betrayal. Only he and Cheryl knew the truth, and Bobby hadn't shot his mouth off to anyone. "What, did Cheryl say something?"

"No, Bobby, Cheryl didn't say anything." He watched closely for Bobby's next reaction. "But your father did."

The kid was cool as a cucumber. "What did he say?"

"That day we went to see him, well after you'd left, he told me that the batteries you put in the smoke detectors were not the same ones he gave you. I know now from Sam that you deliberately switched them, Bobby, and your mother and father are dead because of it. It was no accident, but why did you do it?" Ken wanted to hear from Bobby's own lips about being adopted by Ken and Tristin. It just didn't seem rational.

Bobby kept his poker face and stared out to sea.

Having started down the slippery slope of disclosure, it was too late for Ken to turn back. "And I know about Connie, too," Ken continued, now buoyed by the boy's calm reaction, "because

Tristin overheard you guys yesterday in your room. She was in the bathroom and could hear everything through the vent. Everything, Bobby." Ken now threw Bobby's own words at him, again watching for a reaction. "'I didn't pull Connie off the cliff or burn down our own house just so we could end up back in the pound.' Sound familiar, Bobby?"

Ken then saw a smug, self-satisfied grin on Bobby's face. It wasn't even close to what Ken was expecting. "You don't seem to be taking this too seriously."

Bobby shrugged his shoulders and turned his eyes to watch the waves. "It's kind of hard to take it all very seriously, knowing what I know."

"And what is it you know, Bobby?"

"How did Gil Nortze *really* die, Ken? I mean, was it just that the deck fell down all by itself, or did you *help it along* by cutting the post?" He turned and stared at Ken with cold, vacant eyes. Ken was too shocked to speak. "Oh, I know all about it, Ken. Even heard your own words saying how it would all happen ... before it happened."

"What are you talking about?"

"The video, Ken, the video. I borrowed the camera to shoot some stuff for my school project. I guess you didn't know the sound was on or something, but it was quite a speech, let me tell you." Bobby leaned in close, whispering hoarsely, "and very incriminating." Bobby leaned back. "I have a copy stashed where you'll never find it, but I'll show the police where it is."

Ken then put it all together, and his anger spilled over. "You little bastard. You think you can extort me? Into what, making us adopt you and Cheryl? We don't adopt murderers, Bobby." Ken moved ever closer to Bobby, in his face now. "I know what happened up on that cliff with Gil Nortze and the evidence supports it. Everything else is just wishful thinking by a pissed off neighbor—me. Sure, I wanted that deck gone, and I sabotaged it, but I didn't want Gil Nortze or Margie Swanson going down with it. I made every effort to save them." Every effort to save Margie was more truthful.

From her bedroom window, Cheryl could see that there was some sort of confrontation going on—something she had not anticipated.

"Oh, really," Bobby said, concerned now that his plan was not fleshing itself out as he had expected, but he pressed on. "That might hold up, but not with me saying you wanted Gil dead, and that you knew he was coming back." Bobby cocked his head and looked skyward. "I think I remember overhearing you say you were going to kill him the first chance you got."

Ken became enraged and turned on Bobby, grabbing him by the shirt and jerking him close. "Listen to me, you murdering little sonofabitch. We're going back into the house and I'm calling the police. Tell 'em whatever you want."

Bobby feigned compliance. "Okay, okay. Just let me go."

Ken relaxed his grip, and his defenses. Bobby lunged and hit Ken with his body, forcing him to take a step backwards down the sloping rock. Instinctively and with lightning fast reactions, Ken grabbed Bobby's outstretched arm, trying to pull it enough to regain his balance. When he found himself still at the transition point, Bobby now trying to pry his hand free, Ken didn't give it a second thought. Using what little footing he had beneath him, and along with his own weight, Ken pulled Bobby towards him. Ken went off the cliff backwards, Bobby cartwheeling right over the top of him.

Standing at the window, Cheryl screamed as she watched Ken and her brother disappear over the cliff.

On the way down, Ken managed to turn himself a little in the air, not to see where he was falling, but to check out what was coming in the form of waves. Bobby could only gasp at the rapid acceleration towards a churning ocean, holding his breath all the way down. He should have done differently.

Ken waited until just before hitting the water to take a breath. He hit the water in a very awkward dive, his left side taking the brunt of the force. But with the swirling water, the surface tension was fairly low, so it didn't even knock the breath out of him. The 58° water shocked his system, though.

As for Bobby, he did a face plant from 40 feet into the water, his hands too far apart to make a difference. It was as if he had been hit in the face with a powerful water canon. His body went into mild shock in the cold water, and his blue jeans began to absorb water.

Knowing the depth of the water—about ten feet at this location—and despite the chill surging through him, Ken let his momentum carry him down about four feet below the surface, and then he gave an additional downward pull with his arms to shoot him to the bottom. After Zuma Beach, his reflexes and instincts had taken over naturally. On firm ground but very cold, he sprang up to the surface like an arrow.

Not so knowledgeable as to local conditions, Bobby flailed underwater, its cold grip making itself known, as he tried to fight against both the swirling action of the waves and the undertow a few feet below the surface. His shoes and wet blue jeans were working against any natural buoyancy. Having used up his last breath before he hit the water, he struggled in vain for several critical seconds more, using up valuable residual oxygen in his lungs. When he finally reached the surface, he gasped once for air, keeping his eyes closed. And that's when the next wall of whitewater rolled over him.

Above on the top of the cliff, Cheryl cried and searched for Bobby, finally spotting him. She watched in angst as she saw his head disappear beneath the wall of whitewater.

Ken saw it too, and like Gil Nortze before him, Bobby was on his own. Ken timed the waves and churning whitewater to make his way slowly north, and away from the base of the cliff. With no swim fins and with his slacks, shirt, and shoes on, he was also not very buoyant, using shallow but frequent breaths to help keep him afloat.

At his first opportunity, he pulled his shoes off, unfastened his belt and kicked his slacks off, then tore off his socks, and finally he removed his shirt. He was down to his jockey shorts in water that was chilling him to the bone. But a little cold water did not stop him from doing what he knew had to be done—what he had trained himself over the years to do. Chief among them was maintaining a level head, because it was decision time.

He had two choices: Go for the underwater chamber and wait it out, or try to make it around the headland to his climb-out area.

Cheryl kept her eyes focused on the area where Bobby went under the foam, and she waited to see where he would next surface. "Come on, Bobby," she cried. "Please come up."

By the time Cheryl had given up searching the immediate area where Bobby had gone under, Ken was already past his diving perch and his secret chamber and breast-stroking his way to his exit rock, diving under the onrushing whitewater of each successive wave. With no protection from the elements, he knew his chances for hypothermia were high if he spent too much time in the chilly water. It would just sap whatever strength he had left—strength he needed then or later—for the swim to the climb-out area.

Cheryl made her way north along the edge of the bluff, but she couldn't see directly down into the water until she reached Ken's diving perch. Searching desperately with her eyes, Cheryl began to lose hope. She couldn't spot either Bobby or Ken, and with the waves so big—in her mind—she began to have thoughts that both had perished. She broke down and sobbed.

A few minutes later, she resumed her now-desperate search. On her knees, she peered over the perch close to the edge, closer than she ever wanted to be. But she hung tough, searching back and forth along the base of the cliff and out into the surf beyond, searching for Bobby.

She didn't want to leave because if and when she gave up searching, it meant she had given up on Bobby, the only person in the world who never gave up on her. She sat transfixed by the ocean, trying to figure out how she would survive with him gone. It would be nearly eight years before her trust fund would come through, and she wasn't sure that Ken and Tristin would adopt her. *Maybe with Bobby gone, they'll feel sorry for me.*

"He's gone, Cheryl," the voice behind her said. She turned and saw Ken Easton standing in his bathrobe, alive and well. And very angry. He'd come in around the north side, past the spa and into the house to grab his robe.

The look on Ken's face spoke volumes to Cheryl, but she turned her thoughts to Bobby. "You mean he's dead?" She whimpered, and came to a sitting position facing Ken.

Ken nodded. "Yes, I'm afraid so."

"What happened?" she asked through her tears.

"He tried to push me off the cliff, just like you and he did with Connie."

Cheryl's jaw dropped. *Did Bobby confess? Was that what they were arguing about?* Cheryl began her flow of crocodile tears. "I didn't do anything, Ken. It was Bobby."

"But you helped set it up, didn't you?"

"No, I swear." She wasn't such a convincing liar now.

"And what about the fire, Cheryl. You had nothing to do with that, either, I suppose."

"No, that was Bobby's idea."

"But you went along with it, and both your mother and father died horrible deaths because of it." Ken figured that would be enough to break her, but like Bobby, she gave him only a fierce look, staring in silence.

"I know all about it, Cheryl. How you and Bobby set up me and Tristin so we would adopt you."

Cheryl turned on the fake charm. "That's because I love you both—very much. So now you're not?" she asked, not realizing what a ridiculous question it was at this point in the game.

Ken felt she was actually being serious. His mind was swimming now, caught between his fatherly instincts and his own experience with the two kids. But most of all, his head was dizzy with the whole ordeal he'd gone through for the past six months. "No, Cheryl. You've helped murder three innocent people. I'm going to the police and tell them everything—including my role in sabotaging Gil Nortze's deck."

A change of expression into cold calculation flooded over Cheryl's little freckled face, and Ken felt the chill. It was like the voice of evil speaking with Cheryl's voice. "Are you also going to tell them about how you molested me?" Cheryl said, her dead eyes piercing his very soul. "You remember, Ken, when I was naked that day in the hot tub and you took me into your bedroom?"

Ken remembered that day well. And in that momentary vision, despite what he knew to be the truth, all he saw and felt was a future filled with torment for him and Tristin, and a failed career ahead. "You would do that to me and Tristin, after everything we've done for you?" Ken felt sick with the pain of it.

"You know how it works," Cheryl said, icily. Here she mimicked her conversation with police, heavy on shyness and embarrassment. "He was ... very aroused when he pulled me close to him. His bathrobe was loose and I could feel his, well, you know what on my tummy, officer, and he told me ... not to tell. And then he carried me to the bed ... " She was fabricating the story as she went along.

Anger rose up in Ken once again, and attempts to control it were becoming difficult. "I can pass a lie detector, can you, Cheryl?" He looked at her, waiting for that certainty to sink in.

Cheryl answered with cool detachment, "Perhaps. With all that's happened, though, they'll probably put you in jail first and ask questions later. They'll treat me differently, though. Bobby said so." Her eyes narrowed. "If you go to the police, I'll tell them everything … more than you could ever handle."

At that comment, Ken stepped toward Cheryl in anger. "You little bitch! You blame everything on your brother, Cheryl, but you know what? You're exactly like him … and your father." Ken's increasing anger pumped more adrenaline into his body than any bodysurfing experience.

With that, Cheryl stood and backed up two steps, looking back and down into the churning ocean. "I'm going to kill myself," she threatened. Cheryl looked to Ken, pleading with her eyes for him to beg her not to.

Ken's expression did not change, and he said nothing. Inside, he wished for an instant that she *would* kill herself. It would solve many problems at once.

Cheryl's expression then changed in front of Ken's eyes. Now she was the taunting Lolita, cooing, "When Tristin's not around, you can have me, Ken." She stepped forward, reached out her hand and placed it over Ken's crotch. "She doesn't have to know." And then the chameleon changed again, and she pulled back, her voice once again as cold as ice. "If not, then its sexual assault charges. It's up to you."

Ken's vision of personal doom lasted all of five seconds, his emotions beginning with fury and intensifying from there: Cheryl having the potential to destroy his life with false accusations, or extortion; Cheryl's influence over other human beings on the planet, both in the immediate or distant future; his life with Tristin, and their children, always looking over his shoulder to see if Cheryl was there, waiting in ambush.

At that last image, Ken's eyes glazed over. Something inside his brain finally snapped. He shouted from a few feet away, "Then tell the cops I threw you off the cliff, too." He then moved forward two steps ready to grab Cheryl and launch her backwards into the air. But she jumped back to get away from his grasp, and went back one step too far. She fell over the cliff and screamed all the way down, stopping only when she hit the water forty feet below, flat on her back.

Like Bobby, she should have saved her breath for when she would need it.

Ken Easton stood at the perch and looked down, chest heaving and totally unfazed by the cold wind. Cheryl managed to come to the surface only once, and then she disappeared. As she did, Ken also spotted the dorsal fin and shape of a 15-foot tiger shark heading towards her. He hung his chin down and closed his eyes.

The nightmare was finally over. Ken sank to his knees, burying his face in his hands, and he cried the words, "My God, what have I done?"

61 The Verdict

May 28, 2003

To: John Bascomb
From: Steven Sokkal

Well, John, it's been just over a year since Ken stood on his perch knowing there would be a day of reckoning. I guess it is now the time and place to tie up all the loose ends. I'm not sure how I should end this, as there is much more to tell. So I'll just lay it all out and let you decide for yourself what you think is important. Once again, I apologize for the long delay, but these things don't write themselves.

I spent many, many hours interviewing principles in this case, and I also gathered a lot of information from many sources. Much of what I wrote in the form of specific dialogue and motivation is, however, admittedly my own speculation. I hope you find it more interesting that a dry technical report.

Sam Wynette, Gil Nortze, and Bobby and Cheryl Nortze-Wynette all provided some direct information to both Ken and Tristin, but there was much to fill in. Darcy's neighbor, Marcie Avery, filled in critical details concerning the kids. Her insights into their relationships with Sam and Darcy were especially helpful. Based on the facts at hand, I used my knowledge and experience to fill in the remaining gaps. I hope you find it useful for your purposes.

Of course, the big question is, how do you treat in your screenplay what happened after Ken Easton watched, and did nothing, after Cheryl Nortze-Wynette went over the cliff? Here are a few ideas.

Ken did go to the police the next day—with Tristin and a top-notch criminal defense attorney, Alan Townsend—and Ken confessed all: tormenting Gil Nortze before he went down with his substandard deck; the altercation with Bobby resulting in his death; and even admitting he was so enraged that he was going to throw Cheryl off the cliff, but didn't because she slipped. He also turned over his and Greg McAferty's structural calculations for the overloading of the deck, plus the video/audio evidence from his camcorder.

It was a pretty big load of guilt for Ken to be carrying around, but he knew he also had to immediately tell the police about the kids, as he figured there would surely be a call from the school that day. The vice principal, Mr. Daley, called and left a message that very morning questioning their whereabouts.

The point here is that Ken used pretty sound judgment when faced with such an intractable problem: If you find yourself in a hole, the first thing to do is stop digging.

Townsend came before the police and prosecutors exceptionally well prepared, laying out the many mitigating circumstances for leniency. Ken Easton's one shining bit of hope (not to have the book thrown at him) was realized when he turned himself in and made a full confession. That's always a good strategic move.

Bail was set for $1 million dollars, and he mortgaged his house to come up with the cash bond and pay his lawyer. He was released on his own recognizance principally because of the lack of flight risk. Turning himself in certainly helped in that respect.

Ken and Tristin were married on June 15, 2002 in a private ceremony. It was a decision based mostly on financial and legal considerations, as Tristin could help maintain control of assets while Ken's case made its way through the legal system.

I've read his statements carefully, and there seem to be neither conflicting statements nor any attempt to justify his actions. I consider him to have provided the details in a truthful and forthcoming manner. Numerous and lengthy polygraph sessions failed to show any deception.

So let's move on to the details. Bobby and Cheryl Nortze had, in each of their minds, an idealistic notion of perfection that was not born out by realistic appraisals of people and situations around them. And when that lack of perfection met head on with the current state of their already altered genetic makeup, disaster was not long in coming.

Bobby Wynette was sharp, sharper than most kids his age. And Cheryl was his willing partner and just as culpable in all three murders. But as sharp as Bobby was, he was still just a kid, not realizing that once a critical piece of information had been obtained, other pieces of the puzzle would begin to fall into place. His secret plans and activities depended on not having a critical component exposed and held up to the light of day.

In that regard, Bobby failed a basic prerequisite for criminal success—absolute and lifelong secrecy. The evidence on Bobby's computer was as if he had spilled his guts directly to the police in the interrogation room under a hot lamp. Other evidence corroborated it. What Tristin Barnes supplied was also confirming information. Sam Wynette's deathbed plea to Ken was even allowed to be considered at the evidentiary hearing as an exception to the hearsay rule as an "excited utterance" on Sam's part.

Speaking to the charges first filed against Ken Easton, here's a summary. Ken was at first charged with murder in the second degree for both Gil

Nortze and Cheryl Wynette. These were "charges" based upon what the police believed to be appropriate at the early stage of proceedings against him.

In order for someone to be found *guilty* of two second-degree murders, however, the government would have had to prove—beyond reasonable doubt—that Ken killed both Gil and Cheryl with malice aforethought; and that the killings were premeditated.

And here is where "mitigating circumstances" come into play in the eyes of the law. Strictly speaking, either case would fall under the definition of murder ... technically.

The facts and circumstances in both cases took months to flesh out, and by the end of July, prosecutors were already thinking voluntary man- slaughter instead of murder ... technically. It was deemed "voluntary" at that time primarily because Ken had it in his power to prevent Nortze's death by not sabotaging his deck. Although he gave Nortze verbal warning to get off it just before it collapsed, Ken should have physically removed him, and then told Nortze what he, Ken, had done. The fact that Ken did warn Nortze (in Margie Swanson's presence) would come into play only later as a mitigating circumstance, resulting in a downward movement in the charge. Ken's lawyer argued for a "crime of passion," but it did not at first carry too much weight with regard to Gil Nortze.

As for Cheryl, her role in the game slowly came to light as Ken's lawyer also argued a "crime of passion" defense. In both cases, it was shorthand for jury acquittal, which I will go into later. Whether Ken had actually thrown her off the cliff, or she had slipped and fallen as a result of his lunging at her made little difference, at first, in the eyes of the law. She went over the cliff, and Ken could have prevented that. Or he could have jumped in to save her.

For any other person besides Ken, without his swimming skills and specific knowledge of the local conditions, such lack of heroics would have been instantly forgiven. However, not too many people in the world have Ken's skills and experience, and prosecutors raised the notion as to how he could simply have jumped in and saved Cheryl. But the presence of the shark (Ken passed the polygraph on that one, too) tipped the scales.

In the abstract, jumping off a forty-foot cliff into dangerous waters to save a child not their own, seems, like Detective Sanchez's notion, heroic. In the real world, and in the presence of a tiger shark, it is neither advisable nor mandated. This was yet another example in this case of how murky the line is, at least at times, between acceptable and non-acceptable human behavior in the eyes of the law.

There were, however, many "mitigating circumstances" in both cases, as you can well imagine. It is indeed a rarity to go from charges filed to crime sentencing without adjustments, usually downward.

A good example would have been the case against Bobby Wynette for trying to push Ken Easton off the cliff. Had the boy succeeded and been turned in by Ken (but with Ken nor the police knowing of his murder of Connie and his own parents), he might have been charged with attempted murder. But with factors such as his age, no prior criminal record, and some form of success with a "heat of passion" defense, he probably would have walked off with little or no punishment. Of course, Ken was not ultimately charged with the death of Bobby Wynette, as it was determined to be a clear-cut case of self-defense.

This example drives home the importance of aggravating versus mitigating circumstances—considerations to either increase or decrease one's punishment.

In addition to many such mitigating factors in Ken's overall case, there was one additional consideration with which both the prosecutors and defense attorney wrestled early in the proceedings: What jury would ever convict Ken Easton of either initial "top" charge of second-degree murder for Cheryl Wynette or Gil Nortze, given the mitigating circumstances in both cases?

The nightmare scenario circulating through the prosecutor's office was a jury acquitting Ken Easton altogether on the grounds of justifiable homicide—for both Cheryl and Gil. (That would surely set a precedent for hostile actions against nasty neighbors everywhere!) Juries sometimes like to send messages to the world—called jury nullification—and technicalities be damned. Just don't ask me in writing how I would have voted if I were on Ken Easton's jury, especially in consideration of my own surly, uncooperative, selfish, and tyrannical neighbor with whom I now battle on almost a daily basis, causing me and my family untold misery … .oh, sorry for the digression.

Anyway, it was pretty clear to the prosecutors that they didn't have to take Ken's word that Bobby had spoken the truth about Nortze telling Bobby that, in essence, he had run Valerie Easton's BMW off the cliff. Ken's attorney provided certified lab results showing that the chemical samples taken from Gil Nortze's red Lincoln were "consistent" with those taken from the corroded red streak resembling a butterfly on Valerie's BMW after it had been hauled out of the ocean. It was a butterfly with a hint of color, the color containing molecules organized in specific fashion for the job of painting cars. The manufacturer had used the same identical red paint for that model car year after year.

It was the first major test of Ken's veracity, and he passed with flying colors. So, the prosecutors concluded that it was, indeed, highly likely that Gil Nortze had been the one responsible for Valerie and Tyler Easton's deaths. After that, prosecutors found other reasons to believe that Ken Easton's story was more than credible.

You may recall that I provided expert testimony for the state at the evidentiary hearing that such a firm belief on Ken's part of Gil Nortze's culpability in the death of his wife and son could, but not necessarily would, lead to pre-meditated homicidal thoughts and follow-up actions. It was up to the prosecutors and the judge to decide if, after all Ken had gone through with his Neighbor from Hell (and his demon offspring), Ken's subsequent actions rose to the level of the crime of murder.

Prosecutors also contacted detectives Sanchez and Waxman with Tristin's accusations of the involvement of Bobby and Cheryl in Connie Halperin's death. A more thorough search of the shortest route home without having to use the busy Pacific Coast Highway (and possibly be spotted), ended in the only ravine between Spindrift Road and their house. Searchers discovered Bobby's clothes hidden under the rock. The fibers on his shirt were an identical match to those found on the cliff.

Ken and Tristin had, in fact, helped solve three murders that responsible law enforcement authorities had written off to accidents. This did not go unnoticed in the local newspaper, the *Carmel Pine Cone*, and it was a source of official embarrassment. It would also come into play when Ken's lawyer began plea-bargaining.

As described above, the initial charge is often not the charge one faces before a judge or jury. Plea bargains are the rule, not the exception. In Ken's case, Townsend argued that if Ken was tried for murder in either case, they would take their chances on a sympathetic jury possibly acquitting Ken altogether. It was not, under the circumstances described, all that unlikely.

On the other hand, a little girl is still a little girl, totally innocent or not. While Ken Easton and his lawyer would have taken the case for Nortze's murder to a jury in a heartbeat, even the possibility of juror sympathy for Cheryl Wynette wasn't worth the risk of a trial.

The prosecutors finally caved in to a plea agreement, forcing them into substantial reduction in the charged offenses, thus affecting Ken's ultimate punishment.

At the sentencing hearing in mid-November of 2002, mitigating circumstances won in a shutout. There were just no aggravating circumstances in either filing, unusual but not unprecedented (sympathy for the victim is not an aggravating offense). Also, with Ken's lack of any police record, and the credible, verifiable story he told, it was impossible for the judge to find that Ken Easton was a hardened criminal.

Judge Stanley's words summed up the situation. "You have suffered greatly, Mr. Easton, and I sympathize with what you and your wife have gone through. But the law is the law, and if we let everyone go free who has suffered in life prior to their offense, there wouldn't be many people in jail." Judge Stanley accepted Ken's guilty pleas on two identical counts—involuntary manslaughter for both Cheryl Wynette and Gil Nortze. The sentences were to run concurrently.

Ken is about to complete the first six months of his original one-year sentence at the Soledad Correctional Training Facility in Central California. Normally, inmates have to serve at least 80 percent of their time, but there is also a seldom-used inmate relief to "half-time." Ken qualified for this relief because of his particular case and the unlikely prospect of recidivism. He would receive a day off his sentence for every day of good conduct, and his earliest possible release date was assigned the day he stepped into the prison facility.

It was deemed to be manslaughter on both counts because two humans being died of drowning as a direct result of 1) Ken sabotaging the deck that collapsed into the sea, taking Gil Nortze down with it; and 2) Cheryl falling off the cliff before Ken could throw her off. Although held in abeyance until facts proved otherwise, no charges were ever filed against Ken for Bobby's death.

In Gil Nortze's case, it was deemed involuntary because Ken actually did try to warn the man. If Margie Swanson had not corroborated this, he would surely have been tried for voluntary manslaughter. In Cheryl's case, five seconds of "heat of passion" was the key to the reduced charge. The fact that Ken had not actually touched Cheryl prior to her slipping off the cliff was a minor mitigating circumstance. Again, the prosecutors had to weigh the possibility of jury nullification, and

Ken Easton and his lawyer had to weigh the possibility of conviction.

The mitigating circumstances (plus the fear of jury nullification) made the reduction to involuntary manslaughter in both cases almost a slam-dunk. They say a good compromise is when both parties are dissatisfied, and that's pretty much how the judicial system works.

Although not an accomplished screenwriter like you, as a prison psychologist it is part of my job to also understand human motivations at a deep level. And I think I understand Ken Easton about as well as anyone can.

Ken Easton requested psychological counseling at the outset of his incarceration. He was torn with the guilt of being involved in the deaths of six people (three directly, and three indirectly). With encouragement from a fellow inmate, Ken asked to speak to me, and that began a series of ongoing conversations detailing what I wrote in this report. While much of the time we spent going over events he felt were important— concerns related to his own reactions within very brief intervals of time—to situations as they arose. Highest on the list was how he could have allowed himself to "play God," as he put it, with the lives of Gil and Cheryl Nortze.

In those few seconds deciding the fates of Gil Nortze and his biological daughter, Cheryl, the symbolic life events of Ken Easton passed through his head like a high-speed movie montage.

The butterfly streak had been of unknown origin, making for a significant emotional void in need of filling. It was Gil Nortze's head on that butterfly. Closure was an internal demand on this issue, not a moral choice.

There was Ken's lasting image of Lindy sitting at the edge of the bluff staring down into the turbulent sea, missing Connie. For Ken, that image represented the slaughter of innocents seemingly justified by Bobby's higher, albeit psychopathic purpose.

Ken spoke of a huge wave, approaching with speed and determination, containing within its volume all of the lies and deceits and cunning of related strangers, all with independent agendas. In a slow but constant freefall, Ken felt himself going slow motion down the face of that breaking wave with no gravitationally based limit to its size.

Preventing the freefall into the abyss of despair and madness, Ken's survival instincts simply took over. It was either them or him—now or later. And it was all decided in just a few seconds. In the final analysis, Ken's psyche did not want to revisit later unpleasant events of the same origin.

Does Ken Easton exhibit any signs of becoming a victim of Punctuated Psychogenetic Equilibrium, or PPE? No. What Ken Easton went through was merely typical of ordinary people undergoing enormous strain. The emotional rubber band that snapped in his head in those moments of heated rage was not powerful enough to send a lightning bolt of energy down to his DNA. At least I don't think so.

Ken Easton has been a model prisoner. He has not only kept his nose clean—which I expected—but he has contributed immensely to an important training program at the prison. The prison section he is in is not, as some might imagine, a typical hardcore jail environment. That is a separate facility altogether. He and others are in a guarded vocational training facility. The inmates work in many technical and trade areas to hone their skills prior to their release. Donne & Maris, through Greg McAfterty, donated a dozen computers for use by the prisoners. They strip them down to the bare essentials, and then reconstruct them. Once they've learned the ropes, they are given just the parts to reconstruct into a finished product, with the computer going to the regional public schools.

Ken has all but taken over the computer facility. Every inmate in the program has spent hours—days and weeks, even— trying to outsmart Ken Easton's little acoustic sensors, when they're not building computers. None have succeeded thus far, but the experience gained has provided them valuable real-world experience and hopes for a better future. With a parolee recidivism rate at 70% overall in California, any dent is appreciated.

There has been only one small problem, and I hope it is resolved soon. The computer training program started out with ten inmates and a single instructor/overseer, but it has ballooned to over fifty. This puts the inmate to guard ratio at more than 50:1— an unacceptable figure to the prison guard's union. The union argues that more guards are necessary to supervise the inmates and prevent computer component theft; the administration argues that no more money exists to hire guards for this purpose alone, and if required to do so, the program will cease operation. No one said prison life was easy.

Ken is, overall, a good person with a strong moral compass, concerned with the rights and feelings of others. The fact that he expresses remorse at the deaths of the three Nortzes, yet thinks to this day that the world is a better place without them, shows an understandable pragmatism in the light of horrific events. All he wants—or ever wanted—was the freedom to live his life out on the cliffs of Yankee Point without intrusion. And yet he has accepted his own responsibility surrounding the deaths of two human beings without blaming others. Unless he does something here at the prison to put himself in serious trouble, he will soon be a free man, willing and able to get on with his life. If he makes his release date, Ken will home by the time I return from vacation.

So, give some thought to tying in your upcoming screenplay to Ken's release, because I think we have a good shot at some national TV exposure to talk up an upcoming movie. I'm sure you know of some good publicity firms down in L.A.

that would jump at the opportunity. What is your thinking on that?

I don't know how useful this and the following four topics are for your screenplay, but I'll give them to you, and you can use them as you see fit.

1) Three days after Bobby and Cheryl both died, Ken was in his garden with Jake the Tern. Something startled Jake, and he flew off. And then Ken heard a voice call down to him. When Ken turned around, he saw Gil Nortze standing at the top of the slope and staring down at him. In the few seconds Ken thought he was having a heart attack, he wondered how the man could have possibly survived—maybe carried to a place on the cliffs Ken didn't know about where Nortze climbed to safety.

Nortze shouted down from the top of the slope, "Hi, I'm Harry Nortze. You must be Ken Easton." It turns out it was Gil's younger brother. Funny, huh? Harry Nortze was the lawyer in Atlantic City who helped Gil with his divorce, and he's also a gambler. Margie Swanson brought Harry down to see the property, as he was executor for Gil's estate. It seems that Harry was more interested in cashing out Gil's considerable assets than in seeking wrongful death damages from Ken Easton. I spoke with him by phone and met him face to face on several occasions, and I have to agree with Ken that he's the spitting image of pictures of Gil. But that's where the comparison stops, as he is actually quite a nice person ... for a lawyer. (I would be honored to have such a comparison: Quite a nice person ... for a prison psychologist.) It's just not as funny.

2) Then there's Maria Nortze's journal and the various diaries of George, Duane, and Cecil Nortze. The police found them in Gil's rented Lincoln after his house burned up. According to Margie, he had apparently brought them all to the new house for safekeeping. They were turned over later to Harry Nortze, who couldn't make heads or tails out of them. I could—and did. I used some of it to project the Nortze family mindset—proclivities and motivations of Gil, Bobby, and Cheryl—onto the pages of my report. I also plan on writing a technical paper based on the information inside. "The Psychobiology of Heredity," is the working title. It speaks to possible neurological and biochemical origins of criminal behavior in the DNA molecule, and it is based somewhat upon a colleague's published work in the field of Antisocial Behavior Disorder, or ABD. (FYI copy is attached). You may wish to review it for your screenplay. The behavior typically involves individuals who exhibit the following:

Failure to conform to social norms with respect to lawful behaviors as indicated by repeatedly performing acts that are grounds for arrest; deceitfulness, as indicated by repeated lying, use of aliases, or conning others for personal profit or pleasure; lack of remorse, as indicated by being indifferent to or rationalizing having hurt, mistreated, or stolen from another.

3) The Nortze diaries reveal much about those making the entries, but one cannot make a leap to clear diagnostic conclusions. For example, you don't have to know much about psychology to understand that fire has for hundreds of millennia played an important role in our psychological lives. For some people—pyromaniacs—it is a dominant role. The Nortze "tradition" is not at all typical in this regard, as there seems to be the possible interpretation that fire was merely a convenient means to a successful, albeit destructive end. The fire itself held no intrinsic satisfaction, except mollifying the need to be in complete control. So, in this case at least, pyromania is not considered to be a hereditary behavior. I could be wrong about that, but future studies should decide the matter.

What is important by its absence from the diaries is any reference to personal relationships—bonds and attachments. The lack of such attachments is a red flag for antisocial behavior.

Bobby, Cheryl, and Gil Nortze exhibited, respectively, the classic signs of decreasing levels of antisocial behavior.

Bobby Wynette was a true psychopath, as he acted out with lethal consequences towards others with no signs of remorse. Cheryl Wynette showed signs putting her on the borderline between neurosis and psychosis—commonly referred to as Borderline Personality Disorder, or BPD. Gil Nortze was just an asshole. That's not a technical term, but it surely fits him to a T. There is certainly a better argument for Bobby, and perhaps Cheryl, having active PPE than Gil Nortze.

And 4) Think of Gil, Cheryl and Bobby in terms of Ken Easton's seismic-acoustical model with three levels of concern: 1) <u>N</u>o <u>o</u>bvious <u>p</u>roblems <u>e</u>ncountered (NOPE) but check to be sure (Gil); 2) <u>X</u>-number of <u>p</u>roblems (XP) require immediate expert attention (Cheryl); and 3) imminent, potentially catastrophic threat—GFON! (Bobby).

NOPE, XP, and GFON constraints are not only generally applicable to Gil, Cheryl, and Bobby, respectively, but also applicable to many situations in increasing levels of tension generated within all of us. It's called, "life as we know it." Few are immune to the onset of personal problems, but some are better equipped than others to cope with them without plotting and carrying out murder.

With all these factors in mind, where do all these behaviors—antisocial, sociopathic, and psychopathic—come from? Heredity? Environment? My own theory is that, in the cases of Bobby and Cheryl Nortze, their "evil" behavior was rooted in their genetic makeup, a result of Punctuated Psychogenetic Equilibrium (PPE) somewhere back in his family history. Yet it was only Bobby who exhibited behaviors of the true psychopath, with Cheryl close behind and gaining. And Gil Nortze was not so much patently evil or psychotic, but rather just another screwed up human being who took advantage of people.

So it is Bobby who I look to for answers to the question of the balancing of environmental and genetic factors in human beings. It is my considered opinion (but far from established fact) that while environment played a small roll in Bobby's aberrant behavior, PPE was a major contributing factor. There just wasn't enough in his short life to suggest otherwise.

Once again, PPE is not a diagnosis but a possible phenomenon occurring somewhere along the strands of DNA. And it may be a force relative to weak versus strong. The human brain is a powerful organ for transmitting electrical signals at different power levels. And an extremely powerful emotion or physically traumatic event bringing on intense neurological shockwaves could well prove genetically damaging.

If one were to stretch out all the DNA molecules in an average human body, the length of the DNA is the equivalent distance from the earth to the sun and back. Lots of possibilities there for mutations and beneficial adaptations.

An issue naturally arises as to whether PPE is either a beneficial or ultimately fatal mutation. With three Nortzes gone in so short a time, it may very well be the latter. The question is: How long does it take to eradicate, or hopefully dilute, PPE?

The success or failure of a mutated gene is measured by its ultimate survival. Genes seem to fight for dominance and survival just like whole organisms. If the hereditary line continues, it is successful; if it dies out, it is not. The only surviving direct Nortze descendent is Harry Nortze, Gil's younger brother, and a bachelor. If he marries and has children, the gene could still manifest dominance somewhere down the line.

With Gil, Bobby, and Cheryl gone forever, perhaps they can dig up the remains of Cecil Nortze, grandfather of Gil and son of Duane and Maria, for later DNA analysis and comparison to that of Harry Nortze. I forgot to elaborate earlier on the fact that in 1966, just outside Cambria, Cecil shot two people dead in Gil's presence when Gil was two years old, after they had accused Cecil of cheating at poker. One was Cecil's own son, Toby—Gil's father. The other was Toby's wife, Mary, who was Gil's mother. Harry was just a few months old at the time.

Cecil's diary entry that day read: *"Shot em both. Had to. Only honorable thing to do. Hated Mary's cooking. Toby had it coming for other reasons. Gil and Harry are better off."* And being better off was precisely Gil's take on the fate of his own abandoned children, Bobby and Cheryl.

What those *other reasons* were for Toby Nortze's death are lost to history, as Cecil made no more diary entries prior to his execution in February 1968 at Pelican Bay for double murder.

With the Tet Offensive laying bare overambitious American claims of pending victory in Vietnam, there wasn't much attention paid at the time to a psychotic killer from Cambria.

Gil was orphaned at an early age, so we know nothing about his time in any foster care homes. That would take some time to investigate. Maybe later for the sequel? Just kidding. Although, I must admit to speculating (to myself) how things might have changed if Ken had mentioned "Gil Nortze" by name the first time he and Bobby and Cheryl first met out of the bluff. While previously I ascribed no significant changes in ultimate results, I retain a vision of an alternate reality should the three of them have all gotten together and managed to work things out.

Gil Nortze was a man exhibiting antisocial behavior, but that alone didn't make him inherently evil, or psychotic enough to commit pre-meditated murder. A note on gambling—many fine people in the world gamble, but they are good people nonetheless. It's the addiction (to the detriment of everyone and everything else in their lives) that is the problem.

If we put away all of the people with similar "behaviors" as Gil Nortze, well, paraphrasing Judge Stanley, the world would have more prisons than schools.

On another subject, it is indeed unfortunate that no bodies or parts of Bobby or Cheryl were ever recovered, because DNA preserved for later testing (when the technology is available) might prove enlightening. The best and most interesting results have come from identical sets of twins whose DNA is a perfect match. Some reveal the same behaviors even though they are separated geographically; others reveal different behaviors while growing up together. As far as Bobby and Cheryl Wynette are concerned, we'll never know.

Which brings us to the burning questions: What roles do heredity and environment play on fundamental levels of behavior? What role does severe psychological trauma play in heredity? Is there such an intra-cranial event as Punctuated Psychogenetic Equilibrium? What specific and severe psychological (or physical) trauma triggers PPE? How strong does an emotion have to be to trigger it? How many subsequent generations will be affected?

The simple answers are that no one knows, although there are many investigators in the general field of psychobiology. And what you will have to decide for yourself in writing your screenplay is whether or not Gil Nortze's "evil gene" was active, recessive, or somewhere in between. For reasons described above, I say somewhere in between. It will be interesting to see how this mechanism is depicted on screen. With today's computer graphics, John, I expect a visual extravaganza.

And now we get to your latest email. It leads me to believe that you may be laboring under false assumptions, so I feel that a review of principles is needed here. Since it involves a complicated ethical matter, which I won't go into in detail here, suffice it to say that it is important to me and to the reputation of the prison system that you be made fully aware of the ground rules.

In conversations with prison officials prior to my putting pen to paper, as it were, we all came to an early agreement on the telling of this story. First of all, real names, factual accounts, and actual locations (plus my own speculations) were allowed to be used in writing my "report," with the caveat that this information, in this form, could not be made public without the written consent of Ken Easton and the other people (still living) written about. If you feel any of it useful, by all means use it, but unless Ken Easton is a willing participant (and compensated), any reference to him must be fully disguised and locations shifted so as not to reveal his probable identity. As of a month ago, Ken was keeping his options open, including the writing of his own memoirs. I doubt if that will affect our project.

Secondly, should there be any financial reward on my part (screen rights, books, etc.), all proceeds from my end will go directly towards the vocational programs at Soledad. Having read the "report," officials at Soledad are now very excited about the prospects of a movie (and, of course, the prospect for more program funds), and they have given me great latitude in scheduling my time henceforth. The senior psychologist who hired me said, on more than one occasion, that the California

Department of Corrections can do anything they want to do. If they are not doing it, it is because they don't want to, not because they can't. I am counting on their wanting to do this.

If, however, Ken Easton wants to use information supplied in this "report" (or any other source) for his own purposes, that will be his unrestricted right upon release.

What I'm saying here, John, is that we can't just take what's here and cut and paste it directly into a screenplay with no strings attached. I thought I made that clear, but your email seemed to suggest otherwise. I trust this clears up the matter once and for all.

A few things before I sign off. There's some good news for Ken and Tristin that I just heard about—he won't lose that beautiful house on the cliffs. Tristin even has it all spruced up—new paint outside and in—and waiting for his return. I think they're even doing some remodeling. And that big outfit in San Jose, D&M, is planning on having him at the groundbreaking ceremony on June 10 for the acoustic sensor demonstration project. He's going to be back in business very soon.

Harry and Margie are in some kind of gambling partnership now, but I can't be sure, as it's all very hush-hush. Her B&B is constantly booked solid with gamblers from all over. I do know from personal experience, however, that while she was lousy at online poker, she is a force to be reckoned with face to face. I lost fifty bucks to her in less than five minutes. Don't worry, I won't charge that to the expense account. Besides, the last time I checked, gambling was still illegal in California. And I hope they don't get busted.

And, of course, there is that lot next door. Harry Nortze put the property on the market recently for $1.5 million, and Ken and Tristin snapped it right up. Ken mortgaged the house to make bail, so I don't know where they got the money. But good for them.

Well, John, I guess I've gone on long enough. I'm leaving with my wife and son tomorrow for Puerto Vallarta for that much needed vacation. I hope this finds you well rested from your latest European scouting venture. Read the report while I'm gone, and after I get back we can discuss your screenplay (who knows, maybe a book for me).

/s/ Steven Sokkal

*****

June 5, 2003

Dear Steven,

Having returned to L.A. three days ago, I've been trying to reach you at home while reading your "report." It wasn't until I got into the "note" at the end of Chapter 25 that I remembered a previous email about your vacation and figured out where you are—or were. I then skipped to the last chapter and never went back to read the rest. I'm afraid that last chapter didn't make much sense, but it doesn't really matter.

I trust you and your wife had a nice vacation, and I even gave serious thought to jetting down to PV to find you. It was good that I didn't, because I have a temper and might have punched you in the face.

There is good news, Steven, and there is bad news. First, the bad news: I lied about the good news. You obviously had good intentions, but the road to hell is paved with them.

From the beginning: Your role in our collaboration was supposed to be, per our oral agreement, to write a summary of events that included character sketches and timelines, legal charges and responses, plus your expertise in psychology to help fill in some of the gaps. My role was to take what you provided and fashion it into a screenplay. I've had producers and agents all over me waiting for me to finish, but it's difficult to finish what I can't start. And yes, I did stretch a bit in assuming that taking the people and places written about could be used with, as you put it, "no strings attached." I just didn't feel any obligation to your ethical obligations, in this case to the CDC. Is that so terrible? Hollywood does that all the time.

And now to the meat of it. No wonder it took you so damned long—you wrote a fucking novel! What the hell were you thinking when you went against my direct advice and starting writing all that stuff? ("Don't write a novel!" were, as you wrote, the exact words). Your timing is bloody awful! Taking time to learn Texas Hold'em? We pay script consultants to do that, for Christ's sake. You should have whipped this all out in a month, but instead, you got bogged down in rucs and temescals, seismic crap, acoustic whatever, movie-title headings, lengthy and time-consuming interviews with everyone involved still alive, plus all that unintelligible PPE psychobabble. What's your phrase in Hungarian, Dr. Sokkal, for, "I'm so mad I could spit?"

What I am leading up to is that while you are now enjoying remnants of your tan, your former inmate pal, Ken Easton, just three days ago made a joint announcement. I say "former" because Ken was released three days ago (like you so wisely predicted). And I say "joint" because Ken's publicist, publisher, literary and film agents, lawyer, manager and financial advisor were all in the audience for Ken's appearance on *Good Morning America*. I didn't see it myself, but from what I'm told, he made quite a splash—excuse the pun.

Ken's autobiography, entitled, *Home*, is coming out next week. I'm sure everything's in there you were supposed to write. He scammed you, Steven, into thinking you and I had free reign to tell his story. It seems obvious, at least to me, that he wrote his book in Soledad Prison. Gee, Steven, I seem to remember something about you working there, too. He's also signed a deal with Tri-Star for the movie rights to his autobiography. Movie of the Week on HBO, I guess. Last but not least, he's also scheduled for *Oprah* next week, so maybe someone you know will tape it and will show you a copy upon your return.

For Christ's sake, Steven, didn't you ever poke your head into his cell (or, shock of shocks, ask him) to find that HE HAS BEEN WRITING A BOOK AND TAKING MEETINGS WITH AGENTS AND PUBLICISTS AND FILM PRODUCERS WHILE YOU'VE BEEN JACKING OFF AT YOUR WORD PROCESSOR LIKE GIL NORTZE DURING WOMEN'S APPRECIATION WEEK?

Okay, I am calmer now—but not much. I find myself now locked out of any possible deal for my screenplay—nobody wants to talk to me now. I've already had one unnamed professional disaster in my life, and I thought it would be my last. This was my chance for a big comeback. Thanks for wasting my valuable time. I am now forced to take up a previous offer by family members of Saddam Hussein to write his side of the story. I trust he will be easier to find than Gil Nortze.

BTW (as you computer freaks say): Since the "Books by Crooks" provision of the law dealing with profiting from criminal enterprise was struck down by the California Supreme Court in February, 2002, Ken got a $2 million advance on the whole package. And he's already pre-sold 80,000 copies of *Home* on Amazon.com. Where did you think they got the money to buy that lot next door? Manna from heaven? If only I could have started on the script earlier with your basic historical notes and professional opinions, things might have worked out. They didn't. And I hope prison officials like your report—maybe one of them has an agent you can submit it to.

In conclusion, have a nice life giving meaningless tests to the nearly three-quarters of the criminal tigers who never change their stripes. Don't bother calling or writing. The deal's off.

/s/ John Bascomb
Bel Air, California

*****

June 30, 2003

Dr. Steven J. Sokkal,
Staff Psychologist
Soledad Correction and Training Facility
Soledad, CA 93960

Dear Dr. Sokkal,

Thank you for all you did for me and Tristin, and for the extraordinary amount of time you and I spent together at Soledad. Thanks for listening. Your insights were enormously helpful in getting my head screwed back on straight. It's also good to be home.

I just finished reading your report (and so did Tristin), and we both think it's terrific.

I hope it is not true that whatever it was that exploded like a bolt of lightning in my brain is not permanent and, more importantly, did not trigger some sort of DNA change. Tristin says she's going to keep a close eye on me, looking for "signs of evil," as she puts it. From now on, every time she gives me a weird look I'm going to think of your PPE theory, if not you. I guess I should tell you that Tristin is pregnant, so I'm going to be looking for the signs in our children as well. Chances are pretty small, don't you think?

Your version of events is both compelling and illuminating, and it shows you put a great deal of effort into research and interviews. And your background as a prison psychologist, with experience in human motivation and the like, certainly helps with questions of 'why?' I just didn't know how much until I read it. I now consider the many days we spent together more than worth the effort.

Your screenwriter colleague, John Bascomb, doesn't seem to think so. He sounds pretty pissed off. My agent did some checking up on him. He's been around quite a while, but he got his start around 1986 in the rewrite of the movie, *"Heaven's Gate."* Sounds like he's still trying to live that one down.

I called your number at work, and they said you were on vacation, so I guess you didn't hear the announcement. Enclosed is a copy of my book, *Home*. Unlike your report, I focused pretty much on the general lifestyle aspects, especially the relationship with my then girlfriend, later fiancée, and now wife, Tristin, plus the natural beauty of the whole Monterey Peninsula area. There's a lot about bodysurfing, too. I don't think Mr. Bascomb realized all this when he heard about my appearance on GMA.

In *Home*, I only summarized what happened to the people in my life at the time, so it wasn't until reading your "report" that I realized how complicated my situation really was. If you wouldn't mind, I'd like to show it to my agent (he's in touch with TriStar). I'm sure the details you provided would be a strong basis for a screenplay. If they use your material as a source, of course, you would be amply rewarded—maybe through an option deal of some sort and points on the box office receipts. The vocational training facility at the prison will, I'm sure, make good use of your valuable contribution.

By the way, you might want to add this to your report. When I returned home after being paroled, one of the first things I did was suit up and go bodysurfing. I also decided to pay a visit to my not-so-secret-anymore (thanks to you) chamber and check on the anemones. I'm happy to report they're doing fine. I'm sure it's partly due to the nearby food supply stripped to the bone by all the sea critters, little particles drifting down into their waiting tentacles. It was an adult male skeleton, clinging to the upper rocks, right near the ceiling where the little bit of light comes in. As they say in Malibu, "He's like, totally bleached out, man." It can only be Gil Nortze because of the sapphire ring still around his finger.

From what I could tell, Gil was apparently carried a little north by the current and forced down and under the cliff by one of those 25-footers, and he surfaced inside the chamber during that time of both high tide and high surf. With just enough headroom to breath between rising water levels, he could have survived (suffered might be a more accurate term) for hours before hypothermia set in.

Considering what Valerie and Tyler might have experienced in her own car underwater, I think it was a fitting end for that bastard. The Neighbor from Hell doesn't begin to describe who that man really was, and your account is very much on the mark in that regard. And don't get me started on his demon seeds. Lindy sensed it from the beginning, didn't she? She hated being around those kids.

I contacted the police about finding the skeleton, but so far no one has wanted to risk free diving into the chamber. Not only is it pretty damned dicey in that water at the base of the cliff, but also scuba gear is too bulky to go up into it. They asked me to retrieve the skeleton for ID, but I refused, telling them it was too dangerous. I didn't mention the ring. If they want him so bad, they can get him themselves. I've gone back twice since then and you should have heard the one-way conversations I had with Gil Nortze. He even said I could take a bone and give it to the police for ID by bone marrow DNA (just kidding, so don't send the padded wagon). Maybe you'd like a souvenir sample for that DNA testing you talked about?

As far as your report, I think you should try to get it published, as it reads like a novel. There's a lot of meat in there—much more than in mine, to be honest, and a lot more than Gil can claim on his bones nowadays. If nothing else, at least the general public will be made aware of the acoustic sensor concept, and there might be lives saved. The next big California earthquake should make people sit up and take notice.

Also, since you're so close, why don't you and your wife and son come on down to the Highlands for a barbeque? Tristin wants to meet you. Brad Smiley just finished adding a second story observation room—all glassed in—started while I was "away." You're going to love the view. You can even see my empty lot next door (it'll be that way forever). Jake the Tern and Lindy may also want to say thanks for including them in your story. Jake's wing is much better now. You can also pick up your "souvenir," too.

Margie and Harry are coming back into town. They got married in Vegas last week and plan on moving their "operation" down to Cambria. I hope it works out for them. Like you, I'm curious about any kids they might have, if you know what I mean. Besides, my kids may interact with their kids at some point down the road, and I hope there are no bad influences there. I'll still invite Harry and Margie to the BBQ, as they want to meet you, too.

Oh, BTW: Thanks for the two frogs that came in the manuscript box. Tristin and I both appreciate the kind gesture.

Best of luck in the future. So call me at the number listed on the letterhead and we'll chat.

Ken Easton
Carmel Highlands, California

*****

July 15, 2003

Dear Dr. Sokkal,

I have read your manuscript and find your story compelling on several levels. I would like to discuss your book vis-à-vis a possible relationship with our publishing company. The approval letter by prison officials at the California Department of Corrections is also appreciated. And I am pleased to hear that you and TriStar are now negotiating a book-to-movie option. Good luck on that. It should help book sales. Please contact me directly at (202) 555-3979.

Sincerely,

Mikel Schlessinger
Senior Editor, Random House Publishing Co.

*****

July 30, 2003

To: John Bascomb

Enclosed please find a copy of my publisher's check for $50,000 against book royalties, and a copy of the option payment from TriStar for $25,000. Sorry you didn't read the entire report and quit in such a huff. I sincerely hope things go better for you in Iraq. And here's some non-psychobabble to put in your next screenplay: "Go screw yourself!"

Up Yours Truly,

/s/ Steven J. Sokkal, PhD
Staff Psychologist
Soledad Correction and Training Facility

*****

News Item: December 14, 2003

Associated Press: Saddam Hussein was captured today in a raid near his hometown of Tikrit after evading U.S.-led coalition forces in Iraq for months, according to coalition authorities. He was found in a hidden "spider hole" near a farmhouse and taken into custody without firing a shot. Nearby, a man thought to be an American and claiming to be the official Saddam family biographer was held for questioning.

News Item: December 23, 2003

The Cambrian: A powerful earthquake struck the California central coast yesterday morning, killing two people and injuring nearly fifty in Paso Robles. Forty buildings collapsed or were severely damaged.

The earthquake was also felt in nearby San Simeon, home to the famous Hearst Castle. There were no reports of damage to structures or to its valuable collections.

In Cambria, just ten miles south of the epicenter, the 6.5 magnitude temblor damaged a local doctor's office. Inside the office, an as yet unidentified woman was reportedly thrown from the examining table while undergoing a routine pregnancy evaluation.

According to the attending nurse, the status of the woman is, "slightly injured, but non life-threatening. Her 6-month old twin fetuses—a boy and a girl—seem to have come through the incident unscathed."

The woman was treated and released, and she is expected to make a full recovery.

Note to Reader:

Margie Nortze did make a full recovery. Well, technically, anyway. More on that in my next "report."

/sjs

THE END

Acknowledgments

The usual suspects were at work here, plus a few others. To my publisher, Mikel Schwarz, thanks for sticking by me thin and thinner. To my editor, Tony Stubbs, thanks for all the great story suggestions—you helped make it sing. And to Michael Graham, thanks for another great cover.

A special thanks goes to my former brother-in-law, Dr. Bill Zika, Senior Staff Psychologist at Soledad State Prison. He never knew what hit him, as the story was 99% complete when he was informed of his co-starring, author-by-pseudonym role. As the inspiration for prison psychologist Steven Sokkal, Bill was most helpful in getting several major psychological points—and Soledad Prison policies—clarified. They certainly helped make the story come alive and ring true. Thanks again, Bill. I only ask your advance forgiveness for your unknowing participation in the book sequel.

Thanks to Sydney and Marguerite Temple for their book, *Carmel-by-the-Sea: From Aborigines to Coastal Commission.* I hope you will not seek to revoke the literary license I took with local history.

A final 'thank you' to physicist Adam Sokal of New York University, whose hoax article, "Transgressing the Boundaries: Towards a Transformative Hermeneutics of Quantum Gravity" (published in 1996 in the Spring/Summer issue of *Social Text*), reminded me that if something *sounds* good, and very authoritative, it must be true.